'We cannot live out our dream, you must know that.'

'We can,' Rosamund insisted. ''Til sunset.'

'Nay. 'Twould be the greatest folly.' Oliver's voice was kind, but firm. 'I want to...but no.'

There was a light in his eyes the belied the firmness in his voice. Rosamund saw it and her lips curved. 'Want to...what, Oliver?' she murmured. She reached for his cheek. She touched him. He did not move to reject her, but lay quite still.

'Oliver? What is it you would do? Is it this?' she whispered, very low. She shifted on the grass, and then his mouth was on hers. Rosamund felt the welcoming warmth of his lips move slowly and gently across hers.

She had tried to imagine this kiss. But her wildest imaginings had not prepared her for reality. She had had no experience which had ever hinted that a kiss could be like this. Purest pleasure. She had never felt anything like it. Not even known the human body was capable of feeling such sensations...

Carol Townend is a Yorkshire woman whose nineteenth century forebears were friendly with the Brontë sisters. Perhaps this fact had something to do with the passion for the past that led her to a history degree at London University, and on, eventually, to writing historical novels.

Widely travelled, Carol Townend has explored places as diverse as North America and Sri Lanka, Mexico and the Mediterranean. When not taking refuge from the modern world by reading historical novels or writing her own, she loves to escape to the deep countryside.

Born in 1953, Carol Townend lives with her copywriter husband and young daughter near Kew Gardens.

HISTORICAL NOTE

In medieval times no woman could be lawfully married without the consent of her lord. It was customary for the father of a bride, whether he be serf or freeman, to pay a fine to his lord on his daughter's wedding day. This claim of the lord to exact money from his people was little more than exploitation and was often shamefully abused.

Droit de seigneur—the Right of the First Night— theoretically allowed the lord of the manor to spend the first night with a newly wedded bride. In reality there is little direct evidence of this happening (except in Russia). A theory has been put forward, however, that the merchet was introduced as a way of paying the lord to keep out of the bride's wedding bed. Few people accept this theory and generally the merchet is seen purely as another way in which the lord extracted money from his beleaguered people.

SHATTERED VOWS

Carol Townend

Best wishes

Carol Townend.

MILLS & BOON LIMITED
ETON HOUSE   18-24 PARADISE ROAD
RICHMOND   SURREY   TW9 1SR

First published in Great Britain 1989
by Mills & Boon Limited

© Carol Townend 1989

Australian copyright 1989
Philippine copyright 1989
This edition 1989

ISBN 0 263 76534 2

Set in Times Roman 10 on 10¼ pt.
04-8909-87223 C

Made and printed in Great Britain

CHAPTER ONE

May Day: The Year of Our Lord 1149

ROSAMUND halted mid-scramble at the sight of the grey
stallion on the beach. She was almost at the foot of the
cliffs, working her way down the precipitous track with
more care than was her wont. Seagulls screeched
overhead, flashing across the cloudless azure sky, bright,
soaring arcs of light.

She was wearing her best rose-coloured gown, normally reserved for Sundays, in deference to the holiday.
She had no desire to see it ripped to shreds on the jagged
rocks.

How that would bring Aeffe's anger tumbling down
about her ears! Her stepmother had had to be bribed to
give Rosamund her old rose kirtle with the promise of
a new one from Osric. And that most reluctantly. Between them they had managed to make Rosamund feel
like a beggar. As if she had not earned Aeffe's wretched
cast-offs ten times over! If it were not for the fact that
her other one was in rags, she would have flung it back
in Aeffe's face. Still, it was finer than any she had yet
owned...

Rosamund's blue eyes surveyed the animal narrowly.
She shrugged. It was only a horse. Carefully she picked
her way down the uneven path, one hand holding up
her skirts, the other occasionally clutching at a rock for
balance. She could hear the mournful cry of the gulls
rising shrilly over the hushing waves.

Rosamund straightened and wiped her forehead with
the back of her hand. A trail of dust smeared across her
brow below her circlet of forget-me-nots. She had woven
the flowers for her hair in honour of the holiday. Long

honey-brown hair swirled loose about her face in the
onshore breeze.

''Ello,' she addressed the horse, who had seen her and
whose ears were turned towards her. His reins had been
looped round a large boulder. 'You're a beauty. Where
have you come from? T' castle? Where's your rider?
You're too fine a beast to be left tethered all unattended.
You'd fetch a king's ransom at t' market.'

The girl's low voice was easy on the ear. It proclaimed
both her northern roots and her peasant upbringing. The
war-horse snickered softly in reply and watched her with
huge eyes.

The incline of the cliff path was less steep at the
bottom, and Rosamund came down on to the beach at
a run. There had been a recent rockfall, for a great chunk
of the cliff lay broken on the beach, grass still growing
in the sandy earth that had come down with it. This
place was dangerous and children were warned to avoid
it.

Here was the huge pile of boulders which had tumbled
down last autumn. An attack from a violent rainstorm
and waves the size of Ingerthorpe Castle had combined
to send water cascading down the cliff-side. The ancient
cliff walls, unable to withstand such a determined as-
sault, had been broached. They had thundered down on
to the sands with a mighty roaring that had sounded like
a million ravening beasts.

The rubble thus dropped on the shore almost blocked
this section of the beach off from the fishing village. It
was high and difficult to scale and you could only skirt
round it when the tide was at its lowest—as now.

But Rosamund was not interested in walking to the
village today. She knew what it would be like there, and
had no wish to take part in any May Day celebrations.
She had nothing to celebrate. Everyone would be
drinking and the street would be a river of spilled ale by
nightfall. The Maypole would be set up near the harbour
wall. There'd be coloured ribbons floating in the breeze,
mountebanks, fairings, trinkets, noise, laughter, bustle.
No, she would have no part of that.

She eyed the grey stallion. He was a regal beast. Nothing like the carters' nags who shifted the sacks of flour to and from Baron Geoffrey's mill. They were bony, half-nourished, shapeless creatures. Their coats were dull with dust and lack of care. But this creature had flanks which gleamed in the bright sunlight—she wanted to touch him to see if he was real.

The animal snorted at her and blew through his nose, but his ears were not angry, nor his eyes... Slowly Rosamund moved towards him.

He was real. Warm to the touch. Flesh and blood like her. The grey dwarfed her, but Rosamund was unafraid.

'I wish I'd known you'd be here,' she told him, reaching up to stroke his finely arched neck. 'I would 'ave brought you something to eat. Do you like apples? We 'ave a few left at t' bottom of t' barrel. Aye, 'tis true they're wrinkled, but they still 'ave enough of last summer's sweetness to taste good.'

The grey nuzzled affectionately at her ear.

Rosamund warmed to the animal, but her smile faded as she felt her crown of flowers snatched from her windswept tresses.

'Hey! No, that's not fodder! Stop it!' she protested.

But it was too late. In a swift movement the animal tugged Rosamund's forget-me-not garland free and began to chew with slow deliberation.

Rosamund grabbed for her flowers, but the stallion's head snapped round out of reach. His ears pricked forwards, alert. He had heard something. A man was clattering quickly towards them over the smashed rocks. His movements were angry. Instinct made Rosamund shift back a pace or two, closer to the cliff.

'Get back!' The newcomer was shouting, his voice harsh over the cry of the gulls. 'Don't you dare touch that animal!'

His tone of voice made Rosamund feel guilty. It was imperious, the accent aristocratic and foreign to her ears. But she had done nothing wrong. So she had no need to feel afraid. She watched the young man's hasty approach and cleared her throat. She did not recognise him.

'I've done nowt,' she said, stiffening defensively. 'I've not hurt 'im.' After his voice, her northern accent now sounded thick and clumsy to her ears.

Rosamund's arm was taken in a hard grip and she found herself staring into a pair of flinty grey eyes. They looked her over briefly; then scanned the beach and cliffs before returning to glare at her.

'Who's with you?' the man demanded.

'No one. Ow! You're hurting me!' Rosamund protested.

'And will continue to do so unless you tell me the truth. Who's with you? Who were you going to take him to?'

'No one. I weren't taking him anywhere,' she said, and noticed his lips twitch. 'I were...was...' she corrected herself, 'just talking to him, and then he ate my garland, and then you appeared, and now you are near breaking my arm.' Rosamund winced eloquently.

'He ate...what?' The stranger sounded incredulous.

Rosamund attempted to gesture at the shingle, but his grip was too firm so she pointed with her eyes instead. 'There. See for yourself. You're treading on it.'

She watched those cold, wintry eyes glance down, saw a lock of dark hair fall forward over his brow. His hand relaxed on her arm. But he did not release her.

'Forget-me-nots,' he murmured, as if puzzled, and his voice became almost human.

'Aye. At least they were forget-me-nots this morning. I think they have suffered much since then,' Rosamund told him. She was still wary, but sensed from the change in the stranger's stance that he no longer suspected her of planning to steal his horse. She wondered who he was. His voice was so strange. His was no rough country dialect, but a polished, cultured voice. His clothes were fine enough to mark him noble, and if this was his stallion——

'What are you called?' Abruptly he interrupted her thoughts.

'Rosamund. Rosamund Miller.'

Impatiently he brushed back that errant lock of hair. Wind-ruffled black hair, but clean, not matted and knotted like Alfwold's. 'Aye, I thought so. I have seen you before. You're the miller's daughter,' he stated.

Rosamund nodded. It was easier to understand him now he was not shouting at her.

'I understand your father is not a popular man,' he continued, very directly, watching her reaction.

She flushed. 'Nay.' She did not want to talk about her father. It embarrassed her. She knew how he returned short measures of milled grain, sifting off a little from each milling for his own profit. Her father's dishonesty had always rankled with her, but Osric never heeded Rosamund's objections.

'And you? Am I to know who you are?' she demanded.

He unclamped his hand from her arm. 'My name is Oliver.'

This did not tell her much. She was about to pose another question, but the young man parried it with one of his own.

'Are you dishonest like your father, I wonder?'

'I . . . nay!' she cried, indignant.

A cool gaze swept her up and down, and Rosamund bristled under it. 'No. I do not think you are,' he said at last. 'At least, not to the extent of being a horse thief. Forgive me my suspicions. This horse is all I have, and I must guard him well.'

It seemed politic to ignore the insulting thought that this man considered her capable of some dishonesty—even if he did not think she was out to steal his horse.

She smiled tentatively up at him. She would far rather this man was her friend than her foe. He was tall, over six feet, and strongly built. He had a determined cast to his jaw, and was watching her closely through slate-grey eyes which seemed to miss not a detail. He made Rosamund very conscious of her dishevelled hair, which hung down about her face in rats' tails, tangled by the climb down the cliff and the sea breezes.

She flicked the long brown strands back over her shoulder, feeling oddly threatened, though Oliver had not moved. He said he had seen her before, but she could not recall having seen him. The only time anyone had passed the mill mounted on such a fine horse, they had been in the company of Baron Geoffrey Fitz Neal. Was Oliver part of the Baron's retinue?

He was staring at her with a supercilious expression on his face, as if he was laughing at her. Rosamund forgot her resolve to smile. Forgot the probable difference in their class and responded as she always did when uncertain of herself.

'There's no need to stare at me as though I had crawled out of t' cesspit,' she snapped. 'I 'aven't. No need to look down that long nose of yours at my gown as though it were rags. It's me finest. At least I've made more of an effort for the festival than you've seen fit to. Look at you, all plain, dull colours.'

But Oliver did not rise to the bait as Aeffe usually did. He glanced down at his brown tunic, and fingered the clean cream sleeve of his undershirt with a puzzled expression on his face. 'Festival? What festival?'

Rosamund stared. 'Oh, you can't be so ignorant. You must know what day it is today.'

'No. Remind me.' He sounded mildly interested, as though he were addressing a fractious child.

''Tis May Day,' Rosamund told him, his condescension irritating her.

'May Day. Ah, I see.' He glanced down at the trampled flowers on the shingle. 'These were for your sweetheart and Lance and I between us have ruined them, so you are angry with us. I see I must make reparation.' He smiled.

Rosamund's heart gave a little jump. There were two reasons for this—both astonished her.

The first was that when Oliver smiled at her the hard, bitter lines on his face were erased. His appearance changed to such an extent that she quite forgot how much he had frightened her when she first saw him shouting angrily across the boulders. He was no longer a frowning,

suspicious nobleman, one whom she must outwit if she
were to escape a beating. She looked at him with new
eyes, and saw a young and handsome man who was quite
unlike any lad she had ever spoken to. He was clean for
one thing—he did not smell. She noticed that one of his
white teeth was chipped.

But the second, the most amazing thing of all, was
that this tall stranger seemed to be *apologising* to *her*.
No man had ever apologised to Rosamund in her life.
Had she ever thought about it, she would have supposed
it an impossibility. Men did not apologise. They might
beat, cajole, seduce, command, but they did *not* apologise, for men were never wrong. She goggled up at
Oliver's dark face, speechless with surprise. She *must*
be dreaming. But she could feel the wind lifting her hair;
playing with it. This was real. She was standing on the
edge of the beach; she could feel the shingle beneath her
bare feet and hear the waves. It *was* happening. This
proud man, no peasant's son, was apologising to *her*,
to Rosamund the miller's daughter.

She could forgive him anything after this. Even that
irritating air of condescension. She wanted to savour this
being apologised to, this strange and unusual happening, for as long as she could.

Watching her staring at him with her mouth agape,
Oliver decided the maid must be simple. He reached out
and put a finger under her chin to close her mouth.

'Now, how can I make amends?' he asked, softly.
'What would you have me do?' She might be lacking in
wits, but he had no wish to startle her. Such a pity. For
she was very pretty with those deep, fathomless blue eyes
and that glorious honey-coloured hair. Had she a sweetheart? And how would he treat her, this lover of hers?
Would he be gentle with her, or would he take advantage
of her simple nature and use her before casting her aside?

'What?' Rosamund mumbled. Oliver's gentleness, too,
was new to her. She was uncertain of her ground and
treading warily, lest he should prove to be like other men
after all. He could not be real. Men did not say they
were sorry, men were never gentle with her. Oliver's be-

haviour was so outside her experience, so unlike her father...

He made her spine tingle, as though he were a spirit. With a sudden shudder of excitement Rosamund felt that she had recognised the truth. He was a spirit. Rosamund was suddenly certain that Oliver was not quite human. Had he been summoned up for her as part of this magical day?

He was *not* real. How could he be? Real men did not look so strong, so handsome, or so clean. To her eyes, used as they were to looking on downtrodden, humble peasant men, who had neither time nor means to wash and wear clean clothes, he seemed to shine as brightly as this beautiful noonday.

She sensed a mystery, and her superstitious nature latched on to it and embellished it. The sea was reflected in his grey eyes. Aye, now she understood. The old gods must have brought him to her. It was their day, after all. They had sent him riding in from the sea on his great horse, and for today he was hers. It was not something that she must think about too closely, or question, lest he vanish as the morning mists had done.

She smiled radiantly up into his cool eyes, still silent. 'What reparation can I make?' Oliver repeated, bending to pick up her garland of forget-me-nots so he could give himself time to accustom himself to that smile of hers. Oliver could not remember when a maid had looked at him like this. She was staring at him as though he were a god, and he was human enough to enjoy the sensation. She was so natural; there was no hint of ar-tifice or malice about those rosy lips. And her eyes met his directly, in pure admiration. So unlike the simpering, scheming ladies he had met since his return to this country. Their eyes never fell on him without him being reminded of his lowly status. He read scorn and pity in every glance they sent his way. He had heard their whis-pered taunts, and forced himself to affect insouciance, though he felt like throttling them all.

But now, here he was on the beach, with a common peasant girl, and she was making him feel things he had suppressed. Things that he knew he should be immune to lest they upset the carefully plotted course of his life.

'Anything?' Rosamund asked. She had to make sure he was here for her. Really for her.

Against his better judgement, Oliver found himself nodding.

'I would that you should be my escort,' she was saying. 'Just for today, of course.' And she smiled that smile again. Her voice was low, melodious, her dialect less pronounced now, as though she were imitating him. Who was it had told him that peasants could be splendid lovers but should never be encouraged to talk? They had never heard this girl speak.

'Of course,' he heard himself agreeing. The bright day had caught him in its net too. Hell, why not? He would let her shy admiring smile and honest eyes seduce him from his path. Gladly. But only for a day. That was all she asked. She did not seem to expect or want more, this simple maid. He would be able to forget who he was, and what he was, while basking in the pleasure of that smile. For a day. And tomorrow . . . tomorrow back to Geoffrey. His new master. His cousin.

How Geoffrey would mock him, if he could see him standing thus entranced by the smile of the miller's simple daughter. With such ammunition to fuel him his cousin's baiting would know no bounds. The thought of Geoffrey's mocking face, as he had last seen it laughing with his fellows, twisted Oliver's stomach into an angry knot. The stallion at his side moved uneasily, pawing at the ground. Nay, he would bury his anger, forget his cousin for awhile and enjoy the company of this girl, Rosamund.

The wench must have sensed his flare of anger, for she had stepped back a pace. Her glorious smile had dimmed; she had taken her bottom lip between white teeth and was regarding him with a worried frown. She looked timid, frightened even.

Firmly, Oliver banished the fury from his mind and eyes, and smiled at her. Immediately her large, blue eyes lit up again. Heavens, if he did not watch out for her some other less scrupulous man might come upon her and ... She was simply not fit to be abroad on her own if she smiled at every man she met in such a fashion— particularly on May Day.

He would see her safe till eventide, and then he would return her to the mill. Knowing her father's reputation, he would be out enjoying the festival. There would be no one at the mill to keep an eye on her. Tomorrow she would be safely back at work and be kept too busy to be wandering unprotected all over the countryside. And today—today she would be safe with him.

'I love these little stones,' Rosamund told Oliver, pointing at the broken rocks and shingle brought down by the cliff fall. 'I spend hours here when I can get away. I collect them.' She spoke slowly, making a fair attempt at mimicking his elegant mode of speech. She did not want him to think her completely ignorant. He might ride off and leave her.

'What, these?' Oliver looked askance at the untidy heaps of rock debris.

Rosamund laughed. 'Oh, not just any old stones. The special ones.'

'Of course,' Oliver smiled. He supposed he ought to humour her. Such a waste of a pretty maid ...

'Nay,' Rosamund surprised him by saying. 'I can see you don't understand. Look.' She took one of his strong hands in hers and pulled him over to one of the smaller piles of rubble. She bent and began to sort through the small stones, busily sorting them and setting a few to one side.

Oliver sat back on his heels and watched her, his hands clasped loosely in front of him. Her rich, earthy beauty fascinated him almost as much as did her uncomplicated smile.

She had the posture of a queen. Her rich, golden-brown hair swirled about her shoulders and down her back, a shiny mass swaying in the wind. She had pushed up the sleeves of her pink gown, darned at the elbow, he noticed, to reveal smooth satiny arms. He wanted to touch them, but instead he clasped his hands tightly together and watched the way her workscarred but nimble fingers picked out just a few particular stones. He could see little to distinguish the ones she had chosen from the ones she had rejected. Such a pity...

'Look, Oliver.' She held one up to him. 'No, *really* look. I don't believe you even glanced at it.'

Obediently Oliver lifted the stone from her small palm, dropping his eyes from hers. The pale grey stone was small, almost round, and clearly marked across its surface was a ridged pattern in a spiral shape.

Their eyes met over the stone.

'You see. There are lots of them. You have to search hard to find them, but once you know where to look, there are many. Just waiting to be found.'

Oliver reached past Rosamund and took another stone, a tiny one, from her collection. The same markings. And on them all. It was merely the size that varied. So there was *some* method in it...

'There is a story...' she began and hesitated, suddenly shy.

'Aye?'

'Aye. The priest told it to me. An ancient story. Going back to the times before the Sea Raiders came.' Rosamund paused and flushed.

'Go on,' urged Oliver.

''Tis only a tale for children. I've been told I should not listen to such...' But Oliver's smile encouraged her. That chipped front tooth was visible. It was oddly attractive, that broken tooth. This strong young man was not invulnerable. That broken white tooth proved his humanity.

Her accent firmly in hand, Rosamund continued. 'High up on the cliffs lived a holy lady. A saint. Her name was Hilda. She was renowned for her goodness. She was not a hermit, she did not scorn the common people. They all came to her for help. They brought her their woes, their tribulations, and she dealt with them all. She would see both rich and poor, giving all the benefit of her wisdom. 'Twas said of her that she could solve any problem, however dire.

'Then, one day, the countryside around was visited by a terrible scourge. A plague of poisonous snakes came and overran the village. The snakes were everywhere. There was no escaping them. They hid in loft and barn and cottage, and many people died.

''Twas said by some that the Devil had sent the snakes to torment them. Others said that God was punishing them for their wickedness.

'The people tried to trap the snakes, and many were killed. But more came, and more. It seemed there was no end to them. No one was safe.

'Finally the people went to plead with Saint Hilda that she should intercede on their behalf. She agreed. She went down into the village and drove all the snakes before her with her staff. She herded them up to the top of the cliff as though they were sheep and commanded them to go on over the edge. They did. Every last snake went slithering down to meet its death at the bottom of that terrible cliff,' Rosamund stopped to draw breath.

The young man's grey eyes were fixed on her. His chin rested on one hand. He was chewing his thumb thoughtfully. Rosamund searched his eyes for any trace of mockery. She saw that the grey in his steady eyes was outlined with a soot-black ring, but she could not find any derision there.

'Is that it?' he asked, puzzled.

Rosamund smiled. 'Not quite. These,' she gestured at the tiny swirled stones, 'these are said to be those snakes. The priest explained it. He said that when they fell they curled up tight as hedgehogs so they could roll safely down the cliff. But the tide was in and they all drowned. Here they are. Still curled up. Turned to stone.'

'And you collect them,' Oliver said.

'Aye. You have your horse. He is your finest treasure, is he not?'

Oliver assented.

'Aye. And these are my treasure. They have such a pretty pattern on them. They have no real value, I know, but they are all mine...' Her voice trailed off. Rosamund suddenly felt embarrassed. Why had she told him this?

How he must be laughing at her! 'Oh, how foolish you must think me,' she said, avoiding that cool, penetrating gaze. ''Tis only a tale, I know, but...' She shrugged awkwardly and made to stand up.

Oliver caught at her hand, and she risked a glance. She glimpsed his broken tooth. It only showed when he smiled...

'I have never heard that story. You tell it well.' His thumb moved gently across her fingertips. Her hand trembled and was withdrawn at once.

'I...I'm thirsty,' she announced, her eyes going towards the leather water-bottle hanging from the war-horse's saddle.

Oliver followed her gaze. 'Help yourself, and when you've finished bring me the flask. I'm parched too.'

He watched her patter carefully across the shingle to the huge grey and unhook the flask. He felt confused. It appeared that his assessment of this maiden had been too hasty.

She did not drink, but brought the water straight over to him.

'No. After you,' Oliver insisted, smiling at her rigid sense of class. 'Today I am your squire, am I not?'

'Aye,' she agreed cautiously.

'Then you should not wait on me. Drink. Tell me, Rosamund, what age are you?'

'Sixteen.' She drank, then offered the bottle to him. A gust of wind cloaked both hand and flask with long, silken tresses.

She laughed, tossing her head in a vain attempt to control her hair, but the breeze would not release it and it floated about her—a cloud of rich colour. 'My hair has come alive,' she declared. 'It looks like the snakes being brought back to life.'

Oliver stood up. He was so very tall. He put up a hand and slowly lifted a wind-swept lock aside. His other hand found hers on the flask and Rosamund's laughter died. He was shaking his head slowly, looking into her face. 'It looks nothing of the kind,' he disagreed softly.

'Nay?' she queried. Why was she whispering? Her throat felt parched even though she had just refreshed herself.

'Nay,' he sighed, letting his hand fall away softly so he could feel her hair running over his palm. 'But 'tis a lover's place to whisper compliments...and I am no maid's lover.' His face became remote. He looked down at his hand on hers as if he wondered why it was there. Then he removed the bottle from Rosamund and turned his back on her, tilting his head back to drink.

'Why not?' she asked. The bright day made her bold. Today was not a normal day. If it were she would never even dare lift her eyes to his, so far above her was he. A bird soaring over a lowly worm. But today... 'Why are you no maid's lover?' she persisted recklessly.

Oliver laughed. A bitter sound. It was out before he had time to check himself. 'No one would have *me*,' he told her.

'Why not?' She would. She would rejoice to have him as her lover.

He swung round and faced her. 'I live in the castle. 'Tis a different world in there. You know nothing of that world. 'Tis best it remains so.' He ran a hand over his brow. 'You are not as I thought you were. You are quite able to take care of yourself, and are safe enough here. I think I had better take my leave of you.'

Rosamund's face fell. He was angry. Her impertinent question had angered him. 'Oh, please stay!' she begged. 'I will not pry. Only please stay.'

Oliver had reached Lance, and was already gathering up the reins in one hand, preparing to mount. Seeing her crestfallen expression, Oliver felt himself weakening. He knew he should be on his way. He could not afford to get involved with this girl.

But those blue eyes! They shone like beacons luring him to his doom. The unguarded way they gazed at a man, as though he were the answer to her prayers... He must not look at her. Determinedly, Oliver thrust his foot into the stirrup and threw himself into the saddle. There was no room in his life for her—even if she did possess the most alluring eyes he had ever seen. He must go.

There had been no danger while Oliver had thought her a simpleton—no danger for either of them. She could be as beautiful as an angel, could gaze on him like that forever, protected by her simple state. Some innate sense of honour he had not even known he possessed would have saved them both. But now, now he realised his error. There was danger now. She was as sane and intelligent as he. No disparity of mind to keep them safely separate. He would have the devil's own time resisting the unashamed admiration in her blue eyes. So candid it was purely pagan. He must go.

He gestured to the distant shoreline. 'And what about your lover? Is he not waiting for you further down the beach?' asked Oliver, thinking this would distract her and remove the crestfallen expression from her face. She made no attempt to shield her feelings, everything she felt was scripted with painful clarity across her face.

'Me lover?' she wondered, wrinkling her nose and forgetting her assumed accent in her confusion.

'Aye. Your lover. The one for whom you made the garland.'

'Oh. I see. Nay, I've no lover,' Rosamund admitted, her voice flat. She retrieved the wrecked circlet from the ground and stared at it sadly. Alfwold did not count. He was not a lover. And he never would be, even when they were wed and he...and he...

A cluster of flowers had somehow escaped ruination. Thoughtfully Rosamund plucked them off the garland. The starry golden centres winked up at her.

'Then why the garland?' Oliver wondered.

She smiled and raised her eyes to his. Face and voice well in hand. 'Oh, 'twas only a dream I had. A golden dream for a warm spring day. Here, take this. I think you need to dream a little too.' Gracefully she held out the tiny flowers to him.

She had poise, this peasant maid. He'd give her that. Oliver found himself hesitating. He was glad she was not going to make difficulties. He leaned forward and accepted the flowers, touching her hand briefly with his lips. 'Farewell, Rosamund. I have enjoyed our little dream.'

'And I. Oh—Oliver? Do we have to awaken so soon?' she pleaded wistfully. 'We both know 'tis only a dream...what harm?'

'Rosamund!' His voice held a warning note. She had such pretty lips...

'What harm?' she repeated. 'I will not anger you again. I will not pester you with questions. You were happy enough to keep me company till then.'

'It is not your questions that spur me to leave,' he admitted.

'What then? You seemed content to stay.' Without realising, Rosamund had caught hold of the stirrup.

'I thought you needed my protection,' Oliver admitted stiffly. He could not tell her what he had truly thought...

'Why should I need protecting?'

'I...oh, why indeed?' Oliver stared down at her hand. It clung now to his booted ankle. So small. ''Tis I who need protection from you. A clinging vine I do not want.'

Her clear eyes clouded. 'Only for today,' Rosamund said, reproachfully. 'You agreed. And 'tis only a dream, remember?'

'And tomorrow?' he prompted.

'You will be back at t' castle, and I shall be back at t' mill. We will have woken.'

She said it so simply. Oliver saw her eyes flicker over the blue flowers in his hand.

'And those will have faded.' She shrugged.

Oliver smiled. His hand crept to the pouch at his belt, and he lifted the flap to drop the flowers inside. He held out that hand to her. 'Come then, we'll ride.'

She did not like it. It was too fast, too frightening and too uncomfortable. The stallion's hooves beat like a drum on the damp, compacted sand. Oliver's arm was tight about her waist, and she was confident that he would not let her fall. But the sand looked so very hard. People were not born to ride on these huge creatures.

Oliver's saddle had been designed to hold a knight on in battle. It was shaped so the pommel rose up high in front of the rider—no doubt a good thing if you were a wounded warrior and needed something extra to cling on to. It had not been created to carry two people and consequently Rosamund was perched almost on top of the pommel. It dug into her in the most awkward way. There was nowhere else for her to go unless Oliver moved back a little. She twisted round to try and see if he could.

'What's the matter?' His voice warmed her ear, and they slowed to a bouncing, jarring trot.

Rosamund grimaced and leaned against his arm to glance past him. The saddle back held Oliver firmly in place, allowing little room for manoeuvre. She grinned. 'I think *you* could be dead in that saddle and you'd still stay on this horse, but *I* wish this thing was not so uncomfortable,' she commented, striking the pommel with her fist.

'Impertinent wench,' he said cheerfully and at once slid down from the saddle to walk at her side.

'Oliver!' She shrieked, her stomach turned to water.

The great war-horse tossed his head, and Rosamund wondered if she'd be thrown.

'He'll have me off!' she wailed.

'Not Lance,' Oliver smiled. 'He's trained to suffer the heat of battle calmly. Your screams are nothing after what he's seen and heard.' Oliver's slate-grey eyes sought hers. 'However, not all mounts are so well trained. The first thing you must learn when riding is not to make any unexpected or violent sounds.' He grinned.

'I'm not like to ride again. Riding's for fine ladies, not peasant girls. Oliver, get me off,' she pleaded, in a loud whisper.

His grin widened, but Rosamund was too busy clinging to the saddle to notice. Oliver continued, almost on a monotone, as if chanting plainsong. 'And the second is that that is not the right way to sit in the saddle. Move back into the seat.'

'Sweet Mary, 'elp me,' she cried. The leather creaked and she shifted to obey him. It was that or fly off...

'Aye, that's it. Now let me see if I can adjust the stirrups to your length.'

'Oliver. I beg of you...please get me down. I don't think there's any point you trying to teach me...Oliver! Listen! Please!'

But Oliver had grown deaf. He had her seated properly, with both feet in the stirrups, and before she could make further protest was leading her off down the beach.

Rosamund gripped the leather pommel so hard her knuckles were white. She scowled at Oliver's raven head, and had to force herself to accept the strange motion. It was easier than she had thought. Not so terrifying. She could feel the saddle holding her firmly in place. Lance would not bolt with Oliver at the reins. A seagull shrieked above them and Rosamund spared it a glance.

Oliver was watching her. 'There! I knew you would like it. It can't be that terrifying if you can manage to be looking at the gulls.'

'Nay, 'tis not,' she agreed. ''Twas the saddle, 'twere wrong before.'

'Not made to carry two people,' Oliver explained. ''Tis a horse soldier's saddle.'

'I know,' she told him, and a worrying thought struck her... Only knights had such saddles. She should not be talking to a knight... 'Oliver?'

'Mmmm.' He was patting Lance's neck.

'You're...you're not a knight, are you?' she asked.

His head jerked up. His mouth was a thin line. 'Me? A knight? No, I borrowed this saddle,' he said, twisting his lips. 'Look, my spurs are of base metal. Knights bear gilded ones.'

'Oh, good. That's a relief.' Rosamund sighed, and relaxed.

A sand fly flew past them. Lance's ears twitched.

'He looks as though he is listening to us,' she commented chattily.

'He probably is,' Oliver replied absently.

'It must be wonderful to control him. So strong, so much power at your command,' she went on.

'Aye, there's nothing like it,' he agreed.

'You must feel—invincible! For myself, I find it rather worrying. I've had enough. Oliver, I pray you, will you help me down now. Please, Oliver?'

Oliver was back at her side, pulling her foot from the stirrup. 'You've done well. We'll make a lady of you yet,' he said lightly. 'Kick the other foot free.' He had a strange look on his face.

'It's free,' she told him, and held out her arms.

Taking her by the waist, he set her down. Still with that look in his eyes. He did not let her go, and his eyes wandered slowly over her features. Almost as though she had a secret and he would learn it, she thought. Rosamund was still, waiting for him to speak, conscious of her hands resting lightly on his arms.

'You are a strange maid,' he announced.

'Am I?' The wool of his tunic was so soft to the touch. Rosamund felt no urge to wrench herself out of his hold as she had that day last autumn when Alfwold had sealed their pledge with his kiss. What would Oliver's kiss be like? Not rough and crude and careless of her distaste. Not tainted with the taste of yesterday's fare and reeking of onions, but clean and sweet and pure...

'Aye. That you are. Most ladies would twist their lips and turn away from a mere squire, but you...'

'A squire!' Rosamund interrupted. 'So that's what you are! From your manner I thought you to be a leper at the very least! But a squire! You really are a squire! I am honoured, sir!' Rosamund's eyes sparkled. She attempted a mocking little curtsy, but the effect was rather spoilt as Oliver still had her by the waist.

The bright sun had not chased all the shadows from his eyes. 'You don't know the worst of it,' he went on. His finely chiselled mouth was grim.

'Oh, Oliver. What is the matter with you? You are set to sour the dream. I won't let you. Nothing you say can spoil this. Can't you just accept this lovely day for what it is? And can't we be ourselves for one day in our lives? Our real selves, as we are deep down. Forget that you're a squire, and I'm the miller's daughter. We've no duties to perform today.'

Suddenly, Rosamund remembered Alfwold. A gasp escaped her. She'd given Alfwold her pledge, albeit he was not her choice. Hastily she thrust her unwelcome remembrance to a dark corner of her mind. It could stay there till the morrow. Alfwold had nothing to do with this May Day dream. Alfwold belonged in the real world. She would not allow Alfwold to step into the present and spoil it, any more than she would Oliver's gloomy thoughts.

'Yesterday and tomorrow have no place in our dream. Our dream is now. That's all that matters,' she finished fiercely.

Oliver pulled her close, and put a hand up to stroke the hair from her face. Rosamund moved her head to rub her cheek against his hand and smiled.

'Rosamund, you child.'

She turned her head to kiss his palm, and instantly regretted it, for his eyes flared and he snatched his hand away.

'Don't,' he said gruffly. 'You know nothing about me.'

'I don't have to,' she replied, and meant it. She paused, then, greatly daring, asked, 'Oliver, when are you going to kiss me?'

'I'm not,' he said. He was very stern. She hardly recognised him, his eyes had gone hard, like her little stones. He put her at arm's length, and stepped back. Rosamund was overcome with mortification, and covered her face with her hands.

'I'm sorry,' she muttered, 'I'm not normally like this. I'm not a...a...' She could not bring herself to say it. She peeped through her fingers at him. He was almost smiling. Aye, he was. She could see his broken tooth.

'Rosamund,' he said. The way he pronounced it he made her name sounded important. She knew then that he would let her have her way. He would not sour the dream, but neither must she.

They had wandered along the crescent curve of the cliffs, one on either side of the grey stallion, walking south with the sun on their faces. Oliver removed his boots, so he too could feel the gently warming sand and laugh as the water nibbled at his toes.

'Does Lance not mind the waves?' Rosamund wondered.

'Nay. Though I warrant by now he'd relish some fresh water. We'd best find a stream.'

Rosamund pointed. 'There's one. Our river divides high up in the hills and part of it runs into the sea yonder.'

'*Our* river?' Oliver queried.

'Aye, the one that turns my father's millwheel.'

Oliver grunted and began to lead his horse towards the streamlet.

'There are more little snake-stones here,' Rosamund informed him. 'I came here at the end of last summer and found a fair number.' To her consternation her stomach rumbled loudly. She flushed, and wrapped her arms about her middle to try and hide the sound.

'You need some food,' Oliver commented, grinning at her. He secured Lance's reins so the animal could move freely to graze on the grassy riverbank or drink the clear mountain-water. 'Here, catch.' He threw her one of the saddle-bags, and unhooked the water-bottle.

Not liking to pry into his pack, she hesitated.

'Open it,' he urged. 'There's food inside. We'll share it.'

Rosamund did not need a second bidding. She plumped herself down on the edge of the bank, feet swinging over the side. She pulled out a fresh-baked loaf, some cheese wrapped in fine muslin, cooked meats, a couple of wrinkled russet apples, and a wine-skin.

'This loaf was made with the best flour,' she commented, tearing it in two and attacking her half with sharp teeth. She was ravenous—and this was fare fit for the King. 'We send most of it to the castle, so I don't often taste it. 'Tis delicious, and very soft.' This last was spoken with her mouth full, and it was a few seconds before Rosamund noticed the amusement with which Oliver's grey eyes were regarding her. He had splashed water over himself, she could see it dripping from his face and hands.

'Don't you wash before you eat, Rosamund?' he grinned, coming to sit at her side.

'Oh! Aye! I...I was merely tasting the bread.' Hot with embarrassment, Rosamund dropped her chunk of the loaf and hopped down into the stream, holding her skirts up with one hand and splashing water somewhat ineffectively with the other. Oliver made her colour rise by leaning on his elbow to watch. He broke off a small section of bread and nibbled at it absently.

She tried to ignore him.

'And your forehead. There's an interesting streak of soil smeared right across it,' Oliver added helpfully.

Rosamund glared. More water showered through the air.

'I did wash my face in May-dew this morning,' she said.

'With May-dew? What in the name of all that's holy is May-dew?' he asked.

Rosamund snorted and tossed her head. 'You may live in t' castle, but you don't know it all, do you?'

'Rosamund.' He shook his head. He smiled. With his eyes. Her stomach gave a lurch. She must be hungrier than she thought.

Rosamund started to gabble. ''Tis said that if May-dew is collected early on May Day, and t' face is washed in't, it'll keep t' skin free of blemishes and bring beauty for a whole year. And luck. And you can wipe that 'orrible smile from your face, Oliver. I don't like it.' Giving her face a last frantic dab, she waded to the bank. Oh, how she wished her tongue did not slip so when she was discomposed!

Oliver offered her his hand to help her to her place. 'Tell me, does washing in May-dew mean you never need wash for the rest of the year?' he teased.

Rosamund scowled and gave no answer. He had taken his knife out and had cut several neat slices of meat. Another reminder of the differences between them. Her father would simply have ripped the meat apart, and certainly would never have arranged the slices so daintily on the muslin... She sighed. Oliver indicated that she should take one of the cuts of meat. Just then Rosamund's stomach let her down by howling wolf-like for its share.

She ground her teeth together and turned her head so she did not have to look at him.

'Rosamund, eat.' Something stroked the back of her hand. A caress? Angrily she shrugged it away.

'Rosamund,' he said softly. He had taken her fingers lightly between his, a delicate, courtly gesture, more fitted for a lady than a miller's daughter.

Rosamund steeled herself to try and meet his eyes. She found she could not.

'I'm surprised you want to eat with a peasant like me. We've nowt in common. We even talk different. Watching me eat will probably put you in mind of the pigs at their trough,' she said sulkily.

He took her hand firmly and placed her bread in it. 'Your speech is clear as any noble's when you put your mind to it. Now eat,' he commanded, and then to her intense relief he turned his attention to his own food.

She was acutely conscious of the chasm which yawned between them. Socially they were miles apart. Rosamund did not want to disgust him. She ate her bread and meat more slowly than she had ever eaten in her life. She kept one eye on Oliver and copied the way he took small bites, and chewed his food longer. It was very hard, for she *was* hungry, and it seemed to take a long time before she had blunted the edge of her appetite.

'Better?' he asked, his deep voice startling her.

Reluctantly she replaced the last of the bread in his saddle-bag. 'Aye. Thank you. I was very hungry.'

'So I observed,' he commented drily.

She shot him a sharp look, but his eyes were friendly. She relaxed.

'I thought, only for a minute, of course, that our dream was to be shattered,' she admitted.

He smiled. 'I know you did. But it wasn't.'

'Nay,' Rosamund smiled, and leaned back in the grass watching him with shining eyes.

Oliver stretched out beside her and picked up a strand of her soft hair, idly twirling it round his forefinger. But his grey gaze rested on her face. A distant bell tolled. A bee buzzed past them, lost and heading for the sea. 'It cannot last,' he said, eventually breaking the silence between them.

Rosamund frowned and would have touched his face, but then recalled his cold reaction the last time she had reached out to him. Her hand fell back.

'We cannot live out our dream, you must know that,' he continued, and she noticed his voice was husky.

'We can,' she insisted. ''Til sunset.'

'Nay. 'Twould be the greatest folly.' His voice was kind, but firm. 'I want to...but no.'

There was a light in his eyes that belied the firmness in his voice. Rosamund saw it and her lips curved. 'Want to...what, Oliver?' she murmured. She reached for his cheek. She touched him. He did not move to reject her, but lay quite still.

'Oliver? What is it you would do? Is it this?' she whispered, very low. Her hand slipped up and round his neck. She shifted on the grass, and then his mouth was on hers. She could not tell which one of them had moved to close the gap between them. She did not care. Rosamund felt the welcoming warmth of his lips move slowly and gently across hers.

She had tried to imagine this kiss. Some deep, primitive instinct buried in the core of her had known Oliver's kiss would not be like anyone else's. Somehow she had known she would not shrink from the touch of Oliver's hands on her body.

But her wildest imaginings had not prepared her for reality. She had had no experience which had ever hinted that a kiss could be like this. Purest pleasure. She had never felt anything like it. Not even known the human body was capable of feeling such sensations...

A tingling tide of pleasure flooded her veins. She became conscious of a hungry yearning centred somewhere in her stomach. She wanted to press her young body closer to Oliver's, much closer. She sensed that he could ease that sharp pang which was gnawing at her insides. It felt very much like hunger. But she'd eaten not minutes ago...

Rosamund's free hand went flying to Oliver's cheek, caressed it. She heard him murmur something she could not catch, and felt the weight of his long, lean body shift in the sweet summer grass. But he was holding away from her and she wanted to feel him pushing her deep into the turf. To prolong this wondrous feeling of enchantment. Her hand slipped to his shoulder, to pull him back to her.

He lifted his head. She was flushed, her eyes grown very soft. 'Rosamund,' he whispered, shaking his head. But again his eyes betrayed him. And he did not move away.

She found her voice. It was husky and quite unlike her own. 'Oh,' she managed. She smiled mistily up at him.

He returned her smile and she felt his palm stroke a hot cheek. If she kissed his hand now, he would not reject her. She turned her head and her caress fell on his wrist. The sense of wonder increased when she saw the effect her kiss had on his eyes.

'They've gone almost blue. Quite lovely, like the sky,' she murmured.

'Blue?' His brow wrinkled.

She explained. 'Your eyes. I cannot tell whether they are blue or grey.'

He held her gaze a moment longer, then abruptly tore his eyes from hers and sat up. He combed his hair with his fingers.

'Oliver?' She touched his shoulder.

'No more,' he said curtly.

A sinking sensation in the pit of her stomach.

'No more?'

'You understand me well enough. No more. I knew it would be folly to live out this dream of yours.' He swung round to face her, and Rosamund noticed his eyes were cool grey again. How could she have ever thought them touched with blue?

She twisted a strand of hair round her fingers. 'You dislike me. I am too bold,' she surmised.

'No,' he said, moving towards the stallion.

'What then? You did not like our kisses?' Rosamund's voice held a pleading note. He had liked it. How could he not? It could not have felt like that if he too were not enjoying it...

Oliver did not reply. Strewn about on the grass was the remains of the meal they had shared. He flung the food briskly into his saddle-bag and jerked hard on the strap to secure it.

'You are ashamed to kiss a peasant maid,' she persisted, following him to the war-horse.

Oliver frowned. 'Nay.' He reached for the stallion's reins, had a foot in the stirrup.

She had to clench her hands into fists at her side to stop them reaching out to him. She must attempt to assume some pride. Oliver would expect that. Pride meant something to those in his class. They lived on it. She had never been able to understand it, let alone afford it. Pride was a luxury for the rich. Wasn't it a Deadly Sin too? She sighed. He was going. She wasn't stupid. It seemed that now, for a moment or two, she must pretend that she had some pride.

'Farewell, my Rosamund.'

She stared at him in silence, eyes huge, drinking in the sight of him.

'You have had a lucky escape,' he told her lightly, as he vaulted into the saddle. 'You should be pleased.'

Rosamund cleared her throat, but her voice still came out husky with regret. 'How so?'

She tipped back her head to see his face, but learnt nothing. He was too high up for her to see his eyes properly. She got no joy from his voice either, it was coming out harsh and stiff.

'I'm baseborn. Not even a peasant maid would relish the thought of being kissed by such as me,' he told her.

There was a little silence, during which Rosamund continued to gaze up at him.

'I ... I don't ...' she began.

'I'm a bastard,' he said bluntly. 'How looks your dream now? Shattered, I'll warrant.'

'Nay. 'Tis unbroken. Nothing can damage the dream. How little faith you have in it! I care not for your birth,' she told him.

He stared, and a fleeting expression of pain and regret washed over his face, so swiftly that Rosamund thought she had imagined it. 'Farewell,' he repeated in the soft voice he'd used when he'd kissed her.

'Farewell,' she echoed.

He clapped his heels hard into Lance's sides, and the animal leaped down on to the beach. In a daze, Rosamund took one or two faltering steps in the horse's wake, and then she too found herself on the sands. Staring after him.

Then he was gone. And all she could hear was the cry of the gulls and the gentle rushing of the sea. There was nothing left to prove the dream had ever taken place. Nothing but the prints in the sand made by the hooves of a great grey war-horse as it galloped with the devil at its tail.

The incoming sea sent a wave running up the beach to wash about Rosamund's feet. Soon those deep tracks would all be swept away. Another wave foamed towards her. She saw her discarded garland, a blob of blue on the untidy sands. The wave moved inexorably towards it. Neatly, tidily, it collected the forget-me-nots and carried them from the beach. The wave would carry them towards the deepest oceans where the dragons lived. Rosamund made no move to retrieve her wreath—a memento of a dying dream. She would never see it again.

Rosamund stood motionless at the water's edge and her eyes strained out to sea. The tide crept higher, ever higher till she stood thigh-high in the cold water. Her best pink robe was drenched, saturated with salt, and she did not even notice.

At length the lowering sun took cover behind the tall grey cliffs. It cast weird shadows from the rocks which bordered the land. One of them fell over her. Rosamund shook herself. She felt as though she had been asleep for a thousand years and had woken to find the world a different place. A very different place. She was not sure that she liked it. Her blue eyes moved to gaze blankly at the dying sun. Then back to the sea-filled bay. No hoofprints now.

Slowly, reluctantly, she waded up the sloping shore. She shivered and headed for home.

CHAPTER TWO

'ROSAMUND! Get moving, you lazy wench,' Osric roared. He had locked the wooden gears into position and watched with careful, if bleary, eyes as the mill wheels began to turn. It was barely dawn.

The mill boasted two floors. Rosamund's father, Osric, was on the lower level, ensuring that the mechanism started running smoothly.

Rosamund was occupied in sieving grain on the next level, the 'stone floor', so called because here were housed the great grindstones. That day they were due to start grinding the widow Eva's grain. She had little strength left in her old arms, and her grain had been poorly winnowed—hence Rosamund's frantic sifting. If she did not sift the grain it would not be completely free of chaff and grit, and both her father's grindstone and Eva's flour could be spoiled.

Set amid the boarded floor were the two pairs of grindstones. The heart of the mill, their position in the centre of the wooden structure was symbolic of their vital importance. A good grindstone was almost worth its weight in gold. Rosamund set the grain pouring down the shoe and watched as one of the top stones—the runner—began to rotate over the stationary bedstone. They would only be using one pair of millstones today. The other pair was ground out and awaiting Alfwold's skilled hands.

At the top of the mill a raised platform was used for storage and for sleeping. The sacks of milled flour were heaved up on a hoist at the end of each working day. High up and safe, well out of the way of thieves, be they rodent or man.

The miller slept at the top with his wife and daughter. Rosamund's stepmother, Aeffe, had not yet descended from that chamber. She was rarely up to see the mill begin its daily grind, and, of the three members of the family was the only one ever to sleep through the clattering noises it made.

'Rosamund!' Osric bawled again, impatiently.

His voice was almost drowned out by the rising chatter of wooden cogs and great wheels turning. But Rosamund had learned to jump at the slightest sound her father made. She did so now and dropped the sieve, cursing softly as some of the grain rattled down like hail on to the wooden boards. She hoped he hadn't heard; surely the wooden cogs made more noise than a few specks of grain... If he didn't hound her so, she wouldn't have spilt it.

Today her long hair was neatly bound. She flicked a thick braid back over her shoulder and poked her head through the trapdoor.

'What is it, Father?' she asked. From her vantage point on the stone floor, she could see Osric's shoulders were all bunched up. He was staring morosely into the empty meal bin. Angry again. She hoped he was not going to be in a foul mood all day. If her father was *beginning* the day like this, it did not bode well for her.

'Father?' she repeated. A couple of grains bounced down the aperture, on to his bald head and into the empty bin. Rosamund winced.

A pair of bloodshot eyes turned up to her. 'You clumsy little wretch!' he mouthed in his most unpleasant manner, thin lips twisting. 'Do you think we 'ave grain enough to spare that you can tip it all over t' mill?'

'I'm sorry, Father. I'll sweep it up. It won't go to waste. Did you want me to balance the grindstone for you?'

'Aye. And if you want to keep your 'ide free from birch blisters, you'd better make a better job of it than you did last time,' he threatened.

Rosamund stifled a sigh. Seeing the state he and Aeffe had been in when they returned from the late night revels at the hostelry last eve, she was not surprised at this display of evil temper. It was not uncommon. She had learnt that the best way to avoid a birching was to placate

Osric. Jump to do his bidding. Once she had tried de-
fiance, had even run away. But Osric had caught her,
and brought her back. She hadn't been able to sleep for
a week after that beating. Rosamund had little love for
the man who had sired her, and had a real chance of
escape offered itself she would have snatched at it and
flown the coop.

She grimaced to recall the beating she had been given
that time she'd been dragged back. Aeffe's little barbed
comments had stung as much as her chastised body.

'The devil finds work for idle hands,' Aeffe had
sneered. 'Laziness, me Osric, that's what 'as twisted your
daughter's mind. She's a wicked, wicked girl.' Aeffe's
eyes had shone with malice as she spoke. 'Keep 'er right
busy, Osric me love, and she won't 'ave time for foolish
fancies. I'll teach 'er where 'er duty lies. And think how
our profits will rise...' Aeffe had smiled winningly at
Osric. Osric who denied Aeffe nothing, and his daughter
everything. Osric who never asked his wife to lift a finger
if she didn't want to, but who only had to whisper to
set Rosamund all a-tremble. The thought of her
stepmother deepened the scowl on Rosamund's face.

Seeing it, Osric's tone grew menacing. 'None of your
lip, girl! Get to it!'

Rosamund scurried to obey. She had no choice but to
try and make the best of it. She might have been born
the daughter of a freewoman, but that did not mean she
could really run off and leave. Where should she go?
What should she do?

What use freedom if there was nothing you could do
with it?

At least they never starved her—they needed her strong
to work. I expect if I could work on nothing, they would
give me nothing, she thought bitterly.

Rosamund tilted her head to one side, and with an
expert eye examined the level of the grindstone. She
shifted one of the weights. No, that was no better. She
shifted another. Nor that. 'Father!' she called through
the trap.

'What is it?' Osric snapped. One of his huge ham-like hands was clutching at his forehead. Nursing a monumental hangover, by the look of him, and as usual it was Rosamund who was going to have to bear the brunt of her father's excesses. His usually florid face was the colour of flour paste. His head probably felt as though a war-horse had done a dance on it. At that thought a strange picture took shape and grew in Rosamund's mind. She smiled to herself; a great grey stallion called Lance, and his handsome rider, tall and straight and...oh, this would never do...

'Father!' she yelled.

'No need to shriek like a fishwife. What is it?'

'These grindstones,' Rosamund announced. 'They won't balance any better than the other pair.'

'Oh, blast you for a useless wench! Can you do nothing?' Osric stumped towards the stepladder muttering curses under his breath.

'No, Father. It's not my fault,' Rosamund explained. Her harsh parent shoved her unceremoniously out of the way and bent to peer at the stones. 'The furrows need re-cutting. Same as those.' She pointed at the millstones currently out of use. 'It's a good while since Alfwold was here. Until he dresses *all* the stones properly they will only get worse. Where is he? Was he not due a month back?'

Osric grinned and pinched his daughter's cheek. It was not a loving gesture and it hurt. 'Longing to see your betrothed, are you?' He laughed.

'N...no. I...I...that is...he's normally been here and dressed the stones by the time May is come. Has anything happened to him? Shouldn't he be here by now?' she asked. Rosamund did not want to see Alfwold, but knew it was inevitable. She would rather know when the meeting was to be, than have it sprung on her unexpectedly and be unarmed.

Osric grunted and frowned, moving the weights on top of the runner, first one way, then another. He seemed not to have heard her question. Rosamund watched him. How ugly he had become. He had not always been like this ... Perhaps she was not the only one after all to bear the brunt of her father's excesses. His body had suffered under them too. He was overweight and his chins wobbled when he shook his head like that. He looked unusually pasty today. When he was enraged Rosamund had seen those jowls darken to a deep purple. There were great lines and wrinkles in his forehead—he wore an almost permanent frown. His eyes were shifty, but that was not surprising given what Aeffe had him do. She could not remember the last time she had seen him with clear eyes. Always red and bleary now; always sliding sideways.

'Where's Aeffe?' Osric asked suddenly, looking up from the runner.

'Still abed,' Rosamund replied. She smiled sweetly.

It was a mistake, for her mode of reply brought an unpleasant frown to Osric's face. 'Watch your lip, girl. Your stepmother had a busy time yesterday, she's resting up,' he snapped, and bent low over the stones again.

With his back stooped like that and his large beer gut, he was as round as a wheel. There was no sign of the tall, proud man he had once been. What did Aeffe see in him? She was a pretty woman and could have had almost any of the freemen in the village, but Aeffe had chosen Osric. And Rosamund thought she knew why. Looks had nothing to do with it, nor a good nature— it was money Aeffe craved. And Osric's pilferings kept her well supplied.

'Bone idle, that's what you are. Bone idle,' Osric muttered, his voice holding no trace of affection.

'Father, that's not true. I have been sieving the grain, so it would be ready when——'

'Blast this stone!' Osric broke in, his voice tight with anger. 'And blast Alfwold. Where the hell is the man? He swore blind he would be here this morn. If I managed to get to my feet, then by Christ, so should he!'

Rosamund's heart felt as though it had dropped right through the floor.

'He's here?' she gasped. 'Alfwold's in Eskdale? S...so soon?'

'Aye. I thought that news'd bring t' colour to your cheeks,' Osric sneered.

He knew Rosamund had no liking for the man. The betrothal had been Aeffe's idea. It was a business deal, pure and simple. No reason at all for the girl to have to like the man. *He* liked him. Knew how to put back his ale, did Alfwold. And Aeffe liked him too, she liked those stories he picked up on his travels. Full of them, was Alfwold. That was enough. If Osric and Aeffe could put up with the thought of Alfwold sharing the upper chamber with them, then that was all that mattered.

Rosamund's petty likes and dislikes had nothing to do with it. Business was business, and Aeffe was right to put it first. Osric needed someone who could be relied upon to take over the mill. He was nearing forty. Already old. Aeffe had pointed out to him most clearly that he should be thinking ahead.

He didn't criticise his dear wife for forcing him to ponder on the problems that befell a man in his declining years. He was not afraid to think about his own mortality. Not a bit of it. She was quite right. Someone *did* have to think about these things. It was not the slightest bit gruesome on her part. Wasn't dearest Aeffe much younger than he was? Osric smiled fondly. It was the smile of a doting old man for his young bride. A mere child of eight and twenty, and still a beauty, by God! He was proud to have her. A lucky man.

Osric's brow furrowed, and his eyes clouded. Aeffe was right. He would be dancing with Death before she. She did right to look to her own future. And with Alfwold running the mill as he, Osric, would teach him, then Aeffe would be safe. Aye, 'twas only natural for a woman to plan ahead thus.

Osric grunted and moved a weight one last time.

''Tis no good,' he acknowledged, reluctantly admitting Rosamund had been right. 'We do need Alfwold. I'd thought we might get another day's work out of 'em, but these stones are ground out. Where is that man?'

Rosamund walked blindly away, and stared through the narrow aperture which overlooked the millpond. She saw nothing of the fresh new day. There might as well have been a thick sea fog in off the coast, for all she saw.

'Rosamund!' Her father's harsh voice grew louder till it penetrated at last. 'Rosamund!'

Rosamund's eyes refocused. 'Father?'

'Well? Do you see him?' Osric snapped.

'Who?' Rosamund frowned, trying to drag her wits together. What had her father been asking her? His words floated like fluffy dandelion seeds right over her head.

'Heaven help me, the Lord has seen fit to bless me with a fool instead of a daughter!' Osric sighed heavily. 'Alfwold. Do you see him? I thought you were looking out for him.'

'Oh.' Rosamund's head jerked back to the window. 'Nay. There's no sign of him from here.' Her lips felt oddly stiff.

Osric made an impatient noise which sounded very like a dog growling. 'Get you down t' road a ways, me girl. See if you can find that man o' yours. Drag him from the hostelry if needs be. I've work for 'im,' he ordered.

'That man o' mine,' Rosamund muttered under her breath.

'Rosamund.' Osric's voice was sharp as a needle. 'Did you 'ear me?'

'Aye,' she replied dully. She put her foot on to the top rung of the ladder.

'And Rosamund...'

'Father?' She forced her eyes up to her parent's doughy face.

'Be nice to him. You know what I mean. Nice. He told me 'ow e's been looking forward to seeing you. Don't disappoint 'im, will you?'

'No, Father,' she replied, outwardly the dutiful daughter. Inwardly...

Be *nice* to him. She went down a step. She knew what *that* meant. Another step. Being nice to him meant doing all those things that Aeffe did for Osric in the still reaches of the night. Rosamund was not sure she could be *nice* to Alfwold. Last week she would have taken it for granted. Even the day before yesterday. She had not been brimming with joy at the thought of marrying Alfwold, but she had managed to accept it as inevitable. There had been the slim chance that, given time, she might come to like him. And he might come to treat her well.

Rosamund came out of the mill, and began walking down the road to the tavern, which was situated further downstream. The bright sunlight made her blink after the shade in the mill. She sighed heavily.

Another beautiful day.

This one was not destined to be like yesterday, though. It would be like all the others, all the ordinary, dreamless, hopeless days. She trailed down the road at a snail's pace, having no reason to hurry.

A blackbird trilled from a nearby sycamore. A glorious sound dedicated to a glorious summer to come. But Rosamund had no ears for listening to blackbirds that morning. Deep in thought, she did not see the path ahead, or even feel the earth beneath her unshod feet.

If Alfwold liked her, he might cherish her. Didn't Osric cherish Aeffe as far as he was able? Rosamund would care for Alfwold in return. It had been a long time since Rosamund had had any cherishing. Not since her mother died of the coughing sickness. Her eyes suddenly filled, but Rosamund could not abide self-pity. She blinked hard, closed her mind to the image of her dead mother's face, and marched stolidly on down the track.

Until yesterday Rosamund had hoped that if she succeeded in pleasing Alfwold she might find some of the love she'd always craved. Oh, Alfwold was not handsome, not with that face of his, pitted and scarred by the stone chips which flew from his chisel. How many men were handsome? Not many; life left its marks on everyone one way or another. She thought of wrinkled old Eva. Poverty and misery had scarred her. Of her father. Grown fat and ugly with greed and guilt. In drowning his sorrows he had blurred not only the sharp edges of his mind, but also the contours of his body.

No, Rosamund had not been brought up to expect a handsome husband. The most she could ever pray for was a companion who might come to care for her.

The face of a young man with blue-black hair and sombre grey eyes flashed unasked-for into her mind. Rosamund stopped mid-stride, and stood still as a statue in the middle of the dusty road. Yesterday she had had a dream. Dreams were not meant to colour one's waking hours. They had their own special time, and should stay there safely confined. But this dream had escaped its proper place and walked unbidden into the present. It did not belong here.

Rosamund groaned aloud. A rustling noise came from the ditch by the wayside, but she did not hear it. That wretched dream, urging her to rebellion. It made it more, so much more difficult for her to accept what must be.

She felt sick. Now she could no longer stomach the thought of her forthcoming wedding. They would probably have to carry her kicking to the church door...

A hacking cough had followed the rustling from the roadside. It brought her morose reflections to an abrupt halt. She lifted her head.

Someone was watching her. Someone who had spent the night in the ditch at the side of the road, and was lying there even now, watching her with eyes that were bright and eager. She recognised that dreadful skin at once.

It was Alfwold.

'Oh!' said Rosamund weakly, to cover the shock of seeing him. So ill-favoured. 'I was looking for you. Osric told me to find you. He 'as work for you. But I think you know that already, don't you?' Try as she might, she could not invest the right amount of pleasure into her voice. She knew she must sound cold and unwelcoming.

Alfwold stretched and grimaced. Some of the light went from his eyes. Rosamund flushed guiltily to see that eager look of his fade. She could not help it if she did not love him. She must try. She would try.

Alfwold rubbed his scarred face with blunt fingered hands that were blackened and pockmarked to match his face. 'Aye.' He looked at her, almost shyly. 'You've grown prettier since last I saw you, Rosamund.'

'Oh. Have I? Th...thank you.' She stuttered. She had nothing to say to him. She fiddled with the plaited leather belt at her waist.

Alfwold the stone-dresser climbed out of the ditch and approached his betrothed.

'Nay, Rosamund,' he chided. 'Don't back away from me. Have you no kiss for your betrothed? No warm welcome after all these long weeks?'

Rosamund bit back the denial that rose to her lips. She felt stiff as a wooden doll, but she managed to halt her retreat.

The past winter had not treated Alfwold well. There were new lines and wrinkles in his ruined, dirty-looking face. There were silver threads running through his hair that had not been there before. It was badly in need of a trim. She remembered how she had vowed to try and please him.

This was reality.

She must make of it what she could. Alfwold alone could ease the misery of her slave-like existence with Osric and Aeffe. What use was a mere dream?

So Rosamund smiled and held out her hand to Alfwold. She saw his face lighten. He took hold of it, jerking her close to him.

'Oh.' Rosamund gasped at the unwanted suddenness of it. She was not ready. A strong stench of sour ale assailed her.

'What's amiss?' Alfwold asked, kindly enough.

'Nothing,' she lied, not meeting his eyes.

Alfwold misread the reason for Rosamund's downcast eyes. 'It seems your father was right,' he commented in a pleased voice. 'He swore you were a chaste maid. Seeing you're so comely, I found that 'ard to believe, but maybe 'e's right.'

Rosamund nodded. She was chaste. That at least was not a lie. What could she do? Tell him the real reason for her lowered eyes was that he revolted her?

'Now, Rosamund, your kiss,' he prompted.

Rosamund shut her eyes and bravely angled her head to his. She held her breath.

It was horrible. She had known it would be. But he released her quickly. And now it was he who did not meet her eyes. Oh, God. He knew. His expression...it was all closed up. Alfwold stepped back and silently began brushing bits of leaf and grass from his worn grey tunic and hose. Coarse, workaday fabric. She noticed there was a large rent in one of his sleeves.

Her inability to respond to his kiss betrayed her. One tiny spark of hope flared into life in her breast. Alfwold was not cruel. Would he perhaps release her from her promise?

'Now, lass,' Alfwold said, shouldering his heavy pack of tools. 'Lead on. We'll see what work it is your father 'as for me.'

''Tis but the same as ever,' Rosamund informed him. '*Both* pairs of millstones 'ave lost their furrows.' She grinned suddenly. 'They are as impossible to keep balanced as Father's temper.'

'Come then, we'll talk as we go.' Alfwold smiled at her. She could sense no passion in him. Perhaps he would release her?

Side by side they walked towards the mill.

Alfwold was a stocky man. His height was equal to Rosamund's, but no more. His strength lay mainly in his arms and hands. It was punishing work dressing millstones. It could take up to a fortnight to finish a difficult pair. 'Twas not like whittling a child's toy from wood. It built up the muscles, and Alfwold was reckoned to be as strong as an ox.

Rosamund sent covert glances in his direction. Face and hands had suffered most from his trade. The years of chiselling and hammering had sent thousands of stone and steel darts flying into his skin, scarring the tissue and turning it a dark and dirty colour. One such missile had hit him in the right eye, the eye nearest to Rosamund. It had left him with a red mark there. The permanently dark stain left on the skin of both hands and face made him look as though he never washed. Rosamund knew that that was not his fault. But did he have to reek so of the tavern?

She held out her hands and regarded them. They were clean and white. Workworn, but clean and white compared to his black fists. They were shaking. She curled her fingers so the nails bit into the palm of her hands.

She saw him glance at her. She summoned up a smile for him.

'I missed you, lass, these past weeks,' he commented and paused.

Rosamund said nothing.

'There are several reasons why I want to wed you, lass. Will you listen if I tell 'em to you?'

Rosamund nodded her assent, and as he slowed his pace, matched hers to his.

''Tis a hard road, the one I tread. Always on t' move, from mill to mill, with never a place to call me own. I'm not asking for pity, Rosamund. I want you to know, that's all. Mine's a fine trade to ply when you're young, and t' lust for travel runs fast in your blood. When you're free and proud to own no man your master. The 'ighways stretch out afore you—you feel as though t' world is at your feet, and that you can do owt you like.' Alfwold's grizzled head turned towards the mill down the road. He shifted his heavy pack to a more comfortable position on his shoulders.

'But that time 'as passed for me. T' blood runs more slowly now. The opportunities that I 'ad hoped for, long forgotten, long passed by.

'I need a place where I can settle. This winter past 'as froze me soul to ice, and I thought that I could never be warm again, but wi' you...wi' you... Do you understand what I am telling you, Rosamund?'

'I...I think so. You are saying that you would still wed me,' she said, in a low voice.

'Aye, lass. That I would. I've no young man's passion that you'd want to share. Not now. But if you would try to accept me, I will guard you and keep you safe. I would look after you, and in return...' He hesitated.

'In return...' Rosamund whispered through bloodless lips.

'Let me love you. Truly love you. As a young lover would. Forget my age. I won't 'urt you, Rosamund.'

Rosamund closed her eyes briefly on the red flush that she noticed welling up under Alfwold's blackened and pitted skin.

This was worse than she had thought it would be. He did care for her. This squat and ugly man cared for her. Her wish had been granted. She knew she should accept his terms. She should. Hadn't she prayed for just such a one to care for her and to share her life? What more did she want?

Her blue eyes opened and fell on the wayside shrine at the turn in the road. It was dedicated to Our Lady. Someone had placed a posy of flowers next to the crudely carved and brightly painted statuette. Forget-me-nots. Her stomach lurched. Briefly she closed her eyes.

'Rosamund.' With his voice gone hoarse, Alfwold faced her and gripped her hands in his. 'Let me show you what it can be like,' he begged, kneading her fingers beneath his. 'Tonight. I shall be staying at the mill. We can be wed next week. 'Twill be no shame for us to anticipate our vows by a day or two.'

Rosamund found her voice. 'A week? So soon? Oh, Alfwold, I cannot,' her voice cracked.

The callused fingers tightened over hers. She could not have pulled away, even if she tried.

'You will not wed me, then?' he jerked out.

Rosamund searched his eyes. Brown eyes. Solid and safe and warm. With a terrible hurt hovering in their depths. It was in her power to chase that hurt away. He really did care... It was all she could hope for.

'Alfwold, I will wed you.' She heard herself pronounce her sentence. It was for life. She swallowed and cleared her throat. 'But there is one thing...'

Alfwold's eyes were glowing, but the sight of them did nothing to warm her heart. Rosamund felt as though a sharp frost had crawled through her and now she was paralysed. Frozen solid.

'My sweet lass,' Alfwold smiled. He raised her hands to his lips and kissed them.

'The one thing...' Rosamund reminded him.

'Anything,' he responded, with a pitiful attempt at gallantry.

Rosamund looked at the statue of the Virgin. 'You were right in assuming that I am chaste. I am.'

That much was true at least. Alfwold was nodding and smiling at her. He had no difficulty accepting that truth from her. Now the lie. 'But 'tis no accident that I remain a maid. I have taken a solemn vow to Our Lady, that I shall preserve my virgin state till after my wedding...'

So far so good. He was still nodding and smiling. 'So please, Alfwold, do not press me to lie with you. Not till after the ceremony.' She glanced at him again hesitantly, half expecting him to fly into a rage. If he honoured her 'vow', she might have enough time to get used to the idea, and perhaps by then he would not seem so repellent to her.

'Rosamund. *My* sweet lass. Of course I understand your vow. And I'll 'elp you to honour it. I think 'tis a fine thing in you to 'ave sworn this oath.'

'Oh, thank you.' Rosamund smiled. Her relief was too strong to hide. 'You won't regret it, Alfwold. I am sure it will help me prepare myself better for our wedding day.' And come to terms with it, she added to herself.

'I'm glad that's sorted,' Alfwold told her. 'Now, 'ow long is it since I last dressed them stones for your father? He'll be thinking I'm not coming, if we don't make haste.'

Most people slumbered on in Ingerthorpe Castle. Oliver descended the spiral stairway to the hall and found the cook's boy curled up almost in the wide hearth. The blaze had been banked down last night, and the boy must have edged nearer and nearer the cooling embers in his sleep. No one would be able to rekindle the fire till the lad was roused and shifted.

Oliver suppressed a sigh, and cast weary eyes around the large chamber. It would take some getting used to Baron Geoffrey's castle, and a fortnight was clearly not long enough.

The air in the hall was stale and redolent with the smell of sour wine, spilled ale, rancid fat, and dog. Oliver's nostrils flared in disgust. Well past cock-crow, and the floor still littered with dirty rushes and food debris. The bodies of Fitz Neal's sleeping retainers looked like lumpy sacks of grain tumbled off a cart. Even the hunting dogs still dozed on. It was a far cry from his uncle's well-ordered establishment in the south. By this time everyone would be up and fed. The dogs would be yelping for their exercise, Mass would have been said...

His stomach knotted suddenly in a spasm of homesickness so violent that Oliver had to clench his teeth. He must think of the future. There was nothing to be gained from maudlin reflections. The uncle who had treated him as a son was dead. Nothing would change that. And his aunt had seen fit to send Oliver to his cousin. He could not argue with her.

'Geoffrey needs a squire, Oliver,' his widowed and grieving aunt had announced. 'I am sure he will find you useful, for my beloved Robert taught you all the knightly skills. He would have given you your knighthood in time, for he doted on you. You know we have never let your birth affect the way we have treated you...'

'I know, Aunt, and I am grateful for it,' Oliver had told her stiffly. But he knew, and she knew, that it would be different in his cousin's household. Oliver's experiences abroad had taught him the hard way that the tolerance he took for granted in his late uncle's establishment was far from universal. His aunt's words were meant as a warning, but the fact that they had to be uttered at all had him branded as different. He was an outcast, and most of society might pretend to his face that they did not mind, but he had heard the whispers behind his back, the sniggers. He had seen the furtive glances. He would never be able to take a lady to his wife. A knighthood would have proved his worth. But now Robert de Warenne was dead, and Oliver would have to begin all over again. He would have to convince this cousin of his he would bring honour, not shame, to the knightly estate.

Oliver struggled to conceal his resentment from his aunt.

The Lady Maud de Warenne had made a sound that was suspiciously like a sniff. She looked at him with sad, shadowed eyes, that were huge with the shock and grief of her bereavement.

'Ah, that pride of yours. I see your father's sister in you more and more,' Lady Maud said.

Oliver's lips thinned. 'She was my mother,' he got out.

A sad smile played across Lady Maud's lips. 'If only she'd confessed who it was she'd loved. I've always wondered. But no, Clare never uttered a word. She died taking her secret with her. I liked her. She would have been pleased to see you knighted, Oliver, but . . .' Lady Maud shook her head slowly and never finished her sentence.

'Aunt?' Oliver prompted.

She smiled sadly. ''Twas not to be. 'Tis not within my power to dub you knight. But I shall send you to your cousin. And you will have another chance to earn your place. Twenty-four is somewhat old, I fear, for a squire, but 'twill do you no lasting harm. Take the destrier. Robert would have wanted you to have him. I know you love that animal, and what should I do with a war-horse? Robert should have taken the brute on crusade with him; 'twas not easy getting him enough exercise with both of you fighting the Holy War.'

'There was not much that was holy about that campaign,' Oliver muttered drily.

'Pardon?'

'Nothing, my lady.' Oliver had smiled. 'Lord Robert did not want to risk Lance on the journey,' he explained in a stronger voice.

'So he told me. He risked himself instead. And never came back,' the Lady Maud spoke bitterly.

'My lady...' Oliver began, uncomfortably aware that in her view the wrong man had returned.

The Lady Maud made an impatient gesture and smiled, a shade too brightly. 'I cannot alter the past.' She returned to her former theme. 'But, Oliver, others took their mounts with them...'

'Aye. And none were as prized as Lance, Aunt,' he said.

'Maybe if Robert had taken the beast he'd not have fallen. Ah! What's the use? You may have the animal.' Lady de Warenne finished sharply. 'Every time I see the beast I am reminded of Robert riding him. Of the hours he spent practising his skills. And all for nought. Only to die on foreign soil.' A delicate hand covered her eyes. She shook her head.

'You take Lance. It hurts too much to keep him here. Robert would have wished you to have him. Now go, my boy. Go, before I shame us both by weeping. Farewell.'

So Oliver de Warenne had left the place and the people he loved as his own. No use to beg his aunt to let him stay. She had grief enough of her own to cope with without him whining at his fate.

His cool grey eyes ranged down the length of Geoffrey's hall and over the sleeping bodies. He knew it would be hard. It was not simply that there were no familiar faces. Not simply that he found their dialect almost impossible to understand. These strangers were testing him. Setting him little trials to see how he would react. Teasing him, pushing his temper to the limits. So far he had held himself in check. He would not let them goad him to fury. They would accept him in time. And then his mother's sin would no longer be something to laugh at, to mock at. It would be forgotten and he would be accepted for himself. He would win his golden spurs.

Oliver went to stand over two of the younger lads, and stood for a moment looking down at their sleeping faces.

'John! Matthew! Up with you! Lazy churls! No guard I know of would sleep so long, or so sound. You're only fit to watch swine,' he chided.

Muffled groans and stirrings from the floor. One boy emerged from within his cocooning cloak to frown with ill humour at Oliver. The lad was about fourteen, his lank yellow hair was tousled and unkempt.

'De Warenne,' John groaned. 'Could only be you. You're inhuman,' the boy complained, ''ave pity on us. We must 'ave downed a whole barrel last eve.'

Oliver frowned. The boy's accent was very thick. He spoke lazily. The girl Rosamund's voice had been much clearer, much easier for a southerner to understand. Oliver shrugged. 'No matter if you'd downed a dozen barrels. The work still needs to be done. Arise. You know your duties by now. Waken all these other sluggards. Get the trestles set up. My lord Geoffrey will be down anon.'

Gently, but firmly, Oliver nudged the slothful youth with a booted foot. He had to bite the inside of his cheek to hide his smile as the boys, still grumbling, moved reluctantly to obey him.

'Oh, me 'ead.' This from John.

'Me stomach.' The other lad, Matthew, blinked. He rubbed his eyes with grimy hands. 'Me eyes. Only a peasant would awaken so early. Go away. Let me be.'

Matthew gave a false start of surprise, as if he'd only just noticed Oliver standing over them. Bloodshot eyes gleamed spitefully. 'Oh, 'tis you. Can't say I'm surprised. Get you gone, de Warenne. If it weren't for the fact that you're Fitz Neal's cousin I'd...' Matthew stopped abruptly as Oliver's set expression penetrated his wine-fuddled mind.

'Aye?' Oliver urged, dangerously quiet. His hands on his wide belt, legs slightly apart. 'What would you do, Matthew? Pray enlighten us.'

Matthew looked to his companion for support. John was grinning expectantly. Matthew took courage from his friend's interest. His stricken look vanished. His voice became light and teasing. 'Mind that you asked for this, de Warenne,' warned the boy. 'I'd call you by your real name. The one your mother left for you. You're a bastard in more ways than one. Only a misbegotten churl would kick us awake as you 'ave done after last night's revels. A cold, unfeeling bastard who was probably sired in a barn and that by a...'

A muscle flickered in Oliver's jaw, and his lips thinned. That was all. But it was enough. Matthew seized on it in triumph.

'Aha!' cried Matthew triumphantly. 'I've managed it, as I wagered I would. That's two groats you owe me, John! Did you see t' look on 'is face? He 'as feelings after all!'

'Barely,' the other lad muttered. He climbed out of his cloak, feeling ill at ease. He wished Matthew would not try to goad de Warenne in this way. It had gone on long enough, and John sensed uneasily that one day— if they did actually manage to break through that iron control Oliver seemed to possess—all hell might be let loose on them. He did not like the dangerous gleam in de Warenne's eyes. 'Come on, Matthew, you heard our lord's new squire,' said John. 'We've work to do.'

Oliver spun round on his heel. He would not be drawn. Their baiting would be ignored today, as it had been this past fortnight. They were but boys. Quite soon now they must grow bored with seeking a response from him, and turn to some other wretch for their amusement.

'Boy! Up with you too,' he commanded, coolly prodding the boy in the ashes. 'We'll go to the kitchen to see if there's aught left for us after last night's feast.'

But Matthew had more to say. And by God, he was set on saying it. 'Twas too good to let this one slide...

Matthew scratched an unkempt mop of light brown hair and grinned irrepressibly. 'I saw you on t' beach, de Warenne,' he announced. Then he watched de Warenne and waited.

Oliver checked himself mid-stride, almost imperceptibly, but several pairs of sharp, mocking Yorkshire eyes were on him now and all had taken note. He continued making his way towards the kitchen, determined to show no reaction to this or any taunt they might throw at him.

Matthew's baiting continued. 'Was she pretty, that wench I saw you with?'

Surprise shook John temporarily out of his embarrassment. 'Never!' he exclaimed. 'De Warenne with a maid! You didn't tell me that, Matthew. I don't believe it, who would...'

Gratified with the shock that his accusation had caused, Matthew pressed on. 'I never said she were a maid, John. No lass with what she 'ad to offer could possibly still be a maiden. Aye, saw 'em wi' me own eyes, that I did. Not close up, for I was on t' cliff, but...'

'And who were *you* with?' John interrupted slyly. He had taken note of the set of de Warenne's shoulders. He did not like it. And bastard though he was, de Warenne did rank higher than they. He was Baron Geoffrey's cousin...

Matthew was not so easily deflected from his target. 'I were on t' clifftop,' he repeated doggedly, his cheeks slightly pink. 'De Warenne's hulking great war-horse gave him away. I'd know it anywhere. 'Tis the only grey destrier hereabouts.'

Matthew licked his lips, and probed. 'Was she good, de Warenne? Does she have a liking for the kisses of a bastard squire? How much did you have to pay her for her to...'

'Enough!' A new, decisive voice cut across Matthew's goading as effectively as a knife slicing through warm butter. It was Baron Geoffrey Fitz Neal, Lord of Ingerthorpe Castle. He strode into the hall, following a large beer belly, feet sounding loud on the wooden floor. He had large and perceptive dark eyes which took in the situation at a glance. He clapped Oliver on the shoulder, friendly fashion. 'Good morrow, young cousin! These little pests don't irritate you, do they?'

'They're easily brushed aside,' Oliver replied indifferently.

Fitz Neal's sharp eyes took in Oliver's set shoulders and white mouth. 'Are they, cousin? Are they indeed?'

he murmured softly for Oliver's ears only. 'I thought, for a moment, Matthew had scored a hit.' The Baron turned to his servant.

'You! Scullion! Matthew!'

'Me lord?'

''Tis not your place to goad Oliver,' the Baron said severely. 'Every man has his place here, and you would do well to remember it. Leave it to the women to bitch. God knows there's enough of them here.'

Oliver made a movement with his hand. 'Cousin, I do not need your assistance,' he remarked stiffly.

'Oh, damn that pride of yours, de Warenne. I know that, lad!' Fitz Neal replied.

Oliver gave a little smile at the way his cousin addressed him. Geoffrey was but two years his senior, yet now he made it sound as if he were Oliver's grandsire.

'Let them be, then,' Oliver dismissed them. 'See how pale Matthew has gone. You have terrified the lad.'

His lord grinned. 'Aye, and he does right to be terrified. Anyone who does not know their rightful place here needs to be reminded of it. You may be acting as my squire, but you are of my blood and I will not allow them to forget it. 'Tis not *their* place to mock you. Hear me, Matthew?'

'Aye, me lord.'

'Good lad. Now where's my breakfast?' he roared, turning innocent eyes upon the trestles stacked around the wall. The two boys, happy to have escaped so lightly, sprang to obey their lord.

Oliver stared thoughtfully at his cousin. 'My lord...' he began.

'Cousin, you know my name. Use it,' Geoffrey commanded.

'My thanks. Geoffrey, you say 'tis not their place to make a game of me. It sounds as though you have plans in that direction...' Oliver paused, and arched a brow.

'Aye. If anyone must mock you here, then it must be me! Who else?' Geoffrey emitted a gusty laugh as Oliver smiled. The Baron turned to the trestle table which John had set up on the dais, and plonked himself on one of the few chairs. As lord it was his privilege to be so seated. Most people made do with benches. 'Now fetch me some ale, squire, I would eat!' Baron Geoffrey rubbed strong hands together and his brown eyes followed Oliver as he disappeared in the direction of the kitchen.

Fitz Neal rubbed his chin pensively. He was two years older than Oliver and proud of his birthright. He had the confident manner and assurance of one who had never had cause to question his place in society, being blessed with both position and money. He had always been secure.

Geoffrey's imagination was not large and it did not stir often. He could not begin to comprehend the resentment that his cousin felt at being mocked at for his illegitimacy, but he felt impelled to try. He liked the look of his cousin and hoped that they would become loyal comrades. Oliver had a strong, upright bearing and the makings of a knight.

The dark eyes lightened. He knew why Oliver was being taunted. These knaves were ribbing his cousin to test his mettle—as they always did with newcomers. An initiation ceremony of sorts. Essential if de Warenne was to be accepted. But, hell burn it, the man was his own blood. If anyone was to rib at him, it should be a game of the Baron's own devising—no others in this hold had the right.

Oliver had too much pride. His new squire took himself too seriously. Almost as if he thought himself to be above the sins and failings to which other humans succumbed.

Geoffrey scratched his thinning brown hair. It appeared that his cousin had forgotten the Fitz Neals too were a bastard breed. It was there for all to see in their name. Fitz. That was what it meant. Some forgotten Norman Baron called Neal had fathered a whelp out of wedlock, and their line sprang directly from that illegitimate child.

Everyone knew that. And no one taunted *him* because of it. His family had proved their worth and Geoffrey was proud of his ancestry. It was up to him to remind Oliver of that small but vital point.

My lord Geoffrey's swarthy visage darkened in a scowl. His cousin needed to be brought down a notch or two. Taught a little lesson in humility. In touching on Oliver's bastardy Matthew had instinctively found the weak chink in his cousin's defences. So Oliver was sensitive about his birth, was he? Thought himself immune to human weakness, did he?

Baron Fitz Neal's musing halted as the stair door grated open. There was a little flurry of activity as a tall, well-built dame of elderly years glided into the hall. She was closely followed by a female attendant so quiet and self-effacing that she might as well have been invisible.

With a gentility that sat oddly on his large frame, Geoffrey rose and went to kiss the lady's hand.

'Good morrow, Mother,' he said formally.

The Lady Adeliza smiled. She never troubled to disguise the affection she had for her only surviving son. She had two daughters still living, but all her love was hoarded for her son. 'Geoffrey,' she acknowledged, and let him lead her to her place on the high table.

Geoffrey's scowl returned. His mother and de Warenne's had been sisters. Kinship that was close enough for him to name him cousin. His lady mother had not been ashamed to ally herself with the Fitz Neal family, though all knew their descent stemmed from an illegitimate line. He would teach his arrogant cousin a lesson, and 'twould serve also as his initiation to the Castle. Once and for all.

'Twould have to be a right royal jest to serve its purpose. Geoffrey would think of something. And then, after the jest was played out, he would show his cousin he meant to do well by him. Good men were hard to come by these days.

CHAPTER THREE

'HURRY up with that stew, Rosamund,' grumbled Aeffe, calling out from where she stood combing her yellow hair in the mill doorway. 'I'm famished!'

Rosamund shot her stepmother a barbed glance across the yard, but in the twilight it went unremarked. 'If you stopped preening yourself for one minute, and came out here to the cookhouse to help me, perhaps it wouldn't take so long,' she replied, nettled.

Her comment *was* noted and Rosamund saw Aeffe open her mouth angrily to reply, but just then Alfwold and Osric appeared in the mill doorway too; Rosamund's stepmother shut her mouth sharply and her rebuke went unuttered. Aeffe pursed her thin lips, her eyes bright with dislike. Rosamund knew Aeffe would make her pay for her unguarded comment. But not with Osric and Alfwold at her side. Aeffe was too calculating to risk them thinking her a shrew. She would bide her time and pick her moment, and it would be done in such a way that no one would know what she was about.

'That smells good,' commented Alfwold, crossing the small yard to the cramped hut that served as cookhouse for the miller's family. 'So good that it distracted me from me work and made me lay aside me tools too early for your father's liking.'

Alfwold was happily oblivious of the seething undercurrents which flowed between the two women.

Rosamund smiled and continued stirring the contents of the blackened pot which hung suspended from the central roof beam.

'I hope 'tis to your liking,' she remarked.

'Have you done, girl,' demanded Osric, impatient as his wife. 'Is it ready? I thought fish was quick to cook.'

Under her breath Rosamund muttered, 'It is when it's not been dried as hard as a board.' Aloud she said, 'Almost.' She was grateful the fishing season had started; cooking fishmeat that bore the texture of leather was a thankless task in Osric's mill. She'd not be the only one to welcome fresh fish.

'Bring it over, bring it over. Then you can fetch us a pitcher of ale from the alewife. I've got the thirst of the devil tonight. A *large* pitcher, mind.' Osric's arm was about his wife's waist and they disappeared inside the mill.

Rosamund sighed gently.

'Let me go,' offered Alfwold.

'Oh! Nay. They want me to go,' she replied.

'Give me a kiss, and I'll do it. You've done enough today, me lass.'

She had to will herself not to wince. With a stiff face, and her hand clenched tight on the wooden spoon, she offered him her cheek.

'That's all I get is it?' Alfwold asked.

'M ... my vow,' she reminded him, eyes avoiding his.

'Oh. Aye. For a moment I forgot. Where's the jug?'

Rosamund indicated, and bent her head over the thick fish stew. Out of the corner of her eye she could see him hovering in the doorway. Reluctantly she met his soft brown eyes. There was a question in them.

'Aye?' She waited.

'When we are wed, Rosamund ... I will expect more from you,' he warned. 'You must be prepared to give me more than that ...'

'I know. I will. But you must wait till after we're married.' She stirred the stew with such concentration and vigour that the sooty pot swung almost off its hook.

''Twill all be pulp at that rate,' Alfwold said gently.

'What?'

'The pottage.' He smiled.

'Oh!' Rosamund realised what she had been doing, and quickly removed the spoon from the cauldron. When she looked up again Alfwold had gone, taking the pitcher with him.

'Tomorrow I'll get t' castle and ask my lord how much merchet he'll be wanting for the wedding,' announced Osric with his mouth stuffed full of stew.

Rosamund's hand paused in the middle of serving Aeffe's portion. 'Merchet?' she wondered.

'Aye, you half-wit,' snapped Aeffe. 'Merchet. Though why we should have to pay for the privilege of seeing you wed—I don't know.'

The family were seated round a small table on the ground floor of the mill, to one side of the wooden mechanism which turned the millwheel. It was the danger of fire that caused the cookhouse to be set apart from the mill proper and the family's living quarters. Most people lived in small, wooden houses with the fire for cooking and warming in the centre of the main living area. A few wealthy people lucky enough to have their houses built of stone boasted of proper chimneys. But these dwellings were rare; generally the smoke would wind its way out of the humble cottages by whichever route it chose, leaving roof timbers black with soot.

It was too dangerous to risk placing a fire in the mill. Alfwold had told them of another mill where he had gone to dress the stones. They had had a fire in the mill, and somehow it had caused an explosion which had killed the miller and all his family outright.

'Merchet?' Rosamund repeated dully. Then she remembered. 'Ah! The maiden rent!'

'At last. Takes awhile, but she gets there in the end,' said Aeffe with heavy sarcasm.

Osric grunted. 'Where's that man wi' th' ale?' he mumbled.

'Here, Aeffe, your food,' said Rosamund.

Aeffe paused in combing her lank hair, and looked disdainfully at Rosamund's offering. 'You call that food?' she sneered, jerking the comb through her locks. She was using what Rosamund called her 'lady of the manor voice'. Aeffe's comb caught in a stubborn knot, she wrenched it and it snapped with a loud crack.

Rosamund put up a hand to hide her mouth and strove for gravity.

Aeffe rounded on her. 'Rosamund! You wretch! You've been stealing *my* comb and using it!'

'Nay,' denied Rosamund hotly. ''Twas simply that you pulled too hard on it and—'

'How dare you contradict me?' Aeffe stared in rage at the once-beautiful comb now lying broken in her hand. 'You've been using it on that bush of yours. 'Twas only made for fine, delicate tresses.' Aeffe smoothed her thin hair with a loving hand and sent her eyes shifting craftily in her husband's direction. 'Look, Osric, my best comb, 'tis wrecked.'

'I'll buy you another, me pet,' Osric soothed. Then he remembered the merchet he would be paying. 'Oh. No. You'll have to wait awhile. The bride fine's to be paid.'

Aeffe fumed.

The door banged.

'Ah! Good! Here's Alfwold, wi' t' beer.' Osric belched loudly. 'Pass it over, lad.'

'Here, Alfwold.' Rosamund handed her betrothed his portion. His opportune appearance made her smile brighter than it would otherwise have been.

'You'd think they were wed already,' noted Aeffe, her voice laced with malice.

'Soon will be, me love. That's for certain,' said Osric.

Rosamund bit her lip.

'I still don't see why we have to pay the merchet. Isn't there any way out?' wheedled Aeffe.

'None that I know of,' replied Osric. 'Every father has to pay the lord to see his daughter wed. Yours did.'

Aeffe pouted. 'The pedlar had some lovely combs last time he came...they were very expensive...but if we spend it all on seeing *her* wed...'

'There, there, me love. If there was 'owt I could do to avoid paying it, I would. But wed she must be. You know that,' Osric reminded his wife.

'Aye,' Aeffe responded, spearing a chunk of fish viciously with her knife.

'Osric?' Alfwold interposed. 'I want all to be right in my marrying of Rosamund. If it is any help, I'll pay the maiden rent. I have enough.'

'Oooh,' cried Aeffe, simpering hideously. 'Will you?'

'I...I don't think...' Osric began, but a kick from Aeffe silenced him.

'Oh, Osric, think. He's the one who wants your daughter. Why should you pay to be rid of *her*?' Aeffe argued.

Rosamund stiffened and sat bolt upright on her bench. She stared straight ahead, mouth clamped tight as a clam.

Osric cleared his throat. 'They'll be resting here, me love. Not living elsewhere,' he pointed out.

'Still, why should you pay when Alfwold is happy to?' Aeffe fingered her broken comb. 'Take it. Take Alfwold's money,' she urged.

'Nay, Father. Don't.' Rosamund protested. ''Tis customary for the bride's father to pay, not the husband. Will you deny me what little pride I have?'

'Osric,' Aeffe said, slowly and with emphasis.

Osric grinned at his future son-in-law. 'All right. 'Tis a deal.'

The two men struck hands. Rosamund felt sick with shame. She pushed her meal aside and made to leave the table.

Aeffe masticated her fish. 'I didn't think you were so hot for our Rosamund, Alfwold?' She said it slowly with her thin lips stretched into a knowing leer.

Alfwold's pitted skin darkened. He flashed a guilty smile at Rosamund.

'Oh, Aeffe!' Rosamund tensed, and she flushed too, but with embarrassment.

Aeffe was enjoying herself. 'Did you know, Alfwold, that yesterday, your Rosamund made a garland and went in search of a May Day lover?'

'Aeffe!' Rosamund was shocked. 'I didn't. I only made one because everyone else was making them. You remember? There was Lufu here, with Edwin. We made them together. And then when they had gone, I went for a walk. For a walk. I did not go to meet anyone,' Rosamund insisted.

'Nay?' Aeffe's smile was sickly sweet. Only Rosamund knew she was deliberately stirring. Dear God! So this was to be Aeffe's revenge for that unguarded comment Rosamund had made earlier. She should have known that Aeffe would not let her get away with it . . . Aeffe was trying to wreck her marriage with Alfwold before it had even begun . . . would that woman leave her nothing?

'Forget-me-nots, you chose,' Aeffe said musingly. 'Now why pick those flowers if you have no lover in mind, eh?'

'I *like* forget-me-nots,' protested Rosamund. 'There was no other reason.' She went sick with dread.

'No?'

'No!' shrieked Rosamund. It was true. She had not gone to meet anyone. She had not known the lord's squire would be there. She had never spoken to him before, and would never speak to him again. Oh, this was hopeless . . .

Alfwold's slow voice broke in. 'I know all about the flowers,' he announced.

The two women stared at him.

'Aye?' prompted Aeffe, frowning.

Alfwold smiled. 'Saw 'em on t' wayside shrine where Rosamund had put 'em. She 'as made a vow,' he explained briefly.

Rosamund exhaled slowly. Maybe it would be all right . . .

'A vow,' Osric scoffed, holding his empty drinking vessel out for more ale. 'Rosamund, what nonsense is this?'

'I haven't told my family, Alfwold.' Rosamund looked an appeal at the grindstone dresser. ''Twas a secret vow.'

Alfwold's eyes searched for hers, and it was difficult to meet his gaze, but she managed it. 'I'll honour your secret, lass. 'Twill be safe wi' me,' he swore.

'What *is* going on?' snapped Osric testily. 'Would someone mind telling me what you are talking about?'

Alfwold slapped Osric heartily on the back, and winked at his betrothed. 'Nothing, Osric. Just a private matter between Rosamund and myself, you understand. More ale?'

'Humph!' Osric snorted. His nose was already red with the quantity he'd downed thus far, but he permitted his horn to be refilled as though he'd not tasted ale since Christmas.

Rosamund suppressed a sharp pang of guilt. Thank the Lord that someone had given Our Lady that posy! Alfwold supposed that she had put it there. She did not like to deceive him over this, but it was that or else have Aeffe sour her marriage.

Dear God, it was bad enough to have to marry Alfwold, but the alternatives were far worse. At least with him as her husband there was some chance she might have a half-decent life. She would not allow Aeffe to wreck that one small chance.

While Aeffe sulked, Osric and Alfwold were talking to each other softly.

Osric raised his voice. 'Right then. You can come along wi' me to see Sir Geoffrey. We'll go in't morning.'

'Agreed,' said Alfwold. 'The sooner I'm wed to her, the better.'

Osric paused mid-swig and a trickle of brown ale ran down his flabby chins. 'If you want t' wedding to be soon, you'd best visit abbot in t' morning an' all,' he suggested.

'Oh aye. Why's that?' Alfwold asked.

'T' village priest died a sennight ago. Dropped dead while working 'is strip. We're waiting on t' bishop to send another. 'Th' abbot up at t' monastery's dealing wi' such matters till t' new priest comes.'

Alfwold grinned and looked at Rosamund. 'No need. New priest's arrived. I've met 'im.'

Rosamund's heart, which had risen at the thought of a reprieve, however temporary, sank like a stone dropped down a well.

'Where, Alfwold? Where did you meet him?' she asked.

''E were in t' alehouse. Name of Father Eadric. The bishop's given 'im a parchment to mark his appointment.'

'I didn't know you could read, Alfwold,' Rosamund said, brows lifting.

Alfwold shifted on his bench. 'I can't, lass,' he admitted. 'But I saw t' seals on 'is document. Bright red they are, dangling on blue ribbons.'

Rosamund nodded. 'So this Father Eadric will wed us then?'

'Aye. That 'e will. All we need is t' lord's permission and Father Eadric will wed us at church gate.' His brown eyes grew bright and wandered to the jug of ale. 'That new priest can certainly put away his beer. I've never seen a man of the cloth sink a jar so fast.'

Rosamund pinned a false smile on her face, and took his hint. She passed the brew over to her betrothed.

Three evenings later, she and Alfwold were married. Rosamund's head ached terribly. Father Eadric had rushed the marriage ceremony, gabbling the words. For that mercy she must be thankful. The ordeal had not lasted long.

She suspected that the new priest did not have much learning. The Latin words were probably as incomprehensible to Father Eadric as they were to the rest of them. The last priest had not made a pretence of understanding them either. Only a few very holy men, like the abbot and the bishop, understood God's language.

Rosamund scrubbed at her forehead with the back of her hand. Now Osric and Alfwold were talking about her going to the castle. She struggled to understand what they were telling her. She felt as though the devil had set up an anvil in her brain and was forging chains in there.

'What . . . what did you say?' she asked. 'I don't think I can have heard you aright.'

'You did,' Osric said grimly. 'You did.'

Why was Aeffe smirking so? She'd not looked so pleased since Osric bought her that new gown . . .

'Alfwold, what is it? Why are you looking like that?' Rosamund asked, feeling suddenly as though she was about to be eaten alive. Something was very wrong. As this realisation crept into her aching head, it brought with it a nameless fear which made her heart sink.

'Alfwold?' Her voice rose. Her fingers clenched on the folds of her rose pink gown.

But Alfwold had shut his eyes, as though he could not bear to look at her, and it was Aeffe who spoke. Gleefully. 'You're to go straight to t' castle,' she announced. She was so pleased with what she had to say that she had forgotten her 'lady of the manor' voice and spoke in as broad an accent as Osric. This rather than the actual words she was uttering sent a frisson of fear shivering down Rosamund's spine.

'The castle,' Rosamund echoed, stupidly, not understanding. 'But why?'

Aeffe giggled. 'Apparently Baron Geoffrey has taken a fancy to you. He's waived the wedding fine we owe him on condition that you spend the first night of your married life in his rooms.'

Rosamund's eyes widened.

She turned to her sire, for confirmation. 'F...Father?'

Osric shrugged and nodded without much interest. ''Tis true. Alfwold will accompany you. And then he's to leave you there. He will come and fetch you in the morning,' Osric confirmed callously.

Rosamund's tongue seemed to be cleaved to her palate.

'*After* Sir Geoffrey has finished with you,' Aeffe gloated.

'I don't believe you!' Rosamund choked out. 'You're lying. If this is your idea of a jest, Aeffe, I don't think much of it.'

Osric slapped her sharply in the face. 'Mind your mouth, girl. You forget yourself! This was none of your stepmother's doing.'

'I won't go! I don't believe you. Alfwold, tell me it isn't true!'

Her husband avoided her gaze. 'It is true,' he muttered.

'No!' Rosamund shrieked. 'No! But you'll stand by me, won't you, Alfwold? You won't let them send me to my lord Fitz Neal. You're my husband!'

'Rosamund,' said Alfwold sadly.

And then she knew he would send her. Would not stand by his new wife. Alfwold would let Baron Geoffrey waive the merchet and buy her body for the night, and Alfwold would do nothing. He would do nothing, because he was only a lowly millstone dresser and Baron Geoffrey was his liege lord, and they must obey him.

'But you must do something!' she exclaimed. 'You can't let him *buy* me. As if I was a ... a whore!'

'Aren't you?' Aeffe whispered under her breath for Rosamund's ears only.

Rosamund glared. 'Why didn't you tell me this *before* the ceremony,' she demanded.

''Twould have made no difference. You'd only have worried about it for longer,' Alfwold said, his face creased with concern.

'Don't you think you should have told me? Given me some sort of a choice in the matter, seeing as it's to be my body that you've sold off!' she snapped.

Osric's patience had expired. 'Alfwold, you sort her out. She's your wife now. Come, Aeffe, let's get to the tavern, I could do wi' wetting me lips.'

'Father, you can't just...'

'See you tomorrow, Rosamund, my dear, dear step-daughter,' trilled Aeffe, taking Osric's arm.

Rosamund ground her teeth in fury as Osric and Aeffe turned their backs on her and walked away.

'My God,' said Rosamund in tones of utter disbelief.

'Come, lass,' Alfwold said, very gently. 'I'll take you t' castle now.'

Rosamund felt him take her by the hand and pull her towards the road. There must be some way out.

'What if I refuse to go?' she asked.

He stopped. 'They'd probably hang me,' he said. 'For breaking my oath to Baron Geoffrey.

'Oh.' She believed him.

There was a short silence, while they walked along the path through the fading evening light. Then she asked, 'Whose idea *was* it?'

'Not mine, you can be certain of that,' Alfwold said in swift assurance.

'Aye, but whose? Was it Aeffe?'

'Nay. Osric and I went alone. Baron Geoffrey was in the 'all. He 'ad a chair wi' a back on it. At the 'ead of a large table. We went up, and he asked us what our business was. Osric told him. He asked your name. Osric told him. He asks if you are comely.'

'What?'

'You heard. I tells him you are, and he gives a smile. Seems to think it a great game.'

'A game!' Rosamund exploded.

Alfwold sighed. 'Then he tells us that he will let your father off paying the merchet, if you are brought straight up to the 'all after t' ceremony. He said that he'd never claimed the right of the first night before, but that he was doing it today.'

'"The right of the first night",' she murmured.

'That's what 'e called it.'

'And you accepted it,' Rosamund said bitterly. 'Without a word.'

Alfwold stopped walking and faced her. 'Oh, Rosamund. Not at first I didn't. You must know me better than that. But Baron Geoffrey was dead set on having you...er...on you going up to t' castle,' he amended hastily. 'I 'ad no choice. You're not the only one to have things foisted on you, me lass,' he said.

Rosamund put her face in her hands. 'I wish you'd told me before...'

She felt him remove her hands from her face, and lead her forwards again. 'Rosamund, I know how this must grieve you. Especially with that vow you have made.'

'Vow?' Her brows knotted, and then she remembered the lie she had fabricated. 'Oh, aye. My vow.'

'But I wanted to marry you, lass. I will not hold it against you that you do not come a virgin to our marriage bed.'

'Oh. How kind,' she bit out, drily.

Her sarcasm was lost on him. 'Well, me lass,' he said reasonably, 'don't see how I can blame you. It's not your fault. He'll only have tonight. We will have the rest of our lives.'

'The rest of our lives,' whispered Rosamund dully.

Her eyes suddenly focused on her surroundings, and she realised they had already reached the castle footbridge. Another minute or two to get past the sentries, and she would be inside. At the mercy of Baron Geoffrey Fitz Neal, whose whim it was that she should spend the first night of her marriage with him, and not with her husband. He even thought it funny.

She was very pale.

Rosamund lay quaking in the great bed.

Waiting.

So full of anger and fear, and other quite indefinable emotions that she was oblivious to the luxury of her surroundings.

She could hear, floating up from the hall below, gales of drunken laughter. What kind of a monster was Sir Geoffrey that he should decide to take, sight unseen, an unwilling girl to his bed?

Rosamund had not had to face the devils in those riotous nether regions. The porter at the castle entrance had hailed loudly. This brought an elderly lady running up. Her face, had Rosamund the wit to look at it, was kind and full of sympathy. But terror had frozen Rosamund's wit.

She was led up a wide, twisting stairway past the main hall, and higher still, past another large chamber. She was taken along a cold, dank and badly lit corridor between the castle walls. To this chamber.

She'd been bathed and scrubbed white in a large wooden tub. Hot water. As if that were not extravagance enough, the water was fragrant with the scent of the wild roses which would soon be blooming in the hedgerows. A fragrance she'd normally have favoured.

Rosamund had not noticed. For she had withdrawn from this awful reality where a girl could be taken against

her will and put in a man's room and no one, not even
her husband, would lift a finger to help her.

She felt as stiff as a wooden doll. She allowed the
woman to dry her. She allowed her to comb out and dry
her long, honey-brown hair, and tie it loosely at the nape
of her neck. She allowed herself to be dressed in a soft
blue gown, with a belt for her waist which had gold
threads running through it.

But she did not lift a finger to help.

And now she lay waiting. Numb in mind and body,
blue eyes fixed sightlessly on the one flickering candle
in the wall sconce.

A burst of crude laughter, and her eyes swivelled to
the solid door. Was it her imagination or were the sounds
coming nearer? The sound ebbed, and Rosamund forced
her tense muscles to ease. Her nails were ploughing
furrows in her palms. Deliberately she unclenched her
fingers. Tried to relax.

Then she heard it again. Another wave of sound.
Surely those footsteps *were* surging up the steps now?
Towards the chamber. Rosamund covered her face in
her hands and shrank down under the fine linen and pile
of furs. The furs muffled the angry shouting without.

Someone roared with laughter, a deep belly laugh
which rumbled through the air and brought into
Rosamund's anguished mind the image of a huge bear
of a man with an enormous belly. Her brain went blank
and she could not for a moment recall *what* Baron
Geoffrey Fitz Neal looked like.

She cringed deeper under the coverings and curled up
into a tight ball like a hedgehog. She had never felt such
fear. Rosamund knew that she must be a coward, for
she could not even bring herself to peer out and look at
her would-be seducer.

Rigid with apprehension, she heard the door slam. The
key grated in the lock. More shouts of mocking laughter
from the sots in the corridor. Another of those curt,
angry responses which Rosamund had half registered a
moment ago. Terror-struck though she was, Rosamund
was much puzzled by that angry voice. It was not

somehow in accord with the other hooting sounds those fiends were making. There was a deafening thud. Someone striking his fist violently against the unyielding door. She heard a torrent of furious invective.

How strange.

Merriment *outside* the room, but surely that was anger she was hearing from *within*? Had Sir Geoffrey changed his mind? Did he no longer want her here? Hope and curiosity warred with fear.

Slowly, making as little movement and sound as she could, Rosamund lifted the linen sheet down from over her head.

He was tall. With the build of a warrior. He had his broad back to the bed, and one strong fist struck at the door with such force that the wooden planks bowed under the blow. Someone outside struck up a lewd song, and other sozzled, off-key voices joined the first to make a caterwauling that would drive the devil into flight.

The man lifted his head proudly, as though he would defy them all, tossing his shoulder-length hair into further disarray. Night-black hair. He turned.

'Oliver!' Rosamund cried involuntarily. She sat bolt upright. All the last traces of fear fled in the face of her surprise.

He stared.

'Rosamund.' He said her name very slowly. Then he bowed. 'Welcome to my humble abode.'

'You don't sound very welcoming,' she said, seeing those grey eyes were cold as ice, and as hard as the angry lines on his face.

'To tell true, madam...' he stressed the last word so she would have no doubt it was intended as an insult, 'I don't feel particularly welcoming at the moment. My apologies if that distresses you. I wouldn't want to cause you any distress, would I? Not after this.'

'What...what do you mean?' Rosamund swung her legs over the edge of the bed and stood up.

Oliver's wintry eyes went towards the door. The stumbling footsteps were retreating now. Bored with their momentary diversion, his tormentors staggered down the spiral stairs, the lure of the wine kegs too strong to resist for long.

'Couldn't resist it, could you?' Oliver sneered. 'Couldn't keep the dream safe where it belonged after all?'

'I...I'm sorry?' Rosamund said.

'There's no use playing the innocent with me, I fell for that little game once before. I'm never caught in the same trap twice, my sweet. You would do best to remember that. Never the same trap twice.'

Oliver closed the distance between them and clamped his long fingers round her wrist in a grip of steel. His other hand went roughly to her neck and he released her hair with a jerk that brought tears to her eyes.

'Oliver, don't,' she protested gazing at him through a haze. 'None of this was my doing.'

'Quite the noble lady now, aren't you?' His hand was running down her newly washed hair, his eyes scanning her slender frame, resting for a moment on the gentle swell of her breasts. 'I hope you've been well paid. For I promise you this, by the time I've finished with you, you will have earned every last farthing. Got everything you wanted, have you? And what about Oliver? Is he to have what he wants? Eh, Rosamund?

'Or are you to take on the wiles of fine ladies along with their clothes? Are you going to purse up those pretty lips of yours and sneer down your nose at me. A squire. A poor bastard squire of no account.'

'Oliver,' she whispered in despair.

'Oliver.' He mocked her tone. He took her by the neck and pulled her up against him, his grey eyes never leaving her face.

'What?' he asked. 'No shrinking from me in horror? No twisting away to escape my vile clutches?'

His lips came down on hers, hard and insensitive to the pain he caused. His mouth was bruising, grinding her lips. She could smell the wine he had drunk, but she knew instinctively that he was no drunkard. He was mad with rage at those wretches who locked him in with her, and thought her to be their conspirator.

She had to get through to him. To reach the Oliver who had shared her dream on the beach. This man who imprisoned her head with his hand at her neck, was not the Oliver she knew. She must try to reach that other Oliver. Rosamund made no attempt to struggle—what point? His hard, well-muscled body was too strong for her to resist. So she stood immobile under his hands, a deep feminine wisdom telling her that at the moment she could only reach him by *not* responding. Oliver was not the man to want a puppet. He wanted a real woman, and at the moment he was blinded by anger.

But even now, even though he kissed her in his rage, Oliver was reaching *her*. She could feel a slow, warm glow moving in her belly. Her body was responding to Oliver though he showed her no gentleness. Alfwold with all his careful consideration had never kindled the tiniest spark of response within her. Rosamund stood stone-still, knowing that she would be lost if Oliver realised the effect he was having on her.

At last he lifted his punishing lips from her mouth, His eyes glittered in the candle light. When she raised her shaking hand to examine her ravaged lips she saw his dark brows snap together. Her exploration finished, she drew her fingers away. There was blood on them.

Oliver swore, loudly and fluently in the foreign tongue she knew the nobles used. Then he flung her away from him as though she had the plague, and she tumbled into the pile of furs on the bed.

'God's Body,' he groaned, with apparent remorse. He ran a hand distractedly through his hair.

Rosamund eyed him warily from the bed.

'Oliver,' she began. ''Twas not of my doing. I was brought here against my will.'

'Aye?' he asked coldly, watching her, his face still black as thunder.

The candle sputtered on some impurity in the wax, and to her relief this drew his scowling gaze from her. Automatically he moved to trim the smoking wick, taking his bone-handled dagger from his belt to do so.

'You did not use that on them,' Rosamund observed.

'What! Would you have me stab my lord and cousin!'
Unexpectedly Oliver laughed, glancing at the blade.

That was more like the voice that she knew from the
beach. Rosamund began to relax and tucked her feet
beneath her. But she was not yet sure of him, and when
he drew near her, she scrambled as far back as she could.

'So,' he said softly. 'You claim you are not a party to
this trap my cousin has set me?'

The mattress shifted as he sat on the edge of the bed.

'No. I am a victim of this as much as you,' she told
him. 'I take it we're locked in?'

'We are, my angel.'

Rosamund swallowed. She still did not quite like his
voice. 'You sound as though you're angry with *me*,' she
said.

'I do?'

She nodded.

He rubbed his face and let his breath out in a long
sigh. 'If you say you are innocent of this I will try and
believe you, however much my instincts warn me against
such a course. I am not angry with you, Rosamund. If
only for the sake of what I thought I glimpsed in your
smiles on the beach.

'Now, as you so correctly point out, we are indeed
locked in for the night. I suggest that we make the most
of it, and try and get some sleep. They'll release us in
the morning. There'll be no harm done, and you can go
home again.'

'Back to Alfwold,' she mumbled, bending her head
so her hair fell like a drawn curtain to hide her face.

Oliver frowned. 'Alfwold? Who's he? I seem to recall
you telling me you had no lover.' His voice was kind.

He put out a hand and moved her hair aside, those
grey eyes seeking to read her expression. When she continued gazing at her lap he took her chin and tilted her
face up.

'Rosamund. Who is Alfwold?' He felt the shudder
that passed through her slender frame and felt uneasy.
Was it his touch she found so repellent? Had his rage
driven away that wide-eyed, candid gaze he had found

so appealing? Or was there something else? 'Rosamund,' he repeated.

Silently she lifted up a hand, holding it before him as if she would have him take it. He did so, and his long fingers squeezed hers in gentle reassurance.

It was then that he felt the ring. Without appreciating its significance, at first. He gave it no more than a glance. Then he stared. A thin brass band encircled her wedding finger, winking in the flickering light.

'That was not there before,' he said carefully.

'No.'

'Who put it there? This Alfwold?' he demanded.

'Aye. My husband.'

'Your husband!' Her hand was dropped, and Oliver got to his feet. All trace of sympathy had vanished, his features were stern and hard.

' "No lover", eh? It seems all the world must play me for a fool! First you on the beach, and now Geoffrey,' he said bitterly.

Rosamund made a movement with her hand. 'Alfwold is not, and has never been my lover, Oliver. I did not lie to you. That dream we shared was the most beautiful thing that had ever happened to me. But it was only a dream. When you left me on the beach I had to walk back into reality. And reality, for me, was marriage to Alfwold. Not because I wanted it, not because I chose it, but because the alternative was far, far worse.'

'Do you love him?' He sounded no more than mildly curious. Very cool.

'Nay. But Alfwold is a kind man, kinder than my father to me. And I thought he would care for me. I thought marriage to him would mean I might have some say of my own at last. How foolish I was! To think that I, a mere peasant girl, would have any rights! All my marriage has done is brought me here, an unwilling pawn, in a game of my lord's choosing. I would have fought your cousin off, you know, tooth and nail. I would have resisted him.' Rosamund's chest heaved as all her pent-up anger, and terror, finally found expression in the flood of words pouring from her lips.

'Poor Rosamund,' Oliver said wryly. 'You are as much a victim as I in all of this. Neither of us has been given any choice, have we?'

Rosamund took a steadying breath. 'No.' She smiled. 'But then I should be used to that. I have never been given a choice.'

'Except with our dream,' he suggested softly. She noticed his chipped tooth. She had forgotten all about it. He must be angry no longer.

Rosamund smiled and did not gainsay him. Oliver's tall presence dominated the chamber, and she could not but be aware of how attractive he was. Their gazes locked, and Rosamund found she could not look away. He was so handsome, his skin was clear, not black, not dirty-looking. The only fault she could find in Oliver's appearance was that broken tooth, and she liked to see it, for it was only visible when he smiled...

She flushed. To be shut in here, in this tiny chamber all night with him... and she married to another...

He broke the silence. 'What are you thinking?'

Her flush deepened. 'Oh! Why, I suppose I was thinking how grateful I am that it is you who is with me, and not your cousin.'

He grinned. 'You were scared witless, weren't you? Weren't you hiding under the bedclothes when they threw me in here?'

She put her nose in the air. 'You beast.' Then she caught the gleam in his eyes. 'I was a little scared,' she admitted.

'But now you see 'tis only harmless Oliver, you are relieved,' he said, stretching like a cat.

'Hardly harmless,' she murmured drily, watching him, admiring his soldier's well-honed frame and the careless grace of his movements.

'What?' He yawned and glanced at her.

A smile hovered at the corner of Rosamund's lips. She shook her head. 'I was pleased to find I was to share this room with you, and not your cousin,' she acknowledged, deliberately vague.

'Mmm.' He was not listening. Turning his back on her, he unbuckled his wide leather belt, and dropped it neatly on to a much-battered chest which sat under the wall-light. He pulled off his over-tunic. Then he folded it and that too was set tidily atop the coffer.

Rosamund found herself swallowing. Her mouth had gone dry. She watched, transfixed, as Oliver removed his soft leather boots, his fine linen undershirt, and then, clad only in tightly fitting hose, he padded over to the washbowl. His ablutions complete, he came back to the bed.

'In you get,' he commanded, flicking back the bed-covers for her.

'I ... I ... we can't,' she stammered, suddenly shy. She averted her gaze with difficulty from his well-muscled torso, and strong arms.

'Still afraid, after all, Rosamund?' he taunted softly.

'Nay!'

'Then get in. I'm not about to hurt you.' His grey eyes held an unmistakable challenge, but Rosamund was having none of it.

'Nay.' Craven, she retreated to the bottom edge of the bed and glared at him. 'Are you expecting us to sleep together?' she demanded.

His voice was dry. 'That was the general idea. Have you a better one?'

'But we can't!' she exclaimed.

He shrugged easily and climbed into the bed. He stretched out his long length and lay back on the pillow and watched her. There was a wicked glint in his slate grey eyes.

'Your bed is not big enough for two,' she objected.

Oliver clasped his hands behind his head, and grinned. 'I think 'tis a couch fit for a king. I'll wager you've not seen the like of it before.'

'That's beside t' point. If you were a gentleman, you'd give up t' bed to me and sleep on t' floor,' she objected.

'Why Rosamund,' he said innocently. 'I do believe you're angry. Your accent is showing again.'

Rosamund darted a furious glance at him. 'Oh, I see. You despise me for my peasant's voice, do you? That and my low birth. That's why I must sleep on the floor.' She enunciated with great care, determined he should have no further cause to mock her.

Oliver's lips curved. 'Nay. When have I mocked at your speech?' He lifted a shoulder. 'I merely remark that the dialect is more apparent in your tones when you are angry. I find your voice attractive. 'Tis not high and shrill like most maids—it is most pleasing.'

'For a peasant,' she snapped.

He held out his hand to her. 'Come here,' he said softly.

'If... if you were a gentleman, you'd sleep on the floor,' she repeated.

'But as you know, my Rosamund, I am no gentleman. Now, I have much to do on the morrow, and I propose to get some sleep this night. This is my bed and, while I appreciate that you did not ask to be brought here, I would have you remember that neither did I send for you. I am happy to share my bed with you, but...'

'Oh, are you?' Rosamund cried.

Oliver ignored her and carried on smoothly as though she had not spoken. 'But I had enough of hard floors in the East, and I'll be damned before I give up my bed to you. Sleep where you choose. I care not. Goodnight.'

And with that he turned on his side, pulling the covers over his broad shoulders.

'Hmph!' Rosamund snorted and flounced angrily off the bed.

She went to the door. Tried to open it. A futile gesture and she knew it. She could feel his eyes boring into her back, could imagine the amused, supercilious expression in them. She whirled round to face him, but Oliver had not moved. He lay facing the door, with his eyes firmly shut. The bed occupied almost all of the small chamber, and she could hear his breathing, deep and even. Probably asleep already. Vile, selfish, arrogant male!

The sputtering candle was down to its last inch. Its wick needed tending. Moving softly, so as not to attract

Oliver's attention, or waken him if he were truly asleep, Rosamund picked up his dagger from its resting place on the chest and trimmed it. Her fingers fumbled at the simple task. It was a beeswax candle. They only ever had stinking tallow ones at the mill. She examined the carved hilt on Oliver's dagger and made out an intricate design on it. Was this blade from the far-off East?

Curiously her eyes roamed Oliver's chamber. It might be small, but it was all his own. Imagine having a room to yourself! What luxury. And to sleep in such a bed. Rosamund shot a glance in that direction. It had felt so soft, that bed. She yawned.

She sat down on the rush floor covering close to the bed and tried to get comfortable. Her gaze wandered over her companion's strong features. His face was lightly tanned. The wet spring just passed could not have bronzed him so. One arm lay relaxed on top of the bed-clothes. She admired the shape of it, wondering why she had never noticed before that a man could be beautiful. If she touched his shoulder, ran her fingertips down that arm, what would it feel like? Oliver's hand rested on the edge of the bed, so near that she could see the blue veins under his sun-kissed skin. She remembered him mentioning a crusade. Perhaps the Eastern sun blazed hotter than their own. Or maybe the sea voyage home had burned his skin?

A cold draught whistled under the door and over the floor of the chamber. Rosamund shifted restlessly on the scratchy rush mat, wishing that it were not so hard and lumpy.

She sat up and leaned her arms on her knees. The bed had been so soft, and it was up out of the way of the chilling draughts. She had been a fool not to get in with him. He'd said he wouldn't hurt her. And now she was freezing out here, with only her stubbornness to keep her warm.

She was but an arm's length from Oliver's head. His hair was still tousled and damp from his hurried wash. A stray lock had fallen across his face. She put out a hand and very delicately brushed the lock aside. His eyes opened at once and he looked straight into hers.

Rosamund started, and snatched her hand away. She flushed guiltily.

'Rosamund.' He spoke very low. 'You know you are not afraid of me. You know you cannot sleep on that floor. Why don't you just admit it and come to bed? That way we might at least get *some* sleep. Hmm?'

'I...I...'

He gave a lop-sided grin and took hold of her hand, shifting over in the bed to make room for her. Rosamund stood up slowly, and let him pull her gently towards him. She lowered herself on to the edge of the bed and sat there half-turned towards him. She felt unbearably shy.

He flicked her nose. 'There's no need to look like that. You don't have to face me if you don't wish it.' She felt a warm pressure on her shoulder and then she was lying next to him, with her back to him. The warm hand slid to her waist and was still.

'Sleep well,' he said, huskily.

She could feel the warmth of his body behind her. His clean, masculine scent clung to the pillow. She closed her eyes. It was pleasant to lie here with his hand on her waist. Safe, and yet...not safe. Oliver. She sighed dreamily.

What would it be like sleeping with Alfwold? She did not think she would feel this. She would not lie there wondering what it would feel like to have Alfwold's hand move slowly along her skin, to have it caress her. She shuddered, and Oliver's hand was removed. Rosamund was conscious of a pang of regret.

Nay, she realised, if she lay with Alfwold she would be more like to be biting her tongue to hide her dislike. Trying to prevent herself from crying out to Alfwold that she did not, could not want him.

'Oliver?' she whispered.

'Aye?'

Rosamund rolled over on to her stomach, and leaned on both elbows to look at him. He had remained on his

side, facing her. Their bodies were so close, she tingled.
'How many women have you made love to?'

He raised a dark brow and grinned a crooked grin.
'Enough. Why do you ask?'

'Do you find me pretty?'

'Minx. You know I do.' His eyes were very dark. They
were so near she could see the soot-black ring which de-
fined the grey in them.

'And my lowly birth does not repulse you?'

'Nay.' He gave a little laugh. 'Who am I to cavil at
your birth? You at least were born in wedlock.
Rosamund, what is all this leading to?'

She took a deep breath. She twisted her fingers
together. 'Oliver. I want you to make love to me.'

His face was unreadable, but she saw his lips twitch,
just once. And in his eyes, just for a moment she imagined she'd surprised an eager flare of hunger. He
studied her silently, impartially, she thought, and then
he rolled on to his back and frowned up at the ceiling.

She knew by now she was crimson. 'Aren't you going
to answer me?' she got out.

'I'm thinking,' came the infuriating response.

'Oh,' huffily. 'Well, if you need to think about it...'
She hunched away from him, burying her head in the
pillow, to cool her cheeks. She clutched it to her so he
could not see her shame-filled expression.

The mattress moved under his weight, and Rosamund
felt him lightly touch her head.

'Rosamund,' he said, moving his hand to the nape of
her neck. Somehow he lifted her head round until she
could feel his breath warm on her cheek. 'Open your
eyes. I want to look into them.'

Cringing inside at what she had proposed, Rosamund
slowly obeyed him, dreading the scorn she must see in
his eyes. His gaze was calm and there was no trace of
passion in it.

'Why? I want to know why you want me to make love
to you,' he asked.

Rosamund was curling up with shame. A tight knot twisted her stomach. 'You think 'twas wrong of me to ask you, don't you? I have shocked you,' she blurted.

'You are,' he touched her wedding ring fleetingly, 'a married lady. And married ladies do not usually ask landless squires to make love to them.' The grey eyes gleamed.

He was laughing at her!

'Oh, don't you mock at me like that!' Rosamund cried, tearing his hand from where it still lay resting on her neck, and flinging it from her.

His eyes danced, he grinned, and leaned his dark head on his hand, calmly watching her expressive eyes and face as she worked herself up into a fury to disguise her shame. She was a beauty, this girl, and to have her offer herself to him in such a manner was temptation such as Oliver had never known. He wanted her. He had from the first. But he could not afford to become entangled with a peasant girl. He had plans, and they did not include being shackled to a pair of deep blue eyes and soft welcoming lips.

Oliver frowned. Besides, she *was* married. What was she up to? Perhaps she thought Lord Geoffrey's squire had more to offer than this Alfwold who was her husband. He would let her rant at him a little; perhaps he could learn her motives. Those eyes of hers were not born to deceive.

Rosamund saw Oliver's frown. Misreading it, her anger was fuelled. 'How dare you sit in judgement on me! You do not know what it is like to have to agree to wed someone for whom you feel nothing.'

Oliver shrugged. 'Is he cruel, then, this husband of yours? Will he treat you ill?'

'Nay. Alfwold is not cruel. 'Tis my father who...' She bit her lip, and stopped.

'You are fortunate then, in this husband of yours,' he commented.

Oliver's face held polite, detached interest, and Rosamund felt like slapping it. She groaned. 'Oh, what's the use, you will never understand.'

'Try me,' he suggested softly.

She searched his eyes and dropped her gaze to the gold cross on his naked chest. She licked her lips. 'That...that day on the beach. May Day,' she started hesitantly, and glanced up at him. He smiled. She took it as encouragement.

'I liked you then, I thought you so handsome...' She felt her cheeks sting with colour at this admission. 'I knew 'twas wrong to want to kiss you, but my betrothal to Alfwold was only...well...I wanted to know, to feel what it would be like to kiss a man *I* liked. Someone I had chosen. I did not think it a lie when I told you I had no lover. I never have had a lover. But...but if I ever had the choice I would choose someone like you. Someone who is tall, and strong and proud and...someone whom I desire——'

'You flatter me,' Oliver interrupted drily.

She noticed his mouth was strangely tender. She shook her head.

'Nay. Is it wrong for a woman to admit to desire? Is it wrong for me to wish that once, just once, I might know the pleasure of making love to someone who makes my heart beat loud and the blood rush in my ears? Is that so very wrong?'

He shook his head. 'Just as long as you remember I'm not part of a dream made flesh. Don't expect me to fall in love with you.'

Just then there was a little sputtering noise and the shadows in the room seemed to dance crazily up and down the walls. 'The candle's going out,' she said unnecessarily. For something to say, because she had seen in his face that he *would* make love to her. And now that it had come upon her, this moment she had wished for, she had become a bundle of quivering nerves.

Oliver slid his hand round her neck, and Rosamund felt him shake her hair so it tumbled about her shoulders. 'I shall have to light another,' he said, hoarsely, glancing at the wall sconce. His hand moved on, down to her waist.

'Why?' Rosamund managed.

'So that I can see you,' he told her quietly, 'I want to look at your body, to watch your face.' Pressing a light kiss on her cheek, he vaulted lightly from the bed.

He was only gone a moment or two. Rosamund lay perfectly still. The yellow glow in the chamber grew stronger, the shadows steadied. There was a sudden hiss which told her he had placed the new candle on the heel of the old. Soon, soon she would know what it was like to have a lover. She shivered in trepidation.

And then he was beside her again, taking her gently into his arms. 'You're not cold,' he whispered. 'Are you, Rosamund?'

She shook her head. 'Not cold, no. But I'm a little scared,' she admitted. 'I'm not sure what to do...'

'Hush,' said Oliver, and his lips found hers. It was an oddly chaste kiss, very soft, as though he was afraid he might startle her into changing her mind.

Rosamund began to relax, the knot of shame inside her easing and melting away. It was so good to lie here with his lips moving across hers, so good to feel his arms about her. His fingers were playing in her hair, touching her ears. She gave a tiny sigh and her lips began to respond under his.

He lifted his head, gently stroking her cheek with a large, but gentle hand. Her face was hot under his caress, and, overcome with a sudden shyness, she turned her head from his.

Oliver bent to kiss her neck. Rosamund gasped as an arrow of liquid fire burned its way through her body. Wide-eyed, she put a hand to his head, holding it there in amazement, while she felt the lips and tongue at her neck somehow set her whole body aflame. Without realising it, she was clinging to his naked shoulder, kissing it, tasting him.

'That's better,' he muttered jerkily in her ear. 'I thought for a moment you'd forgotten *you* chose me.'

Rosamund was beyond speech. It was bad enough trying to breathe normally. His lips returned to her mouth, and this time she met his kiss eagerly, her fingers tangling in his springy hair to pull that dark head closer.

She heard him groan, and his pleasure somehow intensified her own. She moved restlessly.

Oliver's hand was shaking as he moved it over her breast. God, he could not remember when a wench had ever felt so responsive. He ached to possess her. He must try to remember that she was a virgin. He must not rush at her like a callow youth and spoil it for her. He wanted her first full loving to be filled with wonder and joy.

Rosamund placed a hand over the one which caressed her breast. 'Can you feel how you make my heart beat faster?' she asked.

Smiling, he replied. 'I can feel more than that, my angel.'

She gave a little laugh. 'I'm no angel. Unless I'm a fallen one. No angel would beg for love.'

'A fallen angel,' he repeated, his eyes on the glossy hair which framed her glowing face. 'Aye. Have you another kiss for me, my beautiful fallen angel?'

For answer she wound her arms round his neck, and reached for his warm and sensuous mouth, willingly losing herself in the heady passion he was arousing. There was no shame in this, only pure enchantment.

Oliver unclasped the belt around her waist. His hands moved down to lift her gown.

He pulled himself free of Rosamund's clinging arms, and smiled when he saw her half-drugged frown of confusion, heard her gasp of dismay. She reached for him again.

'Nay, angel. I must take this gown of yours off. Lovely though it is, I think I will prefer you without it. Lift up your arms. There.'

For a second, Oliver simply stared down at the girl lying, flushed and willing on his bed. He could not move. She was so lovely. Beauty personified.

'Oliver?' Her soft voice sounded uncertain. Her hands fluttered to the linen sheet. She clutched it to her slender body as though she would shield herself from his gaze.

'You were created for loving,' he whispered, and reached for her. He felt her shudder as their bodies touched, and he watched her glowing eyes turn trustingly to his. What was it about this girl? She was irresistible. If Geoffrey but knew what he had given him this night...

Oliver buried his head in her cloud of hair, kissing her through it, pushing the long strands out of the way. All thoughts of his cousin melted from his mind as his body warmed to Rosamund's.

Rosamund could do nothing but cling to him. His kisses filled her senses, leaving room for naught else. Still clad in his hose, Oliver lay half across her body one long leg heavy between hers. Suddenly impatient, she moaned, twisting beneath him, and slid her hands across his broad back.

He was raining soft, biting kisses on her face and neck. His head moved lower, to her breasts, and Rosamund shuddered in unbelievable ecstasy as he kissed first one breast and then the other in light teasing caresses.

'Oliver,' she moaned, clutching wildly at the dark head at her breast. She strained towards him unashamedly, wriggling beneath his lips and body with such abandon that he felt he could contain himself no longer.

His breath was coming fast now too. He eased himself back and, in his eagerness, fumbled at the ties of his hose. Her slender fingers were there before him, swiftly untying the cord and pushing at the material. He held his breath.

'So shocked, Oliver?' He heard her teasing, husky whisper and marvelled anew. 'Remember, I chose you.'

Oliver's lean, hard body moved over hers, and she gasped at the feel of him. Slightly afraid.

'Merciful Heavens, woman! Will you stop wriggling? Or I won't be able to wait 'til you're ready for me.'

Her murmured reply was almost inaudible. 'I'm ready.'

He shook his head at her. 'Not yet, you aren't.' His knee met no resistance and he nudged her legs apart.

Rosamund found herself holding her breath as his long fingers found that secret part of her no man had touched 'til now. Those clever fingers sent her spiralling away into a vortex of agonising ecstasy. She writhed beneath him, aching inside, yearning for release from this exquisite torment, trusting he knew what it was she so needed.

'Please, Oliver, please,' she begged helplessly, unaware even that she spoke. And suddenly Rosamund seemed to explode, and all her nerves from head to toe were molten with longing.

She clung to him, shuddering wildly, and her blue eyes opened wide to stare into the grey ones fixed on hers. She was stunned with pleasure.

'Now?' he whispered.

She nodded mutely.

His lips covered hers. He was very tender. Very controlled. He felt one small hand slip into his a moment before he heard the sharp gasp which accompanied the loss of her maidenhead. No cry of pain. He searched her face. No tears. Just a tiny hand in his. He felt oddly touched.

And then he lowered his head again, and their lips clung. And Oliver forgot the need to take care with her. For they were moving in perfect unison. As though they had been lovers a hundred times together. Their rhythms matched exactly.

Rosamund removed her hand from Oliver's so she could run it down his back, and hold his hips to her. She felt him shudder and gasp her name, whispering incoherent love words in her ear. She was warm all over. In every corner of her body. And Oliver was moving within her, sharing that warmth. Giving his to her. Faster and faster. Slowly taking her with him to a place where the whole world exploded into a million glittering fragments, leaving them lying weak and shattered in each other's arms.

The candle burnt down some way before Oliver made to move away, and when he did Rosamund's sleepy protest gave him pause.

'No. Stay,' she murmured.

He rolled on to his back, and settled her into his arms. 'I'm not going anywhere. We're locked in here, remember.'

'Oh, aye. So we are.' Rosamund snuggled close and pressed her lips to his chest. Affectionately Oliver ruffled her tousled hair.

'Well, my angel, I take it from the smile on your face that you do not regret your request.'

She lifted her long lashes and he felt a pang almost of pain at the adoration he glimpsed in them.

'No regrets,' she replied, knowing it to be a lie. For how could she bear to leave him now?

CHAPTER FOUR

IN THE dense, pre-dawn darkness, Ingerthorpe Castle lay sombre and quiet. Servants snored on in the hall. The pot boy, whose duty it was to light the fire, lay curled up warm with Lord Fitz Neal's favourite bitch and her litter of pups. Only when the first grey streaks of the new day lit up the eastern sky and began to creep over the sea towards the coast would the lad rouse himself.

Rosamund lay warm in her lover's arms, wondering what had disturbed her. She could not see Oliver, but she could feel him. He still slept. His deep, even breathing was the only sound at all in the still, thick blackness. She wondered what hour it was. No twittering of rousing birds to herald daybreak. She moved her head and breathed in the scent of him. Her lover now. So little time left, but she wanted to remember everything about this. His strong arms holding her so secure, those long legs lying casually tangled with hers, the hand at her waist. This feeling of utter peace. She wanted it to last forever.

But when dawn did break she would rise, don her fine new gown and be gone. She would probably not even be able to break her fast with him.

Rosamund rubbed her cheek gently against Oliver's chest. The sensation of peace that had enveloped her was fast evaporating. Her eyes strained in the direction of the window. She relaxed. No light forcing in through the aperture yet. They had some time left . . .

'Rosamund,' Oliver murmured sleepily.

She put a hand to his cheek.

'Aye, lover,' she replied softly.

His grip on her waist tightened. 'Has dawn come so soon?' he wondered.

'Nay. I could not sleep.'

The body alongside hers stirred. She heard a contented yawn and smiled into the darkness, snuggling closer. He stroked her hair.

'So soft,' he muttered, huskily. 'Like you, my angel. All soft and giving. Kiss me, Rosamund.' He held her chin firmly in place. Rosamund felt his lips first on her cheek, and then they travelled tenderly across her face to fasten on her eagerly parted mouth. She melted. Her arm crept round his neck. Her body pressed to his as though this were her last chance at happiness.

And after, when they lay still once more, Rosamund realised that she could see those grey eyes of his smiling into hers.

'Dawn!' she groaned, burrowing her head on his chest.

He did not reply at once. She could feel his hand idly tracing patterns on her back. 'They will release us soon,' he said, coolly.

She lifted her head. 'And you are glad?' she asked, her voice taut with a grief she must not show.

'Glad?' He lifted his broad shoulders. 'I but state a fact. 'Tis dawn, and the little game they forced us to play is ended.'

Rosamund clenched her teeth. 'Is that all it was to you? A game?'

Oliver ruffled her hair, and Rosamund felt her heart contract with longing. His loving had been so tender, so considerate. He must feel something for her...

'A very pleasurable game, my angel.' His voice was low in her ear.

'But only a game?'

'Rosamund, I warned you. I cannot love you,' he stated baldly.

'Cannot, or will not?'

His face took on a closed look, and she knew she had blundered.

'Oh, Oliver. No. Don't turn away from me. I'm sorry. Please, hold me tight. We've such a little time together. I'm sorry, I won't spoil it.'

And then she heard the sound of heavy footsteps pounding on the stairs. Oliver had heard them too. He lay on his back, arms stretched behind his head and a strange expression settled on his features. Rosamund had never seen him look like this. She had seen him turn a cold face to her, grey eyes very remote, but there had always been a glimmer within them to reassure her of his common humanity.

But now... His face was a stony mask of utter indifference. It made her heart miss a beat. Those lips which had kissed her so tenderly, and smiled on her so gently, had become a hard line. To look on him you'd think him wrought of iron, not human flesh and blood.

The door was flung open with sudden violence, and Rosamund's eyes widened as her lord and master stomped heavily into the room, breathing hard. Flushing crimson down to her neck she sat up, clutching the linen bedclothes to her breast.

Oliver remained unmoved.

Her liege lord barely spared her a glance. At once he started to speak to Oliver in French, and Rosamund had no way of comprehending the words. That was the language for nobles, not peasant girls. Baron Fitz Neal's manner, however, told her something. Rosamund's sharp ears detected mockery, there was a question in it.

She had seen her lord before, but never at such close quarters. On the last occasion, he had been mounted on his war-horse and had thundered through the village like a demon from hell scattering animals and peasants alike before him. Open-mouthed with curiosity, she stared. Baron Fitz Neal's dark eyes met hers and he grinned suggestively. Rosamund knew her flush had deepened.

He spoke again, as if urging some reply from his silent cousin reclining casually in the bed.

Oliver's cheeks darkened, and Rosamund saw a muscle tighten in his jaw.

'Wh..what...' she began.

Oliver's eyes rested briefly on her. 'Rosamund, don't gape like a codfish,' he drawled, in English.

Rosamund snapped her mouth shut.

'And Geoffrey,' Oliver continued, 'I think that courtesy demands we speak so the wench can comprehend us, especially as your last comment so closely concerned her.'

Rosamund's liege lord shrugged. 'As you wish, Oliver. Though why we should consider an ignorant little whore like her——'

Rosamund bristled. 'I'm no whore!' she blurted before she had time to consider to whom she was speaking. 'I'll have you know I'd never——' She broke off, aghast.

Baron Geoffrey smirked. 'You mean to tell me I've wasted a virgin on you, Oliver? You lucky dog!' The Baron flung back his head and roared, his laughter ringing loud round the small chamber. Then he straightened. 'Well, Oliver? Aren't you going to thank me for my gift? Innocent wenches are rare jewels among her class.'

'My lord, why thank you for what could have been mine without your aid?' Oliver replied, coldly.

Rosamund stiffened.

'Oh. So the wind sits in that quarter, does it?' the Baron asked, giving Rosamund a thorough scrutiny.

She tilted her chin, her eyes sparkling with anger.

Baron Fitz Neal swaggered up to the bed, and reached past Oliver to grasp hold of that chin. 'Seems to have some spirit,' he commented. 'Possesses a natural aptitude, does she?' He shot Oliver an enquiring glance.

'My lord, 'twould be most unchivalrous of me to answer that,' Oliver replied, face clear as a blank parchment.

'Aha! She does. I knew it.' Baron Geoffrey paused, brown eyes burning Rosamund's skin. 'Her husband spoke the truth. She is comely.' The large hand was removed, and Rosamund's lord turned away. 'I've a mind to try her for myself,' he added casually.

Rosamund sucked in her breath and sent her hand scuttling for Oliver's under the bedclothes. His felt quite cool. When his fingers lightly returned the pressure, she found she could breathe again. He would not let his cousin take her.

'My lord, you jest. What of your lady wife?' Oliver asked.

'My lady wife?' exclaimed my lord. 'What has that to do with it? For heaven's sake, man, you know as well as I that ladies know as much about making love to a fellow as I know about spinning yarn.'

Oliver permitted himself to smile. 'You could teach her,' he suggested. 'Just as you could learn to spin if you set your mind to it.'

'Don't be impertinent!' snapped Rosamund's lord, shocked to his core. 'A lady would be horrified at the mere suggestion. And as for me...' He broke off, the idea too demeaning even to voice.

Rosamund's anger at the way her lord had been discussing her evaporated for a vivid image of him holding distaff and spindle flashed into her mind. She raised a hand to her lips to hide a smile.

'Infernal cheek,' her lord was muttering. He sent Oliver a straight look. 'There's gratitude for you. And to think I have such plans for you. Damned if I don't change my mind.'

His hand reached for the latch, but Oliver was out of bed in a trice, the hand he had been holding cast aside. He reached for his cousin.

'My lord?' His voice was eager. 'You have plans for me, concerning my prospects?'

Lord Geoffrey lifted his eyes, for Oliver topped him by a handspan. 'Aye. I have plans for you. When you have proved yourself, of course,' he confirmed.

'Naturally.' Oliver smiled.

Across the room, Rosamund pulled the covers more closely about her. Forgotten so soon. That was a man for you. To think she had thought that Oliver might actually have felt a fondness for her. Look at him now. So desperate for his advancement that he could stand stark naked grinning at his lord like a simpleton. A feeling of desolation swept over Rosamund.

She reminded herself that she was married. Instead of easing the pain which clawed in her belly, that thought served to increase her misery. Oliver had warned her not to expect anything. He'd told her he didn't want a clinging vine. He'd even told her he couldn't love her. So what did she expect?

Her gaze roamed hungrily over him. So perfectly formed. It made her tingle just to look at him. Oliver pushed back the lock of hair which she remembered brushing aside last eve. So tall, and not an ounce of fat on him anywhere. My lord Geoffrey was flabbily squat and unfit beside Oliver's slender strength. It was strange to think that she had cradled that dark head on her breast. She sighed. It was not simply the loss of a fine lover that made her sigh. Rosamund knew that most men finding themselves in Oliver's place last eve would have taken her without compunction, not minding what she thought. But not Oliver. Their loving had been on equal terms, and she had been vouchsafed a tantalising glimpse of what her life could be like if she lived in a world where men and women respected each other.

Oliver reached for his chausses. 'My lord, you would help to advance a bastard?' He began to dress, all the while his eyes riveted to those of his cousin.

My lord snorted. 'Surely. Why ever not? My own name bears that stain. But you will have to earn your knighthood,' he warned.

Oliver straightened and bowed. 'I will serve you as faithfully as I may.'

Baron Geoffrey leered and Rosamund's heart jumped when he looked in her direction. 'Oh, there's no need to be too extreme. I don't expect complete fidelity.'

'My lord?' Oliver frowned.

Baron Geoffrey strode back to the bed. Rosamund glared at him, hoping he would keep his distance.

'I've a wife for you, Oliver,' announced Baron Geoffrey. 'If you would be a knight, you must marry her.'

'What! Marry Rosamund!' Oliver expostulated. 'But she's already wed, and she's a . . .'

Immediately Rosamund was glaring at her lover, her eyes spitting sparks. How *could* he?

'Nay,' soothed the Baron. 'I wouldn't beggar you with a miller's daughter. There's noble blood in your veins, I'll not see you spliced with a peasant.'

'My lord!' Rosamund burst out, her chest heaving with rage. 'You may consider me a low-born wench who's only fit for bedding, but at least I have some manners. Why, even beggars are not so churlish!'

My lord's face took on a mulish expression and his mouth grew white about the edges. Anger made Rosamund blind to these warnings and she blundered on, her accent becoming more marked. 'I would not dream of speaking in such a way about someone afore their face, my lord! If being noble entitles you to be so inconsiderate, then I tell you I'm proud to be a mere miller's daughter. And I'd not soil meself with the likes of you.'

'Would you not?' her lord asked, cut to the quick. He'd have to teach this wench a lesson. He could not allow his cousin to see him bested by a stupid maid. The Baron's dark eyes fastened greedily on her mouth. Aye, a pretty wench, and he'd have some enjoyment out of teaching her respect for her betters.

Rosamund saw her liege lord lick his lips and for the second time that morning he grasped her chin.

She tensed. There was a movement behind the Baron. 'My lord, ignore this foolish maid. I vow these yokels of yours sound like cackling crows to me—incomprehensible,' Oliver intervened. He placed a friendly hand on his cousin's shoulder. 'I'm unused to this Northern dialect of yours.'

My lord relaxed. He grinned knowledgeably. 'Made it difficult last night, did it, this lack of understanding.'

Oliver spread his hands. 'My lord? What need for words?' He grinned wolfishly.

The Baron's crude laughter rose to the rafters.

Oliver pressed on. 'I confess you have whetted my curiosity. Am I to know the identity of my bride to be?'

'There is a condition, cousin...' Baron Geoffrey announced, watching Oliver keenly.

'I assumed there would be,' answered Oliver, drily. 'Nothing comes free in this life.'

'How true, dear cousin, how true.'

Rosamund bridled at the meaningful glance her lord darted in her direction, but subsided at once when she saw Oliver shake his head swiftly in warning.

The Baron continued. 'I will dub you knight on condition that you wed my sister.'

'But, cousin,' Oliver protested. 'I thought Blanche was promised elsewhere.'

The suspicion of a smile lifted Lord Geoffrey's narrow lips. 'You are presumptuous, Oliver. I was speaking of Cecily, not Blanche. No, it is Cecily I would have you wed.'

There was a pregnant silence. Oliver dragged on that blank face he'd worn so often to hide his feelings. A bastard needed extra shielding in this world if he were to retain some dignity.

Watching him, Rosamund felt some measure of understanding for Oliver's dilemma. It seemed her lord was offering to further Oliver's ambitions, but he was quite blatantly trading on Oliver's illegitimacy. Oliver was being asked to pay some great price for my lord's favour. Instinct told her that that blank face meant he was struggling to hide some deep emotion. But there was more to this awkward pause than that. The hairs were lifting on Rosamund's neck as though an icy blast had chilled her.

'Cecily,' Oliver said eventually. 'I see. And in order to achieve my ambition, I must wed your sister. Cecily.' He shook his head.

'Her birth's better than yours,' the Baron pointed out loftily.

'Aye, but ... Cecily!' Oliver was clearly at a loss for words.

Rosamund's lord gave an exaggerated sigh. 'Not the best reaction to my suggestion, Oliver.'

'My apologies, cousin, but ... Cecily. Why, hell burn you, Geoffrey! She bolts like a frightened colt every time

I go near her. I've not even got one word out of her
yet.'

'It takes time. She's not used to you yet,' Sir Geoffrey
said placatingly.

'Time!' Oliver cried. ''Twill take more than time to
mend what ails *her*!'

'You refuse then,' the Baron said coldly.

'Nay. I have not said so,' Oliver put in hastily. His
grey eyes went to Rosamund sitting wide-eyed and
interested on the bed and he fell silent.

The lord of Ingerthorpe Castle noticed what drew his
cousin's gaze and put his own interpretation on it.

'Cousin, when I told you I did not expect complete
fidelity I did not mean that you should betray your
knightly oath to me, your lord,' he began.

Oliver's head shot round. 'My lord?'

The Baron gestured at the bed. ''Twas your wedding
vows I referred to. No one could expect you to keep them.
Not with Cecily. But I would find her a husband. And
you will be as kind to her as any man alive. You're kin.
No, cousin, I don't expect a man to be faithful to Cecily.
A knight is only answerable to his lord. Keep faith to
me, serve *me* well, and you may take your pleasure where
you like.'

Oliver scowled.

'What is your answer? Do you accept my proposal?'
Baron Geoffrey wondered.

Rosamund's eyes met Oliver's across the space that
separated them. She heard the Baron's derisive snort,
and tilting her chin shifted her gaze to him.

'Speaking eyes, hasn't she?' Fitz Neal commented with
a cynical sneer. 'I can see you don't need words with
that one. Very well, Oliver. If it helps you make up your
mind . . . I'll throw in the lass as part of the deal.

'You can have the knighthood you covet *and* this
wench if you agree to marry Cecily.'

'But, my lord,' Rosamund protested, 'I'm married to
Alfwold.'

The Baron drew himself up to his full height. 'And who is lord here?' he enquired in a dangerously soft voice.

Rosamund drew back. 'Why, you are, my lord, but——'

'Quite so. *I* am lord of this castle. I'll not have a drab of a girl dictate terms to me.' He turned his attention back to his cousin. Rosamund noticed Oliver's hands must have been clenched, for he was slowly flexing and unflexing his fingers.

'Your answer, cousin?'

'I accept your terms. All of them.' Oliver replied. His face was well guarded, but Rosamund knew from his voice that he was livid.

The Baron grinned and dealt Oliver a hearty buffet. 'I knew you'd be my man,' he smiled. 'Here's my hand on it. We have a deal!'

'Aye, damn you. We have a deal,' growled Oliver, and he shook his cousin's hand.

The door had no sooner shut behind her lord than Rosamund let loose her fury.

'You...you bastard! You vile, arrogant knave! How could you? What do you think I am? Do I not have feelings? I hate you! Do you hear me? I hate you!'

'I hear you very well, my angel——'

'Don't you "angel" me! It's not enough for you that I am brought here against my will and mauled and——'

'Hardly mauled, Rosamund.'

His dry tone fuelled her rage. 'And mauled and insulted—called a whore. Oh! Call yourselves men? You're not men, you're rutting swine!'

Oliver closed the gap between them, grabbing her by the wrist. 'You were not averse to sharing my sty last eve,' he pointed out evenly.

Rosamund looked away, too conscious that her body had reacted instantly to his nearness. Her breath had caught in her throat and her cheeks were staining with her slowly warming blood. She would not let him see how he affected her.

Oliver released his hold on her wrist and was winding a soft brown strand of hair round his forefinger. She heard him swallow, and when he spoke there was gentleness in his voice.

'Rosamund——' He bent to retrieve her gown and tossed it at her. 'You'd better dress...' he cleared his throat '...otherwise I shall not be responsible for my actions, and will indeed become the beast you named me. Hurry, for we are expected in the hall.'

He released her hair and, running his finger down her too flushed cheek, turned his back on her.

Rosamund did not need to be told twice. She pulled the gown over her head and got to her feet, shaking out the full skirt to remove the creases. She started at the side lacings.

'Oliver?' she asked. 'What will you do? You can't just keep me here. I'm a married woman, and owe my duty to my husband.'

'Your obedience to your lord comes first.'

'Nay. How can that be? *I'm* no serf. I was born a freewoman. My father was given his freedom when he got tenancy of the mill.'

Oliver frowned when he saw that she was still fumbling with the ties of her gown. 'Haven't you done with your dressing yet?'

'It's the lacings,' she explained. 'They're awkward to get at, and I've never worn a gown with such trailing sleeves. They're getting in the way.'

'Allow me.'

Rosamund stood still as Oliver tightened up the fastenings, jerking and jolting her with his impatience. She watched his tight-lipped face out of the corner of her eye.

'Rosamund, it matters not that you are a freewoman. If the lord commands you, you must obey. His word is law here, you have no choice.'

'No choice,' Rosamund echoed through clenched teeth. 'No choice. I am snatched from my husband. My maidenhead is taken from me. I'm insulted. My lord threatens to take me. And as if that is not enough, he rubs salt into the wound by offering me to you as part of a bargain whereby you achieve your ambitions. And I'm thrown in with the deal in very much the same way as he throws largesse to the children after the harvest supper.

'And you——' Her voice rose, it had an edge to it.

'Aye, Rosamund, what is it I did that was so very wrong?' Oliver wondered, a strange glint in his eyes.

'You have the temerity to accept his terms without so much as a murmur of protest! My God!' She made her voice drip with scorn. 'To think I thought you honest! You are worse than any cheating whore, far worse.' Striving for calm, she reached for the comb on the chest, divided her hair into two sections, and deftly braided it into two long plaits.

'How so?' His voice was cold.

'Whores at least do not involve others in their sordid little deals. You, however...'

'Rosamund, enough!' He raked back his hair. 'If it were not for my intervention you would have become Geoffrey's leman by now. I thought I did right in what I did. Maybe I misread you. Maybe you are angry at a lost opportunity.'

His lips curled. 'After all, who would willingly bed with a bastard squire when their liege lord would have them too?'

'But... but...' Rosamund stuttered.

Oliver's voice rode ruthlessly over hers. 'And as for this choice you seem so intent on... If you tried to put your cracked wits to some use you would have seen that I had no choice either. Do you think I intend remaining a squire forever? I am determined to become a knight, and now at last I am come here and my cousin is giving me a chance. What kind of fool would I be to let a peasant maid come between me and my knighthood? So if you think that having you included in the deal was from any choice of mine, think again. Think again, Rosamund, before you cry to me that all this is not to your liking.'

Rosamund's heart was beating very fast, and she knew she was shaking. She lifted her head and met his glare. 'So,' she said. 'Now we both know exactly where we stand. There need be no more misunderstandings.' She flicked her thick braids over her shoulders. 'Hadn't you better escort me to the hall? You said they will be expecting us.' She paused and sent him a sickly smile. 'I hope I don't shame you, Oliver, for I am only a low-born whore, and I've never lived in a castle before.'

She laid her hand grandly on his arm, for all the world a grand lady, and started to the door. She did not see the sudden smile which quirked Oliver's lips, nor the dawning admiration in his eyes.

Rosamund sat stiffly on the wooden bench, uncomfortably hemmed in and jostled by a black-eyed ladies' maid named Inga and the plump, red-cheeked nurse whose duty it was to keep an eye on the lord's son and heir, Henry. Oliver had led Rosamund to her place, all formality. He had bowed once and abandoned her to her fate, striding off to the high table on the dais where he sat with the lord and his intimates. A slight increase of pressure the moment before he had dropped her hand and Rosamund's eyes had swivelled to his, searching for the smallest glimmer of sympathy. But Oliver turned quickly on his heel and marched off, leaving her to wonder if she had imagined that slight caress.

'I don't know what the world's coming to,' the haughty maid was saying.

'Eh, what's that?' asked the nurse, Marie, through a mouth crammed full of good fresh bread.

Rosamund was elbowed back as Inga made an extravagant gesture which would have seen the ale off the trestle if she hadn't grabbed at the pot.

'It appears our lord has taken to throwing peasants' wives at his squires,' Inga said maliciously.

Rosamund's hand tightened on her drinking vessel.

'And then they are brought to our table, still stinking from their midden, and we are to break bread with them. I don't know how you can stuff that meat away like that, Marie, seated next to this verminous whore.'

The nurse glanced at Rosamund's white face and wiped the back of her mouth with her sleeve. 'Pot calling the kettle black is it?' she remarked lightly.

Inga's eyes flashed, her nostrils flared. Abruptly the maid turned her attention to the groom seated at her other hand.

'Pass t' loaf, love,' Marie said, winking at Rosamund. 'Thank you kindly. Now don't you pay no heed to 'er. She's not even wed, and I can tell you she's no innocent, that one. Hell's teeth! There's not much I can't stomach, but carping hypocrisy sticks in me craw.'

Marie settled back on the bench and drank gustily from her horn. 'Good brew this, why don't you try some? Here, some bread, you've eaten nowt yet, 'ave you?'

Rosamund accepted the proffered bread, and managed to force a smile.

'That's better, love,' approved Marie. 'Never let 'em see 'ow they get to you. It only encourages 'em to make it worse. What you need is some good meat i'side, and then you'll feel better.'

Rosamund warmed to the kindly woman. Mayhap Marie was right. For after taking only a few mouthfuls she found she was better able to take stock of her surroundings. Last night she had been blind to everything but her own terror.

Baron Geoffrey's hall was magnificence itself. A large, round, airy chamber, its roof beams were gaily painted in deep blues and reds. Every available inch of the plastered walls was adorned with pictures and patterns. Rosamund's uncritical eyes did not notice that a film of sooty dirt overlaid all—to her the hall was fit for royalty.

Two trestles filled the central space. The high table was placed on its dais before the wide fireplace, no doubt so the flames could warm the backs of those seated there. Rosamund's eyes were drawn to Oliver, but he was in earnest conversation with his neighbour and did not glance in her direction. Rosamund's table was placed at right angles to the raised high table, and the lowly souls seated thereon had to suffer draughts from two stair-heads. No fire for them.

Something warm brushed across Rosamund's feet and rustled in the rushes. Thinking of rats, she shifted uneasily.

''Tis only the hounds. Throw them a lump o' gristle and they'll go on to t' next person,' Marie suggested. She heaved a great sigh, her ample bosom lifting. 'That's better. Now I've filled up, you tell me about yourself, girl. What do they call you?'

'Rosamund. I'm from the mill.'

'Talk right pretty, don't you, for t' miller's wench?'

'I copy what I hear. *He*...' she indicated Oliver with her eyes '...I, that is, I did not want his mockery. And now I suppose I'll have the mockery of my fellows instead.' Rosamund paused, watching the nurse's kindly face.

The woman smiled. 'I'll make no judgements o' you.'

'Thank you.'

'Go on wi' your tale,' commanded Marie.

Rosamund shrugged. 'Not much to it. Yesterday I was wed to Alfwold—he's a grindstone dresser. And my lord decreed that instead of my father paying the bride fine I should be brought here, to wait upon his pleasure. He...they...locked me in a chamber with his squire. A drunken jest. I was to be freed this morn. But now...my lord will not release me. I am to stay here.'

'A stolen bride!' Marie slapped her thigh and cackled in delighted appreciation.

Rosamund held herself very straight. 'I don't think it amusing, I can assure you.'

'Don't come the noble lady wi' me, lass. I 'ave eyes to see. One sight o' the way you and yon squire keep glancing at each other...you're not averse to him,' Marie commented shrewdly.

Rosamund's stomach tightened. As far as she had seen, Oliver was taking no notice of her at all. 'But I'm married to Alfwold,' she insisted. 'And I ought to go back to him. I'm being treated as though I were no more that a sack of flour to be traded at will.'

'Ah, that's the nobility for you,' Marie agreed. 'No respect for a person's dignity. Remember this, me girl: as far as they're concerned, we're all little more than cattle. Don't start by expecting to be treated any different to the dogs scavenging under t' table. If you do, you'll surely be disappointed.' Marie hesitated.

'Aye?' Rosamund prompted.

Marie looked meaningfully at Oliver. 'And don't expect 'owt from that noble squire. He may be bastard by birth, but just look at the pride in 'im. 'E won't settle for less than a knighthood. He's hot for you now, and you like him...'

Rosamund's gesture of repudiation was ignored.

'Well, make the most on't. It won't last forever. It never does. And when he has finished with you, me girl, you'll be sent packing, and 'e will forget 'e ever knew you. For 'e's of their blood, and they don't 'ave 'earts. Cold as ice. So, if you like 'im, make the most on't.'

Somehow Rosamund managed to keep the smile pinned on her face. Marie's warning had the ring of truth about it.

'I'll remember your advice,' she said lightly. 'And now 'tis your turn. You tell me who everyone is. If I'm to be kept here, I think I'd better know.'

'Brave lass,' approved Marie. She heaved her bulk round to point at the high table. 'My lord you know already. There's his wife, Lady Margaret, next to him.'

Lady Margaret, a fading blonde beauty, was arrayed in a gorgeous red gown which snatched what little colour she had from her face, leaving her pale and wan.

'The lady at me lord's other side is 'is mother. T' Lady Adeliza. My lord takes more heed of her than he does his wife. If she decides to take agin this jest of me lord's then you'll be out of here faster than the winking of an eye.'

The resemblance between the Lady Adeliza and her son was startling. Both were dark, and carried themselves proudly. Rosamund noted that Lord Geoffrey Fitz Neal's tendency to corpulence was inherited from Lady

Adeliza. She sat tall, but there was no hiding her large frame.

'I thought ladies were always delicate,' Rosamund murmured in an undertone.

'Not that one,' laughed Marie. 'Tough as a team of oxen. She'll live to fourscore years, I shouldn't wonder.'

'And who's that pretty girl next to Lady Adeliza?'

'The Lady Blanche,' Marie continued.

'Lord Geoffrey's sister,' Rosamund realised. 'How old is she? She's lovely.'

'Fifteen. And aye, she's a beauty, but too much so for her own good,' Marie said darkly.

'Oh?'

But Marie was not to be drawn. 'And then there's me lord's knights. Sir Gerard is the older one. He's sire to that lad sat next to Henry. And that's Sir Brian who's talking with Oliver de Warenne. But, I forget, you know all about de Warenne, do you not?' Marie teased.

'Don't, Marie.' Rosamund blushed.

There was someone missing from the hall. The Lady Cecily. Oliver's betrothed. 'Pray tell me, where is Lady Cecily?' she asked.

Marie's laughing eyes were quickly veiled. 'She'll be down later. Oh, me God. Listen to them dogs. Methinks 'tis time me lord 'ad a cull. Forever scrapping over t' smallest crumbs.' She bent to peer under the table.

Rosamund glanced towards the lobby. 'No. That noise is coming from the entrance.'

'You're right. That's the porter's voice. Someone's come a mite early to see t' lord,' said Marie.

Rosamund felt Inga prod her in the ribs. 'Maybe 'tis our peasant cockerel come to claim his hen,' she sneered, openly hostile.

Rosamund bit down the gasp of dismay which rose in her throat. Aye. That was Alfwold. She could hear him and . . .

There was a thud, and a scuffle and Alfwold erupted into the hall, blood-red under his scarred skin.

She jumped to her feet, her face a picture of confusion and dismay. 'Alfwold,' she got out, frozen with horror.

'Ugh!' Inga's voice carried clearly over the stunned silence which had fallen. 'The cockerel *has* been wallowing in the mire. Look at his fouled feathers.'

Someone tittered.

Shooting Inga a glance which should have felled her, Rosamund took a step towards her husband. Her feet seemed to be weighted with lead.

Alfwold had seen her, and started towards her, but the guards sprang into life and dived towards him, dragging at his arms.

'Rosamund!' Alfwold yelled. One of the guards hit him violently across the face with the back of his hand.

'Quiet, scum! You wanted to see Lord Geoffrey. Well, now you shall, me lad. Now you shall.'

Helplessly, Rosamund watched as her husband was dragged towards the dais. She felt Marie tugging repeatedly at her gown, trying to force her back on to the bench. Impatiently she pushed that insistent hand aside.

'Ned, must you interrupt my break fast?' drawled the Baron, leaning back in his chair with a sigh.

'Apologies, me lord,' said the Captain of the Guard curtly. 'But this fellow would have it from your own lips. Claims you have his wife held here.'

'*Held* here?' My lord raised a brow, and looked down his nose at the shaking peasant. 'Are you implying that we are holding the woman against her will, my man?'

'I...I...' stuttered Alfwold.

'Come, come, speak up man. Do you see her here? Is she held in chains? Does she languish in the dungeon?' He laughed loudly. The lady Blanche laughed with him.

'You mock me, my lord,' muttered Alfwold stiffly.

Oliver slowly lifted his head to regard Rosamund's husband. An ugly brute. And the thought of those callused hands on her filled him with utter distaste. None the less, the man was her husband. This sweating peasant had accepted responsibility for the wench in a way Oliver never could. To his surprise, Oliver found he felt some measure of sympathy for the man. Perhaps if he spoke up now, and denied his interest in Rosamund publicly, then Geoffrey would be forced to release her and she could return to her home. Maybe he'd still honour their deal...

Oliver rose to his feet, tight-lipped. Rosamund was biting on her finger, her expression telling of confusion, misery and shame in a way that words could never do.

'Oliver,' Geoffrey warned. 'We have a deal now, and 'tis one I want you to honour. Sit down.'

Oliver remained on his feet.

'Oliver, am I to clap you in the guardhouse? Obey your lord!'

'But my lord, I must speak,' Oliver protested. He was achingly aware of Rosamund's wide blue eyes as they crept across from her husband's and encountered his. Her cheeks had lost their healthy glow, she was as pale as an ivory statue, and just as still. Would she welcome his repudiation, if it meant she could regain her freedom?

Lord Fitz Neal was glaring at his recalcitrant kinsman. 'You will be silent when I command you, Oliver. Else you will be no knight of mine! Honour your agreement. Captain!'

'Me lord?'

'Set two of your men to escort my cousin to his room. He wishes to meditate on the advantages of a knight honouring his agreements.'

'Aye, m' lord.'

Rosamund took a shuddering breath and her eyes seemed glued to those broad, well-muscled shoulders. Oliver did not look her way again. Head high, he strolled nonchalantly through the curtained doorway and was escorted out of sight.

Dimly Rosamund could hear an excited buzz of questions. Speculative eyes shifted from Alfwold, to her, and then back to Lord Geoffrey.

The Baron had been muttering in French to the Lady Adeliza. That lady lifted her head.

'Girl!' she cried imperiously, in flawless English. 'Approach the board!'

With pounding heart and shaking hands hidden in the folds of her gown, Rosamund obeyed.

'Stand closer, girl. I would see your features.'

Rosamund stepped so close that the trestle dug into her middle.

Lady Adeliza stared. 'You don't seem afraid, girl.'

Rosamund replied boldly. 'Fear is not uppermost in my mind, my lady.'

Lady Adeliza's dark eyes narrowed, but Rosamund did not think she was angry.

'You like children, do you, girl?' asked Lady Adeliza.

Rosamund's brow wrinkled. She could not see where this was leading. 'Aye, my lady. And my *name* is Rosamund,' she added.

There was a gasp of dismay from behind her.

'Rosamund,' hissed Alfwold. 'Remember who you're speaking to.'

Rosamund did not shift her gaze from Lady Adeliza's. Indeed, she was almost certain that the lady was amused. Her spine stiffened.

'Good,' Lady Adeliza said. 'You do seem honest, at least. And you are vaguely intelligible. Comely, too. I couldn't bear to see another slobbering idiot around the place. You'll do. Marie will show you what your duties are. Away with you, now.' She waved a languid hand in the direction of the lower trestle, and turned her attention to her son. 'Geoffrey, I cannot say I was pleased when I heard what you'd done. But on reflection I think you may have been right. You are too soft with Cecily, she should have been sent to a convent years ago...'

Baron Fitz Neal shook his head in violent denial. 'Nay, mother. 'Twas my fault, and I'll not have her dropped in a well and forgotten.'

Lady Adeliza smiled, and patted the Baron's arm. 'Very well, son. I have agreed. There, are you happy?'

'My lady!' Rosamund broke in.

'Still here, girl? Did I not order you to your place?'

'You did, my lady, but I cannot. I am married to Alfwold,' she said firmly.

'Mmmm. You...are you Alfwold?' asked Lady Adeliza imperiously.

'Me...me lady?' Alfwold stammered.

'I need your wife as a...nurse within the keep. She is required to remain here to fulfil her duties. You will be paid for her services. Should she be dismissed for any reason I will make certain she is brought back safe to you. Satisfied?'

'But, my lady—Rosamund is my wife. Am I not to see her?' blurted poor Alfwold.

'Enough!' barked the Baron, thumping his goblet on the table and spilling a shower of ale over the snowy linen cloth.

'The girl was my vassal long before she became your wife. Her father owes his position at the mill to my favour. There are plenty of others in the village who'd be willing to take over the mill should I say the word.'

Alfwold blanched.

'The point has gone home, my son,' murmured the Lady Adeliza with a smile.

Geoffrey gave Alfwold a direct look. 'I wonder? The man looks a stumbling clod to me.'

'Me lord!' Alfwold strained against the arms that held him. 'Call off your hounds, I can do you no harm here,' he said. Rosamund tensed, recognising an anger in Alfwold that she had never thought to see in him.

The Baron nodded easily and the guards stood off. But Rosamund noticed their watchful eyes, their hands at the ready. They would be at Alfwold's throat in a second should the need arise.

'Me lord.' Alfwold licked his lips nervously. 'Me marred skin proclaims me trade.'

The Baron nodded. 'Stone-dresser,' he surmised.

'Aye. And in pursuing my trade, I get to travel more than most folks. I've seen more than most too. And this civil war has been the excuse for much lawlessness on the part of certain noble tyrants.'

'Alfwold, no,' Rosamund pleaded, wringing her hands. The Baron's face had hardened, the Lady Adeliza raised a brow most eloquent of her disdain.

'I will speak, Rosamund,' Alfwold insisted. He was visibly trembling, but he ploughed on bravely. 'I've seen some cruel things. But never, ever have I seen a man, noble or peasant, that dared to separate a man and his wedded wife. God will damn you for this, me lord! God will damn you,' he raged.

There was a resounding clatter as the Baron jerked to his feet and his chair tipped back on to the tiles.

'God's Blood!' he swore, his face working in fury. 'You dare to upbraid me at my own table. Why, I've had men flogged for less!'

Alfwold gave a smile, which only served to infuriate the Baron further.

'My...my lord.' Rosamund raised her voice. 'He does not mean what he says. He must have drunk too much of the new ale. Alfwold is a good man, not one to flog. If you flog him he won't be able to work for a week, and we'll have no flour in Eskdale.'

'I'll to the abbot,' threatened Alfwold, oblivious of Rosamund's pleading eyes.

'Alfwold, hush,' Rosamund hissed. 'Do you *want* a flogging?'

A movement from the high table caught Rosamund's eye. The Lady Margaret had risen. She was laying a hand gently on her husband's arm. 'My lord,' she murmured.

Rosamund gasped. The Lady Margaret, as all knew, had been married in her youth to another. The Baron had married her for her dowry, and she was some years older than he. But as Lady Margaret turned to soothe her husband Rosamund saw the swollen belly straining the red cloth of my lady's gown. It was sight of this that had torn the gasp from Rosamund's lips. My lady was far gone in pregnancy. Rosamund looked at her pale, strained face. She did not look like to survive the confinement, poor lady.

'My dear,' continued Lady Margaret. 'This angry rage unsettles me.' She put a slender white hand on her belly, and paused for her words to sink in. Her face *did* look very drawn.

'Oh, my dear.' Lord Geoffrey was the image of contrition. 'Sit down again. You must be calm.'

'My lord, such anger...' She paused. 'Such violence...'

The Baron pointed at Alfwold with his knife. 'Count yourself lucky, my man, that I have a delicate and compassionate wife, whose whim I must heed. For her sake I will spare you the lash this day. And mark you, it is only my lady's request that's kept you from the whipping post.' My lord raised his voice. 'Captain!'

'Me lord?'

'Remove this...carcase, and dump it outside the bailey. And if you see as much as a hair of the man's head again, I'm to know at once.'

'As you wish, me lord.'

Alfwold's dark eyes glared at his liege lord as his escort surrounded him.

'I'll to the abbot!' he repeated. His voice trembled.

'Oh, Alfwold, have you no sense? Have done,' begged Rosamund.

'I'll not let these fine folks snatch you from me,' Alfwold declared. 'You're me wife, and Holy Church does not allow any man, not even a lord, to...'

The sharp clout sounded loud in the hall. Rosamund winced and blood trickled down the side of Alfwold's mouth.

'Put a stopper in your gaping maw,' advised the Captain of the Guard. 'You put your teeth at risk.'

'Alfwold,' Rosamund entreated. 'For God's sake begone! They've not done me any hurt. But they will if you persist in this. I'm happy to remain here. Please don't get yourself killed for my sake. 'Tis not worth a man's life. Go! Go!'

Alfwold ceased his struggling and stared at his wife!

'I mean it, Alfwold. I'd not have your blood on my conscience. Please, oh please, go.'

'You're my wife,' he insisted, stubborn as a mule.

'Aye.' She jerked her head towards the high table. 'And he is our lord. What can such as we do against him? Go, I tell you!'

Impatient at this delay, the guards would wait no more. They thrust Alfwold rudely through the portal. Rosamund heard a scuffle, and a grunt of pain. 'I'll to the abb...'

She felt chilled to her vitals, and was shaking. She stared at the swinging curtain which obscured the lobby from her eyes. The struggles and groans moved off and out across the yard outside, gradually diminishing in volume.

She was a prisoner. Slowly she lifted bewildered eyes to the Baron. He was raising his lady's hands tenderly to his lips. He did not look like a man who could separate her from her husband, threaten Alfwold with a flogging, and her father with the loss of his mill. It was true that she was not in chains in the dungeon. She had not been maltreated. She was fed and clothed and...but for all that she remained his prisoner. His to command.

Oblivious to the staring eyes, Rosamund turned blindly for her place. She stumbled, and put out a hand. Someone steadied her.

'There lass,' Marie's reassuring voice penetrated the daze. 'All over now. Leave these gawping clods to entertain each other.'

Rosamund leaned gratefully on Marie's plump arm, tensing slightly when she saw that they had come to stand before Lord Geoffrey.

'Me lord,' Marie bowed her knee.

'Marie.'

'If it pleases you, me lord. I'll show the girl to her duties now. May we have leave to...'

The Baron waved a careless hand. 'Aye. Go. Most like Cecily will be loitering near the stables.' A thought struck him and he leaned forward to peer at Rosamund. 'You don't ride, do you, girl?'

'No, my lord.'

'Good, good. Then you won't be encouraging the Lady Cecily to do so, will you?'

A frown gathered Rosamund's brows. 'No, my lord, but why——'

'Oh get out, girl, get out. You've caused enough trouble for one day,' the Baron told her irritably.

Wise not to argue with him. Though her head was bursting with questions and she could find no answers, Rosamund trailed obediently in Marie's wake and left the hall.

Oliver stretched his long limbs out on his bed, trusting he had read his cousin aright and that his confinement would be of a short duration.

He sighed contentedly. At last. His plans were coming to fruition. He spared a grateful thought for his aunt, the Lady Maud, whose forethought had set his feet on the road to Ingerthorpe and his cousin Geoffrey. A rueful smile tugged at the corner of his well-shaped mouth as he remembered how unwillingly he had left his old home. Lady Maud's instincts had been correct. Lord Geoffrey *was* desperate for good men. Oliver had received a harsh training while on crusade, but it would stand him in good stead now. It gave him an experience none of the other knights, not even Sir Gerard, could rival. They might deride him for his birth, but none could deny he was needed here. With his cousin's support, and his sister to wife, he could finally look forward to a worthwhile future.

The squire stretched languidly, running his commission over in his mind. The men at arms in this northern hold were currently little better than raw recruits. Geoffrey needed Oliver's assistance in moulding them into shape. Presently they fell far short of being an efficient fighting force. Morale was low. They would be hard put to it to defend the castle if it were attacked by a handful of peasants with pitchforks, let alone hold off a real attack from trained soldiers.

'Twas a pity that the other two knights in the hold were not of more use. Sir Gerard had made it plain that as a well-born knight it was beneath his dignity to work hand in glove with a baseborn squire. The younger knight, Sir Brian, had shown willing, but inexperience told against him. Oliver frowned. Sir Brian's eager questions showed a keen mind. Maybe in time . . . He sighed.

His commission would not be easy. One knight overtly hostile, and the other a callow youth.

Hearing the footsteps on the stairs, Oliver sat up, expecting his cousin to walk through the door.

Rosamund stepped into the chamber and Oliver's heart jolted. His ambition was to be met, but it was this young girl who was being forced to pay part of the price. Did she understand that he had not planned this to happen? He wanted her to know that it was never his intention that she should be manipulated in such a way. He held out his hand to her.

'Rosamund, we must talk, you and I.'

Rosamund's face was devoid of expression.

'My Lady Adeliza says you're to accompany me to the upper hall. Lady Cecily is waiting to discuss your betrothal with her,' she announced. To his horror she gave him a clumsy little curtsy.

'Nay, Rosamund,' he protested, rising from his couch.

'You'd best hurry. The Lady Adeliza does not strike me as being a patient lady,' Rosamund advised, not meeting his eyes.

A soft brown tendril of hair had escaped from her braids. Oliver touched it lightly with his forefinger, scowling as she jerked her head away. He caught her by the shoulder and spun her back to him. 'We *will* talk,' he insisted. 'Later. This eve.'

Rosamund's blue eyes lifted to his. 'Aye, *Sir* Oliver. If you command it, I must obey you,' she said bitterly. 'No doubt I shall be made to attend to you as I was last night. And now, your lady awaits you. You must not dally with a peasant maid *now*.'

'What do you mean?' he demanded, conscious of sudden spurt of anger.

Her eyes widened, innocent as an angel's. 'Why, 'tis broad day, *Sir* Oliver. You must take care of your reputation. We're not safely hidden betwixt the sheets now. Your door is ajar. Anyone could enter. Knights don't speak to slaves as though they had wits of their own. What would the Lady Adeliza think if she knew of your liaison with me?'

'Hell curse you, woman! Do you think she doesn't know?'

'Oliver?' Rosamund's voice wavered, he glimpsed a flash of uncertainty.

He smiled grimly. 'That's better. If you'd called me *Sir* Oliver once more I think I'd have beaten you to death!' he admitted.

Rosamund gathered her wits together with an effort. 'So...' she mused thoughtfully, 'the Lady Adeliza knows. Then why on earth is she being so kind to me? She's given me three new gowns—why should she do that if she knows I'm to be lover to her daughter's husband.'

'You'll find out soon enough, my Rosamund,' Oliver told her drily. 'In any event, she probably thinks your own clothes would be thick with lice. The ones she's given you won't carry vermin to spread about the keep.'

Rosamund bit her lips, remembering the woman who'd scrubbed her body and hair so thoroughly before leaving her in Oliver's bed. It irked her to realise he was right. The nobility were known to take baths frequently. When she had first encountered Oliver on the beach, he had seemed so clean to her that he'd shone. How had she appeared to him?

'I'm not yours,' Rosamund protested to cover her rising colour. 'You have no right to call me so. You don't even love me!'

Oliver's grey eyes wandered over her features. 'But who needs love, my angel?' He grinned. 'You look beautiful even when you pout like that. Very kissable.'

'You misbegotten cur! Have you no shame?' Rosamund cried.

'Nay.' Oliver shrugged. 'There is no advantage in it,' he said simply.

Rosamund glared at him. 'Nay? Tell me, Oliver, do you think there is advantage in obeying the Lady Adeliza?'

Oliver inclined his head. 'Most assuredly, angel. The greatest advantage. Lead on. I'm longing to see *my* lady Cecily.'

CHAPTER FIVE

ROSAMUND hesitated by the great portal at the head of the spiral stairs.

'Should . . . should you go first?' she wondered.

Oliver's hand was warm on the small of her back, urging her on.

'You first,' he said coolly. 'The upper hall is the ladies' domain. Announce my arrival to the Lady Adeliza and she will call me in.'

If Rosamund cherished any hopes that the lord's squire might feel something for her, those hopes were crushed when she cast a last glance at Oliver's implacable features.

'How can you be so . . . so unfeeling,' she hissed.

'Unfeeling?' he queried, lifting a dark brow. 'Who am I wronging now?'

'Me . . . and her, the Lady Cecily. How can you do this to us?' she whispered harshly.

'You cannot say I did not warn you, Rosamund. I told you I was not capable of love. You accepted the terms last night. Why have you changed your mind?'

He seemed genuinely puzzled.

'Oh, never mind,' Rosamund snapped. 'Where's the sense in any of this? I'll announce you.'

Casting him a final look of exasperation, Rosamund pushed at the door-hanging and thrust herself into the upper hall. The curtain rings tinkled above a hum of conversation which rose to the domed roof. Several heads turned towards Rosamund. Needles hung suspended over the cloths, flashing as they caught the sunlight. Like weapons.

The Lady Adeliza dropped the work she had been examining. 'What is it, girl? Could you not find him?'

wondered Lord Geoffrey's mother, in her immaculate, aristocratic English.

Inga sniggered and muttered something in an undertone to a sewing companion. The other girl hid her smiling mouth behind a soft, white hand. Rosamund wrestled to keep a scowl from her face.

'Speak up, girl,' prompted Lady Adeliza, a touch of impatience in her voice.

'Oliver de Warenne awaits without, my lady,' she declared in as clear a voice as she could muster.

'Good. Good.' Lady Adeliza clapped her hands sharply. 'Inga!'

'My lady?' Inga jumped swiftly to her feet, with not a trace of her earlier haughtiness in her manner.

'Tell Marie that he has come. She may bring my eldest daughter in now.'

'Aye, my lady, at once.' Inga scuttled to obey, and vanished through a door opposite the one Rosamund had entered.

Rosamund became aware that she was the object of Lady Adeliza's attention. Unconsciously she squared her shoulders and met Lady Adeliza's brooding gaze directly.

'Mmm, I think... Rosamund, isn't it? I think... Rosamund, that you had better wait outside till this er... interview is ended. Then you are to return and Marie will take charge of you.'

'Aye, my lady.'

'Send him in then, and wait on the landing till you are called.'

'My lady.' Rosamund moved swiftly through the door.

Oliver's hand caught at her wrist. 'I'm to go in?' he asked, his thumb tracing a pattern on her soft skin.

She shook him off, irritated at the way her wrist tingled at even this slight contact. 'You might have the decency to hide your eagerness,' she complained. 'But yes, you can go in now. I'm to wait here.'

'Lady Adeliza has much wisdom,' murmured Oliver with a sly grin.

Before Rosamund could form a reply he dropped a careless kiss on her nose, and shouldered his way past the thick curtain.

Rosamund stared at the swinging drapes, her expression sombre. Absently she fingered the place that Oliver had kissed, and tilted her head to one side. It was a fine curtain, a tapestry one, made no doubt by Lady Adeliza's most talented needlewomen. Everything in this castle told of the Fitz Neal family's wealth and standing. Rosamund peered to examine the design and frowned. Now she looked closely, she saw how threadbare and begrimed the hanging was. That was strange. It occurred to Rosamund that though all in the castle from her liege lord down to the lowliest scullion were well fed, there were many signs of neglect in the keep. The landing here was thick with dust. The door-curtain needed to be hung outside and beaten hard; like every other tapestry in the building, it had been bright once, but now it hung grimy and uncared for.

The Fitz Neal family dined off metal plates—lack of monies could not be the cause of this decay. Rosamund shrugged. Why should it matter to her? The castle was still the most magnificent place she had ever seen.

All her life Rosamund had longed to have a taste of such a life. She had cast envious glances up at the castle towering on the clifftop and wondered what it would be like to live there. She had tried to imagine sleeping on a real featherbed, had tried to imagine what a kirtle made of the finest wool would feel like on her skin. She had heard tell of the great feasts held in the hall. She had wished with all her heart that she belonged there, high up in the castle, living with *them*—the nobility.

A murmur of conversation slid past the shielding curtain and escaped into the lobby. The words fell like stones on Rosamund's ears. Some of them she recognised.

'…Cecily…Oliver…' Lady Adeliza's voice drawling a formal introduction.

Rosamund shut her ears, and struggled to pick up the threads of her thoughts. What was the matter with her?

She had been presented with a chance most girls of her class would leap at. She ran her hands down the delicate stuff of her gown. How her dear friend Lufu would envy her this gown! And she had slept on a featherbed, and she had as handsome a lover as one could wish ... why quibble with all that?

Rosamund's mind, though nimble, was untaught. Without the advantages of education she was left fumbling with concepts beyond her reasoning.

Her head jerked up as Oliver's deep voice floated out of the upper hall past the curtain. How she wished she could speak that foreign tongue! Perhaps Marie could teach her some of the more important words. Not that that would help now, for Oliver was speaking so quietly she doubted even those in the chamber with him could hear him.

Rosamund found she had crept up to the door-hanging. Her hand had risen to grasp at the material, she could feel the rough wool under her fingertips, had pushed the hanging aside ...

Her heart contracted painfully. Oliver was down on one knee on the tiled floor. His dark head bent over a slender, white lady's hand. A hand that had never done a proper day's work. Rosamund knew her own hand would seem rough and clumsy beside the delicate one Oliver was so intent on kissing. She forced her eyes up past the milk-white hand to regard the Lady Cecily. Oliver's betrothed wore a green gown and a light filmy veil as befitted her status as daughter of a baron. A dark and swirling mist clouded Rosamund's mind. So strong was the emotion surging through her that she scarcely noted that Lady Cecily's body was slimmer than a wand and too slender to be healthy.

Rosamund's blue eyes were full of shadows as she forced them to come to rest on the Lady Cecily's face. She stifled the gasp that shot to her lips. Pressing her workworn hand hard to her mouth, she stared.

The Lady Cecily looked like a wraith. No one could be so pale and live. Her delicate skin was stretched tight across her cheekbones, almost translucent. Like a fragile flower, one touch and she would be bruised, irreparably damaged. Death sat in Cecily Fitz Neal's eyes. It looked out blindly over the head of the man kneeling in homage at her feet.

Lord Geoffrey's sister was oblivious to Oliver's existence.

Oliver murmured something, in his softest voice and Lady Cecily frowned. Rosamund watched those empty, hollow eyes focus on his face. The lady gave a little start, and at once Marie and the Lady Adeliza were at her side. Steadying her. Lady Cecily's pale blue eyes took on a hunted expression, she moaned and moved restlessly from one foot to the other. With a sickening jolt Rosamund realised that the Lady Cecily was not being steadied. She was being restrained. And she was no match for the two robust women who fettered her with their bare hands.

Oliver caught the Lady Adeliza's eye. He was shaking his head, frowning darkly.

Rosamund bit on her hand, and stifled a laugh that was tinged with hysteria. The ugly surge of feeling that threatened to overwhelm her had vanished. She felt only a deep pity. The Lady Cecily was beautiful, but her beauty did not belong to the living earth. The blacksmith's small son had worn just that look, and he had not lived out last winter's frosts.

This dying girl was to be Oliver's wife. Rosamund had seen enough. And what she had seen sickened her.

Rosamund let the curtain fall back over the doorway and turned instinctively for the window which lighted the lobby. She put her hands on the cold, hard stone and inhaled deeply. The cool air had a tang to it. Blown straight off the sea. She could hear the harsh cry of the sea gulls. If she closed her eyes she could call to mind the sandy beach washed clear by the outgoing tide ... the gulls swooping overhead ... the feel of the warm sun on her face ...

She had a sudden, almost uncontrollable longing to quit the castle. Without willing it, Rosamund had moved to the top step, her body poised as if for flight. Almost anywhere would be better than this place with its sick intrigues; people moved hither and thither like counters in a game.

Even the mill was better than this. Her father's carping and Aeffe's grasping greed were as nothing to this... She thought of flies writhing in webs. And of spiders.

Rosamund's hand clutched at the rope rail. She'd go, and the Devil could fry them all!

There was a sudden rush of air, the curtain rings rattled, and Oliver was at her side, looming huge in the small half-light of the landing. His back was turned towards the narrow window and Rosamund could not read his mood. He stared at her silently for several heartbeats, and then held out his hands to her, palm uppermost, still without uttering a word.

Fool! Fool! a voice in Rosamund's head was screaming. But she placed her hands in his and moved up close to his tall, strong warmth, and did not protest till he had hugged all the breath from her lungs.

'Oliver!' she protested, gasping. 'I shall suffocate!'

'Not you, my Rosamund. You are made of sterner stuff,' he muttered into her shoulder. The iron grip which held her fast relaxed, and she felt him press a burning, biting kiss on her neck, his tongue flickering over her, tasting her.

She giggled. 'You're all right then,' she surmised, and her hand somehow tangled in his hair.

He lifted his head, his eyes on her mouth. 'Kiss me,' he commanded softly, 'and I shall be.'

Rosamund pulled his mouth to hers, her body softening against him. His low groan of pleasure was echoed in her heart, and she knew then that she was not free to escape the castle. Not while he needed her. The castle had spun a web for her, and she was fast in its toils.

'Rosamund! Come in 'ere, lass!'

At the sound of Marie's voice they sprang apart.

'Pity,' Oliver murmured teasingly. He ran his hand down her arm, and lightly squeezed her fingers. 'But we can continue this, later.' And with that he clattered down the stairs whistling, as though he had not a care in the world.

Rosamund stared after him, wondering if she'd just responded to a need that did not exist. Wondering whether Oliver de Warenne did need her. Whether, in fact, he needed anyone.

'Rosamund!' Marie called again, and stuck her head round the door-drapes.

'I'm coming,' Rosamund flung over her shoulder, her face turned pensively towards the empty stairwell. For a moment she thought she'd seen through Oliver's shield. Thought that when he'd held out his hands to her, he was demonstrating that he...Rosamund ran her hand round her neck. She must have been mistaken. For he'd run jauntily enough down the stairs...

'Rosamund! What's keeping you?'

Abandoning her fruitless speculations, Rosamund pushed past the woolen tapestry and entered the upper hall.

There was no sign of Lady Cecily, but Lady Margaret was resting her awkward shape against the closed door opposite, her hand lying on her distended belly. The Baron's wife was watching her mother-in-law, her pale brows puckered.

Rosamund's entry had gone unremarked. Apparently meek, she stood by the door and waited to be instructed, taking full note of what went on about her. Lady Adeliza was surrounded by her ladies. All had bent their heads to their work, a pretty vision of domesticity. Bees in a hive, obeying their queen.

Lady Margaret seemed to reach some decision. She stepped forwards. 'My...my lady?' Her voice was soft and hesitant. She spoke in English.

Lady Adeliza did not even raise her eyes from her work, but she had heard for she replied in the same tongue. 'Margaret. What is it?' She heaved a sigh.

'I'm afraid...' the Baron's wife blurted.

Lady Adeliza's head shot up. 'Oh, Saints preserve us! It's not your first, woman. There's no reason to suppose it will be as hard a labour for you as last time. The midwife explained it gets easier each time. Why, when I had my Blanche it was over in a couple of hours.' Her voice bristled with impatience. 'If you kept yourself busy...' Lady Adeliza gestured at her industrious ladies, 'and saw to your duties in this castle with more diligence, you'd not have time to dwell on such maudlin thoughts.

'And 'tis not as if there's nothing to be done. I've seen how slack things have become since you took over from me as chatelaine.'

Lady Margaret's gentle voice ignored the criticism made by her mother-in-law. 'Nay, my lady, I was not referring to my confinement.'

'Oh?' The silver needle stilled.

'Cecily is not up to this wedding, my lady. You know that as well as I. It is for her that I am afraid.'

'My son wishes it,' said Lady Adeliza curtly. 'He would make amends for causing the fall which lost her her wits. He feels responsible.'

Lady Margaret smiled and came to sit on the stool at her awesome mother-in-law's feet. 'I know that. But, you must see this marriage cannot take place. My lady, Geoffrey is not an unreasonable man. He can be...persuaded. If both you and I were united in our condemnation of this match then he would...'

'I doubt it,' Lady Adeliza said cynically. 'There is more to this than Cecily's wedding.'

'I don't see it. He could send her to a nunnery and——'

'Can you see her delicate constitution thriving better in a dank nunnery? Nay, Margaret, Geoffrey is set on this. There are wild rumours flying about the land. Rumours concerning the Angevin cub. Our king's grip on the kingdom is being shaken. There is trouble brewing and my son must be better prepared. Oliver de Warenne is a godsend to Ingerthorpe Castle——'

'There are others, and they are knights already,' Inga put in jerkily, and then flushed an unbecoming shade of red when both ladies turned their heads in her direction. Inga subsided, muttering an awkward apology.

Rosamund caught Marie's eye, and was amused to see the nurse put a finger to her lips. She was already holding her breath, and needed no warning to tell her that if either of the ladies' eyes fell on her they would cut short their conversation, or else complete it in the French tongue.

Lady Adeliza raised an eloquent brow and continued. 'There is, of course, Sir Gerard, but he's living in the past. And as for Sir Brian...' Her lips sneered, expressing utter contempt.

There was a little gasp and one of the women lifted her head from her work. Lady Blanche. Her blue eyes blazed with such naked hostility that Rosamund almost echoed Blanche's gasp with one of her own. It was apparent Lady Blanche did not share her mother's view of the youngest knight in the keep.

Either Lady Adeliza was deaf, though this did not seem to be likely, or she was insensitive to her daughter's fixed stare. She lifted a claw-like hand to pat Lady Margaret on the arm. 'Nay, our new-found cousin's arrival here was most timely. Most timely. Geoffrey will knight him and have him wedded to our family, for such a tie would prove unbreakable. With the trouble that's coming we need as many good fighters as we can get.'

Lady Margaret's pale eyes searched the older woman's hard face. 'And you would sacrifice poor Cecily in this cause, your own daughter?'

'That girl ceased being my daughter the day her wits were knocked from her skull!' declared Lady Adeliza harshly.

Rosamund saw Lady Blanche wince, but the lady did not raise her head again.

'God's Bones, woman! We're speaking in the peasant's tongue!' realised Lord Geoffrey's mother. 'Why on earth did you address me in it?'

Lady Margaret's eyes slid to where Rosamund was standing. 'Oh, I was worried in case Cecily should hear us and be distressed,' she said lightly.

With a jolt, Rosamund realised that she had been meant to understand the ladies' conversation. Why? Did

Lady Margaret believe Rosamund would plead with
Oliver? Did she think her entreaties would influence him?

'Hmmph!' snorted Lady Adeliza. 'Small matter that
would be! You, er....Rosamund.'

'My lady?' She attempted a curtsy.

'You're to care for my daughter, Lady Cecily.' Lady
Adeliza's wave encompassed Lady Margaret's distended
stomach. 'Marie will soon be too busy caring for a real
infant to have time for a full-grown one.'

'My lady.' Rosamund saw Marie was directing her
towards that closed door.

'Girl!' Lady Adeliza said abruptly.

Rosamund met those hard brown eyes.

'She may be...different, but I'll not have you make
a mock of her. Remember she's a Fitz Neal, and...she's
very sick. Maybe mortal sick.'

Rosamund swallowed down an unexpected lump in her
throat and nodded. Lady Adeliza was not as hard-
hearted as she would like to make out.

Her evening meal long finished, Rosamund set down her
empty ale pot and left the trestle. Oliver was laughing
at some comment of Sir Brian's; out of the corner of
her eye she could see his dark head was flung back, his
face creased with merriment.

As Rosamund wandered aimlessly in the direction of
the castle entrance one of the guards snatched at her
skirts. She looked at him distastefully. His brown eyes
were glazed with too much ale, and his bold smile
promised untold delights.

'Don't look at me like that, pretty lass,' his speech
was slurred, 'I know 'ow to bring a smile to them sad
eyes of yours. I'm as good as the next man.' He smiled
at her winningly and coughed.

Rosamund wrenched her skirts from the guards' hand,
neatly avoiding his next ungainly lunge and stepped
swiftly through into the porter's lodge.

'Nay, Edgar, that one's spoken for,' the porter told
Rosamund's admirer as he stumbled in after her.

Rosamund smiled gratefully at the doorkeeper and, trusting him to fend the soldier off, she ran down the stone steps and into the deserted bailey.

The fresh air made a welcome change after the stuffy atmosphere of hall and ladies' bower. Rosamund remembered seeing a ladder which led up on to the guards' walkway on the castle walls. She altered direction and found it almost immediately. She hitched her long skirts up into one hand and clambered up on to the wooden walkway. Her feet rang hollow on the boards.

'Who's there!' challenged the watchman.

''Tis only me, Rosamund Miller,' she answered.

'Who gave you leave to come up here, lass?' demanded the guard belligerently.

''Twas I,' Oliver replied, from behind Rosamund. He was swathed in a thick fur-lined cloak.

'Oh aye, very good, sir.' The guard changed his tone and saluted.

Oliver took Rosamund's elbow, steering her towards the eastern turret, which overlooked the sea. The wind was strong here, snatching at their words and forcing them to raise their voices.

'I'm sorry,' Rosamund apologised stiffly. 'I did not know I couldn't climb up here. You gave me a fearful start creeping up on me like that.'

'If everyone in the castle decided to stroll about up here, there'd be no room for our soldiers,' Oliver pointed out. 'And I was not creeping up on you. I thought you might have been in trouble, so came hotfoot to your rescue.'

'Trouble, what trouble?' Rosamund shouted over the rushing wind.

'The man who's been ogling you all night. He followed you out here...'

'And you were worried for my reputation, were you, Oliver? A little late. I have no virtue now. I'm a fallen woman. Destroyed. And you know what's to blame for that as well as I! Your ambition! 'Tis that has ruined me!'

She braced herself for an angry retort, but his reply when it came was as calm as could be expected given the wild gusting of the wind.

'Rosamund, come with me.' Oliver put his arm about her waist, and walked her back to the stepladder. The guard clomped past them, his boots drumming loud on the platform. 'We cannot talk here, what with the wind and . . .' Oliver jerked his head in the direction of the heavy-footed lookout, 'other distractions.' There was laughter in his voice.

'Then where . . .?'

'Down you go, I'll hold the ladder for you. That's it.'

Oliver leapt down the last few steps to land at her side with the fluid agility of a wild cat. He took her hand, and pulled her across the yard towards the stables.

'Oh, no!' Rosamund protested, hanging back once there was no doubt of their destination. 'Not Lance! Oliver, you know I don't like riding. It was so uncomfortable last time and I can't ride alone . . .'

Oliver laughed softly, dragging her past the brewhouse and pausing in the yellow lamplight by the stable door. 'Nay, Rosamund. I would speak with you away from the castle. Never fear, I shall not saddle Lance this time. We'll go bareback. And, sweet Rosamund, 'tis time you began to master your fear of horses. A squire's lady must be prepared to learn to ride.'

Rosamund sent him a strange look. 'But, Oliver,' she pointed out sweetly, 'I am no lady. I am one of Baron Geoffrey's humblest vassals. You can't have forgotten my lowly origins already?'

Oliver's eyes gleamed in the lamplight. She heard him curse under his breath. 'Very well,' he growled, 'if you expect to be treated like a baggage.'

Then he had her arm in a bruising grip, and was marching her into Lance's stall. He held her immobile with fiercely glittering eyes, daring her to try and escape while he slipped Lance's bit and bridle on.

She knew she was no match for him. Before she had time to draw breath she was dragged unceremoniously up before him, Lance's coat harsh against her long legs.

'How like you this treatment, baggage?' Oliver grated in her ear.

'How do you think, you hulking lummox!' she jerked back. Then she sobered, and a sly smile spread across her face. 'The drawbridge is up. 'Tis shut for the night. We won't be able to break the curfew.' Her voice was sweet as honey.

Oliver did not see fit to dignify her statement with an answer. Confidently he directed Lance to the gatehouse, calling out a friendly greeting to the man posted there.

Coins chinked. The guard's face split into a wide gap-toothed grin.

'There'll be more for you on our return,' Oliver promised.

And it was as easy as that. With much clanking and grating of metal, the winding mechanism was set in motion, and they were outside the curtain wall of Ingerthorpe Castle before the portcullis had even been fully raised. Outside the man-made haven the sea-breeze stung their hands and faces.

Rosamund glanced back. The crenellated walls were black as pitch, sharply outlined against the star-spangled night sky. At this speed the flaring torch lights receded fast. Oliver's cloak billowed out behind him.

It was so dark trotting along the cliff path. She felt a trickle of unease run down her spine. How could Lance see his way with only the starlight and a thin crescent moon to guide him? She had never, ever ventured up on the cliffs after nightfall. She sent up a little prayer for their safety, hoping fervently that the myths she had heard of monsters and wandering souls out for revenge *were* myths and not true tales.

Oliver smiled grimly to himself. The set of Rosamund's back betrayed her vile mood. As did the way she was trying to prevent her body from resting on his. He sent an unobtrusive command to Lance with his heels, and when the stallion obediently danced sideways Rosamund gave a little gasp and clung to Oliver's encircling arms, sliding back against him. He grinned and pulled Rosamund into the shelter offered by his mantle. It was so much more pleasant to ride down the cliff path with the scent of her in his nostrils and her young body secure in his arms.

Infuriating, stubborn wench. If his cousin knew what he was about, he'd roar his mockery to the treetops. She'd been given to him. No one questioned his right to keep her. Except that poor wretch of a husband. Oliver's face darkened. He must be going soft to be considering the feelings of a filthy stone-dresser.

The gentle churning of the waves as they dropped on to the shore marked their reaching the bottom of the cliffpath. The sea gleamed black as jet. It had captured the moon, for a dancing silver image floated out in the bay, rippling into a multitude of glittering fragments before turning crescent again under the ceaseless, shifting swell. Oliver drew rein and dismounted.

'Why have you brought me here?' Rosamund demanded crossly, as he assisted her from the stallion's back.

He put a finger to her lips. 'Shhh, not a word,' he admonished, and casually made fast his destrier's reins on a rock. Then he carefully removed his leather boots and set them down on the shingle.

'I suggest you do the same unless you want your shoes spoiled by salt,' he advised.

'But what...?'

'Shhh!' Oliver repeated. He stood over her, and Rosamund had no choice but to comply with his advice. When her shoes had been put by his, he took her hand and strode out on to the glistening beach. The cliff wall was a mere stone's throw away.

The retreating seas had left the sand all wet. Starsilvered, it was shining like a polished mirror. Cold on the feet. A crisp breeze in their faces.

'Ol-iv-er,' Rosamund pleaded, stumbling after him.

Abruptly Oliver stopped, eyes narrowed as he searched the cliff wall. 'We're here,' he announced, and pushed her roughly to the fringe of the beach.

'Sit,' he said shortly.

Hugging her arms about her, Rosamund looked at him askance. 'Are you trying to give me lung-fever?' she demanded. 'I'm frozen. You have your cloak, while I . . .'

'Come here, woman.' Oliver spread his fur-lined cloak on the ground.

Rosamund eyed him suspiciously.

''Twill be as soft as our bed at the castle,' he coaxed, stretching his long length on the mantle, and offering her his hand.

'Our bed?' Rosamund asked, pointedly ignoring his hand. 'I thought, *sir*, 'twas yours.'

His sigh was lost on the whispering wind. He sat up and took her by the wrist, forcing her to her knees before him. 'Look, girl, the sand is dry here, we are out of the wind. Why, 'tis almost a cave.'

Rosamund stared mutinously into his dark face. She opened her mouth.

'Not a word, Rosamund. Not one word,' he ordered.

And then somehow he had her lying alongside him on the cloak. He pulled it round them and his arms were like clamps, she could not move. Rosamund stirred uneasily and would have spoken, but his hand came over her mouth. 'Shhh!'

Rosamund was not afraid. But she was angry. She decided not to struggle. Her strength was feeble compared to his, and if she pitted herself against him she could only be the loser. But her body was stiff as a poker in his arms. He must be mad. She wondered what he was about.

For all that it was May, the night air was very chill, but Oliver was warm. Rosamund felt her body begin to relax and steeled herself against it. What was he about?

Unconsciously she burrowed closer to the heat offered by Oliver's body. The hand which was clamped over her mouth lifted and came to rest on her neck. His thumb moved over her skin and she stiffened, realising she was weakening. The thumb stilled.

Her mind was dwelling too much on the tall man who held her. Rosamund listened to the waves breaking on the shore. That was the rattle of the shingle as it was skittered over the sea floor. A seafish playing jacks with shells for counters. Another wave, another. An endless succession of them. The swishing heartbeat of the sea pounding on forever.

Oliver's heartbeat sounded in her ear. Rosamund breathed a soft sigh of pleasure, and before she knew it her hand had crept out and slid around his slim waist. His thumb recommenced its gentle caressing of her neck.

She could feel the long length of his thigh touching hers, and remembered, all too vividly, how it had felt to waken and find her naked limbs tangled with his in the aftermath of love.

Rosamund shifted, pressing her face into his side so she could breathe in the masculine scent that was Oliver, and place a surreptitious kiss on his tunic where his ribcage would be.

His fingers were under her chin, turning her face to the moonlight.

'What are you thinking?' Oliver asked in a husky voice.

Rosamund was glad that the light spared her blushes. 'Oh! I...nothing...you're very warm...that's all.'

'Liar,' he murmured with moon-silvered eyes fastened on her lips.

Rosamund's lips were parted, waiting for his kiss. But instead Oliver's finger trailed lightly over her face and traced the fullness of her lower lip. Her skin grew hot at his touch and Rosamund had to fight down the impulse to clasp his wrist tightly to her lips. She wanted very much to kiss him, but Oliver made no move to fulfil her unspoken desires.

Puzzled, her eyes sought his. Their gazes locked, his silver-grey, dark and unfathomable, hers wide and wondering. Rosamund fancied she read momentary confusion in Oliver's countenance. She heard him exhale sharply and realised they had both been holding their breath.

'You see,' he said, smiling, his broken tooth catching a stray moonbeam. 'When left to ourselves we do not quarrel.'

'I . . . I don't . . .'

'We might even like each other,' he added on a mocking note.

'Aye, of course, but why——?' Rosamund got no farther.

'"Of course", she says.' He shook his head. 'Don't you see? Your position in the castle was turning you into a shrew—no use glaring at me, Rosamund. Every time you come across me you turn on me, berate me. And I'll not have it.'

A cold suspicion curled in her vitals.

'Oh, I grant that you are as pretty a piece as a man could have to liven his nights, but is it worth it? To have you nagging at me, shrieking at me, that is not what I want. There are willing girls aplenty in yonder hold.'

'Why you . . . you . . . conceited——' Rosamund spluttered in fury.

He shook her none too gently and her teeth rattled. 'Hear me out, will you, little wildcat? So I brought you here. To see if we could resurrect at least a fragment of that dream we shared. And I think we did. You quite forgot your anger for a moment, didn't you, Rosamund, my angel?'

'Aye.' Rosamund had to admit it. One minute in his arms—that was all it had taken. And she had been imagining, hoping, dreaming . . .

Oliver pillowed his head on one arm. The other remained about Rosamund's waist. He stared straight up at the stars, and his face was carefully blank. 'So I decided to give you the choice you claim no one has ever given you. You may choose to stay as my lover at the castle, or to go back to the husband who waits for you at the mill.'

Rosamund gasped, and felt the blood drain from her face. The sea played its game with the shingle and shells.

Oliver's deep voice continued. 'I will not force you either way. It is to be your decision entirely. But, Rosamund, I tell you this, if you choose to stay with me, I'll stand no more shrewishness. You know the terms. I am to marry Lady Cecily. I cannot love you, but I will

take care of you. I will not allow any man to insult you.
I will not cast you into the ditch when I am done with
you. You have my word on that. You will be *my* woman.
Mine alone. Well? What is your answer?'

'But Oliver, what about Lord Fitz Neal? *He* "gave"
me to you. I am his vassal. He threatened my father with
loss of the mill if I do not stay. Choice!' She sneered.
'I do not think you give me a choice at all. The Baron
will not permit me to return now. I am part of the
agreement you made with him. A pawn in a chess game
where the squire is determined to be knight!'

Oliver's eyes were still pinned firmly on the starry sky.
She thought he smiled. 'What do you know of chess?'
he asked, and his voice was warm with amusement.

'What, an ignorant savage like me, you mean?'
Rosamund said, stung.

'Careful. You've that nasty edge to your voice again,
my angel,' he mocked.

Rosamund swallowed down a scathing reply. 'Will you
risk losing the game for a worthless pawn?' she
demanded.

'I can deal with that,' Oliver replied confidently.
'Geoffrey only made you part of the deal because he
thought I desired you.'

'And don't you?' she asked in a small voice, before
she could prevent herself.

His teeth gleamed. 'You are the very sum of my desires, Rosamund,' he said smoothly. 'Now will you deign
to tell me whether I am to take you back to the mill . . . or
back to Ingerthorpe Castle? I am curious to know.'

How cool he sounded. How unemotional. He posed
his question in the same tone that he would use if he
asked her whether the day was like to be fair or foul.

Rosamund thought of Alfwold, humble, honest
Alfwold, who had braved his lord's wrath for her sake,
but who none the less left her heart quite unmoved.

Rosamund looked down at the big loose-limbed
warrior at her side. Her eyes scouring his handsome face
for the smallest flicker of emotion. He had not even

glanced in her direction since he'd posed his question. Yet her heart beat fast for him.

Her eyes ran down Oliver's lean length. Her hand lay where she had put it, across his waist. She curled and uncurled her fingers. Through the fabric of tunic and undershirt her sensitive fingers took note of the sudden tightening of that flat stomach. Her lips curved.

Not as indifferent to her as he would have her believe. She moved her hand slowly and provocatively down to his hips. Ah! That brought his head round. Still no word, but his eyes gleamed, watching her.

Rosamund's hand wandered up Oliver's body, and rested on his chest. Her fingers casually drawing circles. He raised his head and covered her hand with his, killing the movement. His eyes had darkened, and she felt his other hand, the one around her waist, tighten.

Her shoulders slumped. But what of it? All these small reactions she had wrung from him were purely physical. Any maid would be able to win such a response from this lusty squire. She sighed.

'Rosamund?' His deep voice urged her answer.

'Why do you give me the choice?' she wondered. 'It seems I am yours for the taking.'

He picked up her hand and examined it, opening up her fingers. 'I thought I explained. I do not think it right that you should be torn away from your family and transplanted to the castle.' He brought her forefinger to his lips and kissed it. 'But there is an...attraction between us, and if you are willing, then I am content. But you must be willing, I'll not force any maid.' He turned his attention to her next finger and kissed that too. 'I can taste salt on your fingers,' he added, huskily.

'I'm surprised that a noble like yourself would waste time considering the views of a simple girl like me,' Rosamund commented.

'Hardly simple, Rosamund! I heard you with Marie. Already you have learned a little French. At the rate you learn...' Oliver grinned wickedly, dropped her hand and moved to cup a firm breast. Rosamund strove to conceal the instant response, the tightening in *her* stomach, her quickening breath, but she knew she had failed by the light in his eyes '...you'll be fluent in a week! We'll make a gentlewoman of you yet!' he finished.

'I'm not sure that I want to be a gentlewoman. Not if it means riding roughshod over other people to gain your own desires,' she announced. The devil! Now he was using her tactics! Proving he could win responses from her too.

Oliver's brows creased. 'I *am* giving you a choice.'

'Aye,' Rosamund agreed, and her voice was puzzled. She fell silent, considering him.

He lifted that thought-stopping hand from her breast and took her hand again. He must be aware how distracting it was.

If only Oliver cared for her. He had been honest with her, telling her plainly that he could never love her. Rosamund was not sure that she believed him.

Rosamund knew no one at the castle would think anything amiss in forcing a peasant girl to stay as the squire's lover. They thought of everyone else as cattle—beasts of burden. Not worthy of any human dignity. Marie had told her so. And she had said that Oliver was like them. He was to be knighted soon. Married to Lady Cecily.

What maid would turn down a chance to be his leman? A golden opportunity for her to taste the life that her humble birth denied her. They no doubt thought her privileged. The Baron knew Oliver had not forced himself on her. He thought she had been seduced. Cynically, Rosamund wondered what the outcome would have been if her lord believed Oliver had raped her. Much the same, she suspected. She was only a chattel.

No, the thought of offering Rosamund a choice had not entered one of those superior, aristocratic minds. Except Oliver's. He was showing her an escape route, and it would appear that he meant it. She really could choose. Why? No squire that she had heard of ever took any account of a vassal's wishes.

There was hope for her in this choice he was offering.

Taking a deep breath, Rosamund smiled deep into his silvery eyes.

'I choose to stay,' she decided, and her voice was as clear as a bell. 'I choose you for my lover, and I choose to stay.'

Oliver caught her to him and pressed a shower of kisses on her nose and cheeks. 'No more carping?' he whispered.

'No carping,' she agreed, smiling like a giddy fool.

'You'll remember I gave you a choice?' He nibbled at her ear.

'I will,' she promised, suddenly reminded of another moment she had shared with him on this very beach. When his cool grey eyes had turned as blue as the sky and she had glimpsed an aching need, a burning regret...

'I will,' she repeated softly.

Two simple words, and Rosamund had flung all sense to the four winds. Her marriage vows were shattered. Alfwold was forgotten. She was utterly changed. No longer an innocent victim. A willing lover. No shred of decency would cling to her now. And all because she believed the flicker of light in those cool eyes came from his heart. The heart that he insisted he did not have. The heart that she prayed she would win.

Rosamund was staking her happiness on a fleeting expression, and if she had misread it she was lost. But if she was right...

She had been lost since that first moment. When she had looked up from the grey stallion chewing her garland to see Oliver, a tall and proud sea god striding angrily towards her. Lost. Thenceforth her marriage to Alfwold had been tainted, doomed.

She loved Oliver. She must do to risk so much merely to be with him. Hoping that perhaps, one day...

Oliver's lips were seeking hers. He moved his mouth gently, barely touching her, nibbling at her lower lip. Rosamund's insides went molten and she clasped his head to hers, her mouth opening to admit his exploring tongue. All rational thought fled. The kiss deepened, hardened, a demanding lover's kiss. Confident and sure. For all his protestations, it was never the kiss of a heartless, passionless man.

Oliver lifted his head. 'Ah, Rosamund, you taste so sweet,' he groaned.

She drew his dark hair through her fingers and it was soft under her palms. She pushed her hands around his neck. She could no longer move. Her bones melted. It was all she could do to pull his head to hers, find that sensitive mouth, and claim another kiss.

Oliver's hand moved to cup her breast, his thumb caressing her through the cloth of her gown. Rosamund moaned, her hand tangling with the cloak on its way to his waist. It took great strength of will to move at all, for her limbs were leaden, heavy with desire.

Oliver's lips were lifted from hers and her eyes flew open. His head was a dark silhouette against the starry backcloth of the heavens. His hair black as night and ruffled by the wind.

Rosamund's searching hand had found the bare flesh of his back beneath his tunic. Strange how such a strong, well-muscled back should feel like softest velvet under her palm.

His eyes glowed down at her. The silver stars had been caught therein. She thought that he smiled.

'Not here,' he said, and his masculine voice was warm but firm.

'What?' Rosamund frowned. She felt him gently remove her wandering hand from his back and enfold it within his. She protested softly and tried to pull his head down.

'Nay, Rosamund,' he chided. 'I'll not take you here on the open beach. Our loving will not be rushed for fear of the chill air, or some wanderer stumbling upon us. We will go to our chamber. Rosamund, enough!' His voice grew hard.

Rosamund gathered her scattered wits together as Oliver eased his long body out of her reach. Silently she stared at him, unaware that the moonlight had revealed her disappointment only too clearly. And more: fear of rejection, fear of not pleasing him, fear of being cast aside.

'Home, Rosamund. Don't look so stricken, my angel. Once safely in our chamber I will prove how much I do desire you.' Oliver pulled her to her feet and into the haven of his mantle. 'I hope we can find our footwear in the gloom.'

Oliver kneed Lance to a faster pace and smiled complacently. It had been a good day for him. The best.

Rosamund sat before him as she had done on the ride down to the beach. Only now her body leaned, happy and relaxed, into his. He put a hand about her slender waist to steady her. She covered it with one of her own, her forearm resting over his, and her fingers weaving round his.

There was a lightness about his heart that Oliver put down to his rising fortunes. At last his ambition was to be realised. The knighthood he had longed for was within his grasp, and he had found his place with his cousin in this northern hold.

That morning the knowledge that he had almost attained his ambition had left him feeling oddly hollow. As though the thing he had grasped and fought for for so long had turned unexpectedly to mist in his hands. His lips twisted. The sudden shock of meeting success after years of grinding oppression must have temporarily stunned him.

Oliver pressed his lips into Rosamund's hair, and felt her fingers tighten over his. He held in his arms the woman he desired most in the world. Married to another, she had elected to stay with him.

A wave of relief had swamped his senses when she had agreed to become his leman. He had not expected it. But then, she was *so* fair, *so* warm, *so* giving. No other wench held a candle to her beauty. He grinned wryly to himself, remembering the effect those wide, blue eyes had on him, even now; remembering the touch of her hands on his back. Even after he had lain with her. Aye, a good day.

'Remarkable.' He realised he had spoken aloud.

Rosamund turned her head at the sound of his voice, presenting him with a moonlit view of her delicate profile. Her lips were slightly parted, and his thoughts returned to the kisses that they had shared. Her teeth showed white as pearls in the starlight.

'Remarkable?' she wondered.

'You, my sweet,' he admitted, surprising himself with his candour. 'I find your beauty remarkable.'

Rosamund's eyes were dark and luminous as they gazed into his. An indefinable emotion churned through Oliver, stirring all his senses. God, how this woman made him want her. No other wench had ever had such an effect on him. He must take care to keep his own eyes shielded, his swirling emotions hidden. She must never know the extent to which she could disturb his composure. The person did not live whom he would trust with his soul's secrets. He was better alone.

'Twas lust. Pure and simple. Nothing more. He'd keep it in its place.

She had agreed to stay. That was enough. He'd take her back to their chamber, and he would succumb once more to her sweet sensuality. And this time, he would know she was his to keep. His enjoyment would not be hobbled by the thought that soon this maid would be lying in another's arms. For she had agreed to be his. He was not to lose her.

Oh, there were common wenches in the castle who were pretty enough to satisfy a man. And one or two of them had sent him bold, inviting looks which told him without words that, were he to press his attentions in their direction, he would not be repulsed. A soft, delicately scented strand of hair fluttered across his cheek; he made no move to brush it aside.

'Oliver, look!'

Rosamund's slender arm was pointing towards the castle gate. Light streamed through the bars from a score of torches. Yellow splashes of light stained the sandy earth. The braziers had been lit atop the towers. At first glance it looked as though the castle was afire.

'Hold Lance's mane,' he advised curtly, his warrior's instincts flaring into life. Lance's easy rocking canter made short work of the cliff path, and Oliver reined in before the raised portcullis.

'What ho!' he called to one of the guards. There were three of them now, watching the entrance. 'What's amiss, why is the gate still open? 'Tis well past curfew now.'

A silver coin described a shining arc in the air. Deftly the man snatched it, and pouched his reward. ''Tis Lord Gilbert of Hewitt. 'E surprised a nest of rebels on 'is land. 'E caught some, killed some, and 'as tracked t'others into Lord Geoffrey's domain.'

Rosamund saw Oliver's keen eyes peer through the arch to assess the throng of horses still massed in the bailey. Her fingers clenched convulsively over his, and for an instant the cool grey gaze met hers.

'Rebels? Surely the Angevin is not trying again?' Oliver mouthed his suspicions looking at the guard. 'I thought his activity was confined to the south.'

'Eh?' The guard gawped stupidly.

'Never mind. My thanks, man.' Oliver swung himself off Lance's back and led his destrier past the stable boys who were struggling with Lord Gilbert's herd of horses.

Rosamund's eyes were round as she took in the chaos all about her. She had never seen so many war-horses before, and all fighting for space in the overcrowded castle yard.

The noise was deafening. There were shouts of exasperation from the grooms struggling to find quarters for the extra horseflesh. Huge hooves threw up clods of mud from the ground of the inner bailey and trampled them back into the earth. Yellow teeth flashed. Rosamund winced. One ill-tempered black brute of a horse took a chunk out of the haunches of another who'd been careless enough to place its rump too close. A scream of pain and rage trumpeted from the victim's mouth. Harness jingled. Profanities split the air.

These beasts were enough to scare off the devil and all his minions. Rosamund had never thought of horses as war machines, more as beasts of burden. But these great hulks were bred to battle. Instruments of war, trained to do violence. To kill. Like the men who rode them. She shuddered and her eyes fell on Oliver.

'I'll stable Lance myself!' the squire bawled to a flus-
tered groom. Rosamund gripped frantically at the grey's
coarse mane, her eyes fixed on Oliver's broad back as
he shouldered his way through the sea of horses. He was
one of them, she thought. All warrior. Another trained
killer. The gentle lover who had covered her in kisses
was blown away like thistledown on the breeze. Quite
gone. Lance was suddenly an island of safety, the only
thing that kept her from sinking down into the wild
thrashing of legs and hooves.

At last they gained the sanctuary of Lance's stall.
Oliver reached for her. Briefly clasped her body to his
for a moment, and a strong hand touched her bloodless
cheek. 'Did you think I'd let you fall beneath their
hooves?'

Rosamund shook her head. 'Nay, but they terrify me.'
She refrained from telling him that he frightened her
too, that his easy competence in the face of such an army
had raised a barricade between them.

''Tis not long since my Lance would have had the same
effect on you. That first time on his back, you went just
as white.'

'I've grown used to him,' Rosamund realised.

'And his master?' Oliver asked with sudden percipi-
ence. 'Have you grown used to him too?'

Rosamund's blood returned in a rush.

Oliver's mocking laughter drove her stumbling to the
stable door to stand with her back to him. If it were not
for the fearful mill of horses without, she'd have stomped
across the bailey and left him there alone.

She heard the clink of Lance's bridle, and knew
without looking that Oliver was making his destrier fast
for the night. She waited. Then she felt a movement
behind her and knew that the warmth on her neck was
Oliver's breath. 'Madam, do you still wait for my
company?' he murmured, voice amused.

'Aye,' she replied, reluctant to admit how the horses
frightened her.

'Our rendezvous will have to wait,' he told her
abruptly.

'I beg your pardon?' Rosamund replied, not following his drift.

Oliver's palm ran down the length of her arm from shoulder to hand. He took her fingers between his, thumb stroking the back of her hand.

'Much as I long to fulfil my promise to you on the beach, my angel, my first duty lies with my lord. There will be a council tonight, and I must attend. So our...er...pleasure will have to wait for another day.'

'Of course I know your duty is to Lord Geoffrey!' Rosamund snapped. 'I'm to expect nothing from you, Oliver, you made that perfectly clear. But I'm only a cowardly peasant, unused to these huge monsters—I merely await your escort across the bailey. I can't move past them without you,' she finished.

Oliver bowed his head, and his voice came soft and mocking. 'Apologies, my angel. To think I was arrogant enough to believe you waited for your pleasure.' His voice chilled. 'And take care, the shrew in you is showing—' he warned.

Rosamund tossed her head crossly. 'You goad me, Oliver. Mayhap I should not have agreed to stay.'

Oliver stiffened and released her hand. 'Do you dare to threaten me?' he asked.

'Oh, no,' Rosamund said innocently. 'How could that be? A mere chattel threaten a squire who'll soon be a knight?'

'Rosamund,' Oliver growled.

'I should have gone,' she announced. 'This is hopeless. You think that in giving me a choice you have made everything right between us. But you grant me no right to pride, and without pride what happens between us is as nothing. I should be gone from this place. You put my soul in jeopardy.'

'Go?' Oliver exclaimed, gripping her fiercely by the shoulders. 'And where shall you go? Back to the husband who loves you?'

'Aye!' Rosamund spat back. 'At least Alfwold does admit he loves me; 'tis more than you ever will. You unfeeling wretch! Why—you're…you're…' Words failed her and she spluttered to a halt.

Oliver's eyes bored into hers. He jerked her closer and glared at her. 'Does your loving Alfwold set your body alight as I do?' he rasped through clenched teeth. 'Do you moan in delight under the press of his stunted and scarred body? Why, I'll warrant this unfeeling squire stirs your blood more than your so-loving husband ever could, if you spent a lifetime in his bed!'

'Why…you…you fatherless swine!' Rosamund spluttered. Her hand came up, and before she knew it she had struck his lean cheek a cracking blow with the flat of her hand.

His grey eyes glittered, cold as the winter sea. Rosamund gasped with horror at what she had done and shrank under his merciless grip. She put up a hand to protect her head from the blow that must surely fall. Peasant maids did not strike their betters in the face and go unpunished.

The blow never came. Warily Rosamund lifted her eyes to Oliver's face. It was a mask of indifference.

'You may well cringe, Rosamund,' he said caustically. 'But, much as you may deserve it, I do not hit women. Now come with me. I shall escort you across the yard, and you can await my pleasure in the chamber.'

'I refuse!' cried Rosamund, though she knew she should have curbed her tongue.

Oliver's reply was very curt. 'You cannot. You made your choice. 'Tis too late to change your mind. You are back in Lord Geoffrey's hold now, and he has given you to me. I want you.'

'That's not enough!' she wailed. 'I was wrong to agree! 'Tis not enough, can you not see?'

''Twill have to be enough, my angel. For 'tis all you'll get from me.'

So saying, the lord's squire steered the miller's daughter through the crowd and drove her to the base of the castle steps. 'Till later, my angel,' he said, and vanished into the throng.

CHAPTER SIX

NIGHT'S shadow hung dark as death over Ingerthorpe Castle. Though the council meeting between Lord Geoffrey Fitz Neal and his new ally, Lord Gilbert of Hewitt, had come at length to a close, no action could be taken till the morrow. But agreements had been made, friendships forged and strategies decided upon.

Seeking what respite they could, bone-weary men sought their pallets, mumbling and murmuring to each other as they scrambled for the best places. There would be no space spare for even a dwarf in the hall that night.

Oliver yawned as he made his way thankfully up the stairs. No hard floor for him. He still occupied the small chamber. Shining golden spurs clanked at his heels. And, swinging at his hips, a leather sword-scabbard proclaimed his new and knightly status to the world. Needing Oliver knighted in the face of the crisis, his cousin had called him to the upper hall and dubbed him there almost before Oliver realised what he'd been about.

'You'll serve me better as a knight, cousin,' the Baron had said briefly. 'Kneel. Come on man, kneel.'

Bemused at the lack of ceremony, Oliver knelt on the hard terracotta tiles, bent his head and received the token buffet. 'Arise, Sir Oliver.' The Baron smiled. 'Here, take you these.' And casually the Baron had thrown the golden spurs, the coveted badge of knighthood at his perplexed former squire. 'Anything amiss, cousin?' Geoffrey had asked.

'Why, no,' Oliver admitted, a doubtful smile rather belatedly lighting his face. ''Tis the suddenness of it. I was not prepared . . . so soon,' he confessed wryly.

'Never mind that, I need your support. We can't have Lord Gilbert thinking my knights to be either bumbling fools or beardless boys. *You* have experience under *your* belt, and it shows. Following Lord Robert to the East has served you well.' Lord Geoffrey put an arm around his tall cousin's shoulders and led him from the upper hall. 'There's a fine sword for you in the armoury, should be just your weight. I'll send Ned for it now.'

'You're very kind, Geoffrey,' Oliver murmured.

'Pssht! Kindness has nothing to do with it,' disclaimed his lord. ''Tis part of the game. Tell me, Sir Oliver, what do you make of Gilbert Hewitt?'

Geoffrey took precedence on the narrow stair; thus Oliver replied to a balding head. 'Too early to say, my lord. I shall consider him during the meeting.'

'Do that,' the Baron flung over his shoulder. 'I've a mind he'll do for Blanche. Best to seal this blossoming friendship, I think. He's a man I'd rather take as friend than foe. Think on't.'

'I will,' Oliver promised.

'And you, cousin, don't forget you still have your part of the bargain to honour...' Geoffrey reminded him, as he pushed open the door to the lower hall.

Oliver had given a stiff little bow of acknowledgement, and the two kinsmen had stepped on to the dais to take their places at the council table.

Now, with the meeting broken up, Oliver's leather scabbard banged against the curving stair wall as he climbed to take his rest. He put his hand to the hilt to steady it. The wall torches had burned almost out, but they lit a face that was grey with fatigue. God knew what hour it was. He felt as though he could sleep for a week, but there was little chance of that. They'd rouse him before cockcrow. He supposed he should be thankful that his billet had not been appropriated for one of Lord Gilbert's comrades-in-arms. A night with the men on those punishing stone flags would be penance indeed.

Oliver's well-shaped lips lifted at the corners. He was a knight now. And to lead the search parties for the traitor's lair. The small chamber in the tower was his to keep. No hard stone bed for him. They wanted him well rested and content, the better to fulfil his commission.

He had reached the door of the chamber, and softly lifted the latch, so as not to disturb the girl that waited for him. No need to waken her. He wondered how she would react to the news that he was now knighted. With respect? With anger? Most maids would be proud to have their lover elevated, but then Rosamund was not like most maids... His unpredictable, unbiddable Rosamund. She would have forgotten their quarrel by now.

Oliver's grey eyes softened momentarily as pleasant images of Rosamund's curving body flashed into his mind. Curse the girl! She was almost too distracting. Their arguments in the stable must have left him at odds with himself for he'd not been able to give the rebels the consideration they'd merited for thinking of her.

He stepped soundlessly into the room and his eyes travelled at once to the bed.

It was empty.

Oliver's dark brows snapped together in a frown and then he shrugged. She was probably paying a visit to the privy down the corridor. He grinned, unbuckled his swordbelt, and began to peel off his tunic.

He leaned back on the bed to wait for her, still smiling. No longer weary. If the wench was awake, he may as well make the most of it. Perhaps if he took her again, he'd be better able to concentrate on the morrow. He wanted his mind clear of confusions, for he had to prove his worth and earn his knighthood. 'Twas no sinecure he had been given. He must work for his honour.

Minutes passed. The knight shifted restlessly on his pallet, and scowled at the door. Devil take the wench! What was keeping her? He rubbed his face and looked about the chamber. He had flung his tunic over the coffer. Rosamund's new garments were peeping out from under his. He could see the rose colour which she favoured, and the blue she'd not yet worn and...

His face darkened and the knight jerked himself upright. A prickling down his neck warned him. He found himself floundering, in the grip of an emotion that was totally bewildering. Oliver strode over to the gowns and rifled through them. They were all there. Nothing amiss. So why this sick feeling at the pit of his stomach?

He swore violently as the realisation hit him with the jarring force of a blow from the quintain in the tiltyard. Rosamund might be bold as brass in his bed, and doff her clothes for him, but Oliver knew with a horrid certainty that she would never, never, step into that corridor unclad. He knew that he was the only man ever to have seen those well-formed limbs naked as God had made them. Her eager loving had been as innocent as it was generous, and he knew with an almost savage pride that it had been for him alone.

And now she'd gone.

One stride carried him to the door. He was down the corridor and wrinkling his nose at the stench in the garderobe before he had time to blink. 'Twas as he thought. The closet yawned emptily at him. No Rosamund.

Oliver stormed back into his chamber and snatched at Rosamund's robes. With an exasperated sigh he threw them aside. No use staring at them. They were all there, every last one. All Lady Adeliza's cast-offs. He rubbed the bridge of his nose, forcing his tired mind to concentrate. What had she been wearing when she'd been brought to the keep? He'd never seen that dress, for they'd bathed and changed her. He had assumed they'd burned her peasant garb but . . . vaguely he remembered seeing a pink bundle jammed into the corner of his chest.

Oliver flung back the lid of his trunk, grimacing as it smashed into the wall. Aye, he'd seen her wearing a gown of just that shade, darned at the elbows it was. He could see her smooth arms, and her hands as she picked up tiny whorled stones from the beach. May Day. She'd said it was her best. Aye, she'd have come to the castle dressed in her finest, with head held high. Proud as a peacock.

Desperately Oliver disembowelled his coffer, spilling its contents over the floor. If ever there had been a pink gown among his gear, there was no trace of it now.

The young knight sat back on his heels and leaned his head in one hand. She had gone. But why leave her new gowns behind? That made no sense that he could find. She'd never see their like again. Unless...Oliver expelled his breath sharply. That pride of hers... He'd seen it in her eyes often enough, though he'd discounted it, because of her village upbringing. It had served to amuse him, her pride. Oliver dragged in another breath of air and almost groaned.

He remembered Rosamund's angry face glaring up at him in Lance's stall. 'I refuse!' she'd cried. 'I was wrong to agree! 'Tis not enough.'

He had commanded her to wait for him. Assumed that she would obey. Weren't peasants bred to obey, as he had been bred to command? And now...

Oliver staggered to his feet and dragged on his tunic, his fingers fumbling in his haste to buckle his sword. He groped for his shining spurs and donned them too.

A wild and unsettling thought spun round and round in his mind. His Rosamund was out there, undefended in the darkness, alone, with only starving wolves and ruthless outlaws for company. The thought of her lying torn and broken in a ditch caused a muffled groan to fall from his lips.

His tiredness forgotten, he strode to the door.

He had to find her, before some terrible ill befell her, and then, by the Rood, he'd teach the wench the wisdom of obedience.

The luckless guard stared with slackened jaw at the fury in the flinty eyes of the man astride the grey stallion. He noted that the glinting yellow spurs proclaimed this one a knight, but knew better than to wonder aloud at the changing moods of his betters. This very eve he had seen the same man riding smiling through the portal with his lover set before him. As merry as any village lad with his lass.

'She...she said you'd finished with 'er...sir,' the sentry stammered.

How you could misjudge a wench, mused the guard. She was no simple lass, that one. The moment she'd offered him the ring to let her out he'd know where he stood with her. She must have been well paid to be throwing rings about so carelessly. A whore. That's what she was.

He'd made it plain he'd let her out without payment if she'd grant him a few moments' joy with her. But the bitch had stuck her nose up in the air—she'd been spoiled by the attentions of this proud knight—and had refused him. She thought herself above pleasuring a mere sentry.

The stern young man did not look impressed. The guard waited for the horseman to speak.

'Finished with her?' The knight's lips thinned. 'I hadn't begun!'

'Aye, and she gave me this to open the road.' The sentry held up his hand. In his dirty palm Rosamund's brass wedding ring winked up at Oliver. 'I thought you must've paid t'lass well for 'er to be giving the likes of me this.'

Oliver's stomach twisted into a painful knot and his face grew grim. 'Lift the portcullis!' he commanded tersely.

'But...but, sir, you know it's against curfew regulations. And your whore's probably warming another's bed by now,' objected the guard.

A muscle flickered in the knight's jaw, but the guard missed the warning signal and blundered on.

'Pick another lass, me lord,' the sentry suggested. 'There's nowt to choose between 'em. And there's plenty o' willin' women right here. No need to go traipsin' to't village. I can recommend——'

'That maid is no whore!' Oliver spat, amazed at his own fury. His spurs dug into Lance's side, and the stallion, unused to such cavalier treatment jibbed, his huge hooves flailing dangerously close to the sentry's feet.

The man paled and scrambled out of harm's way, his back scrunched up against the stone gateway.

'Open up!'

The knight's voice left no room for hesitation, and cursing under his breath, the beleaguered sentry shifted to obey.

Oliver could waste no more time with this witless guard, he had to find Rosamund and bring her back before reveille. He had not taken his oath of fealty lightly. It was the thought of breaking that knightly oath, and losing his honour, that had sent cold sweat trickling down his spine.

As one of Lord Geoffrey's knights he had undertaken to lead the search parties at dawn, hunting for the traitors' hideout. Should he not be there to perform his duty...The word 'deserter' flashed into Oliver's troubled mind.

No baron could afford to let any vassal have such licence that they could shirk their obligations. Considerations of kinship would not help him if he was not back in time. An example would have to be made.

Oliver frowned at the portcullis. It seemed to be taking an age to lift. He flung a complaint at the guard. 'A snail would leave you standing, man! Move!'

The metal gate creaked ponderously upwards.

Oliver's lord had been generous in trusting him so soon with a knighthood. But Oliver was under no illusions as to what was expected of him in return. If he were not back at daybreak, and was seen to have violated the trust given him . . . Geoffrey would have no option but to strip Oliver of his privileges. Oliver would have no honour left, and the disgrace would finish him.

No lord would ever look at him again. For the only thing he possessed was his honour. Aye, 'twas the thought of losing that that he found so disturbing. But it didn't even cross his mind not to search for Rosamund.

The gate was up. In a moment, Oliver had spurred Lance through the gap.

The sentry came to stand in the guardhouse door and caught a last glimpse of the young knight as he turned his destrier's head towards the village and the estuary beyond.

The man watched the horseman ride into the darkness and spat into the dirt at his feet. 'Not so much as a glance behind him or even a wave of thanks,' he grumbled, massaging his aching muscles. 'That's a noble

for you.' Then, suddenly he recalled the generous tip
he'd received from the same rider earlier that evening,
and the man's broad brow wrinkled. He shook his head.
'Nobles,' he repeated contemptuously and spat for the
second time.

With the rough planks of the mill door beneath her
fingers, Rosamund hesitated. No chink of light to shine
a welcome through the cracks. The place looked quite
deserted.

Taking a fortifying breath, she balled her fist and
hammered on the wood.

'Father! Father! Let me in!' she called, and waited.

Still no sign of life.

She tried again. 'Father! Aeffe! Are you there? It's
Rosamund. Open up!'

Rosamund strained her ears at the door. She heard a
thud. Then silence again.

'Father!' Her voice rose a tone or two, and anxiously
Rosamund cast a glance over her shoulder. She could
hear the wind in the trees. An owl hooted from its perch.
She did not like it out here. The walk home to the mill
had exhausted all her stock of bravery; only sheer determination had kept her going. But now she was within
sight of safety, and her eyes and ears were suddenly
opened to the sinister aspects of swaying shadows and
whining winds.

Hitherto her mind had been closed to everything but
her need to escape the confines of the castle. But now,
outside the mill, she was alarmingly aware of her
vulnerability.

'Father!' her voice cracked.

Another thud, and this time—— Blessed relief! A light
crept under the door.

The door was no sooner unbarred than Rosamund
stumbled over the threshold.

'Oh. You're back then, daughter. 'As 'e finished with
you?' came her father's ungracious greeting.

Rosamund straightened her back with an effort. Surely
even her father could not be so callous?

'I *chose* to leave,' she said, and was proud that her voice did not tremble.

Osric grunted and thrust a lighted candle into his daughter's hand. He was already turning for the steps. Rosamund saw Aeffe's pale, sleepy face peering down at them, the upstairs lantern wavering in her grasp.

'Bolt up when you're done, Rosamund,' Osric said, without turning his head.

Aeffe smothered a yawn. 'Is Alfwold back so soon?' she murmured.

'Nay. 'Tis Rosamund,' replied the miller, mounting the stepladder.

'The whore!' Aeffe's voice grew sharp. Then she moderated her tone and employed her softest voice. The one as sweet as honey. 'I'm surprised she dares to show her face here. I heard in the village she was only too glad to pay the price of her merchet. Lady Adeliza gave her pretty gowns, and t'Baron's 'andsome squire loaded 'er wi' jewels that he'd brought with 'im all the way from Constantinople.' Aeffe paused. Her voice became sly and wheedling. 'See if she'll show them to us, my love.'

Rosamund put her hand to her mouth to stifle a hysterical laugh, but it appeared Osric had more sense than his spouse.

'Shut up, wife,' he said succinctly. 'I'm for bed. If you want speech wi' Rosamund, that's up to you.'

Rosamund heard Aeffe's indignant indrawn breath. She sank to her knees and leaned wearily on the grindstones, setting her candle down beside her.

She'd only been gone just over a day, and already the mill showed signs of neglect. The floor had not been swept. The yellow light fell upon food debris spread in sticky lumps where it had been dropped all over the boards. There was much spilt and wasted grain. And both food and grain had been trampled together by heavy careless feet, to form disgusting little mounds which would no doubt be crawling with ants and possibly other, more unpleasant, insects.

'Well, girl?' Aeffe stood before her, hands on her hips. 'Aren't you going to show me your earnings?'

Rosamund gave a tired smile, and shook her head sadly.

Aeffe took a pace forward and eyed her stepdaughter belligerently. 'What! You whore! Where are they, then?' she demanded.

Rosamund got to her feet slowly and spread her hands. 'Nay, Aeffe, you have been told a tale. I've been given no jewels.'

Aeffe's blue eyes narrowed in disbelief. Catching Rosamund unawares, she reached forwards and wrenched open the front of Rosamund's cloak. There was a ripping sound as the clasp resisted her efforts and tore the fabric. Then Aeffe snatched the garment from Rosamund's back and stared with greedy eyes at her stepdaughter's neck.

'Eh!' she cried, on seeing Rosamund's neck un-adorned as ever.

'Aeffe, see, there are no jewels. You're wrong!' Rosamund repeated through clenched teeth.

'Liar!' accused Aeffe, boiling with rage. 'You crafty weasel, you've hid them from me! You've come back dressed in that rag to deceive me!'

'No. No! I'm no liar, Aeffe. There are *no* jewels. I am not a whore. I have not been paid for anything. Let me be, for God's sake. I only want to rest.'

'Whore! Thieving whore!' Aeffe accused.

Rosamund glared at her stepmother. She was fast coming to the end of her tether. She had walked for miles in the dark to reach the mill, she was exhausted and would be insulted by this woman no longer.

'Who are you to call me a whore,' she asked, 'you who are no better than a whore yourself?'

'What?' shrieked Aeffe. 'Why you ungrateful slut! Who kept you on here, though you should have been wed years ago? I did! And what do I get for it...'

Rosamund's nails curled into her palms. 'You only kept me on because you wanted me as unpaid scullion,' she pointed out, 'leaving you free to comb your yellow hair and take your ease. What did you ever do to earn your keep?' she flung back.

Aeffe hissed in fury. Then her pale eyes narrowed and she stared blankly at Rosamund for a moment. Her shoulders slumped, and her eyes slid away like a snake's. She sighed.

Aeffe seemed to have discarded her hostility like an outgrown cloak. A wondering Rosamund wisely bided her time.

'I earn my keep,' the older woman muttered eventually, flinging back her long plait. 'That I do.' The face that turned to Rosamund had grown as haggard as a crone's. 'You think I do not pay for the things that he gives me? You're wrong. I pay all right. I pay with my body and my hands. Doing things that please him. Oh, aye, Rosamund...' Another heavy sigh. 'I pay a heavy price for my keep. But earn it I do. Every last morsel. I earn it. And maybe you are right. Maybe that does make me a whore...'

Aeffe's pale eyes searched her stepdaughter's. 'But what else can I do?' she asked, almost pitifully. 'He's the richest man in't village wi' t' pickings from t' flour, and I aim to keep 'im.'

Rosamund could not ignore the appeal she saw lodged in Aeffe's sad, dead eyes. She was no longer listening to a hated stepmother who'd never even attempted to win a mother's place in her lonely stepchild's heart. Suddenly Rosamund was gazing instead at a once-lovely woman who'd got her own way for years on the strength of her looks. Those looks were fading fast, and she read terror in Aeffe's eyes. Those frightened eyes put Rosamund in mind of someone else. My lady Cecily had worn such a look, though Rosamund knew her terror had a very different root. But to see Aeffe, her hardened stepmother, with her defences down... To see Aeffe blatantly admitting her vulnerability to Rosamund... It shook her to the core.

'I...I...had no inkling,' Rosamund stuttered. 'I thought you must have some liking for my father...'

Aeffe's swift, negative gesture routed Rosamund's false assumption.

Rosamund laid a hand on Aeffe's arm. 'Oh Aeffe, I'm sorry...' she began.

Aeffe glanced in surprise at the hand on her sleeve. 'Don't waste your sympathy on me, me lass,' the miller's wife said shortly.

'Aeffe?' Rosamund removed her hand.

Aeffe sent Rosamund a twisted smile. 'Tell me, are there really no jewels?' she asked.

'No jewels,' Rosamund confirmed. 'But what——?'

'Then you must love 'im,' Aeffe concluded. 'To do it for nowt. Oh, get back to your squire now, girl. Before 'e finds out you're gone and thinks you false. Get back to t' castle while there's time,' Aeffe urged.

'But... but Aeffe, what of Alfwold? What of my husband?'

Aeffe made an impatient sound. She lifted the hand that had lain on her arm. Lifted the empty ring finger between her thumb and forefinger. Stared at it. 'Alfwold went to the abbot. You didn't wear Alfwold's ring for long, did you?' she asked pointedly.

Rosamund's lips twisted. 'I had to bribe the guard to get me out,' she explained.

Aeffe had put her head to one side. She smiled. 'Listen, I hear hoofbeats,' she smirked. 'Far off as yet, but approaching fast on t' castle road.'

Rosamund blenched.

'Are you going to let him fetch you back?'

Rosamund hesitated, staring wildly at the mill door. She snatched up her cloak.

'Answer me, girl! Are you going back with him?' Aeffe demanded.

'Nay... nay I cannot,' Rosamund cried, her heart thudding violently against her ribs. In her haste to reach the door she tripped and stumbled. She gave a desperate moan and jerked at the handle.

'Fool!' Aeffe yelled as Rosamund ran through the doorway. 'He'll not be back this way again. His sort don't need to ask twice you know. He'll find another wench. Fool! Fool!'

With Aeffe's shouts ringing in her ears, Rosamund picked up her skirts and raced across the yard. It was bright enough to see, but if the moon was lighting up the path for her, it would also be lighting up the path for *him*.

The hoofbeats were louder now. He had almost reached the corner by the shrine, and any moment now he would round it, and she would be in his sight. Casting about desperately for cover, Rosamund flung herself off the track, and into the tall foliage that screened the riverbank from view.

She gasped for breath, and put a hand to her breast in an attempt to calm herself. Her eyes were riveted to the path which led up to the mill. She stiffened, and her heart missed a beat. For she could see him quite clearly in the pale light.

He was a dark night rider on a huge war-horse bearing down on the sleeping mill. His blue-black hair gleamed, flying back from his face in tousled disarray. His features were set, carved from granite. An avenging angel. Oliver swooped down from his saddle and dived at the door. A loud crash and a slam that made her start. And then there was only Lance to look at. A horse fit for a king standing unattended in the squalid mill yard— standing with his reins still swinging in the place where the bony carter's nags came to take up their loads for market.

With the blood still pounding in her ears, Rosamund eased away from the shelter offered by the tall reeds and edged her way round the mill, giving it as wide a berth as possible. She had to reach the stepping stones beyond the millpond and cross them before Oliver came back into the yard.

Rosamund had no clear goal in mind. All she knew was that she must escape him, and this was the only path open to her. It was not enough for her that she should be Oliver's lover. And there was Alfwold to consider.

Rosamund's mind ran over the possibilities open to her. She could not hide in the fishing village. Oliver would find her too easily. No one could keep secrets in that tiny community. She could not retrace her steps back to the castle either. That only left the moorland road to York. New territory for her, but perhaps somewhere along the way she could find a safe shelter for what was left of the night. With God's help she'd reach Lufu and Edwin's hut on the edge of the moor. Her former play-mates would let her sleep there.

Glancing furtively over her shoulder as she ran, Rosamund cursed the cloudless skies. The deep millpond shone silver-bright, reflecting with uncanny precision both stars and moon. If he were to come out now, he could not fail to see her. A light breeze rattled the reeds, and the harsh croaking of a frog sounded above her gasping breaths.

She'd rounded the pond now. A few more paces and she'd be at the crossing. Where were those stones? Surely by now...ah! There they were. Pray God that He grant her a second or two to cross the stream. The path on the other side was flanked by flowering hawthorn and shrubby bushes. Even Oliver's sharp eyes wouldn't be able to penetrate that thick screen, and she'd have a chance.

The stepping stones gleamed flat and smooth and white like a necklace of ivory plaques. Rosamund's feet were trembling as she felt her way out over the water. One, two, three... Her fingers became thumbs, she'd dropped her skirts into the water. With a soft moan she hitched them higher. They flapped coldly round her calves. She heard the crashing of the wooden door.

She froze and almost missed her footing. Sent another wide-eyed look in the direction of the mill, but he'd not yet mounted and the building stood between them. Another step, another...

Sobbing her relief, Rosamund stumbled on to the bank. She'd made it. But there was no time to waste. She must not panic. Setting her back resolutely to the mill and the pond, she forced herself to take deep, even breaths. She'd have to pace herself. 'Twas no use running herself out in five minutes. She'd go fast, but steady.

She'd follow this ribbon of track between the shrubs and he would not be able to see her.

She listened as she ran, forcing her feet to settle into a steady rhythm. Her banging heart set the pace. Her throat was dry. Every gulp of air rasped scalding down her windpipe.

She wished her heart would not thud so. A distant rumble of thunder rolled in from the coast, echoing the throbbing of her pulses. She wished she'd had an hour to rest after her walk from the castle to the mill. Then she'd have been able to get away without her chest feeling fit to tear apart.

She heard another series of earth-shaking thunder-claps. The sea storm was roaring fast upon her. Sea storm? To judge from the spangled heavens there was not a cloud within ten miles...

Hands on her heaving breast, Rosamund checked. The thunder stopped abruptly. She heard splashing and a low, urgent voice.

'Steady, Lance! Steady! 'Tis shallow here. That's it. Well done, my fine steed.'

Her blood ran suddenly chill, and she staggered away from the sound of that so familiar voice. He'd be upon her in a moment now. He'd run her down. He'd...

'Psst!'

Rosamund's head snapped round.

'Psst!'

A hawthorn rustled. She heard a yelp of pain, quickly smothered.

'Blast these spikes!' A guttural tone this, she found the accent foreign to her ears, but knew she had heard this man before. She struggled to place him but could not. Her brain felt fevered.

The splashing sounds drew her head inexorably back to the point where the stones reached the bank. By now Lance should be almost across.

'Psst! You want to get away?' whispered the man from the shrubbery.

'I...I...' She hesitated. His face was shrouded by leaves and shadows. Another fear seized her. 'Who are you?

How do I know I can trust you?' she demanded, backing towards the river now. Oliver was preferable to this faceless terror.

She heart a short laugh. ''Tis Father Eadric. Daughter, have you forgot so soon the priest who wed you?'

Rosamund froze.

'F...Father Eadric? What are you doing here?'

'Trying to save your immortal soul. I've been watching your progress from the mill. You're trying to escape your noble lover. You'll never outrun 'im on that road.' The bushes parted and a man stepped on to the track, flinging back his cowl so she could see his face.

'There! Now will you trust me?' asked the priest, his voice strangely tense.

'Oh, thank God! Where?' Rosamund breathed a sigh of relief and relaxed. She crossed herself, amazed that the Almighty should answer her prayers so promptly. 'Thank God!' she repeated.

'Amen to that,' replied the priest, drily.

'Father?' Rosamund frowned.

'Come, my child. Follow me.' Father Eadric melted into the bushes with scarcely a rustle.

Rosamund plunged in after him. The hawthorns snatched at her damp skirts. She jerked them free, not caring that her pink robe was torn.

'His horse cannot follow this route. I doubt that he's seen you, but if he has he'll have to pursue you on foot,' the priest's words came at her in quick succession, like arrows fired from an archer's bow. 'Keep on this path. It winds by the river, heading west. You'll be safe enough here. When you reach the bridge, rejoin the road to the moor at the crossroads.'

Rosamund's brain suddenly balked. The priest seemed to have it all planned. And all she had was questions. 'But...but...Father...aren't *you* going to show me the way? I may get lost. And what are you——?'

'God be with you, my child,' Father Eadric said, suddenly pious. He sketched the sign of the cross in the air above Rosamund's head. Dutifully Rosamund bent her head and her hand echoed the movement the priest had made. When she lifted her head, the scent of hawthorn hung in the air, the branches were still swaying where he had pushed them aside. He had gone as unexpectedly as he had appeared.

She was alone. Standing by the river bank, quite alone.

'Rosamund!' Oliver's voice, hard and furious, made her start. 'Rosamund!' his voice rose. There was a crashing in the bushes behind her.

There was no choice left to her now, but to run. He could not have seen her taking this route, for he'd not left the bank when she'd followed the priest through the thicket. But somehow he was still at her heels. Her hair flew loose from her braids as she fled down the narrow path. It was getting in her eyes. She shoved it with desperate fingers over her shoulder. Thorns and nettles were scratching and stinging her feet. Her flapping cloak caught on a branch, and the clasp that Aeffe had weakened gave way with a sharp crack. Her mantle slipped from her and she could not pause to collect it. He was gaining on her. She could visualise his strong, well-honed body tearing along the track.

'Rosamund! For God's sake, girl! Stop!'

Oliver sounded so desperate that her feet faltered. When he used that tone, she imagined an irresistible pleading look in his eyes.

'Rosamund, please! Stop. You don't understand! Please. Wait at least!'

Rosamund's feet did stop. She hated herself for being so weak. If only he did not sound so desperate. It would be easy then to run. But as it was...

She put a trembling finger to her mouth, and bit it hard. She could not help herself. Slowly and unwillingly she turned. And there he was. A tall figure hurling himself over the ground that separated them, pausing for a fraction of a second to snatch up her cloak.

He halted in front of her. His chest was heaving, his breath fanned her cheeks. Oliver impaled her with those moon-frosted eyes. No pleading there. She should not have stopped. The predator had caught his victim and was about to move in for the kill. Wide-eyed and unable to make good her escape, Rosamund watched him. He held her with his chilling eyes.

Deliberately Oliver dropped Rosamund's cloak to the ground. She blinked, as if waking from a trance, and made as if to run. Too late. His hands clamped on to her shoulders and he shook her like a terrier with a rat.

'Oh! Don't, Oliver,' Rosamund managed to gasp. Her hair unravelled, and fell in a shining cascade about her shoulders and over his arms. 'I had to go. Don't you see? I have made my vows to another man. I'll not be damned for a man who can't even love me!'

'God, Rosamund!' Oliver jerked out. He gave her another hair-tangling shake. 'Did you do it deliberately? You say *you're* damned!' He laughed bitterly. 'Did you know I'd follow you to perdition! You bitch, you knew they were waiting for me, you knew, didn't you? You planned it thus!'

She had never heard him like this. His voice so twisted with loathing and fury as to be unrecognisable. And as for his face... she was blinking up at a total stranger.

An owl hooted nearby, and Oliver's face grew uglier still.

'I'll have my Judas kiss at least,' he grated.

'Oliver, you're hurting me!' Rosamund protested.

'Hurting you!' he exclaimed harshly. 'I could kill you for this!'

Oliver's dark head swooped down in a kiss utterly unlike any she had had from him. It was all hate. His lips bruised her mouth. His hands were curving into her shoulders like the talons of a bird of prey. They would pierce her flesh through the stuff of her gown.

Rosamund felt a sob well up from somewhere deep in her being. He was bruising her soul too. And that hurt far more than the nails she could feel digging deep in her shoulders. As those merciless lips ground ruthlessly into hers, the owl hooted again.

Oliver lifted his head. A twig cracked behind him. A stealthy shadow flitted in and out of Rosamund's line of vision. She would have tensed if she were not already strung tight as a bow-string. Any tighter she would snap.

Oliver's pitiless eyes were on hers. He had taken note of her reaction and his face was somehow expectant, and very, very ugly.

Man-like, the shadow behind Oliver moved.

'Oliver! There's someone——'

Oliver took no heed of Rosamund's whispered warning.

'I want to see your face,' he was saying. 'I want to watch you as you see me betrayed.'

He made no sense. He had not shifted his hands from her shoulders. The shrouded figure was moving through the darkness. Steadily, stealthily, stalking them. Nearer and nearer...

Rosamund shoved frantically at Oliver's broad chest. 'Oliver, look out, I'm certain there's someone behind you!'

'I know, my angel,' he murmured unpleasantly.

'Oh, you stubborn, mule-headed oaf! Why don't you turn and face the danger, instead of glaring at me like that!' she cried.

Oliver's lips twisted. 'And offer *you* a present of my back? I wouldn't turn my back to you, Rosamund, though you were the last person on God's earth. Besides, I told you... I want to see your faithless angel-face as you gloat over how easily the trap was sprung on your impetuous and foolhardy lover. What price did you set on my capture? How much is a man's life to you? One silver shilling? Or perhaps you sold me for thirty pieces?'

Rosamund gasped at the venom in his tone. 'Oliver, I haven't the least idea what you're talking about,' she said clearly, struggling to free herself. Oliver stood solid as an oak and let out a mirthless laugh. Vainly Rosamund pushed at his arms and chest. His feet were rooted to the river bank as though he'd stood there for a hundred years, and his vice-like arms seemed to have grown into her shoulders.

'Oliver!' Her voice cracked on the warning. 'Oh, Sweet Mother, what is happening? Oliver, behind you!'

Oliver's grey eyes were fixed unwaveringly on hers. The muscles in his arm flexed, but he made no other sign that he had heard her. She could feel the strength of those muscles under her fingers. If only he would listen to her. She hated to see his eyes so accusing. She wanted him to stop scouring her confused and apprehensive face, and confront the dark prowling shadows.

She choked down a sob. 'Oliver, please.'

She thought he winced, but no, it must have been a trick of the light. His face was like a stone. Stern as ever.

Rosamund felt rather than saw the sudden movement. There was a heart-sinking thud as the cudgel connected with Oliver's skull. Oliver's eyes flared. His body jerked against hers, and she knew that she had cried out.

'Judas,' he accused hoarsely.

'No, no, no,' Rosamund denied, helpless in the face of overwhelming violence.

Oliver's clouding eyes watched her even now. She saw them change, their momentary confusion and agony rendering him achingly vulnerable.

One of Rosamund's hands shot up past Oliver's ear. She must ward off the cudgel...prevent that pitiless staff from snuffing out the light in his eyes. Oliver extended his arms to hold her away from him so she could not reach out. It flashed into her mind that he was protecting her, and despite the nightmare they found themselves in, this little gesture reached into Rosamund's fear-chilled heart and warmed her.

She clutched at his arms as Oliver's body lunged under the shock of another blow, and the groan that was wrenched from his lips clawed at Rosamund's vitals. His eyes were twin pits of despair. She clutched at his arms to offer him the support of her body, but somehow he still kept her at a distance. Oh, God, she realised with a dawning horror, far from protecting her, he was keeping her from him. He could not bear that their bodies should touch.

Then the taut muscles in his arms went limp. His eyelids dropped to hide the hell behind his eyes. Oliver pitched to the ground like a tree that had been felled by the woodman's axe. Rosamund's legs wobbled and she dropped to her knees.

'Oliver,' she whispered urgently, though she knew from the way he'd fallen that he could not hear her. He lay as still as a corpse. His face was a ghostly blur pointing up to Heaven. She crawled to his head and gingerly reached out a trembling hand to touch his lean cheek.

The undergrowth rustled, and her head snapped up.

'Who...who...' she faltered, and put both her arms protectively across Oliver's inert body. His sword hilt dug into her thigh, and Rosamund stiffened. If she could but draw it and confront them, she'd make these thieves and murderers pay some toll for their sport...

She counted four of them, swathed in shadow. Silent as the grave.

'Don't hurt him, please!' she begged, fumbling at Oliver's sword. It was not difficult to make her voice tremble with fear. It did that without any guile on her part. 'He cannot defend himself!'

One of them flung back his cowl. The gesture struck a chord in her mind.

'Father Eadric?' she asked wonderingly, her fingers freezing on the hilt. She could not attack a priest for all that he consorted with vagabonds.

'The same. Thank you for your help, my child. You may go now. The path you were seeking lies yonder.' The priest lifted his arm and pointed upstream with a bony finger.

'But...but...' Rosamund stuttered, clutching at that dark head.

'Go child,' the priest insisted softly. 'You have no more business here. The less you know, the better. 'Tis for your own sake.'

The other shadows were shifting nearer. Rosamund's hand hovered near Oliver's sword.

'Go,' repeated Father Eadric.

Rosamund eyed the shrouded figures. She swallowed. 'I don't...understand,' she managed.

'Eadric, get rid of 'er,' one of the shadows suggested impatiently, moving to squat by Oliver's feet. The

shadow-man's hair gleamed red as gore and he slapped
Rosamund's hand roughly from the sword belt. He un-
fastened the buckle with cold efficiency, held the blade
to the light, and whistled with approval. He was so en-
grossed in admiring Oliver's sword that he had not noticed the knight's pouch had fallen to the ground.
Rosamund flicked her skirts over it, speaking angrily to
cover this manoeuvre.

'What are you doing?' she demanded.

The thief leered in her direction before turning his attention to Oliver's feet.

Rosamund's blood ran cold.

'What are you doing?' she echoed on a note of rising
hysteria that was no more feigned than her earlier panic-
stricken tones. 'Don't! Leave him alone! What are you
doing?' Her slender arm raised to push at the man, but
the priest intercepted it and flung it back at her.

'Shut up!' growled the man scrabbling at Oliver's
ankles. 'Eadric, get rid of the lass or I'll find a way to
still her tongue—permanently.'

Rosamund saw the unmistakable flash of moonlight
on steel as the man brought out a dagger. The blade set
to work at Oliver's ankles. She heard a sawing sound.

'Oh don't, don't,' she begged, tears starting in her
eyes.

Eadric's large hand was on her shoulder restraining
her. Oliver's jet-black hair was soft under her palms.
Soft and sticky with blood. She felt as though she must
faint with the horror of this, and had to shake herself
to keep her swimming head clear.

The priest spoke softly. 'Why do you not go?' he
asked, curiously. 'I thought you were running to escape
him?'

Rosamund would never trust a soft voice again as long
as she lived. She lifted her bloodless face to him.

'I cannot explain that to you. You would not understand. How could I explain it to you—a priest who keeps
company with scum like these. Strange company for a
man of God, Father.'

One of the hovering shadows barked with laughter.

Eadric chuckled. 'Are you preaching to me, lass? A wench who prefers bedding with knights to bedding with her own husband?'

Rosamund gritted her teeth, discovering with a flash of surprise that anger took the sting out of fear.

'You mistake the matter, sir priest,' she informed him. 'And he is no knight. He is but a...' She broke off abruptly.

The man sawing at Oliver's ankles had finished his grisly work, and let out a shout of triumph. She could hardly bring herself to look. She forced her eyes up and they lit upon the trophies he was brandishing triumphantly. His great fists held aloft...two golden spurs. Rosamund sagged with relief. He had only been sawing through the leather straps which had fixed the spurs to Oliver's boots. Her febrile imagination had had him butchering the unconscious squire. Quartering a living man.

Two *golden* spurs?

Rosamund's jaw dropped as the significance of what she was seeing sank home. Two shining *golden* spurs, not silver ordinary spurs, but gleaming gilded ones. Shining yellow even though bathed in white moonlight. The spurs of a knight. She bent astonished eyes towards the head cradled in her arms.

Eadric was nodding briefly at his companion. 'Good,' he said shortly. 'Give 'em to Tate. Tate...'

The bulkiest of the shadowy figures detached itself from the hawthorns. 'Father Eadric?' He bowed, mockingly.

She was so intent on Oliver that she missed the look that passed between priest and outlaw.

'Enough of that,' snapped the priest. 'You know what you have to do?'

'Aye.'

'Do it then. And remember, Tate, this is no jest we are running now. Can you ride?'

'I've straddled a nag or two in me time,' Tate replied cockily.

'Take our captive's destrier then. He tethered it near the crossing. Do you think you can handle him?'

'Th' 'orse 'asn't been born that I can't handle—one way or t'other,' Tate answered darkly.

'Good. Mark their numbers well. Take care.'

The spurs flashed. Tate plucked them from the air, stowed them in his pouch, and headed off downstream. Back towards the stepping stones, and Lance.

'Tie 'im up,' the fierce priest commanded.

'What are you going to do with him? Where are you taking him?' Rosamund demanded.

She yelped in pain as someone, the godless priest probably, caught her by her hair and yanked her slowly to her feet. She deposited Oliver's head gently on the earth, and deftly twisted Oliver's pouch on to her own belt.

She glared at Eadric. It was an unsympathetic face for one of his vocation. The face of the man who had locked her in marriage to a man she did not love.

'Such concern for a knight, me lass,' mocked Father Eadric. 'And you wedded to... Alfwold, wasn't it?' He shook his head from side to side as if in disapproval.

'You know my husband's name well enough,' muttered Rosamund, with one eye on the still body at her feet. She flinched. Oliver was trussed up like a pig bound for the spit.

Eadric followed her gaze. 'I give you a warning, my daughter. Leave now,' he advised, pulling up his cowl.

'Nay.'

One of the men tightening Oliver's bonds broke in. 'Oh, let her stay if she wishes, *Father* Eadric. We could do with a woman to pass around with t' beer.'

His companion let out a squeal of laughter. It put Rosamund in mind of swine squabbling over their swill.

She felt her face taken in a rude grasp and turned to the light. She shut her eyes, and would not look at the cowled face.

'Nay.' Father Eadric released her. His companions voiced complaints that were as loud as they were vulgar.

'This lass is the miller's daughter,' the cowled figure declared firmly, overbearing their objections. 'We cannot afford to offend the villagers here. 'Tis difficult enough to get enough supplies as it is.' He turned his cowl-shadowed face to Rosamund and spoke coldly. 'Go.'

The other two shadows had Oliver by the shoulders and feet, and were lifting him. Taking him away.

'Nay,' Rosamund groaned, stepping after them. 'Oh, mind his head!' She started forwards and put her hands out to protect her lover's skull, careless of her own safety and the anger that she might rouse in these desperate men. 'You're going to ransom him, aren't you?' she demanded. 'That's why you've not killed him.'

'Maybe,' the hooded man conceded. 'Listen, girl, if you value your skin, you'll go as I suggest.'

Rosamund ignored the sense in his advice. 'You don't want to look after him,' she blurted, taking another step. 'His head is badly split. You won't get any money if he dies, will you? Let me care for him. I'll make sure he lives, and then you'll get your ransom.'

The words had tumbled out in a rush before she had time to consider the folly of what she was suggesting.

Oliver was being hauled up the slight incline away from the river. She scrambled after, keeping as close as she could. She could feel the breath of that unholy priest hot on her neck.

'Very well,' he decided. 'Stay. But don't come whining to me if you're unlucky enough to get raped. I've better things to do than act as wet-nurse to a blunt-witted wench.'

'Oh, thank you!' cried Rosamund, lifting her damp skirts the better to trot beside Oliver.

Father Eadric gave an exasperated laugh. 'You won't be thanking me for long,' he warned. 'Not when you see the accommodation we have to offer. Our camp is nothing like Ingerthorpe Castle.'

'I'll survive,' Rosamund promised.

Another grating laugh. 'We'll have to see about that,' won't we?'

Rosamund's skin prickled uncomfortably. She shot the cowled figure a glance, wondering if he'd meant his remark as a threat. It certainly sounded like one. Her eyes swivelled back to rest anxiously on Oliver's unconscious visage. She'd stay. How could she leave him now?

'Wait!' Rosamund called to the retreating priest. 'Don't just dump us alone in the dark.' The shack was scarcely more than a pit.

Eadric's bony hands stopped trying to force the rusty padlock and the man lifted his head.

'I... I'll need water to bathe his wound, and something to drink, and a light to see by, and bandages, and...'

Eadric's laugh chilled her to the marrow.

Rosamund tilted her chin, determined not to let him see that she was afraid. 'I'm to care for him, remember?' she said.

Another blood-curdling laugh. The warped door of the hovel grated into place. She could no longer see the renegades' glowing camp fire outside the hut. There was the sound of chains clanking on rotten wood. Then silence. A black impenetrable silence, deep as death.

She felt as though they had been buried alive. The brief sight she had caught of their prison had not been encouraging. They'd been thrown into a decaying wooden lean-to, the air within foul with the rotting stench of death. She smiled grimly to herself and jerked on the rope about her ankle. One wooden stake was sound though. The central one and that, naturally, was the one they were bound to. They were well-prepared, these outlaws. Probably using the Angevin cause as an excuse to plunder and pillage.

If it were not for her own breathing, and Oliver's, Rosamund would think they were already dead. Her heart jolted in her breast. She could not hear anything except *her* breathing and the pounding of *her* heart...

Frantically she scrabbled over the stinking floor towards Oliver. Her groping hands found his body unresponsive, and she pressed her ear to his chest. Nothing. With a sob she found his mouth and listened again.

'Oh, thank you, Sweet Lord,' she breathed, as the faint, but distinct flurry of Oliver's breathing stirred against her cheek. For a moment or two it was enough simply to kneel at his side and cling to the security of Oliver's familiar body. Even in a deep swoon his nearness comforted her, calmed some of her fears.

In this ghastly world she had been plunged into, this world where life was held so cheap that men would kill others for the sake of a coin, Oliver's lifeless body offered her some consolation. He represented light and hope and...

Her fingers encountered Oliver's bound wrists. She lifted her head as a thought came to her. She must free his hands. She began to fumble with the knots. But a gale of crude laughter erupted from the direction of the camp-fire, and her fingers faltered in their task. Perhaps not. Not until he was awake and could defend them both. She did not like to think what they would do to her if they discovered she'd freed his hands.

Her head shot up as the door was wrenched open. A feeble light threw a man's face into sharp relief. She recognised the bushy eyebrows, the reddish thinning hair. It was one of the men who had carried Oliver to this encampment. The one who had stolen his sword.

'There's the gear you asked for,' the man grunted, and bent to put several items on the ground.

When he straightened Rosamund realised with a frisson of unease that his eyes were on her, watching with feral cunning.

'Thank you,' replied Rosamund, hoping that he was waiting for her response, and might leave now.

'Anything else you require, little lady,' the man asked, licking his lips. 'I wouldn't want a proper "lady" like you to go missing your...' he sneered at Oliver's recumbent form '...usual comforts.'

Rosamund's grip tightened on Oliver.

'No, thank you,' she said steadily. 'I have all I want. You may go now.'

The man's coarse features became grotesque. His eyes bulged. 'I may go now.' He mocked at her voice, and stepped towards her. 'Why, thank you, madam, for your condescension. I will go, but not before you have thanked me more prettily than that. On your feet, madam.'

'Nay,' Rosamund said, rashly. She found her fingers were curling like hooks into Oliver's neck, and forced herself to unclench them; gently smooth his skin. 'If he were awake,' she continued, 'you would not dare...'

The oaf looked like a fox with that pointed nose and reddish hair of his. And his laugh was more of a bark.

'Ah, but I would dare,' he sneered, filthy hands fastening on her shoulders. 'And get all the more pleasure from seeing a proud knight squirming. Not so fine now, is he, your pretty knight?' He aimed a vicious kick at Oliver's limp form.

'Don't.' Rosamund begged, trying not to breathe in the rank stink of her tormentor.

The cracked and yellow talons tightened cruelly. 'A little kiss, then?' the foxy man suggested.

Rosamund shuddered. 'If you'll let him be...'

She shut her eyes, feeling her flesh shrivel and shrink to escape. But of course she could not escape. She could feel him pressing her to him in the most unwelcome embrace she had ever suffered. She felt his vile claws pawing at her breasts. She would be sick. The bile was rising in her throat, his cavernous maw coming down on her mouth...

'Wulfric!' A voice called from the fireside. 'Be sure you lock 'em up tight!' the voice commanded.

Rosamund staggered in relief, and the loathsome claws lifted from her bosom. Wulfric swore and sent her a look that burnt the clothes from her back. He bent to check Oliver's bonds, wrenching them cruelly tight. He shot Rosamund a look that was all animal. It raised the hairs on the back of her neck. But much to her relief he made for the door meek as a lamb.

He bowed. The lamplight lit up eyes far from meek. 'Till tomorrow, me lady. When the ransom's been brought, we'll see who's to get you then. Eadric owes me one, and I've a mind to collect what's due.'

She waited some time before daring to reach for the provisions Wulfric had left by the door. She wanted to be quite certain he'd gone back to his companions by the fire. She could hear low-voiced mutterings and bursts of wild unruly laughter. Were they planning what they would do with her when they'd sent Oliver back to the castle? She did not think they'd let her go. Not after Eadric's veiled threats, and Wulfric's swearing he'd have her. She'd die rather than submit to them.

In the end it was the thought of Oliver's head wound which nudged her forwards to examine the supplies.

'Ugh.' She wrinkled her nose at the beer. It was sour. There was nowhere near enough water, and no bandages at all, but she was too wise to risk complaining.

Rosamund set the lamp down next to Oliver and gently turned his head to the light. Her brows were furrowed. He'd been unconscious for so long. What if he was dying? Rosamund's knowledge of medicine was limited. She knew how to cope with everyday cuts and scrapes. She could make sleeping draughts and ointments. She'd even helped one of the monks mend a broken leg. But Oliver lay so still. His face had gone the colour of tallow. It was clammy to the touch. If his skull had been smashed she knew there was little she could do for him but pray.

Gently her fingers probed through his raven locks, muttering a litany under her breath. 'Let me not find his head broken. Let him be whole. Let him be whole. Let him be whole.'

Her examination complete, Rosamund knelt back on her heels and regarded him, still frowning. There was no evidence to show his skull was shattered. So why did he not wake? Why was he lying so still? He was so unlike his normal vital self that she could weep. Long, thick lashes lay unfluttering on pale cheeks. A new blue-black growth of beard showed up stark against ashen skin. It scraped against her fingertips.

She sighed. She would have to wait till God saw fit to waken him. And then perhaps they could escape this filthy sty where they'd been immured. And, in the meantime, she could at least make him more comfort-table. Clean away the congealed blood with the water. Keep him warm. Rosamund lifted the edge of her gown, and ripped a strip of fabric from her under-dress. Dipping it in the jug of water, she set to work.

At length she set the bloodied rag aside. He was as clean as she could make him. But there was as yet no sign of the blood returning to his face. His skin still had that waxen look and feel to it. He was cold and so was she. Rosamund's eyes fell on her cloak, lying by the thick central post. She grasped it and stretched out her shivering length under the mantle, tucking it round them both. She wished there was something else they could lie on other than the dank muck embedded into the rush floor covering. She nuzzled closer into Oliver's side, and put her arms about his waist.

'Dear Lord,' Rosamund prayed, 'let Oliver awaken soon. I'm so afraid. And grant that we may find our way safe out of this place. Protect us this night, Lord. Guard our rest. And, Sweet Lord, please don't let Eadric do Oliver harm. I don't mean to question Your Will, Lord, but it seems to me Eadric is a strange servant for You to use. And please, Lord, don't let Oliver be angry with me when he wakes. You know I did not betray him, Lord. Let him trust me. Amen.'

Rosamund burrowed her head back against Oliver's side and tried to sleep.

CHAPTER SEVEN

THERE was not a glimmer of light to be seen. Wondering if he had been struck blind, Oliver moved his head. He groaned. His skull was throbbing fit to split, and the small movement had sent a series of sharp, needling darts of pain shooting down his neck.

He tried to lift his hand to probe the wound which he knew could be the only explanation for such a pounding in his brain, and at once suffered another unpleasant shock, for his wrists had been roped securely together.

He was bemused as to the cause of his bruised and aching condition, but fortunately there did not appear to be anything wrong with his ears. He heard a small gasp, and something warm rustled at his side. Oliver felt his guts turn to water, and he peered vainly into the gloom.

The scent of roses came faintly to his nostrils. He felt himself relax and wondered why. Next came a rusty squeak, and then a dim light glowed muddily from a lantern whose cover had been opened. The horn window of the lamp was yellow with age and caked with filth.

'Oliver?'

A soft feminine voice. Tentative. She sounded afraid. But of what? Of him? He waited for her to make the next move. After all he was the one who was trussed up like a chicken.

'Oliver?' the girl repeated. 'Are...are you in pain?'

She was so close he could feel the softness of her body. Her hand came out to brush his cheek, and Oliver stared at her as though he'd lost his tongue.

He was gazing at a young maid whose eyes were wide with fear. She had long brown hair which must have been hastily twisted into a knot at her neck, for some strands had escaped and were straying about her face. She'd drawn her hand back from him as though the brief contact had stung her and looped her wild locks safely over her ear. She was very pretty. He noticed her hand was trembling terribly, and wondered again what was the cause of such distress. It could not be him. Oliver's nostrils flared. As soon as she'd withdrawn, that oddly comforting fragrance of roses had been replaced by the damp, repugnant stink of mould and rotting vegetation.

'W…won't you even speak to me?' the girl stammered.

Oliver's dark brows knotted. He angled his head round and glanced over his shoulder, but there was no one behind him. Her eyes were searching his. She was talking to him. He ransacked his brain to try and remember what he had done. He could think of nothing. His heart began to beat in slow, heavy strokes which intensified the pain in his brain.

He managed a cautious smile. 'You're not afraid of me, are you?' he asked the girl.

She set the lantern down on the plaited rush matting he was lying on. That too was encrusted with muck, and Oliver realised it must be one of the sources of the fetid stench. He wondered what other rotting horrors lay hidden by the gloom. This hovel he'd been brought to reeked of squalor.

'No. Why should I be afraid of you?'

She appeared startled by his question.

'But I did think that you might still be angry. I didn't do it, you know,' she added.

Oliver was growing more confused by the minute. 'Do what?' he wondered, wishing he could hold his aching head.

'Betray you,' she said.

'Oh. That's reassuring,' Oliver said, playing for time. The blow which had split his skull seemed to have curdled his wits too. He had not the faintest idea what the maid was talking about. It was plain that she knew him, but he could not for the life of him place her. How could he have forgotten such a face? The face of an angel. Some half remembered emotion stirred uneasily in the back of his mind, but he could not grasp it. It was like clutching at a vision which had no substance.

Oliver sighed, deciding it prudent to abandon this somewhat tenuous line of thought. His head ached abominably. 'Did you tie me up?'

'Hardly. Look, they tied me, too.' The girl indicated the thick cord round her ankle.

He stared. Someone had secured her by one slim ankle to a solid post. He realised that both his legs were fastened in the same way. His eyes moved up the post, his mind already busy calculating what hope they had of breaking free. The post looked depressingly strong. It held up what passed for a roof in this misbegotten hovel. However, with a bit of work, they might be able to dig down round the base of the wood—of course the whole rickety structure would collapse, but...

He grinned at the girl as engagingly as he could. 'Is there anything to drink?' he enquired, assessing whether he could trust her or not.

She pulled a face. 'That depends on how thirsty you are. There's sour ale.'

'No fresh water?'

She shook her head. 'No, I bathed your head with that.'

Oliver summoned up another smile. 'Then sour ale it will have to be. Could you...?'

She did not hesitate. Taking the grimy pitcher in one hand, she held it to his lips and slipped her other hand beneath his neck to raise him. Oliver kept his eyes on her face. He noted with relief the rosy flush that stained her cheeks under his steady regard. She had been so pale a moment ago. It could not be him that she feared, thank God.

'Thank you,' he murmured when he'd quenched his thirst. 'I suppose we should be grateful they left your hands free.'

'Oh, it was in their interests to do so. So I could look after you. Keep you alive until——'

Oliver decided. 'I trust you,' he announced abruptly.

The girl tensed. She looked affronted. 'I should think so,' she said. 'Especially after I stayed here, risking life and limb for you.'

'Nay. Don't move away,' Oliver soothed, and laughed. 'You're the sweetest smelling thing in this place. I want you near me.' His eyes narrowed. 'Tell me, what is your name?'

The girl's eyes grew round. Then she gave a strained laugh.

'Oliver. This is no time for childish games. We're prisoners here. We may be killed——'

'I'm not playing a game,' Oliver told her flatly. 'I gather that you know me, and that you expect me to know you——'

'Know me!' she exclaimed. 'Sweet Heavens!'

'—but I don't. This blow I have taken has knocked my senses to the devil. I don't remember anything,' he admitted in as reassuring a tone as he could muster.

'Nothing at all?' she asked incredulously.

'Nothing at all,' he confirmed.

'I don't believe you!'

'You must, for 'tis the truth,' he swore.

'Your name, tell me your name,' she demanded.

Oliver gave a rueful smile. 'Ah, that I do know. 'Tis Oliver.'

'There!' she cried, triumphant. 'You have not lost your memory!'

'I only know my name because I heard you call me by it,' Oliver admitted. 'I know nothing more. I feel I should know you . . .' he ignored her indignant splutter, 'and may wish that I did, but I'll swear any oath you like if it will help you to believe me. *I cannot remember who you are, nor anything about myself either.*' He paused and saw she was chewing her finger. 'Please believe me, and tell me your name,' he cajoled.

She muttered something under her breath.

'What?' he prompted.

'Rosamund!' she hissed. 'My name, as you well know, is Rosamund. But if you must play your foolish games, Oliver, 'tis Rosamund. There, has that pleased you?'

'Rosamund,' he murmured. The name rose easily to his lips. As soon as she had said it he knew she was not misleading him. The maid's name *was* Rosamund. It struck a familiar note in his mind. Any lingering doubts that he might not know this girl were dispelled.

'Do you think, Rosamund, you could unfasten my hands?' he asked.

'I'll try,' she answered. 'The rope is very tight.'

Oliver let out a short laugh. 'You don't need to tell me that. My hands have lost all feeling.'

'Like your heart,' he heard her murmur.

'What's that?' he said at once.

Rosamund coloured, and bent her head over his bonds. 'Nothing. You did warn me that you would not feel affection, but I never thought you'd go as far as this in your efforts to deny it. I can only wonder why you bothered to come after me. Ah, there! They're coming loose. Only a moment now...'

The rope fell away and Oliver shook his hands, wincing as the circulation flowed back into his numb hands, bringing pain in its wake. He flexed his fingers experimentally, and saw that Rosamund was watching him, covertly from under her lashes.

'We're lovers, then,' he shot at random.

Her nose lifted; she looked away.

Oliver laughed softly. 'I see I found the mark with that one,' he commented. 'Well, at least I know one thing about myself. I have good taste in women.'

She sighed. 'Oh, if you must play this game...though how you can jest like this when we're held by a mob of Angevin rebels who seem likely to cut our throats.'

'Angevin rebels?' His grey eyes narrowed. 'Are you sure? I seem to recall something... Oh! Hell and damnation!' He rubbed his temples. 'My head!'

Rosamund's teeth were worrying her lower lip. 'Oh, God, I do believe you're telling the truth,' she declared. 'You can't remember, can you?'

'She believes me,' Oliver remarked drily.

'Aye, I think I do.'

The chain at the door of their prison rattled a warning.

'Hush,' Oliver hissed, flicking the lantern closed and plunging them into sooty blackness. 'Our jailers are coming. 'Tis best they think me out of it.'

'Your hands,' she breathed. 'They're bound to notice.'

'Not with you shielding me,' he countered, pressing her down at his side. 'Stay close.' Oliver's voice lightened. 'Ah, Rosamund, the feel of you. Later you'll have to refresh my memory on certain...er...aspects of our relationship.'

They listened as the door grated open and shut. A creeping footfall on the dirt floor of the hovel. Padding towards its prey. Stalking Rosamund.

'Wake up, girl. 'Tis Wulfric come to claim you.' The feral voice was loud in the stillness.

Rosamund went rigid. Her hands gripped Oliver's convulsively, and he returned the pressure. Oliver's heartbeat was reassuringly loud beneath her ear. He would not let that beast take her. Not even this new Oliver who had no memory. He must possess the same nature, and he would protect her. She knew he would.

'Hey, lass, come 'ere. Move away from that lump o' dog meat, will you?' Wulfric's foot thudded into her thigh.

'Lead him on, I want his weapon,' Oliver sighed into her ear. 'But stay close.'

Rosamund went cold all over, though she knew this was a chance they had to take.

She stirred and stretched with a convincing sigh. 'Who's that?' she murmured sleepily.

The skin-shrivelling paw groped her waist. She allowed the beast to turn her on her back, and almost gagged as the sweat from Wulfric's unwashed body wafted down into her nostrils.

Her hands were up to fend him off before she'd thought to stop them.

'Nay, girl. You don't want it rough, do you?' Wulfric objected. He thrust his hand into her hair to hold her head in place and slapped her hands aside. She felt him clawing at her breasts, bruising the soft flesh, scratching her even through the woollen cloth. She could not endure this much longer. Already Wulfric was groping greedily under her skirts. A moan escaped her, and then Wulfric's hand cracked against her cheek.

'Is that what you want, girl?' he snarled.

She nudged at Oliver's leg with her toes. She made her voice sound calm. 'Nay, Wulfric. I'll not fight you, if you'll but be gentle with me. Only do, pray, remove your sword. The hilt is digging holes in this hip.' She slapped the thigh in question and squirmed, praying that Oliver had sense enough left in his head to follow her lead. She could not bear the suffocating weight of Wulfric's stinking body.

Wulfric gave a grunt and eased off her.

His body twitched, and suddenly there came at her through the inky darkness a strangled wheeze. The blood pounded in her ears.

'Oliver?'

A choking gasp, a frantic gulp, as one of them dragged in some air. Oliver must be at him. It could not be the other way about, for Oliver had had surprise on his side. Her wits were in turmoil as she listened to the threshing and flailing of battling limbs.

The lamp? Where was the lamp?

She gasped as a heavy boot knocked the breath from her body. She had no idea which man it belonged to. Rosamund rolled well out of reach and her hand scrabbled for the lantern. The noises were muted, but were no less horrifying for all that. She fumbled open the shutter.

'Thank Heavens! Oliver!' she sobbed.

He was kneeling astride Wulfric. The thief's face was ground into the dirt and the rope that had so recently bound Oliver's wrists snaked round Wulfric's scrawny neck to throttle him. Oliver was winding it so tightly the man's face grew purple. Rosamund stared frozen with horror at the distended veins in Wulfric's neck. The thief kicked his legs, his nails were broken from his frenzied clawing at the asphyxiating cord. Wulfric kicked again, more feebly this time, and Rosamund covered her face with her hands, and tottered to lean on the upright post.

A hand came down gently on her shoulder. She flinched. The hand was removed.

'Is...is he d...dead?' she shuddered.

Oliver stood beside her, his own sword held firm in his hand, his legs free of the tether. 'You're not sorry for that animal, are you? You know what he'd have done to you if I had been unconscious?'

'I know. But to die for it...' Her voice wavered.

Oliver's grey eyes were sombre. He trailed a long finger down her cheek. She was astonished to note that it was trembling. 'He's not dead,' he reassured her. 'Though I confess I found myself angry enough to murder an army.

You must be very close to my heart to arouse such a fury in me. The thought of him molesting you drove me berserk.'

Rosamund's blue eyes grew very large. She had not expected to hear such an admission from his lips. He was watching her in such a way... her heart leapt at the flicker of light in his eyes. The old Oliver would never... Rosamund took a faltering pace towards him and tentatively rested her head on his broad, strong chest. His arms enfolded her, pulling her up against him. Their bodies touched from chest to thigh and it felt good.

She raised her head and met his grey eyes, her own smiling. 'I knew you'd save me,' she said simply.

Oliver touched her brow with his lips. 'Even though I do not know you?' he teased.

'Aye,' she agreed softly. 'For I think, Oliver, that, though your head has forgotten me, your heart has not.'

Oliver shrugged. 'Possibly,' he allowed.

Rosamund's heart sang.

'Why are you smiling so?' he asked.

'No reason,' she lied.

He kissed her nose. 'Do you mind a man without a memory kissing you?' he wondered.

'Not if it's you,' she admitted. 'I think I am pleased that you have lost your memory, Oliver.'

'Pleased?'

'Mmm. Which do you think it is best to possess, a man's head, or his heart? I think his heart is most worth winning, don't you?' she smiled.

'Rosamund, you make no sense at all.' Oliver shook his head. 'Listen, we must get out of here. Come on, we must tie and gag this scavenging wretch lest he squawks.'

Oliver bent to saw through the rope at her ankle.

'Which?' Rosamund talked to the top of Oliver's dark head. 'Which is best? Head or heart?'

He cast her a look which was half exasperated, half tender. 'Oh, I should think both would be ideal, don't you? Now what have I said? Rosamund? Nay, angel, don't pull that face, 'tis not at all comely.'

Rosamund drew a sharp breath.

'What ails you? Did I hurt your foot?' Oliver asked.

Rosamund stared blankly at him.

'Rosamund?'

'You . . . you called me angel.'

'Aye. What of it?' Enlightenment dawned. 'Ah. I have
it. I must have called you that before,' Oliver realised.

Rosamund nodded.

Her ankle released, Oliver stood up and parried an
imaginary thrust with his sword. 'Good. Maybe my mind
will come back to me soon.'

Rosamund massaged her ankle where the rope had
chafed it and, when she glanced at Oliver again, saw his
lips parted in a satisfied smile. 'See, Rosamund, I may
be short on memory for awhile longer, but I can wield
a sword. You take up his dagger, you may find you need
it later.' The sword described another brilliant arc
through the dank air. 'Ah, but this blade sits well in my
hand.'

'It should do . . .' Rosamund started and then stopped.

'Go on.'

'I . . . er . . . nothing . . . that is . . . aye, you are a fine
swordsman, Oliver,' she commented lamely.

'What am I, Rosamund? Tell me,' he entreated, face
very earnest.

'I . . . I . . . shouldn't we be going?' Rosamund tem-
porised, several thoughts spinning around in her head.
She thought she liked this new Oliver. He was warmer,
seemed less calculating. She was tempted to try and keep
him in this ignorant state as long as possible. She needed
to think. And in the meantime . . .

She looked pointedly at the crooked door. 'They might
send someone else at any moment.'

'Oh. Aye,' he agreed. 'We'll break through the back
here, and then we'll make a run for it.' He began prising
the oak planks of the back wall apart. They were rotten
and all but crumbled under his strong hands. 'There.
And Rosamund, you'll stick as close as a burr, won't
you?'

'Aye, don't worry about me. I can run as fleet as you.
My brain's not been scrambled. Oliver, where are we
headed for?'

Oliver's face was a picture of confusion. 'Oh, fiend take us! I've not the slightest idea where we are! I don't even know the lie of the land. You know the area?'

Rosamund nodded.

'I'll have to rely on you to steer us to a safe harbour,' he admitted. 'Is there an abbey nearby where we can take sanctuary until I can unravel this tangled head of mine?'

'An abbey, oh aye . . .' Rosamund began eagerly. Then she remembered Alfwold. Her husband. He was biding at the abbey for the abbot. She could not take Oliver there. They'd be bound to meet in the guest house, and the whole sorry tale would come out. Oliver would re-alise he was a knight, and his ambitions would rise up to come between them. He'd remember he was promised to the Lady Cecily, and he'd remember that she was married, and that kindling light in those beautiful grey eyes of his would be extinguished forever.

'Nay, nay. We can't go there,' she shook her head, positively.

'Why ever not? It would seem the obvious place to go. No political sympathies among the good brothers...'

Rosamund stared, and then tried to hide the exultant smile which spread across her face. Without realising it, Oliver had just presented her with the best reason in the world for avoiding the abbey. 'You'll not recall their leader,' she said. 'He wears the priestly habit. There may be other rebels wearing the cowl.' And that was no lie. 'We cannot go to the abbey.'

'Where then? Think, Rosamund. And hurry!' Oliver moved with the stealth of a cat to the door and peered through the gap. 'Hurry!' he urged.

Rosamund fiddled with the hilt of Oliver's dagger which she'd stuck into her belt. They could not head for the coast, for Oliver would be bound to spot the castle, and ask questions she had no wish to answer as yet. And there was too much risk he'd be recognised.

'East,' she announced. 'When they find us gone, they will turn west to try to find us. So we must go east. If we can climb Blue Bank and reach the moors, I have friends there who'll shelter us. A shepherd and his wife.'

Her stomach knotted in a sudden nervous spasm. 'If we make it that far,' she added.

Oliver was back at her side, and she saw his eyes were glittering with suppressed excitement. He grasped her hand firmly in his. 'Of course we'll get there,' he said confidently, and Rosamund glimpsed his chipped tooth. He was relishing the challenge of all this. 'Ready?' he asked.

Rosamund gave a slight nod. 'I wish...I'm afraid,' she confessed in a small voice.

Oliver tilted her chin and dropped a swift reassuring kiss on her mouth. 'Don't be. We'll get through to your friends. I am determined we shall. With luck on our side, these beggars will not miss us for some time. It all depends on how long they give our lusty ruffian to...er...complete his business with you.'

Oliver reached to toss aside the wall planks as though they were as light as feathers. Then he was through, dragging Rosamund behind him.

'Which direction?' he hissed.

Rosamund pointed, and whispered back. 'That way. Through the wood, climbing all the time. If we find we're going downhill, we've taken the wrong path. We should come to a waterfall, we can follow the sound of it. And then——'

'That's enough to be going on with. Now let's fly, my angel, and, for God's sake don't make a sound!'

Rosamund could no longer tell whether the moon was shining or not. She thought not, for black shapes were swimming in and out of her line of vision.

'Keep going, Rosamund,' Oliver insisted cruelly, forging on up the woodland track.

The trees were losing their individual outlines, they were blurring together to form one huge dark and dizzying black pit she knew she'd tumble into any minute... Rosamund gasped for breath. He was pitiless. Inhuman. Did the air not sear its way down into his lungs as it did with her? She could hear his breathing had become laboured too. But Oliver had shown no sign of slackening either that relentless pace, or the unyielding grip on her hand. She felt as though he was dragging her to Hell, and wished he'd let her go so she could pause awhile. Oh, why did he not let go of her? A low moan slid from Rosamund's lips before she could retrieve it.

Oliver checked his headlong pace. Praise the Saints! There was some mercy in him then.

'Listen!' he commanded, and shook her by the hand when he perceived she was not really seeing him.

'Wh...what?' Rosamund got out, swaying on her feet and gasping for air.

'The waterfall, can you hear it?'

'No, all I can hear is the sea pounding. We must have gone the wrong way...' She moaned again. 'They'll catch us if we go that way.'

'Rosamund!' Oliver said sharply. 'Pull yourself together. There's been no sign of pursuit.' He dragged on her hand, and forced her stumbling feet to move. 'Can you hear it now?' he asked.

Rosamund tried to listen. She realised the pounding sound was the blood rushing in her ears—not the sea.

'Aye. That's Angel Falls,' she gasped. 'Go on. You'll get to the pool...at the bottom of the waterfall...Keep the water to your right...moorland path veers off left from the spot where...water crashes into the pool... It's a steep climb to the top,' she warned, and stopped to catch her breath.

Oliver was already moving to follow her directions. She would only slow him down now. Rosamund jerked her hand free.

'Rosamund, come on. The more distance we put between us and them the better.' He extended his hand back to her.

'Nay. I can't go any farther. We must have run near twenty leagues,' she protested.

He came back and loured over her. Meagre shreds of moon and starlight filtered down through the leafy canopy above them. A large patch illumined Oliver's broad shoulders. His face was a silver mask.

'You're going on,' he said, in a hard voice.

'I've had enough,' Rosamund declared. 'You can go on without me. It's you they want, not me. They'll leave me alone.'

'Not now you know where their camp is. They'd have to silence you permanently. Nay, Rosamund, you're coming with me.'

'I'll slow you down,' she told him.

Oliver shrugged. 'You're coming,' he said flatly.

'So much concern,' Rosamund mocked.

She saw the silver mask frown. 'Why should I not be concerned for you?' he wondered. 'You have said we are lovers. And I believe you. Should I not look out for my love?'

Rosamund's heart twisted. She threw a hunted look over her shoulder. What if the Angevin rebels had discovered their escape already? What if they had not assumed their route to be to the castle, but were even now tracking them through this wood?

'Oh, for Heaven's sake go on without me. The blow has addled your wits. You would never have been so considerate towards me before you were hit,' she snapped.

'Why ever not?' he asked, apparently startled. 'Surely such a sweet-tempered maid as you obviously are would deserve all my devoted attention?' He grinned, managing to capture her wrist. 'Besides, I need you to show me to your friends' retreat. And who else but my love can I trust to tell me my true identity? Hmm?'

Rosamund felt stabbed to the heart with guilt, and shut her eyes so she would not have to see the confidence scripted so clearly in his.

'I...I...can't,' she wailed, but what it was she was denying she could no longer say.

She felt his hand slide down to squeeze her fingers gently, lovingly, and her heart was wrung anew. She could not bear to lose this new, loving Oliver. If only she could keep him in ignorance of his real identity. Just for a little while. She would not need long. She only wanted to steal an inch from the candleclock of time. Just long enough for her to experience loving, and being loved with no reservations. They would not be knight and miller's daughter, but simply a man and a woman. In love. Now that was a dream worth lying for...

'Very well, my love,' Oliver was saying. 'We'll find a resting place, but I'll not leave you.'

'Oh, Oliver,' she groaned. 'If only you knew how hard this is going to be.'

Oliver smiled down at her and ruffled her hair. ''Twill be easy to continue once you've caught your breath.'

'Nay,' she denied. 'I don't mean that.'

'What then?' Oliver found a fallen tree-trunk and settled her upon his knees. She was staring straight into his eyes. They were looking at her with such candour that she winced. 'My love, what ails you? Is it your feet?' he asked, voice deep with concern, as he bent to examine her shoes.

Curse the Devil that he set such temptation before her! Truly this day had seen her damned...

Rosamund knew she would never be presented with such a chance again. She could not let it go. If she was very careful... but she would have to guard her tongue most carefully. If she let slip his identity, all would be lost.

No matter that she would be living a lie. It would only be for a short time. She thought of Alfwold. He would come to find her. There was no doubt of that. But it might just be possible to snatch at a fragment of happiness before he found them...

Would Alfwold have her branded as adulteress? She did not care. It would be worth it. Far better an hour of true love with this Oliver, than a year as plaything of the ruthless and cold knight that was Oliver de Warenne. Stripped of his ambition and ignorant of the differences between them, he was temptation personified, and she knew she was fallen indeed.

'Angel?' He glanced at her face.

'Oh! I'm sorry, my mind was wandering,' she confessed, with a shy smile. 'My feet are fine enough. But what of your head? It must be very painful.'

Back in the depths of the wood a dog barked.

Oliver gave a crooked smile. 'Aye,' he acknowledged briefly. His silvery eyes wandered over her features so carefully that her cheeks grew warm. It was as though he were seeing her for the first time. Rosamund noticed Oliver's breathing was still ragged. His hand came up and touched the top of her head, combing through her tangled hair.

Rosamund gave a little laugh. 'It must be like a bush,' she said.

She saw him shake his head, his lips smiling. Oliver's fingertips trailed down slowly over her ear, across her cheek. The skin he had touched tingled and Rosamund found breathing had become an almost impossible thing. She knew he was going to kiss her.

He lowered his head gently, tentatively, as though they had never kissed before and he was uncertain as to her response. His mouth was very warm. She felt weak and clung to him. His arm about her waist was a welcome support, for without it she would have slipped from his lap. He held her tight to his chest and his other hand angled her mouth to his.

He lifted his head; his eyes were pools of darkness.

'My Rosamund,' he said huskily. 'You are mine, aren't you? Your lips tell me you are.'

Rosamund remembered Alfwold, but she answered firmly. 'Aye. I'm yours.'

The dark head lowered and he caught her lips in a tender, biting kiss.

'Mine,' he murmured, lips hovering over her mouth. And his kiss changed. It became surer, deeper. She could lose herself in it. Rosamund moaned as a piercingly sweet sensation flooded her veins. He kissed her fiercely, hungrily, as though he would draw her soul to meet his.

When they drew apart both were breathless.

'I needed that,' he admitted. 'I've been wondering what it would be like to kiss you. Angry at myself for not remembering.'

Rosamund reached for him.

'Nay, angel,' he shook his head. ''Tis not the time, nor the place.'

'You've said that to me before,' Rosamund said, before she realised what dangerous water she was stepping into. 'It was this very night. Much earlier.'

'Tonight? No, I do not remember. Tell me about it while we rest.'

Rosamund hesitated, choosing her words with the greatest care. She must not mention either Lance or the castle, for Oliver would immediately want to return to pick up the threads of his lost life. And once back there... her chance of living their dream would be lost forever. 'Do you not remember riding with me to the beach?' she hedged.

'Nay. I cannot remember riding, the beach, or anything. Remind me,' he said vaguely. His hand rubbed at the bridge of his nose.

'Later,' Rosamund decided. 'You've gone very pale, Oliver, and 'tis not just the moonlight that makes you so. You should be resting after a crack on the head like that.'

'We'd no option but to run,' he muttered through his hand. He sighed.

Rosamund gently moved his hand aside and perused his cheeks. They were ashen. His handsome face was taut with suppressed pain, lined with exhaustion. Strong as he was, he was not made of steel. He was as spent as she, quite drained.

'Before I forget, I've something of yours,' she announced brightly. 'Here. Your pouch. I took it to keep those murdering thieves from getting their filthy paws on it. It feels as though you've some money in there.'

'My thanks,' he said dully, taking it from her. His fingers tried, and failed to fasten it back in its place.

'Here let me,' Rosamund pushed his unresisting fingers to one side and completed the task for him. 'Perhaps we should not go any farther tonight. I think... aye... I think we must find a place we can sleep. 'Tis a pity they stole your cloak, Oliver, for it was fur-lined and mine is only wool. But if we curl up together——'

Oliver's hand covered her mouth. 'Hush!' he cut in. 'That dog...'

Rosamund's eyes widened. She could hear it too. An excited yelping bark, such as hounds make when closing in on their quarry...

She peeled Oliver's hand away. 'It's coming this way,' she whispered.

'Aye. A hound hot on a trail. Our trail, do you think?' His eyes had begun to glitter. Summoning up strength from some hidden reserve.

'Oh, no, it couldn't be. They'd be bound to go west, as I said.

'Why?' he demanded.

'Because that's where the castle...oh, damn.' She
should not have mentioned the castle to him. She shot
him a surreptitious glance from under her lashes, but he
was listening for the hound, head tilted to one side.

Oliver pushed Rosamund from his knee and stood up.
He had her tightly by the hand.

'Which way?' he asked curtly.

'There's only one way we can go. Past the pool at the
bottom of the falls and up the path to the top.' Rosamund
indicated the direction with her free hand.

'Lead on.'

Rosamund needed no second bidding. The yelps and
barks were getting nearer with every second that passed.
She could hear the crashing of bodies forcing their way
through the undergrowth towards them. Twigs snapped
and cracked. The outlaws must be very confident that
their quarry was at hand, for they did not trouble to
muffle their approach.

The track was wider here. Oliver and Rosamund were
running side by side, feet pounding in unison.

'We're too much in the open, too visible,' Oliver got
out between breaths.

'Not far now,' Rosamund gasped. 'Listen, the water's
louder. We're almost there. 'Tis less easy for them to
follow from then on. They'll never find the path.'

They ran on, the dog close at their heels, and gaining
with every minute. An owl hooted. Another gave an eerie
reply.

Oliver groaned and muttered, '...their signal for attack
perhaps...'

Rosamund's ears barely caught the sound. The rushing
sound of the waterfall drowned out the rest. They had
reached the edge of a large pool. Its surface was ruffled
by glistening spray which tumbled forcefully down the
steep and stony bank towering like a cliff above them.

Two heads tipped back, looking up the length of the
milk-white, gushing column of water to the summit.
Rosamund blenched. It was steeper than she had remembered it to be. They'd never make it. Not in their
condition. Back down the path, the way they had come,
the noise made by their hunters was growing apace.

Oliver put his lips to her ear. 'Hurry! We'll manage it. Which way?' There was not a trace of doubt in his voice. Grimly determined. It put the heart back in her to hear him speak so. And him so pale...

Rosamund tugged at his hand and stepped boldly into the water, moving across the pool to stand right at the base of the falls. The water splashed on her face and shoulders. They would be soaked from head to foot, but the hounds would lose their scent. A bubble of wild laughter rose to the surface of her mind. If she'd stayed on the bank they'd have been torn to pieces by the hounds. Now they'd probably contract the lung-fever and die of that. Both alternatives were unappealing.

'I'll take my chance with the lung-fever,' she mumbled aloud.

Her shoes slipped on a stone which had been worn smooth by the crashing waters. Oliver was at her side, steadying her with his arm about her waist. The dark waters frothed about their knees, and she pointed at the stony wall which shone like polished jet in front of them. No weeds grew here, the waters were too turbulent. She saw him shoot her a puzzled glance, but there was no time for him to question the wisdom of her directions. Thankful for this mercy, Rosamund waded on. She put her hands out, feeling for a grip on the slippery rock. Her feet found the foothold that she was searching for and she stepped up on to the ledge. Water still lapped about her ankles. Wary of slipping under the powerful rush of water, she moved cautiously. She knew from past experience that the force of it could keep you under, and was violent enough to drown a king's champion. Oliver followed.

Rosamund had discovered this hidden ledge years previously when swimming with Lufu in the shallow pool. They'd been children then, and banned the use of the millpond.

'Millpond's too deep,' Osric had said. 'And I'll not have you disturbing t'eel traps. We lost a good meal last week because of you dislodging them. You can't swim 'ere. Get along wi' you.'

So Rosamund and Lufu had come to swim in the pool created by the roaring force. This pool looked more dangerous than the calm millpond with all its foam and noise. It was exciting. But it was not deep. And there were no eel traps to worry about. It was here that the girls had learnt to swim. Rosamund knew that as long as you did not swim directly under the jet of water you were safe. The concealed ledge ran beneath the surface of the water and along the rockface. If you walked its length you would find yourself walking through the waterfall and landing on the opposite bank. The moorland track, half overgrown, ran on up from there.

Oliver's face shone with spray, he was holding her hand so tightly that it hurt. The sound of their pursuers was completely obliterated. Water was everywhere; it showered their shivering bodies, it streamed into their eyes, it filled their ears, and some of it got into their lungs. Coughing and spluttering, Rosamund pressed on. Inch by careful inch along the narrow ledge.

It felt like drowning. Icy water needles jabbed at her skin. The whole world had melted, turned to water. Suddenly she was lost. Rosamund's feet slid out from under her. The waters closed over her head. She felt nothing, heard nothing, saw nothing, but water. She must have toppled off the ledge and gone under... The pool was so cold she'd gone numb all over.

She could not find her foothold on the ledge, nor feel Oliver's bone-crushing grip. He must have let her go. The cruel waters had claimed her. There was no air to breathe. Only water, cold as the grave, but stifling, drowning.

Oliver hauled on Rosamund's arm. He would pull it from its socket if he had to. Rosamund coughed, groaned, and shook her head to clear the water from her eyes and ears. She opened her eyes. They'd made it to the other side. He'd not let go of her hand. Rosamund sprawled face down in the spray-damp grass, spluttering unprettily. Oliver knelt over her and pushed the wet hair from her face.

She dredged up a smile for him, and some of the tension left his stern features.

'On your feet,' he said harshly. 'Move, Rosamund.'

'I'm dead,' she moaned.

'On your feet. We can't stop yet. If that dog makes it to the pool before we've taken cover then 'twill not matter that we have spoiled our trail. Our struggle through the falls will have been wasted. They will follow us by sight. On your feet.'

'You're inhuman,' Rosamund complained and levered herself upright, hanging on to Oliver's belt for support.

'Practical, my angel, practical.'

Arms wound round each other they staggered away from the pool. Rosamund's legs were shaking. She rallied herself, gritting her teeth, but every time she put her weight on to her feet her legs buckled beneath her. A group of shrubs edged the path. Only a few more feet and they'd be out of sight from the pool.

'Rosamund? Stand firm!' Oliver directed her as her legs crumpled under the strain.

'I . . . I'm trying,' she responded.

Rosamund took another wobbling step, and all but collapsed. If it had not been for Oliver's arms tightening around her, she'd have fallen flat on her face. A shrubby branch combed cheek and hair, and then they were safe. They flopped down thankfully on to the ground behind the clump of gorse. Wet and cold and dripping like a pile of wet linen, but safe.

Rosamund's lungs were bursting. She was dizzy with fatigue, and for a few moments it was all she could do to keep herself from fainting. When finally the swirling mist cleared from her eyes she saw Oliver squatting down on his haunches. The grey eyes were narrowed in concentration as he watched the pool side through the spiky gorse branches. His brows were peaked and frowning.

He swore comprehensively under his breath and his head swung round to her.

'I don't know how the hell they've done it, for I'd swear they did not see us. But *someone* is coming along this track. We've not shaken them off,' he grated through clenched teeth.

'Impossible.' Rosamund's eyes widened. 'Hardly anyone knows about this track, and those men are not native to Eskdale. They cannot know of it.'

'But they do. See for yourself,' Oliver suggested tightly.

By now Rosamund did not need to look. She could
hear the yapping of those too eager dogs which hounded
them. Her shoulders sagged. She could not move. Not
any more. But he could...

Rosamund heaved her head up and directed a pleading
look at those indefatigable grey eyes. 'Please, Oliver,
leave me. I cannot go on. I'm no soldier that I can battle
on like you. I'll be all right. Leave me and follow this
path.'

Oliver's face hardened. In one lithe movement he was
on his feet, he moved to tower over her wilting form.
'Stand,' he commanded.

And because his voice brooked no opposition,
Rosamund obeyed. The black mist came down like a
curtain before her eyes and she swayed. Oliver bent and
scooped her into his arms.

'Oliver! No!' She protested weakly, though her heart
was gladdened at this show of care for her welfare.

'I'll not leave a woman to face a pack of dogs,' he
replied curtly. And her heart sank. He would do as much
for any woman. Not just for her.

Oliver did not speak again. He loped back on to the
track, Rosamund in his arms. Rosamund put an arm
about his neck and clung to his tunic. Her head rested
against his chest. His heart was pounding in her ear. His
long legs covering the ground with relentless energy.

Still the dogs barked and howled in their wake. The
gap between hunter and quarry was closing fast. She
knew Oliver could not keep up this pace for long. No
one could. Amazingly, his stride lengthened and his feet
thundered steadily on. Every step was taking them nearer
to the summit. And every step jarred through her skull
like the smith's hammer on his anvil.

It would not be enough. All his efforts would be wasted
for the dogs had come so close, she could hear their
panting breath. She could almost feel the heat of it on
her dangling calves. Her fingers would no longer
maintain their grip on Oliver's neck and tunic.

A high-pitched shout floated up Blue Bank after them.
It was incomprehensible. Rosamund's ears betrayed her,
she could hear the swishing sea. Wave after wave after

wave. The sound was coming from so far away. Perhaps...after all...they had shaken them off.

Oliver stumbled, instinctively tightening his hold on her. He slowed to a walk. His heartbeat raced on, he took in the air in heaving gasps.

'Stop, you stubborn fool. Stop. Drop me.' Rosamund noted with surprise that her voice was slurred. She sounded drunk.

'Must...go...on...' Oliver gasped.

They were at the top. Mounds of heather grew across their path. The wind up here had whistled all the way from the ice islands. It was so cold it cut into naked flesh like a knife.

Oliver moved on, haltingly. His head was one huge, expanding field of pain. He did not seem to have any control over his legs. He staggered, and attempted to right himself, but his foot moved too slowly, it caught in a treacherous clump of heather. He went down. Heavily.

His last conscious act was to move a hand that seemed as heavy as lead to protect Rosamund's head from being smashed on the ground under him.

A single thought flashed unexpectedly into Oliver's tormented brain. He saw a confusingly stark image of a castle perched on the edge of a cliff. He could see it in his mind's eye as clearly as though he were gazing right at it. There was a view of mile after mile of wave-tossed grey seas.

Oliver knew that there was something he had to do—something he had sworn on his honour to do—and it was connected with that castle. He struggled to hang on to the idea taking shape, but the picture shifted. He could not hold on to it. Like Rosamund's hand, when she plunged under the falls, it threatened to slide from his grasp. Only this time he could not maintain his grip. A thick, blinding fog shrouded all. The cold hand of despair gripped his heart.

'Dawn,' he mumbled incoherently. 'Must be back at dawn. My honour!'

Everything went black. The hand that cradled Rosamund's head could no longer feel the damp tendrils of her hair. It flopped limp and useless into the heather.

Rosamund woke slowly, drowsily content in a soft cocoon of blankets. She tunnelled deeper into the warmth.

'Rosamund?' A young woman's voice, one she recognised. 'Edwin, she's awake at last!' the woman continued, sounding pleased. A low murmur and a man's voice rumbled in response.

Rosamund puzzled half-heartedly over the voices, but felt too slothful to respond. There was nothing to alarm her in either of them. She was so tired, a place where she could sleep and not be disturbed was heaven. The smell of a wood fire drifted into her nostrils. She could hear it crackling as it burned, warming the room.

'Rosamund.' The same woman's voice. Sharper now, accompanied by a hand shaking her shoulder.

Irritably Rosamund shrugged the hand away. 'Want to sleep,' she complained fretfully.

The voice became reproachful. 'Wake up, Rosamund. 'Tis important I speak to you.'

Unwillingly Rosamund opened heavy lids. 'Lufu!' she gasped on seeing who had woken her. The desire to sleep fled, and she sat bolt upright. She had been lying in a double box-bed, and the blankets slipped unchecked from her naked shoulders.

Her friend smiled gently and rearranged the blankets on Rosamund's shoulders. 'You're not clad,' Lufu informed her. 'And while you'll not mind me seeing you...there is Edwin to consider.'

Rosamund's eyes looked past Lufu and encountered wickedly bright hazel ones.

Edwin's wide mouth split into a grin. 'Oh, I'm not complaining. Don't mind me.'

Rosamund put a hand to her brow. 'Lufu? What happened? Why am I...' she began vaguely. Then she stiffened and caught hold of Lufu's arms. 'Oh, dear God! The dogs...the outlaws...did they get him? Where's Oliver?' she demanded hoarsely.

Lufu pointed to the large inert body next to the blazing fire. 'That, I take it, is Oliver.'

Rosamund's whole body jerked and relief flooded through her. His clothes were steaming gently in the heat of the fire. His hair was very dark, his face chalk-white. She could not see whether he was breathing or not. She started to scramble towards him, but Lufu put a firm hand on her chest, and shook her head.

'Nay, Rosamund. You stay put, me lass. I take it from the way you're staring at him that you want us to look after him too...'

Rosamund swallowed and nodded vehemently.

'That's fine, Rose, me lass. That was all I were wantin' to know.'

Rosamund watched as Lufu and Edwin bent over Oliver and began to strip him methodically of his damp clothing. She noticed her own now tattered pink robe was hanging to dry with some other garments on a line near the fire.

'You rest now, we'll deal wi' your lad.'

Rosamund smiled despite herself to hear Lufu call Oliver a lad. 'No,' she protested, clutching a blanket and clambering to her feet. 'I want to help.' But the cramped one roomed cottage shifted and tilted sickeningly and all the colour drained from her face.

'Rosamund, sit down, you daft woman,' Lufu admonished, setting her capable hands on her broad hips.

Weakly Rosamund subsided, her eyes never leaving Oliver's still form. Lufu and Edwin worked briskly, rubbing him dry before wrapping him in one of the grey wool blankets from the bed.

'Shift out of t' way a moment, Rose,' Edwin suggested, as he heaved Oliver into the bed. 'There you are, lass. One dry lad.'

'He...he's very still,' Rosamund touched his cheek. 'And so cold.'

'You warm 'im then,' chuckled Edwin. 'Nay lass, there's no need to sigh and fret over 'im. 'E looks strong as an 'orse. 'E'll be right enough come morning.'

'I hope so. His skin is all clammy.' Rosamund piled more of the coarsely woven blankets over Oliver. She glanced over her shoulder at her two oldest friends. 'Thank you. Thank you for helping us,' she said.

'What 'appened, Rose?' Lufu asked. 'Why didn't you stop when I called you?'

'What?' Rosamund's breath caught.

'I was behind you, all the way up the Blue Bank. I called and called, and Tatters were barkin', but you never stopped. I couldn't make out if 'e...' she jerked her head in Oliver's direction 'were abducting you, or you were going willin' like.'

Rosamund stared blankly at Lufu. 'You mean, it was you! We were running away from you,' she cried incredulously.

Lufu smiled. 'Aye. It seems so.'

'But the outlaws... we heard them in the wood. They were following us. All that crashing about, all that barking...' Her astonished gaze followed Lufu's pointing finger and fell on a small brown mongrel which was noisily chewing on a ham bone.

Lufu lowered her voice. 'She were huntin'. She rarely catches 'owt, and of course her claws have been clipped, but she does enjoy the chase. She's right noisy about it.'

Rosamund gaped. 'So we nigh on killed ourselves, to escape from you?'

Lufu shook her head. 'There *were* strangers abroad in t' forest. I saw 'em. A right shifty-looking crew. But they never got past t' waterfall. How could they know about t' ledge?'

'That's what I thought,' Rosamund admitted. She brushed a dark lock of hair from Oliver's face, and sighed. 'Poor Oliver, he ran all the way up the path for nought. We were coming to you to beg shelter in any case.'

'I 'eard tell you'd been kept at t' castle as squire's lover. Is he t' lord's squire?' enquired Lufu.

Rosamund nodded. 'Aye. He was.'

'And you love 'im?' Lufu said shrewdly.

Rosamund nodded sadly, her eyes travelling over Oliver's still face.

Edwin spoke up. 'Rose, lass, what do you mean 'e *was* t' squire?'

'He's been knighted. I saw his spurs,' she sobbed suddenly, and rubbed her eyes.

Lufu patted Rosamund's arm. 'No need to cry on't. You've a knight for a lover. Many would deem that an honour...'

'But not our Rose,' Edwin cut in from his stool by the fire. His large hands were occupied in whittling the curve of a shepherd's crook. 'She's married. Do you have so little regard for sacred vows, wife?'

Lufu blew him a smiling kiss. ''Tis not the same. We do love each other. Rose 'as never loved Alfwold.'

Rosamund found to her shame that hot tears were coursing down her cheeks. 'He's to marry Lady Cecily,' she blurted. 'He wanted me to live at t' castle. I agreed,' she sniffed. 'But then...but then I found I could not. It hurt too much and I did not want to betray Alfwold. Truly, Lufu, I tried not to break my marriage vows. I...I ran away. I went back to t' mill.' She drew a shuddering breath.

'And...' prompted Lufu.

'Oliver came after me,' Rosamund wailed. 'And we were caught in a trap. Attacked. He was hurt. And now he cannot remember who he is, nor who I am and...and...'

'You are glad for it,' Lufu finished.

Rosamund lifted her head, startled, and looked into Lufu's honest brown eyes. 'How did you know?' she wondered.

Lufu smiled. 'I know you,' she replied.

Rosamund wiped her eyes on the scratchy blanket. It smelt of wood smoke. 'Aye.' She glared defiantly at her friends. 'It's as though I've been given a second chance. And I'm intending to make the most of it.'

She saw Edwin stiffen suspiciously. 'What do you mean, Rose, me lass?' he growled.

Lufu let out a delighted giggle. 'She means she's not going to enlighten our noble friend here as to his identity.'

'You're mad, woman! She'd not be so...' Edwin said. He studied Rosamund's defiant expression and his own changed. Doubt crept into his voice. 'Rose. You don't mean to deceive this knight, do you?'

Rosamund squared her shoulders and met his gaze. 'Aye. That I do,' she admitted.

'You can't, lass!' Edwin exploded. 'Think what they'll do to you when they discover t' truth. You'll be accused of...of...' Words failed him.

Rosamund's hand rested gently on Oliver's ashen cheek. 'I know 'tis very wicked of me. But if I tell him who he is, he'll charge back to t' castle, marry the Lady Cecily and I...I think it would kill me. Especially now...' She hesitated.

'I'll not be a party to this!' Edwin declared stolidly, casting his crook down with a clatter. 'Folks have been put to rot in t' dungeons for less. I've a mind to spend me life on open moor, with heather beneath me feet, not in a black pit on damp prison flags.

'You can get out of here right now, Rosamund. And take your precious knight along wi' you.'

Rosamund tensed.

'Edwin!' Lufu chided. 'We can't throw them out in this state! It would be downright murder wi' 'im in that state! And you know what the penalty is for murder, 'tis far, far worse than prison...'

'I don't know,' grumbled Edwin, subsiding at the glance thrown him by his wife. 'You cast me out of me own bed in t' middle of the night, put strange folks who 'ave no right to be there in me place, and then you tell me what I cannot do. Wife, you're a trial to me. A sore trial.' He shook his head, and pulled at his beard, still muttering.

Lufu winked at Rosamund, and Rosamund hoped Edwin would let Lufu have her way. His bark had always been worse than his bite, and Lufu usually knew how to get round him.

'Rest you,' suggested Lufu. 'And warm your Oliver.'

Edwin glowered at them through lowered brows, but said nothing more.

Rosamund relaxed. It was warm and cosy in the shepherd's hut. She yawned and sank down into the bed, her arms winding round Oliver. She was very tired. 'But what about you?' she protested sleepily. Her eyelids drooped.

Lufu chuckled. 'Don't worry about that, me duck. We'll be fine by t' fire.'

'Oh, we will, will we?' grumbled Edwin without rancour.

Lufu's voice held laughter. 'Aye. And we'll decide what to do in t' morning. Sleep well.'

'Good night Lufu, Edwin.' Rosamund's voice came out muffled. Her lips were pressed against Oliver's torso. 'My thanks.'

She fell at once into a deep and dreamless sleep.

CHAPTER EIGHT

'NAY, Lufu!' Rosamund argued, glaring at her friend with a martial light in her eyes.

Clad in one of Lufu's shifts, Rosamund sat cross-legged on the floor, close to the box-bed, repairing her own gown. Momentarily her gaze softened as it was drawn for perhaps the hundredth time that morning to search Oliver's features. She did not find what she was looking for. He was as still and as grey as a stone.

Her blue eyes returned to meet her friend's. They hardened. 'I'd rather live in sin with Oliver than spend the rest of my life tied in holy wedlock to Alfwold!' she declared heatedly.

It was noon on the next day, and the two girls sat, in fierce dispute, over their work. Edwin had departed to look over his flock, the small mongrel yapping at his heels.

Rosamund heaved a sigh and stabbed her needle viciously into the cloth of her rent dress.

'Rosamund, nay. Show some sense,' Lufu flung back. 'Anyone would think 'twas you who'd been struck witless! You can't keep a knight hidden away. What would you do, put 'im under lock and key?'

Rosamund made an impatient gesture. 'Nay,' she snapped.

Lufu shook her head. 'Nay, for what would be t' point?' She paused. 'And if you did not 'ide 'im away—someone would see 'im and then where would you be? You cannot continue with this deceit! 'Tis impossible madness. You're not thinking straight, Rosamund!'

Rosamund ground her teeth. When Lufu called her by her full name she was angry indeed. Her jaw set in stubborn lines. 'But Lufu,' she argued. ''Twill not be forever. Only 'till he regains his memory...and then...'

'Aye, and then?' prompted Lufu darkly.

'And then I would not prevent him returning to Ingerthorpe Castle,' she finished weakly.

'I'd not taken you for a fool,' Lufu observed, her voice dropping.

Rosamund tossed her head, and her loose brown hair rippled down her shoulders. 'Call me a fool then. I care not. 'Twill be worth it ...'

'Worth it?' Lufu objected, gaping. 'Worth risking your neck for a few days of bliss? No man is worth such a price.'

'*He* is,' Rosamund averred softly.

Lufu snorted. 'And do you think he'll thank you when he remembers? When he finds out how you've deceived him?'

Rosamund's needle was stilled in mid-air.

'Aye, think on't,' Lufu warned cynically. 'You think that he'll thank you for letting him break his knightly vow of obedience to Lord Geoffrey? You'll change your tune then, methinks.' Lufu leaned towards her friend, pointing to emphasise her words. '*He* is a knight. *You* the wife of Alfwold. *He* belongs at t' *castle. You* at t' *mill.*'

'Oh, Lufu,' Rosamund said sadly, subsiding. 'I know. And I think he was beginning to remember some things last eve. When I let slip about the castle he went very quiet. I do know he'll have to go back there some time, of course I do.'

'Aye. Aye. That he will. And for all our sakes, the sooner 'e goes the better,' Lufu replied.

Rosamund looked unseeingly into the fire. 'They're all such schemers at the castle,' she observed with apparent irrelevance.

Lufu snorted. 'Eh, lass, and what 'ave you become? One day in t' castle and you're tarred wi' same brush. What are you at now but scheming? You've changed, Rose. The girl I knew would not even have dreamed of messing wi' the likes of 'im.'

'Oh, you'd be surprised,' Rosamund said drily.

'Eh?'

'Nothing. Lufu, I don't think Oliver likes schemers,' Rosamund said thoughtfully.

Wisely Lufu held her tongue.

Rosamund shrugged. Sad blue eyes met sympathetic brown ones. 'You're right,' she said. 'If it were only me and him involved, I might get away with it. But it's not. There's his oath to consider. I can't wreck his future. And there's you and Edwin. I don't have the right to involve you in this. They might take it out on you...aiding and abetting or some such thing. I see I must tell him the truth.'

Rosamund shifted round to peer anxiously at the figure in the bed. 'Oh, Lufu, do you think he will be well again? He's not going to die, is he? He's been lying like that for ages.'

'He's warm, isn't he?' Lufu asked.

'Aye,' replied Rosamund, touching him.

'And no longer feverish as he was in the night?'

'No, he's not feverish now, thank God. Oh! Look! His eyelids moved! I swear he moved.'

Lufu smiled reassuringly. 'Then he's sleeping himself better. He'll waken soon, no doubt.'

'And then I'll have to tell him,' Rosamund said in the voice of one resigned to doing something against her will.

'Aye,' Lufu agreed. 'That you will.'

Rosamund scanned Oliver's dark features minutely. His brow was cool, dark stubble shadowed his lean cheeks, and his colour was better. But he had yet to waken. A whistling draught from the door brought her brows snapping together. She glanced up.

'Edwin,' Rosamund chided quietly. 'Please shut the door.'

Edwin's guileless face was wearing a most strange expression. A sudden ugly premonition caused the hairs on Rosamund's neck to rise.

'Edwin? You look quite sheepish. What is it?' Lufu teased.

Edwin's embarrassed gaze flickered from Rosamund to Oliver and back again. He coughed.

'I've brought someone to see you,' Edwin admitted, and stood aside.

Rosamund got to her feet. Cold all over.

It was Alfwold. His brown eyes speared her with a greedy hunger that made Rosamund's flesh crawl. She stared at him, speechless with dismay. This man with the greasy hair plastered against his skull was her husband. He looked filthy. He must have been sleeping drunk in the ditch. His tunic was shiny with grease, and his leggings were soiled and torn. Rosamund had mended them only the day before their wedding.

He had been running and his scarred face was dripping with sweat. He revolted her, but it would be cruel of her to let him see. She held herself stiff as a poker, and tried not to shudder.

'Good day, Rosamund,' Alfwold said, for all the world as though they were strangers. At least he was keeping his distance. But the bold gleam in his eyes warned her she could not rely on this.

Rosamund rounded on Lufu. 'You knew!' she accused. 'You knew Edwin had gone to fetch Alfwold!'

But Lufu's face was round with astonishment. 'No...no...I had no idea,' she stammered.

The silence hung between them like a tangible thing. Outside a lamb bleated for its mother. A seagull cried.

Rosamund raised tortured eyes to her husband's scarred and grotesque features. His too revealing gaze was fixed on Oliver's face, and Rosamund's stomach lurched uncomfortably. She read despair in those open brown eyes. And anger. Alfwold knew. She did not like to think how, but there was no doubt Alfwold knew her heart lay with the tall knight who lay unconscious in Lufu's bed. Rosamund sent Edwin a barbed glance.

Alfwold had wrenched his gaze from Oliver. His brown eyes watched her. They were sharp and cunning. They reminded her of Wulfric. There was no doubt that he knew.

Rosamund lifted her chin. 'Good...good day, Alfwold,' she got out.

The stone-dresser and the miller's daughter stared at each other for the space of several heartbeats, Rosamund's defiant stance confirming her guilty love more eloquently than words could ever do. Alfwold's sad, twisted smile was like a gargoyle's. And his eyes were blank and dead.

'So 'tis true then, Rosamund?' he asked in distant tones. His accent sounded very coarse after Oliver's aristocratic drawl.

Strange how quickly you could grow used to things, Rosamund mused. Not long since Oliver's voice was alien to my ears, but now Alfwold's——

''Tis true then that he did not have to force you?' Alfwold cut into her thoughts.

'I was not forced,' Rosamund confirmed.

'So 'e did not hurt you?'

'No.'

Alfwold nodded. 'I'm glad o' that, lass,' he scowled. There was no feeling at all in his voice, and Rosamund wondered if he lied.

He appeared to brighten, and stepped closer. 'But were you willin' to bide at Ingerthorpe wi' 'im? After that first night, I mean? Or did they force you to that?' He sounded merely curious.

Rosamund's heart twisted. Perhaps he did care, after all...

She was assuming that the ghastly lifeless look in his eyes meant he felt nothing. Perhaps she was wrong...

'I was willing,' she admitted, and watched Alfwold's shoulders sag. 'Quite willing.'

'I see,' her husband said, tonelessly, and Rosamund knew she had done him a great hurt.

'Alfwold,' she burst out. 'Forgive me! I did not mean to cause you pain. 'Tis just that I...I...I thought that God would allow me to take a little happiness. But I was wrong. I found...I found I could not stay. I left the castle, ready to come back to you. Truly I did. But Oliver came after me. Then he was attacked and wounded. I could not desert him, so we came here.' She paused to draw breath, and finished on a rush. 'And Lufu knows I have decided to come back to you.'

''Tis true, Alfwold,' Lufu confirmed.

Alfwold's eyes lightened. 'You're coming back to me?' he asked hopefully.

'Aye. I realise it was wrong of me to break my vows,' Rosamund told her husband.

'But you don't love me...do you?'

'I . . . I . . .' Rosamund hesitated, and her eyes swung round to alight on the sleeping form of the man she did love. As if conscious of her regard, Oliver stirred restlessly and muttered in his sleep. A gentle feminine hand fluttered to his temple and he grew calm.

Alfwold made a dismissive sound. 'There's no need to tell lies. Rosamund, before you say 'owt else, I think you'd best hark at this. I've brought news.'

'N . . . news?' Rosamund wondered.

'Aye. And I'm not sure how you'll take it, not now, but . . .' Alfwold shuffled his feet and paused doubtfully.

Alfwold's hesitation and diffidence puzzled Rosamund. Surely he would greet his wife with more . . . more . . .

She had just admitted that she had been willing when she'd sinned against him. An adulteress, and not a victim. Surely Alfwold should want to chastise her? A husband did not accept such things from his wife. He would be within his rights to beat her. She felt suddenly lightheaded. 'Go on,' she urged. 'Your news . . .'

'I've seen the abbot at the monastery,' Alfwold began. His pock-marked skin grew mottled as if he were labouring under some great emotion. 'And the abbot denies all knowledge of the priest, Eadric.' He stopped and his brown eyes were fixed unwaveringly on Rosamund, as though he were waiting for something . . .

'So?' Rosamund said with ill-concealed impatience.

Alfwold swallowed. He opened his mouth, but no sound came out. Edwin came forwards and stepped into the breach. He took Rosamund's arm gently. She frowned up at him. She had still not forgiven him for bringing Alfwold to his cottage. Edwin had betrayed her.

'So?' Rosamund repeated, staring at her husband for enlightenment.

Edwin cleared his throat. 'The man Eadric is no priest,' he announced, smiling grimly at the effect his words had on the two women.

Lufu gasped. Rosamund went the colour of chalk.

'Eadric is a known traitor. He's in the pay of the Angevin faction,' Edwin went on. 'He's been sent to this country to create trouble for King Stephen. To pave the way for Mathilda's son, Henry.'

'He's no priest,' Alfwold repeated. 'He stole his habit from the rightful owner of that document I told you about. You remember, Rosamund? The one hung about wi' wax seals.'

'I remember.' Rosamund's throat was so dry, she could hardly get the words out.

Edwin continued. 'Eadric must 'ave killed the rightful holder of the parchment. Naked body of a man were found on t' moor. They must have got 'im as 'e came down t' moor road from York.'

'Lord ha' mercy,' Lufu gasped, crossing herself.

Edwin put his arm about his wife's shoulders. '"Father" Eadric used 'is stolen identity to gain the confidence of the villagers. You and Alfwold were not wed, Rosamund. The ceremony he presided over were nowt but a sham wedding. A counterfeit. You are a spinster yet.'

Rosamund's legs gave way. She staggered and her hand groped blindly for the bed. She plumped herself down and buried her face in her hands.

'This can't be happening.' Her voice cracked with feeling. 'This can't be true.' The edge of the bed dug into her thighs. It hurt. It was real, hard and solid. 'What are you saying, Edwin? I can't take it in. Are you telling me that I am free? That I have not broken any Holy vows?'

'You have it aright,' Edwin confirmed. 'The abbot has confirmed it. There is no priest Eadric. The abbot knew of a priest named Eadmer whom he thought would get the appointment. But no Eadric.'

'Eadric, Eadmer,' Rosamund repeated. 'They sound alike.'

Alfwold stepped forwards. 'Aye. And they are scripted almost the same. The document was in the dead *Eadmer's* name. The rebel Eadric waved it about as triumphantly as though it were the key to St Peter's gate. My unlettered eyes saw Eadric's name thereon. 'Tis easy to confuse the two. I have no learning.' He reached out a broad, blackened hand for her. 'Rosamund,' he said, pleadingly, trying to capture her gaze.

He wasted his breath. Rosamund had turned to peruse Oliver's dark features, and did not even hear him.

Oliver's eyelids flickered, indicating that he was lost in a deep dream, but there was nothing to show that he was like to waken yet. The new growth of stubble darkened his chin. The muscles in his face were relaxed. He looked so defenceless. Her heart ached. Rosamund stooped over him and tenderly stroked back a wayward lock of hair from his cool forehead. A smile hovered on the edge of her lips. Her eyes were very bright.

'Rosamund?'

Rosamund started as a hand fell on her shoulder. 'Mmm?' she responded absently.

'Don't even think it,' warned Lufu.

Rosamund turned guileless blue eyes on her friend. 'Think what, Lufu dear?' she enquired, all innocence.

'You know. I can see it in your eyes. Now you are free you're thinking you've changed your mind about telling him who he is.' Lufu almost growled at her. 'You're hoping that if he believes himself your equal, and still wants you, that he might offer you marriage.'

'Why, Lufu!' exclaimed Rosamund. She put a hand on her heart. 'I swear no such thought was entering my mind. But now that you mention it . . .' Rosamund's eyes sparked with sudden mischief, 'it does seem a good idea. He might offer for me,' she teased.

To her astonishment Lufu took her seriously.

'Rosamund,' she gritted, 'me patience 'as run right out! I wish you'd pick up your wits from whatever dark corner you left them in.' Lufu took hold of Rosamund to shake some sense into her. Then her eyes softened and she continued more gently, as one would when reasoning with a stubborn child.

She jerked her head towards the bed. 'Your Oliver's a *knight*, lass. You're worlds apart. He's always slept sound on a featherbed, 'twixt fine white linen sheets. While the likes of you and I, me lass, 'ave 'ad to make do wi' straw and coarse homespun. *Sir* Oliver 'as sweet scented beeswax candles aplenty to light his way to bed at night. While the likes of you and I, me love, 'ave to grope about in the mean glimmer and the rancid stench afforded by a spitting tallow light.'

Rosamund felt a rush of tears sting the back of her eyes, and she blinked, averting her face.

Lufu jabbed a workworn finger at Oliver. Her storm of cruel comments continued unabated. 'That knight is not for you, Rosamund. Sweet Saints preserve us! 'Twas bad enough when you simply sought to keep him from finding out who 'e was. But to marry 'im—that's twenty times as bad! What about this Lady Cecily? Didn't you tell me 'e promised Lord Geoffrey 'e would wed 'er? It's probably a hanging offence—folks don't deceive knights into marriage and hope to get away wi' it!'

Rosamund sniffed surreptitiously. 'Don't you think he may have learnt to love me by the time he finds out?' she asked wistfully. 'He might, you know. And if he does love me, he'll forgive me. I shall make him love me,' she declared.

'She's worse than simple!' exploded Edwin, he looked to Alfwold for support, but Alfwold was staring down at a hole in his boots and would not meet his eyes.

'Knights are bred to fight. They are warriors. They love money. They love position. Power. They don't *love* simple peasant lasses, even if they do like 'em to warm t' beds! Love! Do you 'ear me, Rosamund?' Edwin bellowed.

Rosamund smiled. 'I should think they'd hear you right down at Ingerthorpe quayside, Edwin.'

'Aye, well, you do make me mad, Rosamund,' Edwin admitted. 'You can't do this.'

'No, she can't,' Alfwold said thoughtfully. 'Rosamund, I think it would be best if you did marry me. In truth this time. Then all this nonsense would be at an end. You put more than your own life in jeopardy with this foolish fancy of yours. You must wed me, and learn to forget this knight.'

'Never!' cried Rosamund, as an unexpected and wholly unwelcome movement from the bed drew four pairs of eyes to stare with guilt and horror at its occupant.

Oliver's eyes were shut. His breathing deep and even.

'He's awake! He's listening,' mouthed Lufu, white about the mouth. Alfwold too was pale beneath his stained skin. Edwin was gaping, ludicrous in his dismay. Rosamund wanted to laugh. Except it wasn't funny at all. If Oliver were awake, he would have heard everything...

'He sleeps still,' soothed Rosamund, chewing her lower lip. Her sharp blue eyes took in Oliver's dream-flushed cheeks.

Alfwold caught her by the arm, pulling her towards the door.

'Rosamund, marry me,' he insisted on a whisper, sending another uneasy glance in Oliver's direction.

'No,' Rosamund refused and tried to pull free.

'I'll not ask anything of you. Give up this folly, marry me,' Alfwold pleaded. 'I'll clean meself up. I'll never touch another drop of ale. A man gets to need some comfort when 'e's alone in t' world. But wi' you as me wife... Please, Rosamund.'

'No.'

Edwin came forwards and eyed Rosamund belligerently. 'You stupid wench,' he said coldly. 'You'd kill us all, and think nothing on't.'

'No. No, I wouldn't,' Rosamund protested, startled. 'You're jumping to conclusions. I've not said that I... Edwin, your face looks most strange. I hardly recognise you. Edwin!'

The shepherd grabbed her by the arms and marched with her towards the door, Alfwold retreating before them.

'Let go, Edwin! What are you about?' Rosamund cried.

Edwin glowered and thrust her rudely at Alfwold so she was forced to clutch at the stone-dresser's tunic to avoid falling. She felt a surge of hatred rise up in her. She directed an acid glare at Edwin. He had flung her at Alfwold in such a way that she would be bound to reach out for him. No sooner had she staggered against Alfwold than his arm had snaked possessively around her waist. Rosamund stiffened, and sent him a less corrosive, almost apologetic look before attempting to move away.

Alfwold tightened his hold on her. Rosamund's nose wrinkled fastidiously. Alfwold stank. A stench of stale sweat, sour ale and onions hung about his person. And how short he was after... Her stomach began to churn as she struggled to escape him.

'Alfwold,' Edwin said curtly. 'Take her back to t' mill. She's your responsibility.'

'Edwin!' Lufu clasped and unclasped her hands. 'What on earth . . . ?'

'She goes.' Edwin stared defiantly at his wife.

'You can't . . .' Rosamund blurted.

'Aye. I can and I will. You go,' Edwin declared stolidly.

'But she's our friend . . . And do you think that Alfwold can keep her at the mill, if she's a mind to leave?' Two bright spots of colour were stark against Lufu's otherwise pale cheeks.

Edwin laughed unpleasantly. 'No, wife. You miscall her. We cannot call Rosamund our friend now. No friend would risk our necks. She must be stopped.'

'But I never said . . .' Rosamund began helplessly.

Edwin raised his voice and overrode her. 'Alfwold can tie her up and starve her till she agrees to wed him, for all I care.' His merciless eyes travelled with calculating menace towards Oliver. 'And as for him . . .'

Rosamund held her breath. 'You'd not harm him, surely . . . ?'

'Nay, Edwin,' Lufu moaned.

Edwin's shaggy head lifted and Rosamund shuddered to see his face so cold. 'I'm not so eager to hasten my end, I thought I'd made that quite clear,' he said. 'I'll take this knight to t' castle and dump 'im at t' gates. Never fear, Rosamund, your lover will not die. At least not by my hand. But 'e'll live where 'e belongs, up at t' castle. I'll not 'ave 'im 'ere fouling our cottage with 'is "noble" presence.' The hatred in Edwin's voice grated on Rosamund's ears. It astounded her.

'Edwin,' she said gently. 'There's no need to be so afraid. Oliver is a good man, he would not stoop to petty revenge.'

Edwin glowered sullenly. He was not convinced. 'And what do you know, pray, of knightly ways?' he spat.

Rosamund lifted her shoulders. 'Not much, I admit that, but I do know that he . . .'

Edwin spat explosively and raised his eyes heavenwards. 'Alfwold, I pray you, get that madwoman out of my sight, before I change my mind and find I've done murder this day.'

Rosamund dug in her heels. She shot Alfwold an appeal from under her lashes, but the stone-dresser's face was as hard as mill-stone grit.

'Nay! Nay!' she cried desperately. Alfwold was steering her to the door, she could feel the wind on her face. 'Alfwold, I beg you!' But Alfwold was deaf to the prayer in her voice, and blind to the pleading in her eyes. He edged forwards relentlessly, pushing Rosamund backwards towards the door.

Rosamund caught at a cross-beam, and the roughly hewn wood stabbed sharp splinters into her fingers. She scarcely noticed the pain, but clung to the beam as if her life depended on it. Like a drowning woman clinging to a life-saving spar amid a boiling sea. She tore her fingernails, and her fingers began to lose their grip. Alfwold would win in the end. Brute force must win. He might not be as tall as Oliver, but he had the strength of the devil in his thickset ugly body. She was outmatched. Swamped with despair, Rosamund let out a terrible groan. And Alfwold swept her on, as pitiless and inexorable as an avenging god. Past the wooden beam until she stood shaking, helpless with anger, on the uneven doorstep. She screwed up her eyes as a burst of bright sunlight poured down on the purpling heather-clad moor.

Lufu's wail of sheer terror halted Alfwold mid-stride. He craned his thick neck to glance back into the shepherd's hut, and Rosamund felt his body jerk with alarm. Beads of sweat started on to his forehead, and his brown eyes went glazed and stupid with shock.

Rosamund's puzzled eyes followed the direction of Alfwold's stupefied gaze. After the dazzling yellow brightness of the sun it was difficult to pick out what was happening in the gloomy hut...

A tall, dark figure rose up and swam in her bedazzled sight. Rosamund blinked. Her pulses began to race. Alfwold's hands slackened their grip on her forearms. The tall figure took his time approaching the door, and when he got there he stopped to lean his broad shoulders negligently against the door-jamb while he straightened his tunic and clipped his sword belt about his narrow waist. Then his grey eyes lifted and he surveyed them both through narrowed lids.

'Oliver!' Rosamund cried, giddy with relief. She could no more conceal her gladness at the sight of him dressed and on his feet, than she could stop breathing. 'You're awake!' She stumbled towards him. She made as if to reach for him, but recollected herself in time and drew her hands back to her sides.

Her eyes scanned Oliver's lean features. She saw how the dark growth of his beard partially masked the pallor of his skin. His mouth was set in a grim line, and the black brows were drawn together in a scowl. The breath caught in her throat for when her eyes rose finally, inevitably, to meet his, they found those grey eyes already searching hers. And there was something lighting his eyes which she thought she recognised. For she had felt it herself often enough since meeting him. He looked vulnerable, full of longing.

Her fingers itched to touch him, to smooth the frown from his brow, but Rosamund curled her fingers into her palms and set herself to resist temptation. For all that she liked to dream, and for all Edwin's misreading of her motives, Rosamund could not bring herself to deceive Oliver. And she knew that if she touched him without telling him that he was a knight, and thus as far above her as the stars, she would be lost forever.

She wondered whether Oliver had heard anything of the conversation within Edwin's hut. She wondered if perhaps his memory had returned. She shrugged. No matter. She would not take one more step towards him without him knowing the truth. Rosamund knew her heart was there in her eyes for all the world to see, but she did not care.

On the moor, the wind dropped abruptly. The silence hung over them, pregnant with menace. The sun was already warming the air, and despite this Rosamund shivered. She glanced up. High in the blue sky a few scudding clouds were being blown across the roof of the world. A hawk quartered the heather, searching for easy meat. There was nothing alarming in any of these things, so why this horrid prickling of her skin?

The tension crystallising in the sun-warmed air about Edwin's hut could be carved with a knife. Wondering at its source, Rosamund looked at Oliver. He lounged relaxed on the door post, one thumb hooked casually over his belt.

He was waiting for her to take that last step and touch him. He was daring her to move. A muscle flickered in his cheek, and his grey eyes rested on her face. They were clouded with some unfathomable emotion. Try as she might, she could not read his mood. She must tell him *now*. Before she changed her mind.

'*Sir* Oliver?' she began, emphasising his title. She heard him catch his breath. He shut his eyes briefly. 'Are you dizzy?' Rosamund frowned in concern. Some of the tension had left his face when she spoke, but when he opened his eyes they remained clouded. As though he were concussed, and his thoughts had tangled so much he could not unravel them.

'*Sir* Oliver?' he drawled, in his most lordly tones. It served to widen the gap between them.

Rosamund swallowed and nodded. 'Aye,' she confirmed in a small voice.

His eyes smiled. Rosamund's eyes could no longer meet his. They dropped uncertainly to stare at the rapid pulse in Oliver's neck. How much had he heard? Did he think she would betray him?

Oliver's hand bridged the space which yawned between them. He searched one of Rosamund's hands out of its hiding place deep in the folds of her gown. His warm fingers gently prised open her balled fist. She hesitated, then clung convulsively to his hand, but the confusion in her mind was such that she avoided his gaze even so. Thus it was that Rosamund did not see how his stone-grey eyes softened as they rested briefly on her downbent head.

Oliver pulled Rosamund close to his side. She leaned her body into his and relaxed.

'Inside,' Oliver commanded abruptly, looking at Alfwold.

Rosamund's head snapped up. She had not spared Alfwold a thought since Oliver had stepped into her line

of sight. Alfwold's scarred face was rigid, his eyes
staring.

Oliver sighed and shifted to lean some of his weight
on Rosamund. His face grew more pallid than ever. His
finely shaped mouth was white with tension. Rosamund
pushed her shoulder under Oliver's arm to support him
by an arm about the waist. Oliver laid his hand across
her shoulder. 'I'm not out for revenge,' he reassured
them.

Alfwold shot him a glance of mingled disbelief and
hatred.

'Oh, get inside, man, before I keel over. I merely want
to talk with you. I'm hungry, and I could do with a
drink. And then I'll leave you in peace, never fear.'

Alfwold stomped past them.

'I've the thirst of a camel,' Oliver admitted, smiling
oddly at Rosamund.

'A camel? Whatever's that?' Rosamund asked,
looking at him at last, her curiosity sparing her blushes.

Oliver grinned and squeezed her shoulder. That heart-
warming light had appeared in his eyes. His chipped
tooth peeped out at her. 'I'll tell you later,' he promised.
'Now I must sit down. Will you bear my weight? I
confess I'm weak as a kitten.'

'Slow down, Oliver!' begged Rosamund, panting as her
feet slipped for the hundredth time on the steep and rock-
strewn path leading down Blue Bank.

'Almost at the bottom,' Oliver flung over his shoulder
without slackening his pace. 'The falls are just ahead.'

'I know. I'm not deaf. But must we go so fast? My
heart feels as if it's bursting. I don't know how you can
keep this up, especially with that head of yours.'

The water-skin, hanging on a thong from Rosamund's
waist, had slipped and it banged uncomfortably against
her hips with every step she took. Irritably Rosamund
pushed it back into place. She wished now she'd given
in and let Oliver carry it after all.

He had been so weak, back in Lufu's hut. He should
by rights be resting. But he'd made it clear he intended
to get to the castle as soon as possible. Edwin and Lufu
had fed and watered them, but Rosamund could see that

her friends were anxious to be rid of their troublesome guests. The fare they'd been offered had been simple, but good. It had obviously had a miraculous effect on Oliver. The way his long legs covered the ground now, you'd not believe he'd been knocked senseless the day before.

His dark head swung round in response to her earlier comment. 'I don't waste my breath in bleating, that's how I do it.' He spoke with grim determination, but Rosamund saw he was not possessed of super human strength after all. She noted dark rings under his eyes. His hair was damp with sweat.

The roar of the falls grew steadily louder, and Rosamund gritted her teeth to keep up with the pace set by Lord Geoffrey's newest knight. Nimble as a goat, and fleet of foot, he did not seem to have her difficulty with the precipitous route down the bank. It should be easy coming *down* the path, but it was not. What with the stones rolling out from under your feet and pebbles working their way into your shoes...Rosamund swore softly and shook her foot as something dug into her heel.

Oliver turned and offered her his hand. By now they had passed the scrubby gorse bushes and were so near the base of the falls that Rosamund could feel the spray cooling her face.

'You look half-dead,' she commented, closing the gap between them.

'My thanks.' He grimaced ruefully.

Rosamund stared into his clouded grey eyes, and hesitated.

'Rosamund?' His hand moved impatiently.

Smiling to herself, she accepted his help and limped to seat herself on a moss-clad boulder. She dragged off her shoe and began to probe for the offending pebble.

Oliver sank to the ground at her feet and rested his arms on his knees. He bent his head over his arms, breathing heavily.

'Why all this haste?' Rosamund enquired. 'There's no point killing yourself.'

The dark head lifted. 'You must show me the exact location of the renegades' camp.' He spoke wearily. 'And then you must take me back to the castle. I understand

I have duties there which I have been neglecting. The Baron will be relying on my help to muster the forces against the traitors. If I do not—then I shall be deemed a traitor, and my life will be forfeit.' He lifted a brow and gave her a straight look. 'If my continued absence has not already seen me judged guilty, that is,' he added.

Rosamund twisted her thin shoe in her hands. 'Do you not... That is... Has your memory really not returned?' she asked tentatively.

Oliver's handsome face twisted. 'I have a hazy recollection of a grey war-horse...'

'That's Lance!' Rosamund cried. 'He's yours. The rebels took him. I think they went to negotiate your ransom.'

'Then that's another reckoning that I shall have to settle with Eadric's mob. I'll get Lance back.' Oliver hesitated. 'I also keep seeing a castle sprawled atop a cliff. Is that...?'

'Aye! That's Ingerthorpe! You are remembering!' Rosamund's eyes lit up.

'I wish I could remember more,' he admitted. ''Tis very confused, some of it.'

'You must have faith, Oliver.' Rosamund's blue eyes were wide and earnest, her voice soothed. 'You will remember, I know you will.'

Oliver smiled gently. 'Such confidence. So naïve,' he murmured and shook his head. 'Would that I were gifted with your faith. I know that I was given a commission of some importance. And I very much fear I should have been executing it at dawn. But as to the details... It is most likely connected with those swine who clouted me.' He ran his hand gingerly through his hair, fingering his wound. His dark locks became more disordered than ever. 'I pray this Baron Geoffrey is merciful towards forgetful knights.' He swore expressively at the ground. ''Tis not very likely, is it?'

'He might be lenient with *you*,' Rosamund stressed.

'How so?' Oliver lifted his head and looked sharply at her.

'He's your cousin. That's why you're to wed his sister.' She paused. 'She's the Lady Cecily.'

Oliver's cool eyes surveyed her thoughtfully. He linked his hands and rested them on his knees. 'That displeases you, as I recall.'

Rosamund's face scorched with shame. 'You should not have listened to us in the hut,' she accused. ''Twas not an honourable thing to do.'

Oliver's eyes were veiled. ''Twas not something I planned, Rosamund. I was wandering in and out of my wits, and could not help myself. 'Twas nigh on impossible to differentiate between dreaming and reality,' he informed her gently.

Rosamund glared at the shoe in her hand as though she wondered what it was doing there. She jammed it clumsily on to her foot. 'How...how much did you hear?' she asked stiffly, averting her head.

'I learned I am a knight, and I gather I owe my allegiance to Lord Geoffrey at Ingerthorpe. I rather imagine he would be relying on my help to round up those ruffians who addled my brains so efficiently.

'And...what else did you hear?' Rosamund demanded, watching him now with the vigilance of a hawk.

Oliver's eyes widened. 'What else?' His voice became light. 'Oh, nothing of any import,' he shrugged casually.

'Nothing of any import?' Rosamund repeated, mimicking him.

Oliver shook his head. She glimpsed his chipped front tooth.

'Then why did you insist I come back with you?' she demanded tightly.

Slowly Oliver unclasped his hands. Holding her with his eyes he rose up on his knees and reached for her waist. Their eyes were level. His eyes fell to her mouth. 'Because you're my lover, sweet angel?' he suggested huskily.

Rosamund struggled for words, but her mouth had gone dry. She cleared her throat. 'Not because you need me to show you the rebels' encampment?' she offered.

Oliver's lips twitched. He struck his head with the palm of his hand. 'Of course!' he declared, and his eyes twinkled. 'I knew there must be some good reason but, sweet lady, it had quite escaped my mind.'

Rosamund stood up abruptly and moved blindly to the edge of the pool.

'Take care, my sweet,' his deep voice sounded in her ear.

His arm slid about her waist and she was pulled up against him. His lips moved softly on the nape of her neck and she shuddered. It was too easy for him to affect her, and he knew it. Only too well.

'Oh, don't, Oliver, please,' she begged.

She felt him stiffen. 'I'm sorry,' he apologised. 'I thought you had something of a liking for my kisses. When we left the moor you were glad enough to accept my company in place of Alfwold's.'

'Nay, 'tis not that,' Rosamund's voice broke.

'What then? My love?'

She felt him attempt to turn her in his arms, but stood her ground and fixed her eyes on the tumbling water as it thundered into the pool. She could not face him. Her eyes were closed in agony. He sounded so tender, but she knew that he mocked her with false concern.

'Rosamund,' he urged, his hand on her chin forcing her head round.

She took a deep breath and met his questioning gaze squarely. Beads of spray shone in his hair. 'Don't mock me,' she pleaded under her breath. 'Don't make a game of me.' She spoke so low he had to stoop to catch her words.

Oliver's hand tightened under her chin and his eyes darkened. For one heady moment she thought he would refute her low whisper. Then he grinned.

'You have a halo, Rosamund. An angel's halo crowns your hair.' He wiped at some of the dewy droplets which gleamed in pearly strands among Rosamund's thick tresses. She glowed at his touch. Long fingers found her ear and caressed it. Then they traced a path lightly across fiery cheeks to her lips, leaving a burning trail in their wake.

His eyes were bright—with mockery? 'Oh how I hate you,' she declared through her teeth, twisting her head away from his torturing hand. 'I wish you wouldn't touch me!'

Oliver was attempting to look into her eyes. 'I don't believe you.' His eyes gleamed. 'You like it when I touch you...' He bent and demonstrated the truth of his statement by managing to place a soft kiss on her forehead.

Rosamund had put her hand up to his chest, as though to ward him off. Her fingers clutched instead at his tunic. She stood quite still.

'You like it when I kiss you...' He pressed his lips to her hand and then, before she divined his intention and could evade him, his lips were on hers.

Rosamund abandoned the futile pretence as hopeless. She surrendered herself completely to the wonder of his kiss. Oliver's lips burned hers; she felt his forcing her mouth open, exploring the sweetness of her mouth. His kiss became hard. Ruthless. It was a searing, branding kiss and it felt as though he were marking her for his own.

'Don't you?' he demanded, tearing his lips from hers.

Rosamund nodded. 'I think that's why I hate you so much,' she admitted with a shy smile.

He grinned.

'You arrogant swine!' Rosamund lifted her fingers to her bruised lips. 'You hurt me,' she accused, but her eyes betrayed her. They were shining.

Oliver's hand was weaving in her hair. 'Your halo is back,' he said. ''Tis beautiful. Fashioned with a rain-bow's colours.'

Rosamund frowned. 'Halo?' she wondered. Then her brow cleared. 'Ah! The spray! Of course!' she ex-claimed. 'Do you know what this waterfall is called?'

'Nay; if you recall my love, there's not much I do know at the moment.' Oliver's face became bleak.

Rosamund's hand fluttered to caress a lean cheek. 'You will remember,' she asserted.

'I pray that you are right,' he replied.

'You will. You remembered the castle. 'Twill take time, that's all.'

'And in the meantime, what am I supposed to do? I must be mad to think I can bluff my way through all this with only my addled wits to help me,' he said bitterly.

'You've got me. I'll help you. You can trust me,' Rosamund promised.

'Can I?' Oliver asked drily.

Rosamund face flushed with guilt.

'I...I... Of course you can. I'm not deceiving you, am I?'

'Ah, but I woke up and prevented you from being taken back to the mill,' Oliver was swift to point out. ''Tis in your interest to be honest with me now—you know I heard much of what was said.

'I wonder what would have happened if you had had the opportunity to deceive me? If I had not listened, and if Alfwold had not been brought to the hut? An interesting speculation, my love, don't you agree?' His eyes rested on her.

Rosamund glared, and jerked herself out of his arms. Her hair lifted about her shoulders in the slight breeze. She shook her head. 'Nay. I would not. I decided 'twas not right,' she told him.

'Why?' he asked in a low voice. 'Why?'

Her voice became muffled. 'Because...because I want...oh, I cannot tell you. Do not press me on this, Oliver. I cannot say.' She hunched her shoulders on him and turned to face the foaming white waterfall.

She thought he sighed.

'Very well, Rosamund,' he said. She fancied there was disappointment in his deep voice, but his next words were prosaic enough to dispel the impression. 'Now, angel. The camp. We have rested enough.'

'Do you not like the waterfall?' Rosamund asked brightly.

'Of course I do. But I have to redeem myself if I want to keep my position.'

Rosamund faced him. 'It's called Angel Falls.'

'That's very interesting, Rosamund. Now come on.' He took her hand. Not listening at all. His eyes were mapping out their route across the stream.

Rosamund ignored the pull on her hand. 'Do you want to know why it's called that?' she asked.

'Later, later,' he said impatiently.

'I'll tell you now,' she insisted, snatching her hand free.

'Rosamund!' he warned. His hand rubbed his stubbly chin. His lips were set in a grim line.

'I'll tell you now. A beautiful lady with the face of an angel once lived at the top of the falls. She fell in love...'

'Good God, Rosamund!' Oliver exploded. ''Tis no time for telling tales!' He reached for her hand and dragged her over to the pool. 'Go on,' he urged. 'The ledge...'

Rosamund faced him defiantly. The words tumbled in a babbling torrent from her lips, like water forcing its way through a broken dam. 'The lady fell in love, and her love was requited, but it was a love that was doomed. Her father was ambitious. He refused to let her marry her humble lover and she married instead some merchant from Scarborough.'

Oliver made a movement of exasperation.

'I've nearly done,' she said.

'Good. Spit it out, then,' he said with resignation. 'And then we can be on our way.'

'Aye. Thank you. The lovers could not bear to be separated and they would meet secretly here at the base of the falls. But the rich merchant found out and let it be known that he would kill the lady's penniless lover. He laid a trap for them. He waited. Here. The two lovers agreed to meet at noon to say a last farewell. And the merchant sat waiting.' Rosamund watched Oliver carefully from under her lashes.

'Go on,' he said, listening now despite himself.

'They did meet. Only this time they met at the top,' Rosamund pointed upwards.

Oliver's eyes wandered up the length of the frothing cascade to the summit. They narrowed, flickering back to Rosamund's.

She smiled sweetly. 'Eventually the merchant found them. At the bottom of the pool. Their bodies were entwined together so tightly that they could not be separated. And that is why at noontide on a hot and sunny day, like the one they died on, 'tis said you can see the shape of an angel's wings shining through the spray. So, Angel Falls. 'Tis God's own memorial to their true love.'

'What are you trying to say to me, Rosamund?' Oliver demanded tightly.

Rosamund opened her eyes. 'Why nothing, *Sir* Oliver.' She made her voice light. ''Tis but a pretty story.'

Oliver hustled her towards the ledge.

'I like the tale,' Rosamund insisted. 'I think it's lovely to think that two people would prefer to die together rather than live apart.'

'I've never heard anything more ridiculous in my life,' Oliver growled. 'I swear you made it all up. Now get along with you. Heaven help me that I am forced to put my trust in you!'

'But you do, don't you?'

'What else can I do? I have no alternative,' he replied with devastating frankness.

At his tone Rosamund's eyes filled with dismay.

'I have a hazy recollection of meeting a young maid on a beach...' Oliver began unexpectedly. 'It seemed part of a dream, a fevered dream I had while I was out of my head. Now let me tell it to you. You can judge whether 'tis a true tale or not.'

Rosamund tensed. Oliver's eyes were as cool as the water behind them. He picked up a strand of her hair and weighed it idly in his palm.

'She was most comely, that maiden on the beach. Her robe was pink, like yours. She had rich honey-brown hair which flowed like silk, and the body of an angel. But 'twas her eyes which struck me most.'

Oliver stared at the eyes in question, and whispered softly. 'Big blue eyes, bright as jewels, but far, far more lovely than any hard gem could ever be.' He paused and, dropping both his gaze and her lock of hair, turned abruptly to frown blackly at the churning water in the pool. 'But they lie, those eyes, they lie,' he said harshly.

Rosamund swallowed down a choking lump in her throat. 'L...lie?' she stammered.

'Aye. Most prettily they lie. But 'tis a lie for all that. For though the maiden on the beach had all the beauty a girl could wish, her chiefest attraction to me was those honest, smiling eyes.' He whirled round to face her, his fingers biting into shoulders. 'In my dream, I had given up hope of finding a woman with such frankness in her eyes, Rosamund. Till that day I had read many things in women's eyes. I had seen scorn, calculation, greed, indifference—to name but a few. But never such directness. Your seeming honesty quite unmanned me.'

'So you do remember,' Rosamund got out through still lips, inwardly wincing at his words.

'That much I do,' Oliver conceded. 'I remember the beach, and you. Your beautiful deep blue eyes. Your innocence, your guilelessness. I wanted to keep you by me.' He took a breath. 'And now I find you are no different from the others. You would lie, and cheat to gain your ends, just the same. Women!' he said bitterly.

Rosamund's heart sank like a stone, but she rallied herself. 'Did you hear me tell Lufu I would be honest with you? Did you?' she demanded.

Oliver watched her with eyes that seemed a million leagues away. 'Aye. While you thought yourself married to the stone-cutter. And you changed your tune as soon as you thought you had a chance of snaring a knight, didn't you?'

'Nay! Nay! That was Lufu's thought, not mine,' denied Rosamund, her voice unusually high.

'Was it really, my love?' Oliver drawled, very dry. 'I confess I am instantly reassured by your protestations.' He sighed heavily. 'Now, much as I admire the charm of this place, much as I like your Angel Falls, 'tis time we moved on. Do you think you could set your calculating little mind to finding the encampment?'

She gritted her teeth to keep her temper. She protested. 'But Oliver, why on earth did you stop Alfwold taking me back to the mill, if you thought so badly of me?'

Oliver's dark face was impassive, his eyes hard as slate.

'The direction of the camp, sweet angel,' he prompted, raising his voice over the rushing waters. He nudged her inexorably towards the ledge.

'I'm not one of your men!' she yelled. 'Don't you use that voice on me!'

'No, you're not, are you?' His gaze swept her from head to toe. She was very conscious of the spray beginning to dampen her robe. When dry her pink dress was the most modest of gowns, but now it was wet it clung to her shape in the most revealing manner. Huffily Rosamund pulled on the strings of her cloak, and hunched herself more securely within its concealing folds. Oliver's lips twitched, but Rosamund could take no comfort from that, for his voice and eyes remained stony.

'The camp,' he repeated.

'Aye. I'll show you t' rebels' camp,' Rosamund's accent betrayed both anger and distress. 'But there's no need for us to take a soaking. I can point its location out from this side of t' river. As we're on foot, 'tis easier to get back t' castle if we stay on the north bank,' she explained. 'This way.' She held out her hand, flushed, and withdrew it hastily into her mantle. 'This way.'

Rosamund's head jerked up and she stalked off, Oliver close at her heels. The roar of Angel Falls muted and then was lost as other sounds swelled to take its place. On she marched, along the river bank. She heard the sound of the river itself as it bubbled along to fill her father's millpond, the sound of the gulls, the everyday sounds of villagers at work on their strip fields, of oxen clinking in their yokes.

Ahead of them, the river Esk flowed through the village which had been her home for every one of her sixteen years. It wound on from there to mingle with the unfathomable waters of the sea. Rosamund could visualise it every foot of the way. How strange that everything remained the same. She felt so different, she had half expected everything else to have changed too.

She did not need to look over her shoulder to see Oliver. He was keeping so close, she could feel his breath on her neck.

She shrugged her shoulders impatiently. 'Do you have to walk on my heels?' she complained.

His low answer warmed her ear. 'I like to have you within easy reach, my love.'

Rosamund felt her heart contract in sudden understanding. He didn't trust her. He wanted her where he could grab her, lest she decide to betray him.

Her nose inched higher. 'We're almost at the camp,' she said. 'Thereafter we will take the cliff path to the castle. 'Tis by far the most direct route.'

'How good of you to tell me,' Oliver remarked, dry as dust. 'Is that to put me off my guard?'

She did glance over her shoulder at that, and sent him a glare which should have burnt him to a cinder. He smiled at her, a cold smile which did not warm his eyes.

Rosamund swivelled her eyes round to the path, determined not to look his way again.

They'd passed the mill and were cutting across the clifftop towards the castle. There was little in the way of cover up here. No shrubs. Hardly any vegetation. The misshapen lines of a few wind-bent trees told those who had eyes to see that, up here, the east wind reigned supreme.

Oliver's head no longer throbbed in that thought-hobbling way. The clear air seemed to have swept the cobwebs from his brain. His long legs covered the ground easily, confidently. His face was relaxed.

When Rosamund and Oliver had stalked past the mill, the sense of urgency had permitted Oliver only the most cursory glance. But that had been enough to set his spirits soaring. He recognised the mill. And something had shifted in the back of Oliver's mind, clicking into place. Something which had him turning instinctively for the shortcut to the castle.

He was remembering. Slowly, too slowly for his liking, but his memory *was* returning. When Rosamund had pointed out the direction of the rebels' encampment he'd been able to work out the location of that in relation to Lord Geoffrey's castle as well.

He altered his stride to avoid stumbling in a cluster of coney holes. So some larger forms of wildlife managed to eke out an existence on these wind-blasted heights. It could not be easy, but, judging by the number of holes which dotted the coarse grass, the rabbits at least were successful. A pair of them must have escaped from the abbey's coney garth and established a flourishing warren.

It was a poacher's paradise. Oliver's eyes lit on a tell-tale net lying tangled and torn where its owner must have sited it some months earlier, its fibres rotting and in need of repair. Had it been forgotten? Or had the thief been caught by the Baron's warrener? Though the animals were wild they belonged by rights to the lord, and any taking them would be accused of poaching.

Oliver's gaze sharpened and he cocked his head to one side.

'Half a dozen horses,' he murmured tersely. 'Coming this way at a gallop.'

'There!' Rosamund pointed unnecessarily. 'They're coming right at us! They're like to run us down!' she cried in alarm and clutched at Oliver, her antagonism forgotten.

Oliver thrust Rosamund behind him and stood, legs braced slightly apart, facing the oncoming troop. His hand hovered over his sword hilt.

'My lord's men?' he demanded, curtly.

'Aye, I think so.' Rosamund screwed up her eyes. 'Aye, I recognise Sir Brian Martell on the black gelding at their head,' she confirmed. 'My lord's youngest knight.' She tightened her hold on the soft fabric of Oliver's tunic.

Oliver peered at her over his shoulder. 'Keep your head up, angel,' he advised. 'We must brazen this one out. I don't want them mistaking fear for guilt.' She felt him peel her hand from his tunic.

Rosamund sent him a worried look. 'But I am afraid,' she whispered.

'Don't be. I'll...' But he never finished his sentence.

Hooves drummed loudly on the hard earth. There was a jingle of spurs and harness, and with a flourish the small troop drew rein a mere sword's length away.

'Sir Brian.' Oliver inclined his head, cool as you please.

'De Warenne,' replied the mounted knight, bright as a poppy, with a scarlet tunic over his mail coat. With his brown hair and most of his features hidden under a steel helm he was very much the implacable warrior.

Rosamund stiffened. Sir Brian had avoided using Oliver's title. She could not decide from his face whether it had been accidental or deliberate. Oliver appeared not to have noticed Sir Brian's omission.

'You're in command of this troop?' Oliver enquired in English.

The young knight gave his assent. He doffed his helmet, and balanced it on the pommel of his saddle. He pushed back his mail coif as a mixture of expressions crossed his youthful face. He looked uncomfortable and embarrassed, as though he knew that he should make the next move but was uncertain as to what was the best course of action.

Oliver was running an experienced eye over the steaming horses. Their barrel chests were still heaving. 'If you wish my cousin's horses to return to the stable in the same condition that they left it, you might take some heed of the terrain you ride over.'

Sir Brian's jaw dropped. 'Eh?' he said, stupidly.

Oliver gestured impatiently at the honeycomb of rabbit holes. 'The warren, man,' he explained. 'It only takes one wrong step, and you've got a screaming horse with a broken leg, and lost Geoffrey a valuable asset.'

The young man's face went red to match his surcoat.

'I don't expect you've had the pleasure of finishing off a horse, have you?' Oliver asked pleasantly.

'Nay.'

Sir Brian seemed to recollect that it was he who should be taking the initiative, for he drew himself up in the saddle and opened his mouth to speak.

Oliver was there before him. 'Not the easiest task,' he said, frowning reminiscently. 'Very messy. And Brian, lad——'

Rosamund hid a smile at the young knight's discomfiture.

'De Warenne?' Red to his ears, the mounted man eyed Oliver warily.

'One thing more. Never lead a troop of horses to a flat-out gallop unless it is absolutely necessary. Think of the poor beasts labouring under the combined weight of you, and all your armour. You exhaust their reserves, and then when you come to need it most, you'll find your mount doesn't even have a trot left in him, never mind a gallop.'

Sir Brian Martell cleared the obstruction from his throat. 'De Warenne...' He hesitated and glanced at the mounted men, seeming to draw strength from their presence. 'These knights owe fealty to Lord Gilbert Hewitt. We have combined our forces and were charged with the task of finding you and bringing you in...' His voice faltered and stopped. He shifted in his saddle as though he had a thistle in his hose.

Oliver's cool grey eyes met Sir Brian's and held them. A strange smile twisted his lips.

'Bringing me in, Martell?' Oliver asked. 'Surely you're not asking me to surrender my sword to you?' he murmured, his eyes not wavering from the younger knight's countenance. 'Is there a charge against me?'

Martell's eyes slid away first. 'Nay, no charge,' he blustered. 'But . . . but there are grounds for suspicion, and before my lord was wounded he commanded . . .'

Sir Brian got no farther. Oliver strode to Martell's gelding and snatched at the bridle.

'My cousin is hurt, you say?' he bit out.

The young knight nodded.

'Badly?'

'I . . . I think so. My Lady Margaret was so distraught that her babe has started, and 'tis not yet her full time . . .'

Oliver swore comprehensively.

'Give me a horse,' he demanded, his keen eyes ranging over the troop. Two of them were but youths, they wore no mail and their arms were light. He addressed the one who was mounted on a stocky-looking roan. 'You, sir. A knight?' he asked briefly.

'Nay, sir. Squire,' replied the lad.

'Yours will do then. I mustn't offend a fellow knight by taking his horse, must I, Martell?'

Sir Brian made a choking sound.

Oliver flung himself into the saddle, and turned the roan's head towards the distant castle. 'You can follow on foot,' he told the squire.

'Aye, sir,' the youth saluted. He came to stand beside Rosamund, looking her up and down with a leering light in his eyes. He would be glad to escort the knight's pretty playmate back to the castle, that he would.

Rosamund's cloak had slipped. She was so taken up in following the gist of the conversation that she had not noticed the fellow's insolent gaze rested on her damp, and too revealing gown.

'Oliver?' her soft voice asked. 'I'm to follow after?'

Oliver spared her a glance. 'Aye, you follow . . .' His eyes sharpened as they took in the squire's ardent gaze.

He might be only a lad, but the way he was looking at Rosamund...

Oliver's fine lips thinned. 'Nay,' he said shortly, reaching down his hand. 'You ride before me.'

CHAPTER NINE

THE Lady Adeliza was standing on the steps by the castle door, clad entirely in black from head to toe. As the small troop rattled into the already crammed and jostling bailey, Rosamund glimpsed her exchanging words with Sir Gerard. Sir Gerard's face was pinched. He was opening and shutting his mouth, but no sound came out.

A squire stood at Sir Gerard's elbow. He plucked at the knight's sleeve, gabbling wildly. He seemed to have forgotten his polished French phrases and expressed his agitation in his native tongue. The elderly knight's grizzled head moved from side to side. Heeding the lady...the squire...the lady... Another man erupted from the seething yard and stood before the harassed knight. Sir Gerard put his hand to his greying head. 'M...m...must think. Must th...think. Need a minute alone to think,' he was muttering disjointedly.

Sir Brian reined in, and jumping from his mount, executed a courtly bow.

'Merciful Heavens! What now?' Lady Adeliza cried from her perch. Her voice cracked.

'I've found your nephew, ma'am,' Sir Brian announced.

Rosamund's jaw dropped as she assimilated the change that had taken place in the Lady Adeliza. The lady was wringing veined hands at her breast, her eyes were wild, her black garb flapped about untidily in the breeze. She looked like an elderly rook whose rookery was being threatened by the woodcutter's axe.

Behind Rosamund, Oliver slid from his saddle. Rosamund had to hold fast to the pommel to keep her seat.

'My lady!' Oliver sketched a bow. 'How fares my cousin?'

'He lives yet. But no thanks to you. Traitor!' My lady croaked.

Rosamund saw Oliver's shoulders stiffen.

Sir Brian came forwards a pace. 'My lady, 'tis not proven,' he began awkwardly.

'Not proven!' cried the Lady Adeliza harshly. 'My poor son has barely dubbed him and he's off consorting in the woods with those blackguards!'

'Nay!' Rosamund burst out. ''Twas not so! They hurt him!' Several heads turned curiously in the direction of her flushed countenance.

'Who speaks?' demanded Lady Adeliza haughtily. She affected to search for the source of the interruption. Her dark eyes located Rosamund and impaled her with a well-tried glare which had successfully felled many a maid with more claims to pretension than Rosamund. Rosamund subsided, crimson. She wanted to hide herself, but she was still stranded high and dry up on the sturdy roan.

'De Warenne,' continued Lady Adeliza. 'You disgrace your mother's name.'

'My lady,' Oliver interposed. His voice was low. 'I swear to you on my mother's name, I have not betrayed our house.'

The Lady Adeliza made a sound that was suspiciously like a snort. 'Ha! 'Tis strange how your arrival, nephew, on this Northern shore coincided with the first sighting of these rebels. Two weeks you've been here. My lord of Hewitt tells me that was when his men first noticed these Angevin scum.' She lifted a brow, enquiring.

Oliver shook his head, frowning. 'I knew nothing of them till last eve,' he said, carefully.

Lady Adeliza's eyes were piercing. 'And the attack this morning on my son...so carefully calculated...almost as if they had first-hand knowledge of Ingerthorpe...as if someone had gone over to them—with information.'

'Never, my lady. I swore an oath to your son and I mean to honour it.' Oliver averred swiftly. He had gone very pale, but did not quail under his aunt's penetrating glare.

'They hurt you, you say?' probed Lady Adeliza.

Oliver nodded, his eyes wary. 'Aye.'

'Hmm.' She looked thoughtful. 'And did you talk?' she threw at him, suddenly sharp as a bodkin.

Oliver drew himself to his full height. 'My lady? I think I misunderstand you.'

'I think not, De Warenne,' replied his aunt. 'Well? Did you talk?'

Rosamund flung one look at Oliver's set features and jumped instantly to his defence. 'He did not betray you! He would not! He is an honourable knight! Did they not come to you with the ransom demand? Did they not send you his spurs as a token that they had him held captive?'

Lady Adeliza's eyes took in every detail of Rosamund's appearance. Very conscious of her torn and sullied gown, her tangled hair, Rosamund glared back. Hands still at the pommel, she tossed her head, thanking God that the roan stood firm. Lady Adeliza's features were bland. She lifted a wrinkled white hand to hide a quiver of her lips. To Rosamund's surprise she was favoured with a reply.

'Aye. They did demand a ransom. But after the attack when my son was wounded, some thought the demand to have been a ruse. 'Twas suggested that you had thrown your lot in with the rebels, nephew.' Lady Adeliza's eyes gleamed. 'You have a most fierce ally in that wench of yours, de Warenne,' she commented drily.

Oliver shrugged carelessly. 'Aye. It appears the maid is much struck with the notion of having a knight as a lover. 'Tis not in her interests to see me disgraced,' he added with cold cynicism.

Rosamund stared at him. 'Oliver!' she cried, shocked.

Oliver's eyes lifted to hers. ''Twill save you the trouble of finding another protector, especially now you are not wed after all.' He reached up and lifted Rosamund to the ground, slapping her dismissively on the buttocks. 'Get to the ladies' chamber, Rosamund,' he commanded her. 'You'll be needed there to help my lady.'

Rosamund's eyes glittered in fury. 'Which lady do you mean me to help?' she ground out. 'My Lady Margaret, or *your* Lady Cecily?'

'Whoever needs it most, of course,' Oliver sighed wearily. He turned on his heel leaving her scowling at his broad back. 'And now, Sir Gerard. Quickly. Tell me where we stand with these rebels,' he said briskly.

Sir Gerard hesitated and glanced at Lady Adeliza.

Lady Adeliza lifted her shoulders. Her eyes had not left Rosamund. 'Oh, do as he says, Gerard. He at least is capable of making a decision. Give him back his spurs. Someone has to take over here. My son cannot be moved, and Lord Hewitt has not yet returned.' She met the older knight's shifting eyes, her own hard and dark as jet. 'No one else is fit for command.'

'My lady,' protested Sir Gerard, puffing out his chest indignantly.

'Take over, de Warenne. I trust you'll not disappoint your aunt.' Lady Adeliza favoured him with a thin smile.

'Your servant, as ever, my lady,' responded Oliver, inclining his head.

Rosamund ground her teeth. So he had time to play the gallant with his aunt, had he? While Rosamund was dismissed as though she were only a child. Bitterly, Rosamund watched him turn to the older of the knights.

'Come, Gerard, accompany me to the armoury. What was their strength when they attacked? How many men did we lose? And where the devil is Hewitt?' Oliver's deep voice was stern, his demeanour unruffled. He marched coolly away towards the low armoury built against the west wall. Not even a backwards glance. Rosamund shivered.

She could still see Oliver's dark head make its way easily through the throng—Sir Gerard hopping alongside stammering into one ear, and the squire who'd lately clung to Sir Gerard now hanging on Oliver's arm, busily filling Oliver's other ear with his chatter. Oliver had ears for everyone but Rosamund.

Oliver directed an order at the squire. The lad flashed Oliver a look of intense relief and his face split into a smile. Then he was off, running, keen as hound to do his master's bidding. A groom panted up. Rosamund's eyes were bleak as she watched him claim Oliver's attention.

There was an ache in her heart while her eyes followed Oliver's progress across the sun-filled bailey, but she could not look away. His bitter comments had hit her

like a spear thrust through her vitals. He did not trust
her. He must have heard every word she'd uttered in
Lufu's hut. Oh, why could she not have kept her foolish
fantasies to herself? Then he would not have given ear
to Lufu's wild suggestion that she trick him into marriage. He thought she was intent only on ensnaring a
knight.

Had she admitted that she loved him? Rosamund
cudgelled her brains to remember her exact words, but
her mind was too agitated to think straight. Even if she
had, in Oliver's present frame of mind he would think
it only a ploy to trap him into marriage. Rosamund let
out a groan.

What would happen to her now? Would he discard
her as his lover? No. No. That must not happen. She
did not care if he did not wed her. Let him wed the Lady
Cecily. But he must keep her as his lover.

A small smile hovered at the edge of her lips. She could
take some comfort from the fact that he had stopped
Alfwold carrying her back to the mill. And at the falls
he had kissed her. He must have mistrusted her even
then—and yet he had kissed her. So he desired her even
without trust. That would have to do. Rosamund's eyes
prickled with tears and her view of the castle yard suddenly misted over. She was but a beggar and she could
not afford to be choosy.

'Come, girl.' Lady Adeliza's voice made her start.
Rosamund tore her eyes from Oliver's tall form, and
eyed her lady in surprise. Lady Adeliza sounded almost
kind.

'We must leave them to do their work. I think *that*
one knows what he is about, don't you?' Lady Adeliza
smiled and lowered her voice confidentially. 'I confess
I was most relieved to see him back. I have no knowledge
of military matters. Naturally it was never my domain.
But when Sir Gerard did not seem to have the first idea
how to proceed, I was forced to intervene. Ghastly,
ghastly,' she shuddered expressively. Then she
brightened. 'However, I'm glad to see my nephew can
handle such affairs. My son was in doubts as to de
Warenne's integrity but you, my dear, apparently are
not.' Lady Adeliza raised an eyebrow.

'N...no, my lady. You are right to trust him,' Rosamund assured her.

Lady Adeliza's face softened and her gaze followed Oliver as he bent his head under the armoury door lintel and vanished inside. 'I see much of my wilful sister in him,' she admitted on a wistful note. Then her voice hardened. 'Now, girl—what's your name?'

'Rosamund, my lady,' Rosamund replied.

'Rosamund. Of course. Well, Rosamund, we cannot neglect our duties either. Do you know aught of healing?'

Gone was the wild, worried woman who had greeted the troop a few minutes ago. In her place stood the Lady Adeliza Fitz Neal. Proud, confident, and assured.

Rosamund nodded. 'A little, my lady. I know which herbs to use, and how to mix...'

'Good, good,' Lady Adeliza cut in shortly. 'And you won't faint at the first sight of blood?'

'No, my lady,' Rosamund said firmly.

Lady Adeliza stalked through the portal to the lobby, and began to ascend the stairs. 'At last!' she said fervently. 'A wench with a sensible head on her. You will follow my directions. I need someone to assist me with my son.

'Marie is too taken up with poor Margaret's confinement to be of any use with Geoffrey. Blanche took one look, turned as pale as her name and dropped like one dead. And as for Cecily...'

Lady Adeliza peered down the spiral at Rosamund as though to assure herself she was still there. 'Of course one can't expect Cecily to *do* anything, but one would at least have hoped she wouldn't cause yet more pother by running off screeching. I had to send two of my other ladies off searching for her. No men to spare today, as you see.' Lady Adeliza stopped at the top of the stairs to catch her breath.

'It must have been very trying,' Rosamund murmured inadequately.

'Trying!' exclaimed her lady with feeling. 'Of course it was trying! But now you're here we can concentrate on my son, and leave de Warenne to deal with those rebels. And while we're about it I want you to explain to me how it is you are so certain my dear sister's son

is no traitor. I feel instinctively that he is not, but Baron
Geoffrey will want more than that. He will not be pleased
to hear his garrison had been entrusted to a suspected
traitor on the strength of a woman's instinct. He will
want proof.'

Rosamund leaned her throbbing head wearily on the
trestle in the deserted hall, worn out with tending her
lord day and night, and so exhausted that she had swayed
on her feet and the Lady Adeliza had dismissed her.

'Go and eat, girl,' Baron Geoffrey's mother had ordered. 'You're no good to me if you swoon. There's sweet
wine in the store. Go on. And don't come back till you're
rested. Geoffrey is quiet now. I can manage for awhile.'

Rosamund had not argued. Her eyes felt dry and
scratchy. She squinted at the tiny dust motes floating in
the light. It must be sunny outside. She moved her head,
let out a weary sigh and closed bleary eyes, too fatigued
to care that the trestle's surface was covered with half-
eaten meals and no one had come to clear them. For
two days now, cleaning had been a luxury the occupants
of Ingerthorpe Castle had had to forfeit. The women
seemed to be preparing for a siege. There were no ladies
sewing in the upper chamber. Supplies were being
counted, medicines and bandages were hunted out from
dusty stores, and wounds were tended.

The soldiers would gobble down their food, and go
unsmiling back to their duties. Warriors fighting a local
war, with nothing on their minds but winning. 'Twas
kill or be killed for them.

And Oliver? Where was he? She'd not seen him since
he'd ridden into the compound with her on that squire's
roan. When was that? Yesterday? The day before?

Rosamund rubbed her forehead, and despite the dis-
comfort of her seat felt herself slide slowly into sleep.

She could only have been dozing for a moment when
she surfaced again. She felt something light brush over
her head. A hand? She murmured drowsily, but her brain
was too fogged, her body too exhausted for movement.
Then came the unmistakable sound of someone creeping
furtively towards the stairwell. A spur jingled.

Rosamund sat bolt upright. The door closed softly behind the tall figure of a mailed knight. She had been too late to discern his features, but the sudden pulsing of the blood in her veins told her what she wanted to now.

'Oliver!' she whispered under her breath. Tired? She was not tired. She dived across the hall and up the stairs, not even certain of what she would say when she caught up with him.

But his long legs were too quick for her. By the time Rosamund arrived panting at the top she could hear Oliver's voice coming in hushed tones from the small chamber currently occupied by the wounded lord. Lady Adeliza had insisted that her daughter-in-law's confinement should take place in the main bedchamber. She had brought her son to this small room—little better than Oliver's, save for the fact that a fireplace took up the whole of one wall, and a large tapestry depicting a hunting scene hung behind the bed.

'Oh, he rambles yet,' Rosamund heard Lady Adeliza tell him. 'But I have hopes, nephew. I think he'll pull through. Your wench—what's her name?'

'My wench, my lady?' Oliver sounded wary.

Lady Adeliza let out a cackle. 'You know very well who I mean. Rosamund. The miller's beautiful daughter.'

'So you do know her name,' Oliver said softly.

'Touché, de Warenne. A hit,' Lady Adeliza said appreciatively.

'What of Rosamund, my lady?'

'You mar your handsome looks by scowling, de Warenne,' Lady Adeliza said sharply. Her voice lowered. 'She has been more use to me these past days than all my other ladies put together.'

'I'm glad of that, my lady...' Oliver responded.

'Who's there?' demanded the Baron's voice peremptorily. 'Who speaks?'

Rosamund pushed open the door and entered the bedchamber, pushing past Oliver to draw closer to the sick bed.

Oliver was annoyed to find he had tensed. He was acutely conscious of Rosamund's sweeping skirts brushing past him. He wanted to snatch her to him and

hold her close, so he could remind himself of the soft
warmth of her body, and inhale the subtle fragrance of
the wild rose which she washed into her hair. He put his
arms firmly behind his back and laced his fingers
together. Trying for composure. He had been too much
in the rough company of soldiers. Aye, that was it. He
must be missing feminine company...

Oliver succeeded in sparing Rosamund only the
briefest of glances, and affected to turn his attention back
to his cousin. But his eyes were as keen as a scout's and
he'd made the most of that short glimpse, observing
every detail of her appearance.

Rosamund was wearing a blue gown he had not seen
her in before. A lady's gown. It must be one of the ones
Lady Adeliza had given her. The colour became her well.
It emphasised the vivid blue of those startling eyes. Her
thick hair was neatly braided, but she was pale and had
dark shadows under her eyes. She'd darted him a glance
from under her long lashes, and her lips trembled. He
wanted to kiss them.

Oliver stared fixedly at his cousin, though every nerve
in his body was conscious of Rosamund. In contrast to
Rosamund's wan face, Lord Geoffrey's colour was high.
His brown hair was drenched with sweat, and he was
struggling like a demon to rise. Oliver watched his cousin
with a worried frown gathering on his brow.

'Nay, Geoffrey,' admonished Lady Adeliza, with a
firm hand on her son's chest. 'Be still, or you'll undo
all our good work.'

'Who's there? Mother? You've not let de Warenne in
here, have you?' The Baron pushed feverishly at his
mother's restraining hands.

The anxious look faded from Oliver's face. His
expression became shuttered.

'Aye, cousin. I'm here,' Oliver replied. 'That does not
worry you, surely?'

Baron Geoffrey spluttered. 'Out! Out!' he cried.
'Mother, get rid of him! He's planned it all, don't you
see? He's after my lands!' The Baron was upright now,
his chest and belly heaving with the effort. Almost out
of the bed.

Lady Adeliza sent an appealing glance to Rosamund. No words were necessary. Rosamund ran at once to the bed, and between them the two women held down the sick man and forced him back under the covers.

'He'll kill me. And get the title. Broke his bond. A man who breaks his word...capable of anything. Sneaked out of the castle...no intention of fulfilling his obligations!'

'That's not true, my lord,' Oliver insisted quietly.

'You should have been back at dawn. Why weren't you?' the Baron asked, his voice hoarse.

Oliver probed the scar on his head and grinned ruefully. 'Bodily weakness prevented me, my lord,' he admitted.

Lord Geoffrey's eyes slid to rest on Rosamund. They were surprisingly clear. 'Bodily weakness, eh? That's one way of putting it, I suppose.'

Oliver's skin darkened. 'If I had not gone after her, my lord, I would never have found the rebel camp.'

Lord Geoffrey's eyes glittered, dangerous again. 'Aye. And that's when you betrayed me!' he accused. 'You want me dead so you can get my title!'

Lady Adeliza made a sound of pure exasperation. 'Nonsense, Geoffrey. You're raving. And in any case, your sons would be next in line,' Lady Adeliza pointed out with brisk common sense.

'Sons? Sons? I've only one. Henry. And he'll kill him too, to get his filthy hands on my lands. Betrayed!'

Lady Adeliza glanced at her nephew. Oliver's face was set hard and pale as Death himself.

'I'll go,' offered Oliver, stiffly.

Lady Adeliza shook her head, and her veil rippled with the movement. 'Pay no heed to him. It's the fever speaking. Feel his head, he's as hot as a smithy.'

Baron Geoffrey groaned, his head flopped back on to the pillow. His face gleamed with perspiration. The short struggle had sapped all of his strength.

Lady Adeliza wiped her son's forehead tenderly with her veil. 'Why, I told him last night his wife was safely delivered of another boy, and he's not even remembered that,' she told her nephew. 'If he can't take *that* in, his mind's too clouded with sickness for other matters.'

'My lady, I think I'd best remove myself,' Oliver said coldly.

'Very well, very well,' agreed Lady Adeliza. 'Come back tonight. He may be restored by then and I shall be sure to tell him how much we have relied on you both these past...' Her head tipped to one side, listening. 'What's that noise?' she asked sharply. 'Rosamund, you go and tell them to be quiet down there. My son needs peace and quiet,' she snapped.

'Aye, my lady.' Rosamund moved to the door.

'Nay,' Oliver caught at Rosamund's arm, and she lifted questioning eyes to his, 'I'll go. 'Tis the men celebrating, and methinks they'll not heed a maid.'

'Celebrating?' Lady Adeliza grated, lifting her head. ''Tis over then?'

'Aye, my lady, for now. I came to inform you. We have routed the rebels. Their camp is destroyed.'

'Did you slaughter the lot?' Lady Adeliza demanded, her eyes bright with gruesome relish.

'We killed a few. It could not be helped. But we took many captives.' Oliver's fingers still burned Rosamund's arm.

'Where've you put 'em?' Lady Adeliza demanded in her forthright manner. 'In the dungeons?'

'Aye. When Geoffrey is fit again he will want to question them,' Oliver explained, with his eyes glued on Rosamund's. 'My Lord of Hewitt has his prisoners too,' he added.

'You've done well, very well, de Warenne,' Lady Adeliza praised.

'I thank you, my lady,' replied Oliver formally.

His eyes roamed over Rosamund's features with hungry intensity. His look told Rosamund how much he still desired her and she felt herself flush with hot colour. Rosamund stared back, hoping for something more in those cool grey depths. Then, finding she'd unthinkingly put her hand on his, her gaze fell and she jerked herself out of his grasp. He was arrogant enough already. She'd not fuel it further.

'You'll be back to see your cousin tonight, de Warenne?' reminded the Lady Adeliza with a smile for him.

Oliver nodded. 'My lady.' He bowed, and the door clicked shut behind him.

Rosamund approached her lady with her head lowered to hide her eyes. 'How...how...can I help, my lady?' she asked huskily.

Lady Adeliza had taken note of Rosamund's high colour and she pursed her lips together thoughtfully.

'A fine young man,' she commented, slyly. 'He will make a handsome husband for my Cecily, will he not, Rosamund?'

Rosamund stared blindly out of the window.

'Rosamund?' Lady Adeliza's voice rose. 'I spoke to you. Did you not hear?'

Rosamund gulped and tried to find her tongue. She could not meet Lady Adeliza's penetrating brown eyes. 'I...I heard, my lady,' she confirmed at last.

'Well? Your verdict?'

The room was very still.

'The...the Lady Cecily should be pleased to marry him,' Rosamund got out.

'Aye. So she should.' Lady Adeliza's voice grew faint. She began to mumble to herself as she bent over her son's perspiration-streaked face. Rosamund was too immersed in her own thoughts to notice.

'So would any real woman. But Cecily is not...and she is not pleased. I do not want to force either of them...bah...what a mess.' The Lady Adeliza sighed and fell silent.

Rosamund recovered herself. 'I beg your pardon, my lady?' she asked.

'Nothing child, nothing. 'Twas nought but the ramblings of a tired old woman.'

Rosamund selected a cloth from the cooling water and wrung it out. 'Here, my lady,' she offered. 'Let me do that. 'Tis your turn to rest now. I've had my rest.'

'You're a sensible woman, Rosamund,' observed Lady Adeliza, heaving herself to her feet.

Rosamund gave her a straight look. 'For a peasant, you mean?' Her voice was very dry.

Lady Adeliza's lips twitched. 'You're an impudent chit,' she announced. 'But you'll do. You'll do.'

Rosamund crept cautiously down the spiral stairs. She hesitated as she passed the closed door of Oliver de Warenne's chamber. She lifted her hand and moved her fingers over the rough wood. She listened. She could hear only wind and distant waves. No sound from his chamber. The hall below was equally quiet. She wondered what hour it was. The lack of noise told Rosamund that she had been released from her duties too late to partake of the nightly revels. The soldiers had finished celebrating their success. Rosamund did not mind. She did not feel that she had anything worth celebrating.

Lord Geoffrey was sleeping peacefully now. His fever had left him late that afternoon. And apart from a brief walk around the outer bailey, Rosamund had watched over her lord most of the day. Rosamund knew she should be pleased; her hard work had not been wasted. Lord Geoffrey was well. The Lady Adeliza regarded her with much favour. For three more days they'd worked as one to save her son. In total she'd spent five days nursing her lord in his sickbed. Lady Adeliza was grateful, and she was not one to let her debts go unsettled.

Rosamund hoped Lady Adeliza would secure her a permanent position in the castle. Then she need never return to her father and Aeffe. Surely that should be a cause for jubilation? She could wear fine clothes and eat good food every day now.

But Rosamund felt nothing; she was empty, drained. The look she'd last seen in Alfwold's eyes would haunt her forever. His disappointment in losing both her and his future at the mill had scarred him to the soul. Even if she was not to wed him, she could never be free of that. His sorrow would turn to bitterness and... Rosamund sighed. A good man soured.

Her hand pressed on the heavy oak door. Rosamund had not seen Oliver to speak to for three days now. Too taken up with her nursing, she had had to snatch at meals and sleep. Eating on the run, and sleeping on the long, hard bench at the foot of the Baron's bed.

And now, at last, Lady Adeliza had waved her away. 'Get to bed, Rosamund. My son needs you no more. Our thanks,' Lady Adeliza said dismissively.

Rosamund stared at Oliver's door, wondering whether he was sleeping already. She could see him as clearly as if the door were transparent. His dark hair would be tousled, his long limbs sprawled out across the bed.

Get to bed. Lady Adeliza's parting words echoed through Rosamund's mind. The question was...which bed? Should she be joining the other ladies in the women's quarters or...?

Her hand slid up to find the latch, but she did not lift it. She curled her fingers round the metal so it dug into her palms. She bit her lip in an agony of indecision. Should she go in? If only she had been able to speak to him. Then she might have some idea what was expected of her. If only she had the right to lift that latch and go to him... She sighed sadly, and her hand released the latch without a rattle and fell to her side.

She could assume nothing. She had no rights. It was the Lady Cecily who would have the rights... Her head bowed, Rosamund picked up the blue fabric of her skirts to trail dispiritedly down towards the hall door, feeling her way with one hand. The wind had extinguished the wall torch.

A door clanged in the bowels of the castle. Quick footsteps on the stairs above. Rosamund scurried on.

'Rosamund? Is that you?' a familiar masculine voice demanded from the landing above.

She froze. 'Aye, sir,' she replied, her heart beginning to thump.

His dark shape landed lightly beside her. 'Give me your hand, I can't see a thing,' Oliver ordered.

Tentatively Rosamund put out a hand and lightly touched his chest. His fingers gripped her.

'Where the devil are you off to now?' The grip tightened fractionally. 'You weren't running away again, were you?' he asked.

'R...running away? Nay, sir,' she replied. 'I was g...going to b...bed.'

'You're going the wrong way,' he told her. 'Our bed's up there.'

'Oh.'

'Oh,' he mocked her. She felt him tug at her hand.
'Come on, Rosamund.'

Rosamund hung back.

'Nay Rosamund, I won't have you playing the coy
maid tonight,' he announced. He stooped and, scooping
her into his arms, took the winding stairs two at a time.

'Oliver!' protested Rosamund, clutching desperately
at his neck. She was certain he'd miss his footing in the
dark. 'Be careful!'

Laughter rumbled in his chest. 'At last! I thought
you'd lost your memory too!'

'I beg your pardon?' Rosamund frowned.

'You've seen fit to remember my name,' he explained.
'You were so formal I thought you'd forgotten it.'

Reaching his door, Oliver kneed it open and carried
her through. He kicked it shut behind them.

The wall candle was lit there, and Rosamund saw his
face clearly. He was panting and slightly flushed, and
his eyes were shining.

'I shall have to get in better shape, if I'm going to
have to carry you to my chamber every night,' he remarked with a grin, and his chipped tooth gleamed white.

Rosamund's heart began to race. That slow hollow
ache started in her belly. 'Every night?' she commented,
trying to harden her voice. 'Your lady wife would not
think much of that. Put me down, please, Sir Oliver,'
she begged, suddenly painfully aware that while he held
her those searching grey eyes might glean too much from
her expression.

'As you wish, my lady,' he replied, with a smirk on
his lips. He moved to stand by the bed, bent to his knees,
and lowered her slowly on to the mattress. Remaining
on his knees by the bed, he did not let go of her.
Rosamund squirmed under his penetrating gaze, and
lowered her eyes self-consciously. She felt shy as a maid
who'd never been kissed.

'I had hoped...' Oliver began huskily '...that, now,
you would be pleased to...' He stopped and his fingers
pulled insistently at her chin forcing her bashful gaze to
his. 'Rosamund, I prefer watching your eyes to the top
of your head.'

Rosamund trembled. He was going to kiss her. She could tell by the way his voice had deepened. Oliver's hand on her back moved to bring her towards him. Rosamund heard herself give an inarticulate murmur and swayed towards him on the edge of the bed. His first kiss fell on her cheek and then he was kissing her neck, feverishly, hungrily, as though he was starving. She could feel his fingers loosening her braids, fanning out her hair. He buried his head in its softness and she heard him mutter her name.

She was clinging to his shoulder, one hand holding his head. His lips moved across her throat, and Rosamund found she'd arched her head back in an unconsciously provocative gesture. Abruptly the kisses stopped.

She felt him pull back. 'Oliver?' she queried, and her voice was as shaky as her body.

'Oh, God. How I've missed you. Rosamund, *my* Rosamund,' he said fiercely, and his lips reached for hers.

So eager was Rosamund for that kiss that she slipped to her knees before him, and then they were kneeling on the floor together. Arms clinging, lips together in a kiss which robbed Rosamund of all her strength and made her body melt willingly against his. She could taste sweet wine on his tongue. Her eyes closed.

'Rosamund,' Oliver mumbled, half lifting his lips.

'Mmm?'

'What's wrong with the bed?'

Rosamund shrugged and pressed her lips more closely to his. She could not bear that the kiss should end.

Oliver lifted his head. Rosamund gave a little murmur of protest and her fingers tightened their hold on his head.

'Nay, my sweet love, not on the floor.' There was laughter in his voice.

Rosamund lifted her eyelids and found herself staring into eyes that smiled so tenderly she could almost think... His expression altered subtly and the moment passed.

'Up you get. There. That's better.' Oliver lay her back on the bed and sat down beside her.

A long-fingered hand smoothed her hair, idly playing with a shining tress. He was watching her, something about his manner made her uneasy. He was hiding something.

'What is it, Oliver?' she asked, taking hold of the hand in her hair.

Oliver shook his hand free and stood up. 'I've some wine over there, would you care for some?' he asked, lightly.

Rosamund was not deceived by his casual manner. She noticed a muscle had clenched in his jaw. 'Wine?' she repeated, stupidly.

'Aye, wine.' Oliver replied roughly, tossing back a lock of dark hair from his forehead.

He seemed to be avoiding her eyes. Rosamund brought her hand to her lips. 'Oh…er…wine. Aye…th…thank you,' she said, wondering at his game.

Oliver turned to a tray set on his travelling chest. He held himself stiffly, and his knuckles were white on the neck of the wine-skin. 'You're to wed me in the morning, Rosamund,' he announced gruffly.

Rosamund's eyes widened. She sat up. That stiff, broad back told her nothing. If only she could see his eyes…

Her throat closed up, and she could not speak.

'Well?' Oliver demanded, staring fixedly at the blank wall in front of him as though he'd lost the power of motivation. His voice was as taut as a bow string.

She cleared her throat. 'Are…are you asking me, or telling me?' she got out.

He paused. 'Asking.'

Rosamund slipped from the bed and came to stand behind him. She put both arms round his waist and hugged him, leaning her cheek against his strong back. 'Oh, yes. I'll marry you. Please.' She pressed a series of warm kisses on to his tunic, and felt some of the tension ebb from his body. Her lips curved into an understanding smile. Her brave, proud knight did not find it easy to ask.

He turned in the circle of her arms, looked at her, eyes haunted.

'You're willing?' he asked, a trace of hesitancy evident in his tone.

'Of course,' she reassured him. Her blue eyes were aglow with happiness. Then a shower of objections tumbled into her mind. Rosamund's bright smile dimmed. 'But what of you? How can you possibly want to wed me? I'm only the miller's daughter. I have no dowry to offer. There's no advancement to be gained by wedding me. I thought your memory had returned. Don't you remember you made a solemn agreement? You'll be dishonoured if you break it. Or have you forgotten that?'

Oliver grinned. His eyes lost that haunted expression. 'Nay, my love, I've not forgotten a thing. I remember it all.' He cast the wine-skin back on to the tray and swept her over on to the bed. 'And we'll be wedded in the morn.'

He pressed eager lips to hers.

'But . . . but . . . you'll be ruined,' Rosamund objected, using all her willpower to twist away from that beautiful, distracting mouth.

He shook his dark head. ''Tis all agreed. I've asked for you. My cousin has consented. Lady Adeliza has given us her blessing too.' His voice took on an edge of laughter. 'And when the Lady Adeliza does that—why, 'tis tantamount to a command, as you should know by now. She said she'd not have her daughter terrified into an early grave.'

Rosamund shivered. 'Lady Cecily's not long for this world in any case . . .'

Oliver's expression sobered. 'I know. She has the wasting sickness. Poor lady, her life has been one sad trial from start to end. Lady Adeliza has persuaded my cousin she should not be coerced into anything. She'll have a place here as long as she lives.

'Lady Adeliza seems to think you a more fitting partner for me. She holds you in great esteem. You have a formidable ally there, my love.' His voice went husky. 'Now Rosamund . . . please?' He lowered his head.

'Oliver,' she moaned, and let his lips find hers. She sighed happily as his mouth moved over hers. Her blood tingled and her toes curled. Suddenly Rosamund gasped and broke free. She'd gone milky white.

'God, but you were ever a wriggler,' Oliver commented without rancour. 'What now? If it's Alfwold you're worried about, don't be. I've recommended him to my cousin as the next tenant of your father's mill. That way he can stay at the mill—the village could do with a permanent stone-dresser in any case.'

Rosamund stared at Oliver. She hugged him. 'Oh, thank you! I was worried. He is so kind, you see, and it seemed dreadful that we should be the ones to send him back to trudging lonely highways. He hated it. But now he will be able to help my father, and he will have some standing in the village.' She paused and grimaced. 'And one day the villagers will have an honest miller who gives them their full measures.'

Flushing, she dropped her voice and confessed. 'Nay, Oliver, though this kindness of yours does relieve my mind, 'twas not of Alfwold that I thought.'

'Nay?'

She hesitated. 'I'll be a l...lady. 'Tis an honour I'd not thought of. I don't think I can...'

'You can and will,' he stated firmly.

'But...a lady!'

'You'll not be too much of one, I trust.' Oliver smiled, and kissed her nose.

'Then I'll be named——'

'The Lady Rosamund de Warenne,' he finished for her. He kissed her neck.

'Oh, Oliver! I can't. 'Tis not right,' she wailed, stunned by her extraordinary rise in fortune. 'I only know about two words of that language you speak.'

His arms tightened on her. 'You'll soon learn.'

'Nay! Nay! You must be daft thinking we can wed. You can't really want me.'

'I do want you. Why, you silly wench, I'd even give Lance to Geoffrey if it meant I could have you. But fortunately Lady Adeliza took my part and that wasn't necessary.'

Her heart lifted. She was sure of him, but she'd have him admit it. She opened her eyes at him, and said wryly, 'Me, the miller's daughter, rather than your destrier. Sir, I am flattered.'

He looked disconcerted. 'Rosamund?'

'Luck is on your side isn't it, Oliver? You have your war-horse back unharmed *and*——'

'Not quite unharmed,' Oliver told her. 'Those ignorant brutes have damaged his mouth. They've had a whip on him too. I'll be the first to admit that Lance needs firm handling, but they've mangled him.'

Rosamund touched a lean cheek. 'I'm sorry, Oliver. Will he heal?'

'Aye. But I'm glad he was with them for no longer. They'd have ruined him.'

Rosamund heaved a sigh. 'Ah well, that diminishes my value then,' she said lightly. 'To be rated higher than a war-horse was, perhaps, too much to expect. But I see now my true worth. 'Tis a little more than a broken nag.'

A grin edged round Oliver's lips. 'I do want to marry you, Rosamund.'

'Why?'

'Why?' Oliver stalled. A dark flush ran up under his skin.

'Aye, tell me. I have to know.' Her eyes misted. 'You've not said it yet. Do you love me?'

A warm hand slid to rest on her breast. 'I'll love you all you want,' he agreed instantly, moving his thumb.

Rosamund threw his hand away. 'That's not what I mean, and well you know it! Why are you marrying me?'

Oliver shrugged carelessly. His lips curved. 'You're not wed, and I might have made you pregnant. I'll not see a child of mine suffer the indignities of bastardy that I have had to suffer.'

Rosamund stared at him. 'I don't believe you,' she said flatly. 'I think you love me. You said you could never love, but I don't believe you. I think you're in love with me, but you're too scared to admit it.'

Oliver snorted. 'Scared . . . I?'

'Aye. You. My brave knight. A courageous warrior on the battlefield, but in the bedchamber . . . a coward.' Her low voice pleaded. 'Admit it, Oliver. Admit you love me. Please. I love you so much it hurts. I need you to love me. I can't marry you without your love. I'll need your love to support me if I'm to learn to be a lady.'

A muscle flickered in Oliver's jaw. 'Maids!' he exclaimed. 'Always greedy for more. I told you I could not love. I warned you. You will have position, good food, fine clothes, money. Isn't that enough?'

Rosamund closed her eyes. 'Give me strength,' she cried. 'You great oaf! Do you really think those things matter? Oh, only a fool would turn down the chance to sleep 'twixt smooth, clean linen sheets like these, and drink sweet wine like yours. But I was not born to this, Oliver. I will never be a real lady. Not without your love. I need your love. I will need your love to support me. To help me, to teach me—to forgive me when I make mistakes.'

Rosamund put her hands on either side of his face. 'Without it, we cannot wed,' she said earnestly.

Silence. Clouded grey eyes looked deep into hers.

'And I do love you so very much, Oliver,' she whispered.

Oliver stared at her. He swallowed. There was pain lurking in the depths of his gaze. Rosamund could see his inner struggle reflected in his face. She waited.

'And I love you,' he murmured in a cracked voice.

Rosamund let out her breath, unaware that she had been holding it. She smiled up at him with tender eyes.

Oliver's eyes darkened. The grey in them was tinted now with the pure blue of the sky. His lips twisted. 'Though why on earth I should pick on a nagging wench such as you... I'd rather fight a host of rebels than wrestle words with you. But if you need the words...'

Rosamund's eyes sparkled. 'I do.'

Oliver twisted her hair round his fingers and stared at it. 'I'm no troubadour that can mouth pretty words, my angel. I know I love you. I've loved you from the first, I think, but I wouldn't admit it even to myself.' He kissed her ear. 'I should have known it when you ran away,' he muttered. 'I was hot with rage, for you'd dented my pride. I wanted you back. But it was more than that. I was also afraid—desperately afraid that some harm would come to you. I don't remember feeling like that about anyone else. A bastard has to steel himself against all feeling early on, and I thought I'd got myself well protected. But you... from the first you were so easy to talk to. You'd no haughty airs, and such guileless eyes.

You crept under my guard and before I knew it, my heart had fallen into your keeping.'

Rosamund smiled. 'I'll treasure it,' she promised.

Oliver's eyes searched hers. He nodded slowly, satisfied at what he saw there, and gave a rueful grin. 'It took a blow from a rebel's cudgel to knock some sense into me. I'd not been used to trusting myself to others. But back there, in that squalid hut, there was nothing but you between me and oblivion. A little maid, and me with my senses blown to the winds, struggling to escape from those outlaws. I trusted you completely. At the time it seemed perfectly natural that I should do so. I never doubted you or our love for a second. I knew I could trust you with my life.'

She hesitated, remembering a moment when her integrity had been sorely tested. 'I almost failed you. There was a time when I...'

'When you thought you could deceive me,' Oliver completed her sentence. 'I know. I overheard some parts of that in Lufu's hut.'

She bit her lip. 'I'm sorry for it.'

'Nay, angel. When it came to it, you were honest with me,' he reminded her.

Rosamund put a hand to her brow.

'When I stopped Alfwold taking you back to the mill,' Oliver explained, 'you were not to know I'd heard your conversation and knew I was a knight. Yet you deliberately called me *Sir* Oliver.'

He sighed and gripped her hard. 'It was all so clear to me then. But gradually, the more my wits cleared, the more difficult I found it. For years I'd striven with no goal in mind save winning my golden spurs. I thought there was nought else worth the having. And suddenly my ambition was tarnished, worthless. I wanted your love. As memory crowded back I found to my horror that I had made commitments that would keep me from you. I had no desire to honour them, if it meant that you were to be insulted by becoming my whore. And unless I broke my vows to my cousin, that was all that I could offer you.'

Rosamund looked thoughtful. 'But it never came to that. I wonder if you would have broken your agreement for me?'

Oliver gave her a straight look. 'When I went to my cousin to ask for you, I went prepared for a nasty wrangle. But as you say, it was not necessary, thanks to my success with the rebels and your winning over the formidable Lady Adeliza. Yours was the greater victory, I think.'

His smile lightened even the depths of his eyes. 'And so tomorrow, thanks to both our efforts, we will wed.'

'Aye,' Rosamund whispered, inexplicably shy.

'When you look at me like that, Rosamund, all the words fly out of my head,' he told her softly.

Rosamund slid her hand round his neck and pulled his dark head towards her. 'Do they?' she asked kissing him briefly on the lips, and drawing back a little. 'I think I've had enough words for now.' Her lips curved, and her hand went to the lacings of his tunic.

Oliver lifted a brow. 'What can you mean, my lady? Surely you are not inviting my advances? 'Tis not suitable for a lady to proposition a knight, even if they are to be wed.'

Rosamund pulled a face. 'But I, Oliver, have much to learn. I was not born a lady,' she reminded him.

'Thank God for that,' Oliver said fervently, his fingers at the fastenings of her gown. 'And angel, there are some lessons that I would prefer you not to learn at all.'

'You mean you want me to be Rosamund Miller inside the bedchamber and Lady Rosamund de Warenne without?'

'Precisely,' Oliver murmured, eyes on her lips.

'I'm not sure I can manage that. It sounds very difficult.'

'We'd better practise then,' he suggested with a grin. 'Kiss me, Rosamund.'

'But I know all about being Rosamund,' she teased. ''Tis the lady part I'm not sure of.'

'In case you hadn't noticed, we're in the bedchamber now, my angel,' Oliver said, resorting in desperation to logic.

Smiling, Rosamund tugged his head down. 'So we are, my love. So we are.'

VOWS   *LaVyrle Spencer*   £2.99

When high-spirited Emily meets her father's new business rival,
Tom, sparks fly, and create a blend of pride and passion in this
compelling and memorable novel.

LOTUS MOON   *Janice Kaiser*   £2.99

This novel vividly captures the futility of the Vietnam War and the
legacy it left. Haunting memories of the beautiful Lotus Moon fuel
Buck Michael's dangerous obsession, which only Amanda Parr can
help overcome.

SECOND TIME LUCKY   *Eleanor Woods*   £2.75

Danielle has been married twice. Now, as a young, beautiful widow,
can she back-track to the first husband whose life she left in ruins
with her eternal quest for entertainment and the high life?

**These three new titles will be out in bookshops from
September 1989.**

W⊕RLDWIDE

*Available from Boots, Martins, John Menzies, W.H. Smith, Woolworths
and other paperback stockists.*

An irresistible
offer from
MILLS & BOON